STARSHIP OF THE ANCIENTS: BOOK 3

REBEL WORLDS

A K DUBOFF

www.akduboff.com

Published by Epic Realms Press
Cover by Robert Rajszczak

ISBN-10: 1965614108
ISBN-13: 978-1965614105

0 9 8 7 6 5 4 3 2 1

Produced in the United States of America

TABLE OF CONTENTS

1 1
2 11
3 21
4 31
5 44
6 50
7 57
8 63
9 74
10 83
11 93
12 100
13 107
14 119
15 128
16 139
17 152
18 164
19 169
20 181
21 192
22 201
23 212
24 217
25 234
26 246
27 253
28 263
29 274
30 283
31 294
32 306
33 315
34 323
35 339
36 350
37 359

38.. 365
39...370
40..378
ADDITIONAL READING.. 385
AUTHORS' NOTES... 386
ABOUT THE AUTHOR 387

ו

DOES EVERYONE DESERVE a second chance? For most of his life, Evan would have advocated for a shot at redemption. He'd done enough questionable things that the opportunity to atone appealed to him. Yet, as he watched the camera feed of Roman Santano in his holding cell, Evan had serious doubts about Roman ever being able to redress his past brutality. Their most recent conversation had only underscored that point.

Though Roman had lost some of his original bluster over the week since his capture, the smug twist of his lips and hard gaze reminded Evan of the ruthless, superior attitude he'd observed with the Noche Syndicate's senior leaders. No doubt, Roman had been immersed in that culture for his entire life. It would take a major revelation to break free from that ingrained mindset.

"What's your assessment?" Chancellor Conroy asked, drawing Evan's attention from the monitor.

Evan crossed his arms. "That it wasn't a joke when he said that he reserved the right to stab me in the back—and I think he meant it literally."

"Have you changed your mind about sparing his life?"

"He's still more valuable alive than dead—for now. There's

a lot of important information buried in that warped mind. We just need to get him to share it."

The older man clasped his hands behind his back. "I'm not a fan of torture."

"No, I meant bargaining with him. There has to be *something* he wants badly enough to be willing to talk."

"How's that going?"

Evan rubbed a wet spot on his shirt. "Well, he spit on me and told me to 'go to hell', so we have a ways to go."

"That's not promising."

"These things take time."

"Say you *do* get him to talk. How will we know if he's telling the truth?"

Evan had honed his ability to read people over the course of his career, but he'd found he was even more in tune with those feelings since his exposure to the Korani tech. And it was through those enhanced senses that he knew the chancellor was more concerned than he was letting on. "I'll know," Evan said.

Conroy arched an eyebrow. "For that matter, how do I know that *you're* not going to use that information against *me*?"

"You don't. If you'd rather I walk away, I'm happy to oblige."

"No, we're not playing that game again. Get him to talk. But I'd like it if you came to me before making any commitments."

"I'll keep you posted."

"Also, Zaris agreed to hold the other dissidents on one of her ships," Conroy said. "We transferred them this morning."

The UPDF squad leader Red and remaining members of her team had been captured following Evan's confrontation with Roman, and it had been clear they weren't going to let go of the fight anytime soon. Keeping them in lockup was really the only option. "I think that's for the best—especially separating them from Roman."

"They very well may have succeeded in their mission if it wasn't for you."

"A lot of things could have gone differently."

"Well, we're here now. We have a difficult path ahead, but we *are* making progress," Conroy continued.

"I'll take your word for it."

The chancellor frowned but eventually inclined his head. "Loyalty is won through action, not words."

"I look forward to seeing what you do."

—   —   —

Reverberations and thuds from demolition work overhead filled Tobin Mori's office. Even with sound isolating earphones, he still felt the vibrations through his chair and desk.

Listening to near-constant construction noise in the building over the past year was grating on Tobin's nerves. But in the last month, everything else had gone so spectacularly bad that the maddening din now felt like a torturous punishment for his failures.

Tobin massaged the inner corners of his eyes, hoping to relieve the aches of staring at data tables for too many hours. It didn't.

He instead looked out the single window at the back of his office—his one connection to the outside physical world. Though a narrow opening, he did have a partial view of the United Mall, the landscaped park space surrounding the capitol and other legislative buildings at the center of government on Terrax. Trees and grass were hard to come by in some parts of the Commonwealth's capital city, so he appreciated being able to see green whenever he could spare a few moments away from his screen.

A soft alert chime sounded on his earphones, drawing his attention back to work. His heart skipped a beat when he saw the message on his omni.

Most of his communications with Chancellor Conroy were via encrypted text exchanges, but they did speak on voice calls on rare occasions; the encrypted interstellar relays made the calls difficult to trace, but there was still a risk. He reluctantly answered.

"Sir, we really shouldn't talk like this anymore," Tobin said. The last time they'd spoken had been right after the doomed *Stratum* colony ship had departed, back when there'd been so much hope and it had seemed like all of their carefully laid plans were coming together. That optimism seemed so foolhardy in hindsight.

"This couldn't be a text exchange. I need to hear the conviction in your voice."

A flush rose on Tobin's cheeks. "Are you doubting me, after everything?"

"I just need confirmation that you're still in this."

Fighting off his initial insult to the question, Tobin could understand the chancellor's perspective. They'd been laying plans for years. Countless things had gone wrong. It would be understandable for a person to lose faith in the efforts, and—in a way—it was respectful of Conroy to ask him if he wanted out.

"No turning back now, sir," he said.

"Good. Are you safe?"

"As much as I can be. What's going on there?" The recent communications had been sporadic, with Conroy temporarily losing his base on Aethos in the fight for the planet. Tobin had yet to hear the whole story, only that Rostov and the Syndicate had collaborated to sabotage the mission.

"We have the ship. We're trying to replace the supplies we lost in the crash. I'm building a following."

"That's good to hear." How more people had possibly gotten to the planet was a big question, but Tobin didn't want to prolong the call, knowing the risks. The important thing was that Conroy was alive. "You will always have my support, sir. Do you need anything else?"

"I need the final evidence," Conroy said. "Have you been able to get it?"

"No," Tobin admitted reluctantly. He'd been carrying around a data cloner for months, but he hadn't had the right opportunity to install it in Rostov's office.

"I understand what I'm asking of you, but we need it now. Everything is about to move very quickly."

"Yes, sir. I'll find a way."

"Be careful, Tobin. Everyone is on edge."

The call ended, and Tobin immediately wiped it from his communication logs. He leaned back in his seat, his pulse heavy in his ears.

Are we really nearing the end? He'd been living a double life for so long that he could no longer remember what it was like to not feel anxious all the time.

The front he needed to maintain with Rostov grated on his soul. Every time someone spoke ill of Conroy—often multiple times a day—he needed to smile and play along. Listening to them disparage and smear his hero fueled him to push through the discomfort. Tobin was the man on the inside. Conroy was counting on him to access the secret information no one else in the chancellor's network could obtain.

Despite the risks, Tobin would do anything to support the rightful leader of the Commonwealth. Conroy had been his mentor for the last decade, graciously sharing his knowledge and opening his connections to Tobin as he'd grown into himself and his role. He'd been a father figure in many ways, and he could tell that Conroy regarded him with equal fondness. Tobin had been on track to rise in Conroy's administration, and then Rostov had done the unthinkable.

Though Tobin put on a friendly face each day, he couldn't wait to see Rostov called out as a usurper. The man was a monster. Monsters needed to be slain.

Tobin touched his belt, which contained a hidden compartment where he'd been carrying around a Dupe chip for months. The small gadget was his answer to getting the information Conroy wanted, but installing it had proved challenging. Attach a Dupe to someone else's omni or computer terminal, and all data running through the device could be routed to another recipient without the victim knowing that anything was amiss.

He'd bought a set of them on the black market and had been trying to get one installed in Rostov's executive offices since earlier that year. The chancellor had substantial security, naturally, and visitors were almost never left alone in any of the rooms with sensitive electronic equipment. Tobin had been trying to contrive the right circumstances to get in, but he was realizing that there would be no perfect time. He'd just have to go for it… somehow.

Tobin's desktop lit up with a summons from Rostov's Chief of Staff, Lucy Morell. *A sign from the universe if there ever was one.*

He took a few deep breaths to calm his nerves and then headed for the executive administrative offices in the neighboring building.

The construction noise was louder in the hallway, and a thin film of dust had settled onto the floor tiles, likely shaken loose from the ceiling. As annoying as the din was while working, Tobin appreciated the cover it offered when he needed to gather information. A person wearing a hard hat and safety vest was invisible walking through a hallway when there was a construction project going on nearby, and he'd been able to eavesdrop on rather interesting conversations without anyone taking notice.

Now, though, he needed to be his consummate, suited-professional self. He got along well enough with Lucy, though she was one of those no-nonsense people who was more likely to issue a stern glare than a smile.

He took a skybridge to the building housing the chancellor's office and rode the elevator to the upper floor. The entrance to the executive area was a two-story rotunda finished in marble and ornate woodwork on the upper floor. One wall was a bank of windows curving around the bottom of the dome, offering a perfectly centered view of a massive stone globe on the southern side of the United Mall park. The ten-meter-tall planet supposedly represented *all* planets of the Commonwealth, but cynics said it was a monument to Terrax itself.

A young aide, identified with a sky-blue sash, was waiting for Tobin.

"Good afternoon. Ms. Morell wanted to see me?" Tobin greeted.

"Yes. She's finishing up another meeting now and will be with you shortly. Please, follow me." The aide extended her arm and pivoted ninety degrees on her heel with dancer-like precision.

Tobin followed several paces back, taking the opportunity to look for new people or other changes since his last visit. There were several new aides he didn't recognize, though that role typically had high turnover. The furnishings and core staff were as he remembered.

The aide opened a wooden door and held it for him to enter. "You may wait for Ms. Morell in her office."

Tobin stepped inside. The office was surprisingly large, with a desk as well as a seating area. It was finished in wood and high-end textiles, following a blue and gold color scheme. Its most notable design element, though, was a life-sized painting on the back wall behind the desk, depicting a female warrior with armor that exaggerated every curve and was far too low-cut to serve any practical purpose. A very strange choice for a government office, in Tobin's opinion—but it looked expensive, so perhaps it had been a gift from an important donor.

"May I get you any refreshment?" the aide asked.

"No, thank you."

The door closed behind Tobin, leaving him alone. In Lucy Morell's office.

Stars alive, is this for real? While Rostov's office would have been preferable, his top aide's office next door would be on the same local network, so it was a sufficient place to plant the Dupe.

Tobin immediately flipped the antique physical latch on the door as a precaution. He reasoned that trying to explain a 'malfunctioning' lock on an old door was better than someone walking in on him mid-subterfuge.

He unclasped his belt to access the hidden slot where he'd

stashed a Dupe. The chip was only the size of his smallest fingernail and translucent, making it difficult to both see and handle.

Carefully gripping the device between his thumb and forefinger, Tobin laid down on the floor under the desk. He found an exposed hardline cable and placed the Dupe in a shadowed place that would be difficult to spot. It adhered like a nearly invisible sticker, perfectly blending into the rest of the equipment. Nanites within the device would burrow through the cable's sheath to form a direct connection to the computer. Since it worked through those hardline communications, there were no wireless signals to be detected through the regular security sweeps—one of the reasons the devices were so prized.

Standing up, he pulled out his omni to initiate the sync with the device. The one-time connection would activate it, and then all subsequent data running through the terminal could be routed to the receiver of his choosing.

A progress bar appeared on his omni screen, indicating the status of the sync. It advanced, frustratingly slow.

The door handle rattled. Someone was clearly trying to enter, but the lock was holding.

Tobin's pulse spiked. He decided that staying quiet was his best move for the moment. The sync was almost complete.

The handle rattled again, followed by a knock.

"Is it stuck?" Tobin asked, trying to act casual.

"Why won't this damn thing open?" an annoyed, muffled female voice said.

Tobin glanced at the sync, still not complete. "One sec, I'll take a look."

Another knock, more insistent.

"I'll try it from this side!" Tobin called, louder.

The progress bar was agonizingly slow but nearing the end.

Did syncing always take this long?

His heart pounded in his ears. Losing his cool now wouldn't help. He took a deep breath but nearly choked when another firm rap sounded at the door.

At last, the sync was complete. Tobin quickly closed out of the interface. He dashed across the room to unlock and open the door.

Lucy stood framed in the doorway, her hair slicked into a sleek bun high on her head and wearing a dark-blue skirted outfit well-suited to her matronly figure. She glowered at him. "Why was this locked?"

"Uh, looks like the latch was loose. It must have dropped down when the door closed." He tried to demonstrate the antique mechanism.

She looked him over, her eyes lingering on his flushed cheeks and the belt he'd incorrectly re-clasped in his haste, before she glanced up at the suggestive painting behind him. "This is a government office. Have a little decorum." Whatever conclusion she'd drawn wasn't favorable, but it was better than the truth. "The chancellor is waiting. Come on."

Tobin hurriedly fixed his belt and straightened his jacket. "What does Rostov want to talk about?"

"He has a new assignment for you."

"Anything interesting?"

Lucy led the way into the hall. "You're about to find out."

2

EVAN DEPARTED THE underground base feeling no more confident than when he'd arrived. In the week since returning to Aethos with Zaris and her corsairs, he'd been fully in the observation mode that had been his default as an undercover investigator. Every sight, every conversation fed into a larger vision of his circumstances.

His honest assessment was that Conroy was making up a plan as he went along. In all fairness, the chancellor had admitted as much. The previous plan had shattered with the destruction of the colony ship—people, supplies, technology. They were trying to get back on track. But they couldn't remain in limbo indefinitely.

Tensions were mounting. People were antsy. And that's when it could turn dangerous.

The muggy weather didn't help. Evan was struck by the oppressive humidity the moment he stepped outside. He'd started to get used to the planet's environment during his initial trek with Anya, but their subsequent travels had reset his internal gauge.

Eager to get back to the comfort aboard the *Asamar*, Evan headed across the field toward the parked starship. He was only a third of the way across when angry shouts caught his attention.

A dozen men were gathered at a makeshift camp along the northern edge of the field. Though the firepit wasn't currently in use, the group was hanging out at a set of logs positioned around a stone ring. Half of the men were seated and the rest were on their feet. Two near the center of the group were squaring off.

One man held his arms wide, and the other reached under his jacket for something unseen. Instinct told Evan it was a weapon.

Don't do it. As the words formed in his mind, his skin tingled and heat spread from his core.

Trees surrounding the incident bowed as though blown by a gust of wind, leaves rustling and branches swaying. But Evan soon realized that it wasn't a movement of the air. The trees themselves were vibrating.

A hum of energy swelled, making Evan's fine hairs stand on end. Buzzing rang in his ears as pressure built in his head. An electrical tingle danced across his fingertips. He sensed the power coming from the ground, traveling all the way through him. It was his to command, ready to be unleashed.

Stop fighting. As the words filled his mind, the two men abruptly froze mid-taunt.

The onlookers glanced around in confusion. It took Evan a few seconds to realize what had happened. Through subconscious intention, he'd gripped them in an invisible vise. Evan hadn't consciously planned for that to happen, but it's what he had *wanted*.

The two men seemed unaware of what was happening to them, as though they were in a trance.

We see you, a voice whispered in his mind.

Evan's heart leaped at the sudden presence. It had come from inside his mind… but it wasn't part of himself.

His concentration broken, the two men snapped free from the invisible vise. They continued their argument as though there'd been no interruption.

"You're taking it all for yourself?"

"You had your chance."

"You can't take everything!" The first man lunged for the other.

Now knowing that it was possible, Evan tried to restrain them again—purposefully this time.

The man who'd been mid-lunge dropped to the ground as he froze but his body kept moving. His opponent went rigid, his eyes glazed over.

It's telepathic control, not physical, Evan realized as he assessed the reaction. *But how does the telepathy work?*

He released the two men from his hold and jogged over.

Other people were already coming to address the commotion. Samor was the first to react. "Gentlemen, everyone will get fed. Let's keep it friendly."

"You heard him. Back off!" Tarek growled, storming across the field. His face was flushed and his shoulders squared in the way Evan had seen when he was gearing up for a fight.

As Evan arrived, the man who'd fallen was back on his feet and brushing off his clothes. "What happened?"

"You're so drunk you can't stay upright," his opponent shot back.

"I haven't had a sip since we got to this confounded place."

"I tripped you," Evan jumped in.

The two men turned to face him, confused.

"You're clearly wondering how. Well, I can give you another demonstration if you want to get better acquainted with the ground."

The man indistinctly grumbled something that offered an unfavorable graphic image.

Evan loomed over the man. "What did you say?"

"I said you can go—"

"Enough!" Samor bellowed. "No one will be wishing ill of anyone today."

Tarek stepped in to take the problem man by the neck of his jacket. "If what you've been given isn't good enough for you, then you'll get nothing at all." He roughly dragged him away.

The other onlookers dispersed.

"Thanks for the assist," Samor said once they were alone.

"No problem," Evan told him. Truthfully, though, it *was* problematic. He didn't want to be seen as taking sides, and he wasn't sure how his actions might have come across.

"What did you do back there?" Samor asked tentatively.

"I'm not sure. I'm still trying to figure out how this alien tech works and what I can do with it."

"I heard that it wasn't all the Korani."

"Yeah, that's true. I don't know how to separate the two." Evan couldn't decide if the Syndicate's interface serum or the bizarre 'primal energy' situation was more unnerving. At least the Syndicate's product had been used by humans before. He didn't know what interfacing with the primal energy would mean for his health or sanity. For that matter, he didn't rightly know when he was even tapping into the power.

Samor nodded thoughtfully. "It is very interesting what fate dealt you. I trust you will find a way through."

"It's that or give up, right?"

"And we both know you're not doing that."

Feeling the renewed weight of his responsibility and

unexpected power, Evan excused himself. The *Asamar* had become his refuge. More importantly, that's where Anya was waiting. No doubt, his latest telepathic feat would pique her scientific curiosity.

When he arrived on the ship, Anya was in none of the usual daytime places—flight deck or lounge room.

"Anya?" he called out.

Sam's voice filled the room. "She is in her lab."

"When did we get that?"

"It has been an ongoing project over the last week," the AI replied. "I will illuminate a path for you."

Lights pulsed down the corridor. Evan followed them to the lift. Down one deck and heading toward the aft of the starship, he arrived at a sealed doorway. He waved his hand over the controls, and a chime sounded.

The door slid open to reveal a well-equipped scientific research lab, complete with work surfaces, sample holders, and complex-looking equipment Evan couldn't begin to identify.

Anya was seated in a tall swivel-chair at one of the workbenches. She beamed at him. "Hey! What do you think?"

"Wow, you've been busy."

"I decided that having a full set of scientific equipment would be really handy. Sensors can tell us a lot, but learning some things requires hands-on experimentation."

"I absolutely agree."

She smiled at him coyly. "Strictly professionally speaking."

"Of course."

"Well, I'm pretty well set up now, in any case. It's taken a lot longer to construct everything than your work with Sam, but we got there."

"Anya has been very patient with me. I cannot see into her mind in the same way as I can yours, Evan, but Conroy's library yielded a wealth of information. Combined with Anya's guidance, I was able to construct a variety of scientific instruments."

"First project is a deeper analysis of those weird rocks Zaris got on Pavia," Anya said.

"On that note, something interesting just happened outside." Evan told her about the run-in with Zaris' corsairs and the apparent telepathic link.

Anya took in the words with her usual professional focus. Her brows furrowed slightly and she pursed her lips in thought. "It made sense that you were able to interface with Roman during your fight, because he also had the primer. But it's interesting that you were able to influence these people, too."

"Does that mean I can do it with *anyone*, or have people picked up some of the nanites from the environment on Aethos?"

"A good question, and something I'd want to investigate under proper experimental conditions when I get the chance."

"I should probably play around with my abilities more," Evan admitted. "I'm just not used to having this kind of power. I don't want to inadvertently hurt anyone."

"You've been able to do the most under duress. Getting conscious control might be more difficult."

"I'll keep working on it."

"I'll help you in any way I can."

"Thanks."

She stood up behind her workstation. "How did it go with Conroy?"

"That part was fine. My conversation with Roman... Still not sure what to make of that guy."

"What's your read?"

"He's a cornered man who'll say anything to further his

personal objectives."

"And those are…?"

"Complicated. More than anything, he wants to be acknowledged and accepted. I'd actually feel bad for the guy if he hadn't been so intent on killing me."

She scoffed. "Yeah, great start to a friendship."

"I wasn't going for 'buddies'. I just want him as a resource—extract information from him to serve our own goals. I know he's mostly just playing along, but there *is* a genuinely strained relationship with his brother. The search for praise from someone who'll never grant it is a crack ready to be wedged open."

"Well, I hope I never see him again. He pointed a gun at me one too many times." She scrunched her brows. "Actually, even *once* was too many, and it's been a lot more than that."

"I've spent a lot of time in the moral gray. I've learned to see the value of an asset while despising the person."

She shook her head. "I hope he's worth it."

"So far, he's given just enough to keep us talking. He knows what he's doing."

She came around the work table to stand directly in front of him. "Do you have a plan?"

"Getting there." He placed his hands on her hips. "But regardless of what happens with Roman or Conroy, I think we should have plans of our own. Fallback contingencies."

"That's a very good idea."

"We have Haven."

"I could think of worse places—especially since Sam could help us build it out."

"Since I appear to be part of your plans," the AI intoned, "I would like to again express my desire to locate the Korani."

"I know, Sam. We got a little side-tracked with the future

of humanity," Evan said.

"I don't mean to minimize your conflicts. However, humans are currently grappling with a political disagreement. Is it not also important for you to investigate the Korani's disappearance to rule out a potential planet- or civilization-ending threat?"

"Sam's right," Anya said. "There's the signal on Terrax. We should figure out what that is."

"That *would* be very nice to know," Evan agreed. "There's a lot to consider. How many factions are we dealing with, and who's aligned with whom?"

"We need to be careful about who gets access to this ship," Anya said. "Who can we trust?"

"I don't trust anyone other than you." Their growing bond simultaneously brought him joy and apprehension. He hadn't allowed himself to get close to anyone in a long time, and Anya now held real power over him.

She gently ran her hand down his arm. "Same. Marta is no doubt out there looking for the ship, and I don't want anything bad to happen to Sam."

"I appreciate your concern," the AI said. "However, I have significant weaponry to protect myself."

"Are you willing to fight, Sam?" Evan asked. "Things could get messy. We seem to have wandered into the middle of a brewing civil war."

"Noted. Your analysis that certain human factions would wish to possess the *Asamar* and strip me of my autonomy is a significant concern. Nonetheless, I remain confident in your leadership."

"The fact is, Sam, that Anya and I are more or less two nobodies in the Commonwealth," Evan continued. "We don't have any real influence."

"You have sway where it matters. I will take necessary actions to protect my own interests and ensure your safety."

"What about Roman?" Evan asked. "Do we have to worry about you being overtaken again—by him or someone else who's had the primer?"

"I should note that even with the additional Korani presence, he was unsuccessful in forcing me to comply with his demands. The primer is not what should concern you, but rather the unseen influence behind power. Roman had a darkness within him that was easy for those with ill intentions to exploit."

"He's the kind of person Rostov would love to turn," Anya pointed out.

"I wonder what the Korani learned from him while they were merged?" Evan mused.

"That entity is now locked away, but you do have another resource," Sam said.

Anya brightened. "Oh! Part of the Korani is in the animals and plants, right?"

"Correct. Though they are very different from my original people, they are wise and observant and may be able to give you answers I cannot."

"Have you tried to communicate with them yourself?" Anya asked.

"Yes, but they don't have interest in me. I think you organics might have better luck."

Evan sighed. "This whole 'you organics' thing, Sam... No."

"Have I offended you?"

"It's just not the nicest phrase."

"I apologize. Would you prefer 'mono-biologics'?"

Evan and Anya exchanged glances. "We'll keep working on it," she said.

"Well, I'd love to get the Korani perspective on this," Evan said. "How do you talk with them here on Aethos, Sam?"

"It's not that simple. They are no longer in the form of my makers. I *can* communicate with them, but they are not my people."

"What have they told you?"

"They have spoken of their existence on this world. They have no information about what happened to Koranis or why they are here. They have no memory of their origins before they gave themselves to this planet."

"That means they're invested in this world. They'll probably be willing to help us protect it," Anya said.

Evan frowned. "I just find it hard to believe that there's no record anywhere. How they got here, or how they merged with the planet—or whatever you want to call it."

"I can infer that they took a ship," Sam said. "I believe that its wreckage may be some of the artifacts humans discovered here."

It made sense. "Do you think they'd be willing to speak with me?" Evan asked.

"Yes, they have been eager to properly meet you."

"I think that's our next step, then."

"I will guide you," Sam said. "But you should prepare yourself for the experience. There are many aspects to my creators, and some voices are louder than others. Roman listened to a dark influence I would not consider a good representation of my people, but different factions within the collective will try to appeal to different parts of you. Are you willing to open your mind, Evan?"

"It's as open as it's ever going to be. Tell me how to talk to them."

ZARIS FIDGETED IN her seat inside one of the hab tents erected near Conroy's bunker. She'd been staying with the bulk of her crew aboard the *Invictus* orbiting the planet, and Tarek had been sticking near Conroy planetside to make sure everything was in order. But with reports of infighting, remaining at a distance was no longer an option.

"Are people starving down here or something?" she asked.

Tarek shook his head. "Tensions are high. The crew is eager for action."

"We always spend plenty of time sitting around between jobs. Is it the heat and humidity driving them crazy?" After less than half an hour back on the planet, she was already feeling it. Something about the air feeling like a wet, weighted blanket wrapped around her chest made her antsy.

"A bigger issue is Conroy's team. They're keeping watch on everything we do, like they expect us to steal."

"*Has* anyone stolen?"

"I can't say for certain."

"There's your problem."

"We don't have issues like that on the *Invictus*."

"It's not just our ship's crew down here, and not everyone

here is on the same team. This temporary alliance doesn't make us friends. People are trying to look out for themselves and their tribe."

Tarek nodded. "Good point. The two guys that got into it were both ours but from different ship crews."

Zaris flourished her hand with vindication. "Which brings us back to the point. Why am I here?"

"You're the face of this operation. The crew listens to you."

"If they won't listen to you, too, then you have no business being my first officer."

He clenched his jaw and took a measured breath. "I can take care of it. But I thought you'd want to be involved."

I'm already involved in more than I want. She sighed. "Tarek, I have no interest in policing petty spats."

"Fine, but I need to know what to tell them."

"About what?"

"The plan. A timeline. Anything!"

"To be determined."

He glared at her. "How long are we going to wait around for others to decide our fate?"

"That's the question, isn't it?" She stood up. "Call me when there's a *real* problem."

Before he had time to fully articulate a response, she stormed out of the tent.

Zaris knew she was being a little unfair to her first officer, but the truth was that her involvement in crew conflicts would lead nowhere positive. Inevitably, she'd wind up taking a side in each argument, which would only further the rifts. It was imperative that she remain a neutral figurehead. Tarek could be an enforcer, but he must remain separate from her oversight authority.

Being in the open air offered temporary relief from the

weight she shouldered. Tarek's concerns were perfectly valid, which didn't make her job any easier. She *didn't* know when a plan might be formulated, and she'd already handed over more control than she'd ever wanted to surrender. Even if her crew *wanted* to leave, they'd be facing months of transit through normal space and had insufficient supplies to make that journey without severe rationing.

We need to all get along. But I need a seat at the table. She'd been promised that much when she'd signed up. Which meant either they hadn't been planning at all, or she'd been cut out of the discussions. Neither option was good.

As she fumed about her predicament, Zaris spotted Evan and Anya leaving the *Asamar* on the other side of the field. If anyone could offer insights into prospective planning activities, it would be them.

Zaris set an intercept course and trekked across the field. She waved at them as she approached, and they slowed their pace.

"Zaris, what are you doing down here?" Evan asked when she was within earshot.

She shrugged. "You know, just making sure the world wasn't falling apart."

"Is this about the fight?"

She eyed him, surprised he would jump to that question. "You heard about that?"

"I was there."

Well, that figures. At least this would give her an opportunity to get another perspective to contrast Tarek's account of the events. "How bad was it?"

Evan glanced at Anya and they exchanged a knowing look. "Just bored people wanting action."

Zaris frowned. "What aren't you telling me?"

"It's nothing about the fight. I'm just figuring out my new abilities."

"Meaning?"

"He stopped the fight," Anya jumped in.

"I assisted its resolution," Evan said. "It wasn't a big deal."

It was obvious to Zaris that he was skipping over a big portion of the story. She could guess what might be going unsaid. "You used that alien nanite stuff on them?"

"Something happened, yes. We were just on our way to try to find out what might be going on."

"Where are you going?"

"Into the forest."

"Why?"

"To talk to the planet."

She blinked at him. "Wait, what?"

"He's going to try to commune with the Korani who've melded with Aethos' environment," Anya explained.

"Oh. That's… weird."

"Weird or not, Sam thinks it's worthwhile, so I'm going to try."

Zaris tapped her foot. She still didn't know what to make of the alien tech or Evan's mysterious abilities, but learning as much as she could about them seemed like a good idea. "May I come with you?"

Both Evan's and Anya's brows shot up with surprise. Evan pointed over his shoulder to a backpack. "It's going to be a hike."

"I'm up for it," she said with a confident tone that didn't entirely reflect her true feelings.

Anya shrugged and looked at Evan.

He sighed. "As long as you keep up, you can come along. But it's only to observe."

— — —

Evan was prepared to regret allowing Zaris to come along, but she had no difficulty matching his brisk pace, even wearing a pack filled with the survival supplies he'd insisted she bring in case they ran into trouble. She had kept unusually quiet during their hour-long hike away from camp.

Given their newfound access to transportation vehicles, it felt a little counterintuitive to be setting off on foot through the forest again. However, Sam had emphasized the need for Evan to 'acclimate' and avail himself to the alien collective consciousness in the environment, and walking to the destination was the best way to do that.

The place Sam had identified was several kilometers to the northeast. Evan followed a route on a wrist-mounted map Sam had fabricated for that purpose, which was remotely linked to Sam's sensor suite. The alien ship was able to capture clear readings where other human technology struggled to cut through the interference. With his new knowledge about the world, Evan now realized that the 'interference' that had plagued the colony expedition's planning was actually the alien presence he was now seeking out. It made perfect sense that Sam, with his shared ancestry, would have no difficulty navigating the world.

Being out in the forest again had a somewhat calming effect, though Evan couldn't relax while being vigilant about his surroundings.

As they walked, Evan noticed regular rustling in the bushes several meters from their path, following their route and remaining at a consistent distance. They were being followed.

His pulse spiked as a reflexive response, his memories of

the planet's vicious creatures still fresh in his mind. However, his newly attuned senses told him that this wasn't a serious threat. All the same, he wanted to know what was there.

"We're being tailed," he whispered to Anya.

She glanced in the direction he'd seen the movement. "I thought so."

Zaris perked up. "Everything okay?"

"Yeah, it's fine. Come over here." Evan motioned to his right side, which would place himself between her and the unseen creature.

Anya's hand moved to a handgun at her hip, and she nodded to Evan.

Evan suspected it was one of the panthers tracking them. He couldn't feel the animal in the way that he'd experienced a telepathic link with others. All the same, he tried to reach out with his mind. *"We are only here to talk."*

A creature abruptly burst through the trees, a mass of leaves and vines. It rolled and clawed through the underbrush, as though the vines were a dozen legs.

Evan recoiled at the unexpected sight. *Is it a plant or animal?*

It didn't matter. The thing was hurdling toward them.

Anya fired.

The pulse blast struck one of the vine tentacles, sending a ripple radiating through the creature's body. The mass of apparent foliage let out a rumbling bray of wounded surprise.

As abruptly as it had come, it tumbled back into the trees and disappeared.

Evan stood in stunned silence for a few seconds. "What the hell was that thing?"

"An extremely well-camouflaged giant spider," Anya stated.

"Wait, *what*?" Evan blinked at her.

"Yeah, we saw a few in the survey. They were never aggressive toward the drones—don't like electronics, it seems—so they didn't seem like a big deal."

"That thing was as tall as me!"

She shrugged. "It's all show."

"How can you be so calm?!" Zaris exclaimed. "I've seen a lot of crazy things, but I've never seen *that*!"

"After you've visited enough planets, you get used to things trying to eat you," Anya said.

Zaris pinched the bridge of her nose. "This. This is why I don't leave space."

"I hate to break it to you, but there are some pretty nasty creatures in the void, too..."

"No. I don't want to know anything about them."

"That doesn't mean they won't exist," Anya pointed out.

"Ignorance is bliss, right?" Zaris shook her head. "I want to go back to a place where being eaten isn't a consideration."

"Sorry, but that's not an option," Anya told her. "Humans are a prospective menu item pretty much everywhere."

Zaris frowned. "Anya, you're really not helping."

"Hey, *you* asked to come along."

Evan held up his hands. "No one is getting eaten today! Come on." He set off along their path.

—

Evan maintained a brisker pace for the rest of the hike, hoping to wind Zaris enough to prevent further argument. The plan worked, to his relief, granting a peaceful final stretch of their journey.

When they reached the destination indicated on the map,

Evan spotted a field nestled against an impressive rock formation wrapping around two sides. The air was calm in the protected hollow and even the wildlife seemed quieter here.

Initially, Evan was unsure why Sam had singled out this place. But as he took in his surroundings, Evan soon felt a shift in the energy. It vibrated with a subtle electrical charge that not only prickled his skin but resonated in his very core.

"Do you feel that?" he asked the two women.

"I don't think so," Anya replied while Zaris shook her head.

"You should stay back," he told them.

Anya motioned to Zaris, and they retreated to the tree line.

Evan stood in the center of the clearing. He closed his eyes, opening his senses. Soft floral and woody aromas wafted on the soft breeze. Bird songs and haunting animal calls immersed him in the environment.

"I'm here," he said in his mind, sending the message out to the unseen beings lurking in the forest.

A presence stirred at the edge of his mind. His skin prickled as he was abruptly overcome with the sensation of being watched. However, there wasn't one vantage—it was as though the trees themselves were now intently focused. He had been an accessory in this environment, but in an instant he'd become the centerpiece. It was like he was being truly *seen* for the first time.

"We see you. You have changed," a voice said in his mind. The message swirled and swelled like wind, an impression more than true words. He recognized it as the voice he'd heard earlier while breaking up the fight.

"Do you mean how I was Touched?" Evan asked.

"Yes. But there is more."

He could sense the sentient presence evaluating his body

and mind. His defensive, protective instincts wanted to close off the probe, but he willed himself to relax and submit to the process. Though he had no reason to trust this modified Korani consciousness, he *did* trust Sam. And if Sam told him that these beings meant no harm, then he would do what was necessary to build a relationship.

After a minute or two of standing in silence while the alien consciousness conducted its evaluation, Evan sensed the beings relax their probing.

"You are not like the others who came to this world," they said.

"Every human is unique."

"They wish to take. You want to learn."

The comment was the opening Evan had been looking for. *"I do want to learn. I want to understand how you came to be what you are now."*

"We only know what we are, not what once was."

Sam had warned about the memory of the collective consciousness not including the Korani's history, but Evan still wanted to see how much he could glean. *"Can you show me what you know of this world?"*

"We will try."

Images filled Evan's mind, taking him on a journey across forests, plains, and sea. With each change in location, he was fully immersed in the environment—not simply observing it, but being a *part* of it.

Power flowed within each place he was shown—unseen to the untrained eye, but a monumental force, nonetheless. In those locations, the wildlife was bigger and stronger, the trees more majestic. Life thrived on the power. The Korani had dispersed to those sites around the planet. Only a handful of guardians remained.

The guardians.

New images filled Evan's mind. In a rush, he was tumbling through a thick section of jungle. Trees and vines bent out of his way, twisting to clear a path rather than breaking. He was one with the place, protecting it because it was an extension of himself. He fed on the power of the land.

There was so much to take in. Too much.

His eyes shot open. Sucking in a sharp breath, he made a conscious effort to calm his racing heart.

When he could breathe normally again, he turned around to address Anya and Zaris. "That wasn't what I was expecting."

"Did you talk to them?" Anya asked.

"More like 'communicate' than 'talk', but yes. And I think it's all starting to make sense to me now."

Zaris eyed him skeptically. "You got that much out of talking to a tree for a few minutes?"

Anya glared at her.

Zaris held up her hand defensively and took a step back.

"The telepathic communications don't happen at the same speed as spoken word," Evan explained. "I feel like it's been hours. They showed me the planet. I think I understand what the Korani did here."

The two women looked at him expectantly. "And?" Anya prompted.

"It would be easier to show you than try to explain it with words. But I need Sam's help."

4

BEING BACK IN the underground bunker was like returning home for Conroy—but that former sanctuary had been tainted by the attack, and his people would never fully recover. They'd lost too many friends, who'd become more like family in their years of hiding. That kind of loss couldn't be forgotten, but it could become fuel. His job as their leader was to harness their bitterness and anger and transform it into action.

How to act was now the question. Though the addition of Zaris' corsairs had granted precious numbers to support their cause, Conroy couldn't trust that those rogues were any more than casually aligned with his current objectives. Only those truly committed to a vision could be trusted. *Can I gain their allegiance?*

In many ways, that would be his first test. They were a loyal enough bunch to have committed to Zaris and followed her to a remote world on nothing more than a promise, so they *could* believe in a vision. Whether or not he could sell them on his dreams for the Commonwealth's future remained to be seen.

That inspiration needed to be instilled sooner than later. "That fight today wasn't a good sign," Conroy mused to his head of security.

"Whenever you get a large group of people together, run-ins are bound to happen," Samor replied.

"It was more than that, and you know it."

Samor nodded. "We may have *food*, but some of it is a lot more appetizing. Not to mention the other supplies."

"I thought Zaris said her people came with provisions?"

"They did… but now they're not satisfied with *what* they have after seeing the alternatives."

"What's their request?"

"The tone from earlier was more like a 'demand', though that was just a random guy, not anyone with a leadership voice. He was saying that we should pool everything and 'share'. What he really meant is that they want a free-for-all to grab the good stuff and leave us with whatever is left over."

Conroy shook his head. "I won't do that to our people."

"Obviously. But we need to come up with a strategy fast, because I expect this discontent will only get worse. And they outnumber us by a significant margin, so we really don't want to find ourselves in a disagreement."

"No, definitely not," Conroy said. "What will it take to make these people happy?"

"You know as well as I do that they'll invent new reasons to complain as soon as one need is met."

"What do they *really* want?"

"To be well-fed and feel safe," Samor replied.

"We're surrounded by food."

"Many of these people have never seen a tree outside of a planter box. They don't have the know-how to process the natural resources around here, and we don't have the staff to hand-hold them through the process."

"How long would it take to get them equipped?" Conroy asked.

"My point, sir, is that *no* amount of training would make the endeavor worthwhile for now."

"There was a time in our history when 'living off the land' was the only way of life for humans. Now, too many expect everything to come from a box."

Samor shrugged. "What can I say?"

Conroy nodded. "We need supplies—the kind of supplies we were supposed to get from the colony ship. But where can we get them now?"

—   —   —

Returning to the *Asamar*, Evan's mind was still full of the images. A diagram, of sorts, was forming—not quite a map, but an illustration of hotspots around Aethos. His telepathic link with the alien consciousness had revealed a living network on the planet. Whatever 'primal energies' he'd encountered on Pavia also existed on Aethos, and the Korani had surrendered their corporeal forms to blend with them.

"Sam, I need you to pull this information from my mind," Evan requested as he stepped into the lounge room, followed by Anya and Zaris.

"It seems like it was a productive chat with the beings controlling this world," the AI replied.

The phrasing caught Evan by surprise. Before, Sam had spoken about the Korani settlers as inhabitants at one with the world—but not in *control*. "There wasn't a lot of talking. But I want to show Anya and Zaris what they shared with me, if you can translate what's in my head to a visual."

Evan sensed a little pressure and a tingle as the AI assessed the information through the telepathic interface.

"Interesting," Sam said. "This is more than they were

willing to share with me."

"I'd really love to see what you're talking about," Anya interjected.

"Give me a few minutes to parse this," the AI requested.

Zaris crossed her arms. "How could the planet tell you *anything*, Evan?"

"Telepathy is a series of electrical signals like other forms of communication," Sam told her. "These trees just happen to be better at sharing their thoughts."

"I think we should listen to the sentient ship on this one," Evan said.

Anya nodded pensively. "There are many communications in the natural world we don't fully understand. For a long time, humans thought that animals were restricted to body language and limited vocalizations. But there's a lot more going on that's difficult for us to perceive."

"I have completed my visual model," Sam announced.

The large screen integrated into the lounge room's wall illuminated with a semi-translucent image of a planet. Evan had seen Aethos from space enough times to recognize the continents. However, this rendering also included features beneath the surface.

A dozen or so patches around the planet were rendered in bright blue, and a complex web of finer conduits connected those hot spots. The active zones corresponded to the locations Evan had been shown in his strange telepathic communion— not that he had seen those places with his own eyes, but he could *feel* that they were the correct locations.

As he studied the planet, Evan couldn't shake the feeling that he was looking at the diagram of an organism rather than a planet. *Maybe the former Korani really are in 'control' of this place.*

He set aside that point and tried to focus on the core discussion. "The cave where we found the *Asamar* and the nearby valley are only one area with concentrated alien signatures. I'm sure these places look familiar to you, Anya."

She nodded. "Yes. These overlay with the odd energy readings we'd observed during the mission evaluation. Plus a few others I haven't seen."

"And you'd written off those readings as being naturally occurring. And then we thought maybe it was just the alien tech."

"Right."

"Well, it seems that you were right both times. Based on what we saw on Pavia," Evan intentionally didn't mention Temple World in Zaris' presence, "and have observed here on Aethos, it appears there are certain planets with these so-called 'primal energies'. Quite possibly, Koranis had them, too."

"I can confirm," Sam said. "However, those energy wells are no longer active on the planet, based on our visit. I can't say when or why they dispersed in the intervening six thousand years."

"Could it have something to do with the 'glassing' we saw?" Anya asked.

Evan nodded. "That's what I'm wondering. Whatever weapon was used to destroy Koranis, it might not have been targeting just the Korani living on the surface."

"Wait, hold on," Zaris said, holding up her hands. "Are you saying that there's some kind of planet-killing weapon that can destroy these 'energy sources', or whatever they are?"

"Whatever happened with that weapon occurred thousands of years ago," Evan said. "What I'm trying to understand is how the pieces connect. The nanites. The 'primal energies'. The alien devices. We know that the nanites can function off-world with the help of a controller—like my bracelet—but what are the limitations? Did the Korani make the energy wells, or is it the other way around?"

"The primal energies are older than the Korani," Sam said. "The ancient texts of my makers document and revere them. As I explained before, the nanites at the foundational level of Korani tech—including this ship—are modeled after those energies. And what you are observing on this world pre-date any Korani exploration of this planet."

"But that doesn't mean they weren't seeded," Anya murmured.

"What do you mean?" Evan asked.

Her brows scrunched up. "I don't know, just thinking out loud. When science observes identical things on multiple planets, we generally assume a panspermia origin—that there was a common ancestral source for that material, and it was distributed to the various destinations."

"From meteors or whatnot?"

"Right. That would be an example of natural origin. But it's also possible that the distribution could have been directed—especially given the self-propagating nature of this technology."

Evan focused on her. "Are you suggesting that there might be an even more ancient alien race that sent out 'seeds' for what we're now calling the 'primal energies'?"

"A half-formed and unsupported guess at this point, but yes."

Zaris passed her gaze between them, blinking with her jaw slack. "Is this how you two always spend your free time?"

Evan ignored her. "It *would* explain how we found such similar things on worlds that were so far apart." He kept the statement vague, knowing that Anya would fill in the blanks with Temple World and the other planets they'd identified with the star map.

"I agree with the assessment," Sam chimed in. "The Korani had what you might characterize as religious reverence for the primal energies, but it was also accepted that the power had come from *somewhere*. There were many theories about the origin, and a particular sect hoped to one day travel to that place—"

Evan snapped to attention. "Whoa, Sam, that would have been helpful to mention before."

"Why?"

"Because you may have just explained where the Korani went when they left Koranis. What if they finally located the 'source' and went to find it?"

Anya nodded along with his reasoning. "It would be a compelling reason, but that still doesn't explain what happened to the planet. There's no debate that it was destroyed."

"I wasn't questioning that at all," Evan countered. "Let me ask you, Sam, did the Korani ever target a world for settlement that *didn't* have these primal energies?"

"No."

"Do the Korani need that energy to live?"

"Not constant exposure, but the nanites at the center of all Korani technological functions would eventually fail without access."

Evan flourished his hand. "There you go."

Anya tapped her finger while she thought. "I hadn't considered that angle before."

"Neither had I," Evan admitted. "Koranis was the homeworld for the Korani, but they might have been a new iteration of life, just like the creatures on Aethos transformed from the Korani settlers."

"It's an amazing lifecycle, if it's true," Anya said, her voice bright with wonder and excitement. "We normally think about evolution on the scale of hundreds of thousands or millions of years, but that kind of rapid adaptation would allow a species to have exceptional exploration and growth!"

Zaris held up her hands. "I'm not sure what you two are going on about, but what does this have to do with anything?"

Evan turned to face her. "Because everyone in the Commonwealth wants to use this Korani technology—the *Asamar*'s jump drive, the fabrication tech, these nanites that essentially give us telepathy and telekinesis. But considering that the homeworld of its creators was destroyed, there's a very real possibility that this very technology was related to their demise. And before we allow it to spread around the Commonwealth, wouldn't it be good to know where it originated and if it's dangerous?"

Zaris crossed her arms. "Okay, that's a valid point."

"What we've been piecing together today about the Korani—and potentially an even older alien race—are all important clues to that larger picture," Anya explained.

"Unfortunately, too much of it is still hypothetical," Evan said. "I do think we're getting somewhere toward understanding how they colonized other planets, but there's still the big outstanding question about why the Korani needed to leave their homeworld."

"I can't shake the feeling that they knew they were going to be attacked and left proactively," Anya contended.

"I agree with Anya," Sam stated.

"Let's assume that the 'primal energy' was intentionally spread to different worlds," Anya continued. "If that force was vital to my way of life, I think I'd want to hunt down its source."

"In military operations, you would fall back to basecamp if

you're facing a threat that's too big to take on. I think that general approach could apply at the civilization level," Evan agreed.

"That all hinges on Koranis itself being an outpost," Anya pointed out.

"It's just a gut feeling. The collective consciousness on this world doesn't remember their previous form, so why would the Korani be any different?"

Zaris shrugged. "It all sounds like a lot of wild leaps to me."

Maybe it was. But wild leaps had become Evan's life in recent weeks. Before he could articulate a response, Sam cut in again. "Evan, Chancellor Conroy is calling."

"Answer." He took a deep breath. "Chancellor, what can I do for you?"

Conroy's voice came over the speaker. "Evan, there's something I'd like to discuss with you. Can you come back to the bunker?"

Though he'd had enough meetings about official business and the future of humanity for the day, declining wasn't really an option. "Sure, I'll head over." He ended the call.

"I'll stay here and start digging into this new data," Anya said.

Zaris took a step toward the door. "And *I* need to make sure Tarek has gotten the crew to behave."

"I'll walk you out," Evan told her. He was about to leave, but the expectant look from Anya made it clear he couldn't depart without a proper goodbye. Though he didn't want to rub the new relationship in Zaris' face, keeping Anya happy was his bigger concern. He went to give her a quick kiss farewell, but she grabbed the back of his neck and held him to draw it out.

As they finally parted, Anya shot a territorial look in Zaris' direction before bringing her gaze back to him. "I'll see you soon."

"Yeah…" He headed for the exit before it could get even more awkward.

As they descended the ramp off the ship, Zaris came alongside him. "Looks like everything is going well with you two."

"I wouldn't want to do any of this without her."

Zaris raised her eyebrows. "I see."

"She knows you and I have a history. So…"

"Yeah, I gathered that. Well, she has nothing to worry about from me."

I hope she means that. Despite her words, there was still something in Zaris' expression that spoke to unresolved feelings Evan didn't need muddying an already complicated dynamic. "I'll let you know if Conroy tells me anything you should be aware of."

"Thanks." Zaris turned to go, then hesitated. "Hey, Evan… Thanks for taking me with you today."

"Sure. Anytime."

"I needed a reminder that there's more to life than being a ship captain."

"There sure is."

— — —

Anya's scalp tingled. She got the feeling whenever she was really engaged in a project—some kind of physical response to her hyper-focus. She hadn't experienced that 'in-the-zone' feeling for months, and she relished the sensation again.

Her latest project was revisiting the serum analysis she'd previously attempted based on Evan's blood sample. Working with that single specimen and with limited information about the underlying Korani nanites, her previous research attempt had promptly hit a dead end. Now, though, she had a much better understanding of the alien technology, giving her a better sense of which elements to analyze.

The revelations about the Korani's integration into Aethos had given her new ideas about what to look for at the micro and nano levels. Biological systems often mirrored each other, so macro expressions could indicate interactions at tiny, unseen levels—much like how a mycelium network in the forest floor resembled neurons in a brain.

So, if the planet has different hot zones of activity, what does that mean for a person? She mused. "Hey, Sam… Do you have a body scan of Evan?"

"Yes, several."

"Could you filter for the kind of energy signatures like those in the hot zones around Aethos and look for similar energy in Evan?"

"One moment."

After several seconds, a three-dimensional rendering appeared on the holoprojector, showing a translucent human figure with bright blue highlights in various places. There was so much more than Anya had anticipated. The strongest concentration was in the head, with another large cluster between the stomach and heart, and smaller hot spots on the hands. Each zone was connected to the others through fine filaments that were only visible under magnification.

"Can you explain what this is showing, Sam? Are these bright spots nanite activity?"

"Not exactly. It appears that Evan's cells are emitting this particular form of energy."

Anya's breath caught in her throat. "Has there been a

change to his mitochondrial function?"

"I do not have a sufficient baseline scan to accurately determine biological modifications."

Despite the AI's hedging on the point, Anya could think of no other explanation other than Evan's very cells changing to enable production of the exotic energy. She'd been operating on the assumption that the alien nanites would persist as an independent entity within a body, but actually fusing with the host to change its own cells' functions… that was more in line with her observations in the field about Aethos' wildlife, and it would also explain why she'd been unable to isolate the effects during her testing of the individual nanites.

As she thought through the implications, she was reminded of an old phrase. *They become more than the sum of their parts.*

The nanites were never intended to exist on their own—they would merge with a host and become something new entirely.

But that meant she was facing an even more shocking possibility. *Evan isn't entirely human anymore.*

That was a bold leap and not one she took lightly. It would take more study, and she needed to apply the same scientific rigor and testing she would with any other experimental investigation. "There's a lot going on with all of this, Sam. Can you help me parse it?"

"Certainly. My evolving understanding of human biology and your goals for this research have also better equipped me to evaluate the data and offer further research suggestions."

"What have you got for me?"

"I believe your first investigative query is about the so-called 'serum' the Syndicate uses to interface with Korani tech, correct?"

Anya nodded. "That's at the core of it, yes."

"Well, the rock sample Zaris obtained seems to be the key. Would you like me to walk you through my analysis?"

"Please do." Anya settled in at the workstation in front of the wall screen. This could very well be the most consequential research of her career, and she didn't want to miss any detail.

5

LUCK COULD BE a fickle beast, but Marta couldn't deny that she'd been *extremely* lucky. When Pavia had been attacked by the traitor's fleet, it had seemed like a disaster in the making. But the short-term loss had all been worthwhile if the information displayed before her was accurate.

"Are you sure it's self-replicating?" she asked Sarin, the lead scientist who'd been tasked with analyzing the nanite sample retrieved from the alien ship.

"Certain," Sarin replied, bobbing her head—a behavioral tick that Marta found more annoying than deferential.

"How soon can you begin scaling?"

"That will depend on how much material can be salvaged from Pavia. These *will* self-replicate, but they require a suitable material to feed them."

Of course. It can never be simple. Marta didn't let her frustration show. "We'll have mining operations up and running again soon."

"Yes, ma'am. We'll be ready." Sarin excused herself, leaving Marta to her thoughts.

Alone in the room, the pressure of the situation closed in on her. She couldn't afford to show weakness or doubt around others, but she allowed herself a rare moment to fear for her future.

Despite her spoken assurances that the mining operations would resume soon, they were nowhere near their former production capacity at Pavia. The attack itself hadn't caused insurmountable damage, but the awakened alien tech beneath the planet's surface had destroyed most of their human infrastructure. Without lifts or loading bays, getting material off-world would be a challenge—but they didn't even have *access* to the mines right now after the cave-in. But admitting that the materials they needed were buried under dozens of meters of unstable rubble would unleash a shitstorm she wasn't sure she'd have the fortitude to weather.

She went to the window in her office. Looking down from the orbital station above Pavia, there was little indication of how much damage had been dealt to their operation. It wasn't just the loss of their facility—more critically, there'd been a major blow to the crew's morale. For years, the Syndicate had projected an aura of control. They had mastered alien technology to wield as a mighty spectacle, performing feats no mere humans could achieve.

Keeping that tech within a small circle within their family and trusted advisors had enabled them to command loyalty and respect. They were revered.

But that illusion had been shattered. They'd had no control when the alien devices had awoken from their long slumber. Marta and her compatriots had been helpless in that decisive moment, and that undermined everything they'd built over the past few decades.

All that work, undone in a matter of minutes. That was the unfortunate nature of power.

Though she allowed herself this brief time to fear the loss

of her station and what might come next, it was a temporary break. To regain power, she must project power.

Reopening the mine would require more time and planning, but she wasn't without options. Replicating the alien nanites was the most promising lead they had at the moment, so she'd have to find another source for the materials they needed. Since she'd require Marcus' signoff, the plan had to be solid before she presented it to him.

Shoving all doubts and apprehension to the back of her mind, she sat down at her desk and got to work.

The Syndicate's resources were far-reaching and deep. Despite their larger enterprise being classified as a criminal organization by the official authorities, the Santano family had their hands in a number of legitimate businesses, which could serve as fronts for their operations when needed. With their involvement hidden through layers and layers of shell companies and false identities, tracking down the true owners was next to impossible. It was through this network that materials from Pavia had been distributed to various outposts across the Commonwealth.

She looked over the inventory across the various locations. According to Sarin's assessment, they'd need a significant amount of the pavite they extracted from the Pavian rocks in order to make more of the jump drive nanites. Most outposts only had a smattering of the material—and even all of them combined would be insufficient. Except for one place.

It would be a big ask. But she had to try.

Marta struck an authoritative pose behind her desk and called Marcus.

Her brother promptly answered the vidcall. "Marta, is this a social call or a request?"

They never called just to chat. "I need access to our pavite storehouse on Rilen," she announced without preamble.

Marcus scoffed and leaned back in his seat. "That's not your territory."

"I run the Syndicate as much as you do, Marcus."

"We keep certain operations siloed for a reason."

"Until production on Pavia can ramp up again, we'll need to rely on our stores. Situations like this are why we built up a stockpile."

"We can't afford to lose this, too. The Lux—"

"There will be plenty left for that synthesis. If you want the jump drive this year, then this is the only way."

"Do you have a timeline?"

"The team is ready to scale whenever they have the material."

He rubbed his chin. "I would never insult you by saying you're anything like Roman, but I have to be honest... I wasn't pleased with how you handled Pavia."

Like he would have done any better. We couldn't have seen that coming. She kept her expression calm and composed. "I recognize those failings. Aside from that, I think my results speak for themselves."

"Historically."

"Give me this chance to get everything back on track."

Marcus sighed. "It was all falling into place, Marta. Why has so much gone sideways in the past few weeks?"

"Because we trusted outsiders." Specifically, Marcus had struck a deal with Rostov without talking it through with the rest of the family. They'd always kept the Syndicate's operations within a tight group, but Marcus' grand aspirations in the last few years had put them all at risk.

"It was a means to an end. You know that," he shot back.

"A long play for an opportunity that may never come."

"Oh, Marta, I would *make* the opportunity. Rostov is just keeping the seat warm." His eyes gleamed with the insatiable thirst for power he rarely showed so openly.

The unbridled ambition chilled her, but to indicate any concern would only paint her as an obstacle. "I'll play my part."

"I know you will. If the stock on Rilen is what you need, take it. But I want it replaced ASAP."

"I will. Thank you." She ended the call before her composure broke.

Her hand was trembling as she pulled it away from the comm controls. He shouldn't make her nervous through a screen; she knew better. But she'd seen those hard eyes up close too many times before—had seen what he could do when he was pushed.

Marta reached under her desk to access a hidden compartment near her left knee. Palming open the lock, she reached inside to retrieve a metal box.

She opened the case. The syringe gleamed enticingly in the lamp light. Her skin prickled in anticipation.

When did it become an addiction? The priming had been a perfunctory matter of policy at first—more of a family tradition than anything she would have incorporated into her regular routine. But once she'd begun the regular injections, they'd eventually become a core part of her identity.

She loaded a fresh vial. The clink of the glass against metal sent another anticipatory tingle through her. She inserted the syringe to her neck and pushed the plunger. A refreshing, exhilarating warmth filled her veins.

She relaxed into her chair, savoring the energy rush. Almost immediately, her senses sharpened.

Marcus has his ambitions, but that won't stop me from pursuing my own. Marta tapped a quick entry on the comm, opening a voice channel to her lead researcher. "Sarin, you'll have the pavite within the week."

"That's excellent news," the engineer replied with a bright tone. "Where did—?"

"The logistics aren't your concern."

"Yes, ma'am."

"Now, tell me… How long will it take to synthesize enough material to jump an entire ship?"

6

RETURNING TO MEET Conroy in the bunker, Evan queued up a string of ways to say 'no'. Whenever the chancellor wanted to talk, it was almost always to make an unreasonable request that plunged Evan's life into further chaos. If there was any option to head off additional complications, he'd take it.

However, Conroy's opening words when Evan entered his office disarmed him. "Evan, we're low on supplies, and we need to be provisioned for the fight ahead."

It's true, and there's no way around it. Evan nodded. "Yes, we are. And where do you propose we get these supplies?"

"I have connections. The problem is how to get everything from there to here."

Evan nearly walked out of the room. "I didn't come back here to be your delivery driver."

"Hear me out. I can arrange for everything we need to be picked up at a supply depot, but we have no way to get there. You have a ship that could jump there and back before we have a chance to miss you."

"I don't want to risk the *Asamar.*"

"Its jump drive can be transferred to any vessel, right?"

The suggestion was technically feasible, but the entire

exercise came with risks. Nonetheless, it was also clear that they couldn't stay on Aethos forever. Evan was eager to advance their mission—and that meant having sufficient equipment and supplies to get through the next phase.

"It would need to be one of Zaris' ships," Evan said after some consideration. "But there's no way I'm handing over that jump tech to them without supervision."

"All right, then the two of you can go. We just need materials transported from a pickup point to here. How you go about it is on you."

"I'm your logistics guy now, huh?"

"I understand a lot of roles have been placed on you, Evan. But frankly, you're the only one who can get from Aethos to anywhere else in less than two months. I know it's inconvenient, but I hope you'll help with this."

"If I do, it will delay things with Roman."

Conroy shrugged. "A little more time to sit and marinate in his own thoughts might be beneficial."

Isolation and boredom did have a place in an interrogator's toolkit, though Evan wasn't sure Roman would be moved. Nonetheless, delaying their next chat by a few days was unlikely to impact his efforts. "Fine. Make the arrangements."

—

Evan found Zaris in the makeshift camp where the corsairs had been settled for the past week. The people around camp looked Evan over with expressions ranging from suspicion to awe. Word was clearly spreading about his unusual abilities. After spending most of his career trying to keep a low profile and blend in, being recognizable was uncomfortable.

Zaris was hanging around the empty firepit at the center of

the campsite. She stood up as he approached. "What now?"

"Let's chat." He motioned her away from the others.

They went to the edge of the tree line, well beyond earshot of the corsairs.

"We have a supply problem we need to solve," he began. "I need your help."

"Well, well… That sounds like the opening to a negotiation."

"It's an honest, good-faith request. I hope you'll respond in kind."

She placed her hands on her hips, a smirk twisting her lips. "This relationship has become a little one-sided. Seems like you're the one always coming to *me* for help."

"Zaris, does everything have to be a contest with you?"

She sighed. "What do you need?"

"Replacements for the supplies that were lost when the colony ship exploded. Conroy's people are low on necessities. And it sounds like you could stand to stock up on things that would make a longer stay more comfortable for your people, too."

"That would be nice, yeah. But where are we supposed to get that stuff?"

"Conroy will set it up. You provide the ship. I have the jump drive. Quick hop there and back—what do you say?"

She nodded slowly, pursing her lips. "I say it sounds too easy. There has to be a catch."

"He claims it'll be a simple pick-up."

"And do you believe that?"

"I can hope that we've had enough trouble that the universe owes us one."

"So, no." She sighed. "Well, if we take the *Invictus*, at least we'll have sufficient firepower if we run into trouble."

"That's my thought."

"You're not worried about me running off with everything after the pickup?" Her smirk gave away that she was only joking.

"We've had a pretty good run since our reunion. I'd like to keep it that way."

"Me too." She glanced across the field toward camp. "You know, when we were reintroduced—with you being the real you—I had low expectations. I mean, the whole thing about Conroy and crazy alien tech was an absolutely *wild* story, but it's all been true. I want to see how this all plays out."

He smiled. "A front row seat to history in the making, right?"

"Yeah. But make no mistake—my allegiance is to what's in the best interest of my people. I know for certain that's not what the Syndicate is peddling. But…" She dropped her voice. "Between us, I still have my doubts about Conroy. He's just currently better than the alternative."

Evan nodded. "We're on the same page. Come on, let's go prep to head out."

— — —

Anya's head was spinning from the revelations from her recent discoveries. *How am I supposed to tell Evan about what this is doing to him?*

She still didn't know enough about the alien technology to make a clear assessment, but the preliminary findings were astounding. Foremost, she was curious if the modifications to his cells were complete or if this was simply the beginning of a longer-term transformation.

Deep in thought, Anya nearly fell out of her seat when Evan entered the lab. "How's it going?" he greeted.

"You're quite fascinating under a microscope."

"Just what every man wants to hear."

She pushed back from her workbench. "You know, it might be helpful to have a sample of Roman's blood to compare with yours."

"I'll see what I can do about that."

Anya pushed back from her workbench. "Why so serious? What did Conroy have to say?"

"You know the fight I mentioned earlier today?"

"Yeah…"

"Well, it sounds like it was a symptom of a bigger problem. Supplies are running short."

"I thought Zaris was equipped for *months*—"

"She's said a lot of things that were a version of a truth."

Anya crossed her arms. "Meaning?"

"They brought enough with them to *survive*, but the food stores are the kind of rations that make a MealPak look like fine dining."

"The planet has more than enough to feed everyone."

"I know. But the problem is that we would need people down here to harvest. And the people we have aren't comfortable foraging, not to mention the tents they're staying in right now were never meant for extended habitation."

"Meaning, we'd need a more comfortable, permanent camp to use the planet's resources, but no one wants to put in the effort to make that happen," Anya surmised.

"I could assist with fabricating lodging, food, and supplies," Sam offered.

Evan shook his head. "Sam, you're amazing, but if we turn you into a manufacturing facility, you might have even more people wanting your secrets than the interest in your jump drive."

"What's the plan, then?" Anya asked.

"I'm going on a supply run."

"Where?"

"Conroy is going to arrange pickup at an outpost somewhere."

"Are we taking the *Asamar*?" Anya asked.

"I'm going with Zaris on the *Invictus*."

She tilted her head. "Is that so?"

"There's a lot to pick up, and we don't want to reveal the *Asamar* to any more people. Using a normal human ship makes the most sense."

Anya sighed. "Right."

"And," he continued, "I don't want to leave the *Asamar* unattended."

"I don't require supervision, you know," the ship's AI chimed in.

"It's not about you, Sam," Evan assured him. "I just think it's better to have one of us around so no one tries anything."

Anya didn't like the idea of being left behind as a babysitter—especially not with Evan and Zaris going off together. She hated that she had any jealous feelings, but she recognized that the stress of their situation was coloring her perception. "Fine."

Evan's brows knitted. "I know it's not ideal."

"I just want to see a real action plan, Evan. Right now, it feels like we're running in circles. Does Conroy *actually* have a strategy to… I dunno, do whatever it is he's planning?"

"That's a concern for me, too. I think he intends to go after Rostov and retake command of the Commonwealth."

"Yeah, well," she shook her head, "that's a really big ambition."

"It is."

"Do you think we can do it?"

"I don't know," Evan admitted. "But there's a next to zero chance of success without getting more supplies. So, I need to make this run. If he *still* doesn't get in gear, we can make our own plans."

"There are plans we should be making, regardless."

"About…?"

"The bigger mission. We need to locate the original Korani. If you were the ambassador to that alien race, Evan, imagine the sway you would hold. You could have a real say in how this technology gets deployed."

Evan frowned. "I don't want that role."

"But who better? You've interfaced with it. You know what it can do. And you've spent time in both law enforcement and with people who couldn't care less about laws. Is there anyone else who's experienced those three sides of this?"

He sighed. "I'll need you to keep me honest."

She gazed into his eyes. "I promised before to be with you every step of the way, and I will. Now, go get those supplies we need so we can take on the bad guys."

7

TOBIN RUBBED HIS eyes, but his head still ached from trying to understand the information Rostov had given him to analyze.

At first glance, the documents for his latest assignment had appeared to be financial records. Tobin had initially assumed it must be government business, but it had quickly become clear that the numbers were related to some kind of private sector enterprise. Whatever it was, the operations were far-reaching and dealt with huge financial figures.

The longer he studied the information, a picture became clearer in his mind. These records were for the Noche Syndicate and its various holdings. And their network was vaster than he could have imagined.

No wonder Rostov wanted to work with them, Tobin realized.

He'd been on the periphery of those discussions, and what little he'd learned was deeply concerning. It appeared Rostov might be building himself a private military force to carry out his bidding without pesky checks and balances like parliamentary approval. What he might intend to do with that power remained unclear, but the fact that it was even a possibility made Tobin's skin crawl.

He was willing to kill Conroy to get this position. What else could he do? Anything, really. Trying to execute the sitting leading leader of an interstellar government was about as serious as it got.

The most concerning elements of all, though, were these documents fanned across Tobin's touch-surface desktop. *Why did Rostov show these to me?*

Sensitive details in the documents painted an indirect yet clear line between Rostov's administration and the Syndicate. Seeing that information was dangerous, let alone being in possession of it. But there was one reason Rostov might have sent it…

Tobin's heart dropped. *He wants me implicated. This is leverage.*

His worry turned to anger in a flash.

Rostov had a habit of roping people into his orbit, but Tobin refused to be controlled. However, he couldn't simply tell Rostov 'no'. He still had another job to do—more important responsibilities, for someone actually worthy of his allegiance.

But Rostov had made a mistake. In an effort to capture him, he'd handed Tobin a weapon that could be thrown back in his face. It was the kind of hubris he'd come to expect from Rostov and his ilk, and it was oh so fitting that it would contribute to his downfall.

Tobin made a copy of the records to store in his obfuscated files for relaying to Conroy.

Next, he still had to piece together a response to Rostov's nebulous assignment. The instructions had simply been, 'Analyze this operation for future growth potential.' It was clearly a test, and Tobin was pretty sure he could read between the lines. Rostov was *really* asking where the government could offer strategic funding to ensure the Syndicate's market dominance, and thereby create a symbiotic relationship of power and control.

The entire scheme was devious and underhanded—not that Tobin thought murderers would behave any better. The relentless search for more power was an obsession. At least, he'd never been able to come up with an explanation for *why* they did the things they did. Sport? Looking for their next thrill?

It didn't matter. Regardless of motivation, Tobin was one of the few who could get proof of their indiscretions. And they'd need evidence that would not only hold up under legal scrutiny, but also in the court of public opinion. They needed to get the *people* on Conroy's side, or no number of official declarations would carry weight.

With the end goals in mind, Tobin prepared his report to Rostov. He rooted it in fact, drawing the obvious conclusions. But this analysis needed to stand out. He included the information that Rostov was asking-without-asking to really go above and beyond with his delivery. This report needed to solidify Tobin as an indispensable advisor and demonstrate his commitment to fulfilling Rostov's grandest visions.

When he had completed the write-up and added the final polish to his satisfaction, Tobin submitted the document via a secure file transfer.

He didn't need to wait long for his reward.

>>Well done,<< said a text message from Rostov. >>It's like you read my mind.<<

>>That's my job, sir.<<

>>I'm working on closing the deal.<<

>>Standing by,<< Tobin texted back. And he would be. He was logging each of the communications for his archive, and

all of it was gold.

The rest of the day turned into his usual tedium of following legislative news, reviewing reports, and logging updates on active projects. He was just about to wrap up for the evening when a coded message came through on his secondary channel—the one Conroy used for communications.

Tobin opened it: >>Need supplies. Can you arrange pickup?<<

While the request seemed simple on the surface, the list of items was long, including large volumes of many things.

Is he serious? Tobin groaned.

He took a steadying breath. After years of sneaking around, his pulse still spiked every time he got a message through the back channels, but he'd gotten better at coping with the stress. The work was important, but his life was tied to their success. Maintaining a cool head is what would keep him alive.

>>That's going to take a little time to arrange,<< he told the chancellor.

>>Tomorrow?<<

Tobin swore under his breath. There was only one place that *might* be able to fulfill the order in that short a time. But how did Conroy intend to get there? >>Who's picking it up?<< Tobin wrote back.

Conroy sent him the contact information for a captain named Zaris Alva. Tobin ran a quick search on her, finding a colorful record. There was no way the place he had in mind would deal with someone like her.

>>Won't fly. Who else?<<

Conroy sent another profile. This one Tobin recognized as the man who'd been added as a last-minute addition on the *Stratum*. He was the pilot of the new alien ship. But he had the same credentialing issues. >>No. I need a clean government contact.<<

>>There's no one who isn't supposed to be dead. Can you find a workaround?<<

Tobin sighed. He could build an entire fake profile for the two people, but that would be an incredible amount of work—

>>I know you'll figure it out. Thank you,<< Conroy said before Tobin could launch an objection.

He knew he should still push back, but he didn't have the heart to deny Conroy after the recent setbacks and losses. If making sure the crew on Aethos had food and other necessities meant staying up all night to create fake backstories that would stand up to official scrutiny, then that was the role he'd play.

The first step was to send the order request to the supply depot so they could start fulfilling it. He left the recipients blank for now, knowing the depot would follow up with a request for that information—which Tobin would have to invent.

He set up the purchase details and arranged payment, making a note of the various codes needed for verification.

Tobin then built out the fake profiles for Evan and Zaris. Depot security would want to verify their identities, and Tobin would need to override the real information in the system. That kind of data manipulation was his specialty, but it was trickier when dealing with a remote versus local system. He'd have to set up a remote handshake to force an update of the depot's records.

Working well into the wee hours of the morning, Tobin eventually completed the new profiles. He just needed to get that information into the supply outpost's system.

Tobin started up a vidcall. "Hey, I just wanted to confirm my recent order."

The depot supervisor appeared wholly unenthused with his work. "Identifier?"

Tobin electronically sent the credentials. The data link was what he needed as an open conduit for the update. He initiated the transfer.

"I have your order here. Everything looks good on our end," the supervisor said.

Tobin needed more time. "Great. Could you read off the inventory to me?"

"Dude, there's like a hundred things on here. I don't have time for that shit."

The link abruptly severed.

No! Did it finish sending? He couldn't be sure.

Tobin tried to call again, but he was sent straight to the automated answering system. With the late hour and having skipped dinner, Tobin was torn between punching something and curling up under a blanket. Neither of those would be productive, so he did the only thing he could and sent a warning to Conroy. >>Order is in, but not sure about the altered ident. Nothing more I can do now.<<

>>We'll have to risk it.<<

Tobin's stomach knotted. If the transfer hadn't finished, there'd be trouble. The codes might get them through the door, but it would only mean they were walking into a trap.

8

STEPPING ONTO THE *Invictus*' flight deck, Evan was relieved to see that Tarek was absent. While the man was no doubt an excellent first officer for Zaris, Evan had found himself on the receiving end of a weapon one too many times to want to venture out with him on this critical mission; handling Zaris would be tricky enough.

Zaris occupied the center command chair, one of her legs casually propped on a nearby console. She straightened as he entered. "Welcome back."

"Hopefully, this trip will be less eventful."

"It's hardly an outing if you're not getting shot at." She gestured for him to take the seat on her right, normally occupied by Tarek.

"We have very different definitions." Evan sat down.

"Callie, what's our status?" Zaris asked the young woman sitting at the front station.

"Ready to depart on your command."

Zaris turned to Evan. "All we need is a jump drive."

Transferring the system to the *Invictus* still made Evan a little nervous, but that's what the mission demanded. On their previous jump as a fleet, Sam had simply needed to expand the jump field to encompass all of the ships—but the *Asamar* had remained the central control vessel. For this journey, Sam would control the jump via his link to Evan's shuttle—which they'd decided to name the *Mara*—docked in the hangar.

"All right, Sam, we're ready whenever you are," Evan said.

"Transferring the drive system now."

A stream of golden particles flowed from the moon to the *Invictus*. They swirled around the ship to form the same kind of dazzling latticework Evan had come to recognize on the *Asamar*. Somehow, it seemed even more alien and wondrous surrounding this human-made ship.

"Not sure I'll ever get used to this," Zaris murmured.

Even stranger than watching the sight, Evan now *felt* it in a way he hadn't on their previous jumps. He wondered whether that was a psychosomatic response from familiarity or whether his recent brush with the 'primal energies' had unlocked a deeper connection to the tech.

"Ready to jump," Sam announced.

Zaris waved her hand. "Let's go."

Golden light enveloped the ship as the nano-lattice spun. The vessel slipped into the spatial distortion, entering the now familiar realm outside normal reality. The crew took a collective gasp of awe as they soared through the dark tunnel adorned with bursts of abstract light. Seeing their reaction, Evan was surprised to realize he'd already gotten used to the wondrous sight.

I never thought something so incredible could start feeling ordinary.

The outside scene resolved into a starscape. As the ship turned to the left, a transit ring came into view.

"Right on course," Callie announced, breaking from her mesmerized trance.

"Set our destination," Zaris ordered. Quieter, she added to Evan, "You've ruined me. How can we go back to normal gate travel after that?"

"It's a real problem." That was the risk with any progress; once a new, better way became possible, the tried and true felt like a massive step backward. Zaris' comment had only reinforced Evan's concerns about the alien technology working its way into the Commonwealth. Once it was out there, they'd never be able to rein it in.

The gate came to life with spinning lights. When the portal formed, Callie directed the *Invictus* inside.

Evan's skin prickled with electrical energy as the ship passed through into the tunnel across space.

The transit lasted less than a minute. As soon as they exited on the other side, the tone on the flight deck turned serious.

"Send a welcome ping with our ident codes," Zaris instructed.

"Aye," Callie acknowledged, her hands flying over the front controls.

Conroy had provided access credentials. Supposedly, he had a contact in the supply depot who'd help them out without asking questions. A simple pickup, there and back to Aethos. Easy.

"Codes acknowledged," Callie announced.

Evan relaxed a little. "Good. Let's get this over with."

They were soon within visual range of a sprawling station. Four branches fanned out in a star shape with a large mouth at their juncture, leading into an interior hangar. A dozen small to medium-sized vessels were visible through the opening.

"We're not fitting in there," Callie assessed.

"They've gotta have an exterior dock," Zaris said. "Find out what's what."

Callie made some entries on her console, then frowned. "They're requesting an inspection before they'll grant docking clearance."

Zaris sighed. "Is Conroy setting us up?"

"I really hope not," Evan murmured. Truthfully, he was prepared for any possibility.

"Well, no way I'm letting randos on board to get up in our business. Maybe we can take a shuttle over to get this sorted?"

Evan nodded. "Probably the best option."

'Best' was relative, of course. Not having the *Invictus* docked would mean less access to backup. However, keeping the ship at a distance would offer better cover if they got into a firefight—

Evan shook his head to clear the thought. *Everything will be fine. Don't overthink it.*

He followed Zaris to the hangar bay, where they prepped her largest cargo shuttle. They wouldn't be able to carry all of the supplies on their shopping list in one go, but they could ferry everything over multiple trips if they weren't able to work out a satisfactory docking arrangement for the *Invictus*.

Zaris piloted the shuttle from the *Invictus* to the central bay of the spacedock, following instructions from the station's controller. The protocols seemed professional and in line with normal space station operations, so there was still a chance they wouldn't have any trouble.

They docked on a pad on the right side of the hangar, cordoned off from the rest of the facility's operations. A sign with instructions about 'inspection' was mounted to the bulkhead, but Evan couldn't read the details.

"I'll let you do the talking," Zaris said as she powered down the shuttle.

"Fine," Evan agreed, though he had no idea what he was

supposed to say. Nothing about Conroy's instructions had indicated that there'd be any negotiating or inspections. *Maybe he didn't tell them what ship would be coming and they don't want to get robbed by pirates?* he speculated, knowing full well that was wishful thinking.

Evan's sole comfort was the two Korani bracelets, granting him a measure of offensive and defensive abilities his opponents would not easily detect. Hopefully, that wouldn't be necessary.

Dropping the back hatch, Evan and Zaris exited slowly.

As soon as they were clear from the ship, four guards with rifles ambushed them.

Wonderful. Evan held out his hands and put on his best diplomatic smile. "Hey, that's not necessary. We're all friends here. Let's just—"

"Stay where you are," a man said in a firm tone, stepping out from behind a stack of crates. His short-cropped, dark hair and firm brow gave the impression of former military, though he may just be seasoned private security.

"You saw our codes," Evan said. "We're just here to get our stuff and then we'll be on our way."

"Is that so? Just walk in here and leave?"

"Yeah... That's generally how these things work."

"If you think you can buy us off, you're mistaken."

Evan blinked at him. "Sorry, what?"

The man crossed his arms. "You don't see the problem?"

"I'm sorry, I have no idea what you're talking about."

"Unbelievable." He scoffed and took a few steps away before coming back. "I don't know what you came here expecting, but you're not going anywhere."

— — —

Zaris gripped her sidearm inside her jacket. It was unclear what kind of trouble they'd wandered into, but she wanted to be ready. "What's the issue?"

"Come with me," said the man, likely the dockmaster. He turned to leave.

"We'd rather stay by our shuttle," Evan objected, to Zaris' relief.

"And I'd rather be playing Aertrix right now, but life isn't fair." The dockmaster didn't stop walking.

Zaris remained in place, curious how Evan would handle the situation. If it was up to her, she'd just rob these people if they didn't want to cooperate.

"Can you please explain your concern?" Evan asked, taking only a single step after the man.

The dockmaster sighed and spun around. "Who's the captain of your ship?"

"I am," Zaris volunteered.

"That's an… interesting registration you have."

Zaris tensed. The conversation had started out on shaky ground and was only going downhill. She'd been through plenty of inspections, and her forged registration credentials had never caused any problems before. "You'll have to be more specific."

The man tapped a device on his wrist, and a holoprojection filled the air between them, displaying a schematic of the *Invictus*' exterior. "See, this ship has really gotten around. But it seems like every time it pulls into port, it's under a different name."

"That seems unlikely," Zaris lied. However, it wasn't *every* port visit—sometimes, they'd hold onto a registration for several months, covering multiple stops.

"Well, would you like to explain the active bounty?"

Shit! She struggled to keep a straight face. She hadn't expected their recent indiscretions to be reported to the authorities. While the Syndicate's close ties to Rostov's administration changed the equation, it was still a bold move for one crime organization to officially report a run-in with another. Unless... "What are the charges?"

"Grand theft. Destruction of property. Personal endangerment—"

This guy's about to get firsthand experience with all of that.

"—And sedition."

She gaped at him. "What the hell? That's absurd!"

"Take it up with the Security Corps. Now, come with me quietly and I'll let them know you cooperated."

The guards tensed, ready for a challenge.

"Stop," Evan commanded. He didn't raise his voice, but there was a gravitas to his tone Zaris hadn't heard before, instantly snapping her to attention and prickling her skin.

The dockmaster froze in place. Then, he slowly turned around. His expression was blank, with an almost serene faraway look in his eyes.

"You're going to give us what we came for," Evan stated.

What do I have to give? Zaris thought in a momentary panic, only to realize he wasn't talking to her. *Of course, I knew that.* She shouldn't have been confused at all.

Buzzing filled her ears as pressure mounted in her head. She recognized that Evan must be exerting some kind of telepathic control, but even knowing that, she remained compelled to carry out his command.

The dockmaster led them to the back of the bay. The guards with him seemed to be in the same trance-like state.

When the group reached an office, the dockmaster

stopped, his face pinched. "What did I come here for…?"

"To get us our supplies," Evan reminded him.

The man's eyes brightened with recognition. "That's right! No…" He rounded on Evan. "We have nothing for you. You don't belong here."

Uh oh. Zaris ducked aside as the other members of the group broke from their daze and aimed their weapons.

Evan raised his right hand. The metal bracelet dissolved into a cloud of golden specks, swirling around each other like a swarm of insects. They fanned out into a curved wall separating Evan and Zaris from the dock workers.

A series of pulse blasts from their weapons struck the shield, harmlessly scattering across its surface. However, the telepathy hadn't held, so Zaris didn't trust that the shield trick would last, either.

These people had insulted her character, and that royally pissed her off. If they were going to ruin her day, she'd drag them down with her.

Zaris swept her gaze around the hangar, looking for the right target. She spotted a plastic crate and squeezed off several shots. The crate split down its side, spilling its contents of brown beans across the floor. It wouldn't hurt anyone, but it would slow down their pursuit. Moreover, it would be a pain in the ass to pick up. She flashed a smug smile at the dockmaster.

"Come on!" Evan urged. "We're not getting anything from these guys."

"Like hell we aren't!"

— — —

Evan dashed toward their shuttle. Zaris, however, was

running perpendicular to him, toward a stack of small crates on the ground.

The angry mob was giving chase. They had no time for a detour.

"Zaris!"

She grabbed the most accessible crate and hefted it. She struggled with the weight but managed to hobble back in Evan's direction.

He covered her with suppressive fire and a nanite shield. "You're insane!" he shouted at her.

"Yeah, I hear that a lot." With a groan, she hoisted the crate onto the ship.

Evan fired one last shot toward their pursuers before he jumped into the shuttle after her. He sealed the hatch. "Get us out of here!"

"On it."

The shuttle powered up and smoothly glided toward the exit. However, a massive door was closing in front of the force field.

"Zaris…"

"I can clear it," she said, concentrating on the path ahead.

The shuttle flipped on its side, sending Evan's stomach into his throat as the internal grav simulators took a moment to compensate for the sudden shift. He gripped a handhold, doing his own mental math on their clearance and not liking the odds.

With a sudden burst of speed, the shuttle surged through the opening, mere meters on each side.

"Told you," Zaris snarked.

"Yeah." Evan could finally breathe again. "Good flying."

"Thank you." She frowned. "Ah, shit. They're firing on us."

Three seconds later, the shuttle rocked with the concussive

force of an energy weapon blast.

Evan slid into the seat next to her on the flight deck. "Shields?"

"Holding for now," Zaris said. "But a couple more of those and we'll be toast."

The comm chirped. "Need a little help?" Callie asked.

"Light 'em up!" Zaris confirmed.

Several blasts fired from the *Invictus* as it moved between the shuttle and the station.

The station continued firing. One clipped the aft of the shuttle, sending a shudder through the vessel and lighting up the control panel with warnings.

"Three of the starboard maneuvering thrusters are damaged," Evan reported. "Time for more fancy flying."

"I've got it."

Zaris banked the shuttle toward the *Invictus'* bay. The craft was sluggish in its response, and she grimaced as she tried to get in on the correct vector.

"Do I need to point out that we're headed for a wall?" Evan asked as the large ship's hull loomed in front of them.

"I see that, thank you." Zaris flipped several switches and tried the steering yolk again.

This time, the shuttle finally corrected its course. But they were coming in fast.

The shuttle slipped through the force field and slammed down on the deck, throwing Evan against his flight harness. The friction spun the vessel to the side, and they slid to a stop in a shower of sparks.

Zaris calmly powered down the shuttle like everything had been business as usual.

Evan let out a relieved sigh, thankful to be back on solid ground. "Well, that could have gone better."

"At least we didn't leave with nothing." Zaris headed to the back of the shuttle, and Evan followed.

"What'd you get?"

Zaris popped open the crate. "It's…" Her brows knitted. "Support brackets, maybe?" She held up a plastic triangular component. The parts were packed tightly inside the crate in orderly rows and columns.

"Great. We can hang shelves to display all the supplies we don't have."

"Yeah." She tossed the bracket back into the crate, frowning. "Clearly, we need a new plan."

9

ANYA STRETCHED HER arms above her head and soaked in the sun on her face. It had been months since she'd locked herself in a research lab for any meaningful length of time, and that felt like a strange practice now.

You don't learn everything important from lab experiments. That had been her philosophy from the last part of her career, but she'd come to realize that there was an important balance between the theoretical and practical. Controlled trials and models did have their place.

In this particular investigation, she'd need every venue and subject she could get her hands on. Solving the mystery of the Korani tech wasn't just a matter of biology—it was an intersection of multiple scientific disciplines, plus some new fields that humans hadn't even invented yet. She relished being on the forefront of the research, but it was a daunting task made more stressful because of her feelings for Evan. Whatever was happening to him, she wanted to do everything she could to ensure his wellbeing.

She spotted some of the people from Zaris' crew across the field, heading away from the camp in the direction of the *Asamar*. Almost everyone had stayed away thus far, whether it was out of wariness or if they'd been instructed to keep their distance.

Figures they'd get curious as soon as I'm here alone, she thought. Positioning herself by the ramp, she waited to see if they'd come any closer.

The two men and a woman took a direct path, waving as they approached.

Ten meters out, one of the men called, "You're the scientist, right?"

Anya nodded. "I'm *a* scientist. What do you need?"

"You know about, like, plants and stuff?" the woman questioned.

"I do."

"We heard there was some good fruit around here, but Tarek said we shouldn't leave the field," the first man continued. "Conroy's people don't want to share the fresh stuff. Can you help us get some?"

The story wasn't quite what Anya had been hearing about the supply allocation difficulties. However, she liked to reward industriousness.

"I can show you what's safe, but I don't want to cause any conflict," she said. "Whatever you find, you eat it out there and don't make a scene at camp. Agreed?"

The three nodded eagerly.

"Okay. I'll show you some spots that aren't too far from here, and Conroy's people aren't using those groves. But if anyone asks, I wasn't the one to show you."

The first man smiled. "We never spoke."

"Good."

Anya returned to the *Asamar* to check in with Sam, letting him know to stay locked up and not allow anyone onboard until she returned. She grabbed a bag to gather some fruit for herself, as well as her handgun and a knife.

Returning to the three waiting people, the first man introduced himself as Garet, the woman was Mary, and the other man was Tim. It turned out that they were crewmembers from one of the companion ships in Zaris' little fleet, the *Rising Sun*.

"Wow, talk about getting dropped into the middle of a mess," Anya commented as she led them toward the first grove. "An alien ship. Conroy. You've had a lot thrown at you."

"Yeah, it's just been little pieces here and there," Mary said. "I thought the whole thing was made up until I saw your ship."

"It's not *mine*, exactly."

"You're living on board it, though, right?"

"I am," she admitted.

"That's so cool," Garet said, his eyes bright with wonder. "I always loved movies and stuff about aliens. Fantasizing about all the cool tech. I'm so envious."

"They can do some pretty exciting things," she told him. "I wish I knew a lot more than I did. I deal mostly with animals in my work, some plants. I sure wish I knew more about comm systems and that sort of thing."

Garet lit up. "Comms are my specialty!"

Tim snickered. "He says he works comms, but what he really does is just look at signal noise and try to make sense of it."

"Is that so?"

"Hey, there's way more to my job than the guys who just answer calls!" Garet shot back. "When was the last time you found a ship hiding from scan?"

Anya was already way ahead of them in her thinking. "Garet, if I had a bunch of scan data with signals captured from various places, would you be able to pick out what's different about them?"

"Sure, that's easy. But don't you have an AI for that?"

"An AI doesn't look at things in the same way as a human. It's more… linear thinking," Anya explained. "I'm looking for the kind of connections that aren't readily apparent."

"I have literally nothing else going on right now. I would love to take a look."

She nodded. "All right, let's get a tasty snack, and then we'll check it out."

Anya showed the trio three different places where they could gather fruits and some edible greens to break up their monotonous rations. After pointing out the potential dangers in the area, she led them back to the settlement. Tim and Mary returned to their camp, and she invited Garet on board the *Asamar* to get his thoughts on her work.

The young man looked around the ship with a slack jaw as she escorted him to her new lab. "It's absolutely incredible."

With all of Sam's renovations to make the ship more comfortable for human passengers, Anya didn't find the interior to be particularly alien or exciting anymore. "The most impressive part is Sam."

"The AI?" Garet's eyes somehow got even wider. "Can I… talk to it?"

"Greetings," Sam intoned.

Garet jumped, and then a grin split his face. "An alien AI! For real!"

"*You* are the alien to me."

"Ah, I can't believe this is happening!"

"Deep breath, Garet," Anya soothed, amused and heartened by his enthusiastic reaction. It was a good reminder that she was dealing with incredible technology she shouldn't take for granted.

"Anya, may I ask the reason you have brought this visitor?" Sam inquired.

"Garet has experience with communications systems and deciphering signals, so I thought he might be a helpful, fresh set of eyes on our research project."

"Excellent idea. Would you like me to pull up the scan data in your lab?"

"That'd be great. We'll be right there."

Garet's expression dropped. "No tour?"

"Let me see how useful you are first. If you earn your keep, I'll consider it."

The project files were fanned out on screens around Anya's lab when they entered. Garet immediately started a slow circuit of the room, studying the data. "Where did you record this?"

"The where and what doesn't matter right now," Anya replied. "I want to know what you can make of it."

There were a lot of rumors swirling around camp, but few people knew the specifics about the Korani tech and exactly what they had in their possession. Anya wanted to see if Garet might actually be able to offer helpful insights before she gave away too many details.

He made the rounds again and scratched the stubble on his chin. "I see evidence of electromagnetic field manipulation. There's a signal that changes the properties. It's like there's a base state and an active state. When the signal is active, it fluctuates. And then it goes back to baseline. But what's controlling it?"

His preliminary assessment was high-level, but he had picked up on the correct components. "What if I told you that these readings were captured while someone was controlling alien nanites to rearrange matter?"

Garet's brows shot up. "Holy crap, is this about Evan?"

Word really does move quickly around camp. Anya nodded. "I'm trying to figure out how the nanites work. Rather, the alien tech, in general. It's bigger than just a few devices. I want to understand the impacts of this technology on a global scale."

His eyes remained wide with excitement. "I can absolutely see how this stuff might scale up. Do you have any specific examples you could show me?"

She was already in it now, so she brought up data about one of the planets with the odd signal they'd observed, leaving off its exact location and identifying information. "I'm curious if this has anything to do with the other signals we've observed. Is it the same kind of active operating field, or is it broadcasting a message, or…?"

Garet looked over the new information intently. "This is definitely more of a broadcast than a localized field. I'm picking up common elements in the background, but this active channel is different."

That was something. "Can you tell if the broadcast is being directed anywhere particular?"

"It would be helpful to know where it was coming from."

"If I may offer a suggestion?" Sam chimed in.

"Go for it," Anya said.

"I can assemble an allegorical model of the data. I will maintain the relative positions of bodies from the real scenario but present it in an anonymized structure."

"Perfect, Sam. Do it."

"I'm not going to tell anyone," Garet muttered.

"Whatever your intentions, people have ways of extracting information. Consider it for your own safety."

"Whatever you say."

Sam completed his new model and brought it up on the screen. It showed the various planets where they had observed the signals. Looking at it all laid out and the targets highlighted, she was relieved that Terrax wasn't named.

"Okay, based on this, I think we need to run a trace for this field signature in these places." Garet pointed at the various parameters.

Anya placed her hand on his shoulder. "All right, Garet, now we're on the trail. Let's see where it leads."

—   —   —

Convincing Marcus to grant her the pavite rocks in their storehouse on Rilen was only the first step. Now, Marta needed to collect the materials. Normally, she'd delegate such a menial task to a member of her staff. However, after the unfortunate business with Roman and his lost shipment several months back, she wanted to oversee the operation herself.

To get the process moving, she sent a written request to the facility manager at the Rilen base—one of her cousins. Armond was diligent and capable, but his temper was as sharp as his wit. While his high performance standards served their business interests well, Marta usually made a point of steering clear from him whenever possible.

Not five minutes after sending her request, it was clear she wouldn't have that luxury this time when a vidcall from Armond popped up on her omni.

She answered. "Hi, did you—"

"All those rocks are already allocated for production," Armond said without any hint of greeting.

"You have my orders."

"I don't answer to you, Marta. I have my own business interests to worry about."

"But you *do* answer to Marcus, and he approved this

request."

"Well, I can't fulfill it. Do you have any idea what this would do to our production schedule?"

"I have an important project to complete, and I need these materials."

"It's not my problem that you lost Pavia—"

She glowered at him through the screen. "Without Pavia, you'd still be getting drunk in a dive bar, bringing home a different woman every night."

"Ah, you're making me miss the good ol' days!"

Marta swallowed her disgust, knowing that slinging insults wouldn't get her what she wanted. "Armond, I don't want to have a problem here. I understand your position, but I promise that you'll want in on what I'm doing." She hadn't intended to give away anything about her project, but giving a little teaser might move the conversation along. She understood people like Armond—highly transactional with their relationships, banking favors and trading secrets. Fortunately, she was rich in both.

"A new product line?" he asked.

"Yes, but not in the way you're thinking. This one isn't a drug. It's a device. One that, if I'm successful, will make the gate system obsolete."

His eyes widened. "You're joking."

She shook her head slowly, her lips curling into a smile. "I promise you, if you help me out now, you'll be at the front of the line to get one when I roll it out."

"Enticing, but… how do I know you're not full of shit?"

"Because I don't waste my time on pointless exercises, Armond. Now, do I need Marcus to have a talk with you?"

"No, I've got you."

"Excellent." She was about to hang up. "Oh, and I'll need

to bring my big ship for the pickup. Open the main door for me, would you?"

He sputtered in protest for a few seconds before fading out. The battle was won. Reluctantly, he nodded. "Fine. We'll have it waiting for you."

"Good. We don't have a problem, after all."

10

EVAN WASN'T SURPRISED the mission had gone so poorly. They hadn't planned. He hadn't verified any information. *I shouldn't have taken Conroy at his word.*

Though the chancellor spoke of his network of helpers, how much could he actually accomplish from Aethos? The planet was too far removed, and any coordination had to go through intermediaries. There were too many break points in communications and logistics. Until the team on Aethos could take direct action, there was no real control.

I let myself get complacent. I know better. But the setback wasn't the end. He'd find another way.

"We can't go back emptyhanded," Evan stated, sitting down across from Zaris in her office.

Zaris sighed and leaned back in her chair, propping her booted feet on the desk. "What do you propose?"

"Getting supplies just like we normally would."

"By 'we' you mean…"

"Yes, *you*. Where do you stock up your ships?"

"A well-connected man like you, I'd thought you'd know."

He sighed. "My guess is the trading post on Markeesh for the really big runs, but you probably have a bunch of smaller suppliers for specialty goods—the kind of people who'd get you staples if you ask nicely enough and the pay is right."

"Good assumptions." She eyed him. "Speaking of which, how are we paying for all this?"

That *was* a good question. The original assignment had been to go to a specific location to pick up the cargo, and everything was supposed to have been pre-arranged. Conroy hadn't specified the manner of payment, so Evan had assumed there was some kind of electronic funds transfer happening behind the scenes. Dealing with these other vendors might not be as straightforward.

"How do you normally pay?" Evan asked.

"Direct transfer from a private wallet. Nothing fancy."

The system was pretty standard in the more remote regions of the Commonwealth. While credit transfers were more common around the core worlds using the central banking system, freelance traders often used a form of personal credit bookkeeping. The monetary value was stored and tracked on an electronic 'wallet', which could receive deposits and withdrawals just like the central system—but there was no record of the transaction outside the two devices.

Technically, the currency exchange rate was supposed to be one-to-one with standard credits on the official banking network, but traders often applied a modifier as a negotiating tactic. Evan had seen some transactions at three-times the standard rate when a trader really wanted to get creative with their accounting. He could only imagine what kind of markup they might face with this kind of ask.

"I need to check with Conroy, see what our options are," Evan said.

Zaris held up her omni. "I've got the inventory checklist for our pickup. Want me to make some calls and see what I can source?"

"You'd do that?"

She smiled. "Only if you admit that you need me."

"On this matter, I do, yes," he conceded. "I can't be anywhere near this." His reputation was shot, and most people thought he was dead. Any call from him would be rejected immediately.

"And there's something else…"

He crossed his arms. "What?"

"Be honest… You like my company." She held up her thumb and forefinger a millimeter apart. "Just a little bit."

"You are rapidly making me rethink my opinion."

"Oh, come on!"

"It's true, there are more objectionable people I could travel with."

Zaris scrunched up her nose. "I'm not sold on your tone."

He took a calming breath. "Zaris, despite nearly getting each other killed multiple times, our recent adventures have had their fun moments, and I'm glad you were my first call when I had nowhere else to turn. I appreciate everything you've done." He paused, gauging her reaction. "How was that?"

She pursed her lips, eyes narrowed slightly. "Okay, I accept."

"Thank you. Now, if you'll excuse me." He left the office and headed down to his shuttle, where he could have a private conversation.

He didn't like it when Zaris got cutesy with him like that; it felt like an intentional encroachment on his relationship with Anya. While it was true that part of him *had* enjoyed these recent exploits with Zaris, he didn't want her thinking it was anything more than a professional friendship.

Evan settled onto the *Mara*'s flight deck. "Sam, change of plans." He filled the AI in on their trouble at the supply depot.

"Let's call up Conroy and see what he has to say."

"Certainly, Evan. I will also search available directories and message boards for potential leads on what we need."

"Thanks, Sam."

A secure comm connection appeared on the screen, and Evan initiated the link.

Rebeka answered. "Evan, is everything okay?"

"We're fine, but the pickup didn't go to plan. I need to speak with Conroy."

"Sure, just a minute."

The screen went blank and returned several seconds later with Conroy in his office. "Rebeka tells me there was trouble?"

Evan recapped the events, watching the furrow between the chancellor's brows deepen with each detail. "So, we can try to source everything ourselves, but using Zaris' contacts is going to cost us," he concluded.

"I'm sorry, Evan, I'd hoped everything was in order," Conroy said. "I can arrange a funds transfer. But I don't like the idea of Zaris touching that money."

"I agree. I do think she's being genuine with us, but that kind of potential payday is a bigger temptation than I'd want to risk. Sam, do you think you could set me up with a wallet?"

"Yes, I can scavenge enough from this shuttle to manufacture a device. Chancellor, if you are agreeable, I will function as the intermediary for the funds transfer and key the device to Evan's biometrics."

"It's good enough," Conroy said. He didn't look entirely pleased, but nothing about the situation was ideal. "Just let me know how much you need."

"All right, I'll report back soon."

Evan returned to Zaris' office.

She flashed a smug grin as soon as he walked in. "If you

didn't love me already, you will now."

"Good news?"

"I've got a line on where we can get everything from the list, not a terrible markup, and all in one stop."

"What's the catch?"

"Eh." She winced. "It's a trade rather than a purchase."

"What did you promise them, Zaris?"

"A weapons shipment."

"You… what?" He stared at her, jaw slack.

"Okay, hear me out. This whole thing with Conroy is going to come down to a fight eventually, right? Well, he's going to need soldiers. And these guys are the best. We use a little inside intel from Conroy's contacts in the core worlds about where a UPDF re-supplier is going to be, and just like that you have a well-outfitted mercenary crew ready to fight for the future of the Commonwealth."

"That's…" He crossed his arms. "I can't believe I'm saying this, but that's actually not a bad idea."

"Right?"

"I'm not sure Conroy will go for it, though."

"Well, Conroy has been living in a bubble for his whole life, and the time in hiding on Aethos hasn't helped. There are a lot of harsh realities about how the galaxy works that he needs to come to grips with."

Evan understood her sentiment, and he didn't disagree. "How does this future trade work? Do we have to give them anything now?"

"Just a modest fee to cover their acquisition costs, and we'll square-up once we have a lead on the right supply target."

"What did you tell them to get them to agree to those terms?"

"I told them I'm working with people who are actively

trying to dismantle the Noche Syndicate. They signed up on the spot."

"Seriously, that's all it took?"

"Evan, you were working on the other side. I don't think you appreciate the kind of hold the Syndicate has in my industry. People remain loyal because they're terrified about what would happen to them if they step out of line. But no one actually *wants* them in power. And the prospect of them getting cozy with Rostov is the final straw."

"I find it hard to believe it's that simple," Evan said.

"Most things are. It's the people in charge that make them complicated."

— — —

Despite her assurances to Evan that the trade was a done deal, Zaris knew better than to walk into the meeting with high expectations.

They'd jumped to a remote gate and then transited to Markeesh. As Evan had guessed, it was one of her go-to locations for deals large and small.

The planet had become a hub for commerce due to its central location—as far as the outer realms were concerned—and unique configuration. The planet had a climate suitable to agricultural growing conditions over a large territory, and the rest of the land had been smartly developed for manufacturing industries, making it one of the few worlds that was truly self-sufficient. It also had six moons, which had been heavily mined in the early days of the colony. Those activities had left behind tunnels and caverns, which had been repurposed into habitable structures. Now, they were a series of thriving bazaars, with each moon offering different specializations.

Zaris' most frequented market, and their current destination, was the moon known as Health—a practical name to denote its goods related to basic necessities like food, medical supplies, and personal sundries. The other moons dealt, respectively, with weapons and security, ships and parts, textiles and furnishings, and electronics and computer equipment. The final moon, Bliss, focused on entertainment and 'human services', which included everything from restaurants and clubs to brothels and darker things she'd made a point to pretend didn't exist.

Since it was set up for commerce, the port was able to accommodate the *Invictus* without them needing to take a shuttle. That was just as well, since her preferred transport shuttle was down for repairs following their recent firefight.

Descending the gangway with Evan, Zaris led the way down an escalator from the port to the underground structure. There'd been significant excavation on this moon following the original mining activity, merging many of the tunnels into large storage warehouses.

Her contact, Vinny, ran one of the warehouses. As a full-service provider, he kept a large inventory of the basics on hand, but he also had partnerships with the more specialized traders so he could quickly pull together a client's order by sourcing from all the moons. A fleet of drone transporters ferried the items, and they could be seen constantly flitting around the corridors.

"Would you like to tell me how a glorified grocer has an interest in military hardware?" Evan asked.

"Evan, you're the last person who should need an explanation about putting up a front."

He kept walking, keeping his attention straight ahead, but it was clear Zaris' comment had landed. "I thought there was a whole moon with people dedicated to that stuff?"

"Sure, and everyone knows what *they* do. When you need more finesse… Well, it's nice to have those people, too."

"The kind of shipment they want as payment is not exactly *subtle*."

"Would you like me to request their full ten-year business plan?"

He sighed. "Never mind. Let's just get our stuff."

The corridor opened into a massive cavern. Towers of crates filled the center of the space, separated into islands with pathways in between. Automated equipment zipped between the stacks, retrieving items to bring to various checkpoints.

"Vinny said he was going to set aside everything for us." Zaris headed toward the closest station.

Evan looked around the space. "I remember coming to a place like this with my parents back when I was a kid."

"They were merchants?"

He nodded. "They bought a small cargo runner when I was eight. That ship became our home."

"Huh. I wouldn't have pegged you as a space kid."

"I think it was one of the reasons I was able to do the undercover work. I'd been enough places in my life to find a way to settle in anywhere. It was about the journey for me, never the destination."

"Not for me." She could probably learn something from his perspective; life happened quickly enough without trying to speed it along.

They arrived at the service station, and Zaris entered the identifying number she'd been given when she'd arranged the order. The screen flashed a message reading, 'A representative will be with you shortly.'

It better be the boss man himself, with how much we're

about to give them, she thought to herself.

Two minutes later, she did, indeed, see Vinny approaching. He was a broad, solidly built man on the upper side of middle age, with dark eyes and thick brows.

He smiled broadly as he neared, softening his otherwise stern appearance. "Zaris! My, how long has it been?"

"Long enough, my friend." She placed a hand on Evan's shoulder. "This is Evan, my associate. He's the intermediary in the deal."

"The dead man, right." Vinny looked him over. "It sounds like you have quite the tale."

"I'm not sure what Zaris has told you about me, but everyone's story is interesting when it's told the right way."

It was a smart answer on his part. In truth, Zaris hadn't told Vinny much at all, beyond confirming the available details about Evan's identity that had been circulating since he broke cover. Vinny was fishing. She smiled in support of Evan's statement. "We've all worn many hats in life. You know all about that, don't you, Vinny?"

The big man chuckled. "I do."

Zaris didn't know his complete history, but he'd served time in the UPDF and had worked as a military contractor for a time afterward. At some point, he'd publicly stepped away for a quiet retirement as a trader. In reality, he'd simply gone underground with his business, making the setting for this front all the more appropriate. Zaris' paths had crossed with his on a few occasions, and she'd found him to be honorable to his own code—even though those rules might seem harsh to the rest of society.

"We have a deal to discuss," Zaris continued. "Where's a good place to talk?"

"Follow me."

Vinny led them across the warehouse to a side tunnel where the origins of the structure as a mine were especially evident, with exposed rock walls and ceiling. He opened a metal door and motioned them inside a room equipped with an oval metal table and six chairs.

Evan hesitated a little at the door but went in, selecting a seat at the head of the table where he could see the door and could get to it without having to go around the table. Zaris followed his example and took the same spot on the other side.

Vinny closed the door, glancing between the two of them, and let out a soft tsk. He went around the far side, facing the door. "When Zaris said you're planning to take on the Syndicate, I thought she was joking. But when she told me you were involved, Evan, I became intrigued. Word of Alex's betrayal made the rounds."

"I can think of a lot more interesting topics," Evan said.

"You underestimate yourself," Vinny said. "See, you did something that no one else had ever been brave enough to do. You showed that the Syndicate *does* have weaknesses. To put it bluntly, you pulled one over on them. You did what many had considered impossible."

So, he's a damn inspirational hero, huh? Zaris crossed her arms and leaned back in the seat. The conversation was about to get interesting.

11

THE SIMPLE SUPPLY run that Conroy had described was thoroughly out the airlock at this point. Evan wasn't sure if he'd stumbled into an interrogation or a job interview, but this was definitely not a standard supply pickup.

"Vinny, I was doing a job," Evan said. "I don't want to cause trouble now, but it keeps finding me."

"Well, it's the kind of trouble that gets my blood pumping," Vinny said, leaning forward. "I hear you have an inside track on Commonwealth intel?"

Vinny was smart not to say what he was really asking: whether Evan could supply logistical details for military weapons shipments. Evan answered in an equally vague way. "I know someone who knows people."

"And is your contact interested in a trade?"

Unsurprisingly, Conroy had *not* been pleased with the suggestion, initially. However, after walking him through the potential benefits of an alliance, he'd started to come around. But only partially.

"While your initial proposal was intriguing, I have a counter-offer," Evan said.

Zaris' brows shot up and she glared at him accusingly. He

hadn't run any of it by her, which may have been a mistake. But she'd made the original deal without checking with him, and he was concerned that she'd modify the terms again if he said anything before the face-to-face with their potential partner.

"What are your terms?" Vinny asked. His expression was the unreadable neutral of someone experienced with negotiations.

"Rather than giving you logistics info, how about we get you the items ourselves?"

Zaris nearly fell out of her chair at the other end of the table.

Vinny tilted his head, still not giving away his feelings. "And how might you do that?"

What Evan didn't dare explain was that Sam could fabricate whatever items they needed to close the deal. Both Conroy and the AI had agreed, though neither was thrilled with the concept. Still, they agreed it would be a net gain for the larger movement.

Instead, Evan said, "We already stole some. They're just sitting in a warehouse waiting for the right owner to put them to good use."

"No. I want them from the source. No deal," Vinny said. "Zaris, you told me he had an inside line. You lied to me. And you know how I feel about liars."

"Whoa, Vinny!" She held up her hands defensively. "I didn't mean any disrespect. You'll still get the goods. What's the issue?"

"It's not about the merchandise. You should know better than that. It's about having current intel. Information is power. What you're telling me is that you got lucky before and got your hands on some goods, but now you know nothing more

than an average chump off the street. That has no value to me."
He stood up. "Now, I need to figure out what to do with you."
He stormed around the table and left. The door bolted behind
him.

The nanite bracelets on Evan's wrists warmed against his
skin in response to his worry. He'd rip the door from its frame
and cut a path to the exit if that's what it took, but he wasn't
willing to give up on the deal yet.

He placed his hands on the table and kept his voice as level
as he could, figuring that they would be under observation.
"Zaris, you said these were friends of yours."

"I don't think I used that word. Pretty sure I said 'business
associates'. You know full well that associates are just as likely
to shoot you as help you."

He wanted to wipe his hands down his face, but he settled
for taking a deep breath. "We need those supplies. There has to
be a way for us to come to a mutually beneficial deal."

"I'm thinking." Zaris jumped to her feet and paced back
and forth for three laps before stopping, a devious gleam filling
her eyes as she smiled. "Oh, I've got it!" She ran around to
where Evan was seated and leaned down to whisper into his
ear.

He listened to her idea—bold, creative, and reckless, just
like most of her concepts. "*That's* your solution?" Evan asked.

"Good, isn't it?"

"I need to ask, Zaris," he whispered, "and please be
honest… Do you have a death-wish?"

She laughed. "What? No! Why would you ask that?"

"Because it sounds like a great way to get us un-alived."

On cue, Vinny returned. "What are you two cooking up?"

Evan swore under his breath. He'd figured that Vinny or
his associates would be watching, but he'd expected that he and

Zaris would be left for longer to really ramp up their anxiety. He wanted more time to plot his response. But before Evan could say anything, Zaris jumped in.

"Say, what did you think of Chancellor Conroy back in the day?"

Vinny shrugged. "A politician is a politician. But I preferred him to Rostov."

"You did, huh?" She smiled. "Well, what if I told you that Conroy is alive and you could have a front seat to a revolution?"

Vinny chuckled. "I'd say you have my attention."

Zaris grinned at Evan. "See? I told you."

— — —

Conroy gaped at Evan through the screen. "You agreed to *what*?! That isn't what we'd discussed." Not only was it not the plan, it wasn't even in the same star system of ideas.

"Well, sir, this is what happens when you send out people to do your work for you without a backup plan. We make it up on the fly."

Conroy took in a slow breath through his nose. His cheeks burned, and he hoped he didn't look too flushed over the video feed. "Point taken."

"But I think this could actually be beneficial. Spreading the seeds for your return now will turn up the temperature on Rostov. People make mistakes when the pressure is on."

Regardless of what information made its way back to Rostov, there was now the issue of what Vinny—the mercenary masquerading as a trader—might do with the knowledge of Conroy's intended return to power. A man like that could do real damage… or be a major asset.

"What, exactly, was promised with this arrangement, Evan?" Conroy asked.

"He provided the supplies we needed, down to every last MealPak. In exchange, he wants an inside track on your offensive plans to take the Commonwealth. I told him that the intention is for the transfer of power to be peaceful, and he laughed in my face. They don't like Rostov, or the direction things are going, and they especially hate the Syndicate. If we provide the weapons, he'll provide the people to help handle the opposition and get to keep a portion of whatever is liberated from enemy forces."

"You're asking me to authorize these mercenaries to seize and keep UPDF military assets. How is that any different from Rostov's deal with the Syndicate?"

"It's not, other than these guys are on your side. Look, I can call the whole thing off. There are other places we can get food and spare electronics parts. But I need to ask, where were you planning to recruit fighters? Because you *will* need a militia. Zaris' corsairs aren't enough, and you already agreed to bring *them* into this deal."

The words struck true. Conroy had been avoiding that reality because he didn't like the idea of anyone getting hurt or killed in his name. But the fact of the matter was thousands had already died. Vinny and his fighters were a tool, just like any other personnel asset. Uniforms and banners and titles didn't matter now. It was about people coming together for a common cause. Since Rostov wasn't playing by the rules, they couldn't expect to win against him by following convention. Unexpected partnerships—like with Zaris and Vinny—was the kind of novel approach that would give them a chance.

"I'm glad it's you and Zaris out there."

The younger man looked at him through the screen. "Does

that mean we have a deal?"

"It does," Conroy assented. "I need to stop thinking like the leader I was and begin acting like the leader I need to be."

Evan nodded. "Consider it done. We need to stay the night to get everything loaded. We'll be back tomorrow."

"Thank you, Evan."

"Thank me when it's over." The commlink ended.

Conroy sighed and leaned back in his seat. It was clear to him that they were past the time of any simple, easy assignments. Their work in the shadows over the last five years was bleeding over to the light, and he could no longer operate like he was a man in exile. He needed to rise again as a leader—the kind of man worthy of governing billions.

While the deal Evan and Zaris had brokered was not part of the plan, it was the push he needed. No more waiting for solutions to come to him. He needed to actively seek them out.

While Tobin's research had yielded some actionable results, more information was needed for Conroy to take the final steps to his public return. Information they needed from an outside source. Unfortunately, there were few places to turn for such confidential details.

Samor walked up as Conroy was glaring at his desktop screen, evaluating the options. "Did someone die?" Samor asked.

Conroy leaned back in his chair. "No, I was just debating how best to *avoid* more death."

The soldier sat down across from him. "What's the problem?"

"Everything. But, specifically, I have a lead on some rather damning evidence against Rostov, but it's unvetted. I need corroboration before it would be prudent to act."

"That is tricky."

"Our informant network is at its limits. I need an outsider to us—and yet on the inside for Rostov. And the person who comes to mind…" He let out a long breath.

"Who?"

"Julian Rojas. Anya's father."

Samor's brows shot up. "I hadn't considered that connection."

"I haven't been able to *stop* thinking about it. He's been in Rostov's orbit for nearly two decades. And if anyone has a chance to get him to divulge information, it's his daughter."

"The daughter he allowed to go on the *Stratum*. Either he doesn't know the plans, or she's not that precious to him."

Conroy had been working the angles on that issue for weeks. Though he had no biological children of his own, he couldn't imagine sacrificing his child, no matter the political pressure. *Something* else had to be going on, but he didn't have all the pieces to work it out. "We could ask Anya to reconnect. Julian wanted to meet, from what I was told."

Samor nodded. "I can offer no better suggestion."

"All right. I'll see if she's willing to help."

12

ANYA SHOOK HER head. "No."

"I know it's awkward," Conroy reiterated, "but—"

"It doesn't matter," she cut in. "He sent me to die. So he's dead to me."

The chancellor bowed his head. "I can understand how your feelings toward your father are a little complicated right now—"

"Complicated? No. 'Complicated' is when you're with your boyfriend at a wedding and run into your ex, only to find out he's your current boyfriend's college roommate. What's going on with my dad is a deep betrayal that shakes the very foundation of your core. The kind of thing that changes your entire perspective on life. But you know all about that, don't you, sir?"

Conroy's face twisted. She'd struck a nerve with that one. A man couldn't survive an attempted assassination perpetrated by a close friend and professional confidant without leaving a lasting wound. "You want answers, don't you?"

He did have her there. Beneath the anger that simmered whenever she thought about her father, a large part of her just wanted to know 'why'. Despite how it looked, it all might be a terrible misunderstanding. She didn't want to believe he was evil—it would take a truly evil person to knowingly send his only child to her death—so maybe there was more to it? She'd have no chance of getting any answers without having another conversation.

"He might not tell me anything," Anya said.

The tension eased in Conroy's shoulders as he realized that Anya was starting to come around. "I can coach you. His reactions to certain questions would be telling, even if he doesn't say a word."

"When would I reach out?"

"No time like the present."

Her heart skipped a beat. "I think I need to work up the courage."

"No, delaying will only make you prone to overthinking. I'll be right here, helping you navigate every turn."

Tension seized her chest. Anya turned away from the chancellor, suddenly unable to draw a full breath. "I don't know…" She wasn't sure why she was so nervous. *Is it that he won't answer me… or what he might say?*

"Anya, I wouldn't ask this of you if it wasn't important," Conroy said.

This is ridiculous. I don't need a coach to talk to my own dad. She nodded. "Fine. But I'm driving the conversation. You're just here to observe."

"Agreed." Conroy sat and motioned to indicate he'd be quiet.

He's just dad. Don't overthink it. Anya took a deep breath and let it out slowly.

She initiated the vidcall.

Despite her self-assurances, tension seized her chest again while a three-dimensional star symbol pulsed and spun at the center of the screen, indicating a connection was in progress.

Her father's face filled the screen a few moments later. Unlike the previous time she'd called, he was in his office with daylight visible through the window behind him. "Anya, I'm glad you called." There was that unsettling tone again—the right words but missing enthusiasm.

"Hi, Dad," she struggled to keep her own voice chipper, "I wanted to talk to you about that meeting."

"Good. I hate to think about you being so far from home."

"I didn't say where I was."

"You're not on Praxis, are you?"

"No."

"Then anywhere is far, my dear." He paused. "Is a meeting on Constella still out of the question?"

"Too much Syndicate business there for my taste."

"As I recall, you don't have a much higher opinion of politicians."

"Some are better than others."

"You're being evasive and contrary. I thought we were past that when you grew out of your teens."

"Well, Dad, can you think of any reasons why I might be on edge?" she asked pointedly.

He stared at her through the screen. "It must have been jarring to find out the colony ship you were supposed to be on went missing."

"How did *you* feel? You recommended me for it. You thought I was on that ship."

His expression hardened. "You *were*, weren't you?"

"I think you already know the answer to that."

"Ah." He pulled back from the camera a little. "Conroy always knew how to talk a good game, but the man had an allergy to the truth. Be careful what you believe."

"Do you mean Chancellor Conroy? He—"

"Anya, spare me. He's in the room with you, isn't he?"

Her heart leaped into her throat. She involuntarily glanced at where Conroy was seated.

Julian noticed her eye movement and nodded. "You were supposed to be safe, Anya. I never would have put you in harm's way. The only reason you're in danger now is because of Conroy's actions."

Anya decided to go for it. "If you knew that the mission was doomed, why send me at all?"

"No one was supposed to die, Anya. And you're a brilliant scientist. We needed an insightful mind like yours on the world."

"The ship was shot down!"

"You thought that was intentional? Is that what he told you?"

Anya glanced at Conroy again, and his expression was stoic.

"It's too complicated to explain over a vidcall. Let's meet in person and I'll explain everything."

She didn't trust him after recent events, but there remained an unsettling aspect of his demeanor she couldn't quite place. With nothing to lose, she decided to make a more personal bid. "Do you remember when we used to stargaze when I was little?"

His expression softened for a moment before turning stoic again. "Of course. You liked the shooting stars."

To her recollection, that had never been a notable part of their time outside. The memories that stood out most were their talks about life on other worlds. Other kids liked the bright streaks of meteors, but that wasn't her. And he should know that.

Was he just drunk those times and misremembering? Anya decided not to give any indication that his answer was strange and set up another test to confirm something was, indeed, off. "Those nights inspired me to follow this career path." True. "But it really wasn't until that summer I volunteered at the nature preserve when I realized how much I wanted to study all the forms of life across different worlds." Mostly accurate, except for her brief interest in being a vet instead. "No matter where I go, the pendant you gave me for graduation makes me remember those old nights with you." Fiction—he had actually gifted her a bracelet, which she almost never wore because he'd never bothered to learn her taste, instead equating cost to value.

"I'm glad you have those memories and still think about those good times, Anya."

She struggled to keep a neutral expression, deciding on a bashful smile to hide her concern. "Yeah, me too." *What in the planets is going on? How has he forgotten so much?* Unless there was another explanation. "Say, Dad, I need to think about the best place for this meeting, okay? I'll be in touch."

"Anya—"

"Give my love to mom." She hung up, immediately glaring at Conroy. "Did you lie to us about the *Stratum* getting shot down by the escort cruiser?"

"No, Anya. They did it. Maybe it wasn't the plan—he may have been telling the truth about that—but the rest was lies."

"I'm not surprised." Anya leaned back in her seat. "That's not him."

Conroy's eyes softened with compassion. "It's difficult to see a different side of people we love—"

"No, I mean, that's *not him*. It looks like him and that's his voice, but that is *not* my father."

"Anya—"

"I know my dad. Something has been off since my first talk with him, and I couldn't place it. But I know now. It's not him."

Conroy gazed at her the way someone would look upon a child insisting they had an imaginary friend. "People change."

She shook her head. "Not like this. I can't explain it. It's like he's an imposter. I know something is off, as crazy as that sounds."

"We've seen some very unlikely things. I just…"

"You don't have to believe me. But I'm telling you, whoever we just talked to isn't Julian Rojas."

— — —

Rostov studied the face of his longtime advisor through the screen. He could read him as well as anyone, and he recognized the truth in his words. *We have a real problem.*

"I didn't mean for you to get in the middle of this," Rostov said.

"Anya was always too curious for her own good." Julian shook his head. "This is bigger than me."

Good man. It wasn't often Rostov found people willing to do *anything* to help the greater cause, but Julian Rojas had proved himself to be committed beyond measure. His work as a liaison with the Syndicate had been invaluable to Rostov's mightier ambitions, paving the way for the revolution he envisioned with the Commonwealth. Soon, they would throw off the shackles that had been holding them back from taking a true step forward for humanity.

"Anya isn't a concern on her own," Rostov mused. "We need to find out who she's working with."

"She still refuses to say anything about where she is or how she got there."

"No surprise. Given that she was on Aethos, it's a fair assumption Conroy is involved, at least. He'll be the one calling the shots, no matter who else might be involved."

"Now that he has the ship, he'll be a lot more difficult to eliminate."

Rostov nodded thoughtfully. "Difficult, but not impossible. He'll want to make a move eventually. He can't hide forever."

"If Anya *is* close to him, she might be able to lead us to him."

"You need to give her enough to make her think you're sympathetic," Rostov instructed. "It's a balancing act, but that should be well within your skillset."

"I understand," Julian acknowledged.

Rostov was sometimes surprised how agreeable Julian had been to his more unsavory suggestions over the last two years, but he wasn't about to question the man's attitude when it was so beneficial to his own goals. They were so close now. All the pieces were inching into place. They just needed one final push for their master plan to be complete.

"Stay vigilant, my friend," Rostov said. "We will reap the rewards for our sacrifices very soon."

13

FOR THE FIRST time in weeks, Evan felt like everything was falling into place. They had food, transportation, and security—but most importantly, a plan was coming together. Whether it was a *good* plan remained to be seen as events played out.

He was still apprehensive. Trusting others was difficult for him after so many years of only being able to rely on himself. Yet, Anya had reminded him how powerful it was to have a partner through the tough times. He'd missed that camaraderie from his military days, and he was excited to recapture that dynamic.

He smiled at Zaris as the *Invictus* arrived in orbit above Aethos. "Welcome home."

"Thank the stars for that!" she exclaimed, letting out a long sigh.

Evan was anxious to get back to Aethos' surface and see Anya, so he said his goodbyes and took the *Mara* down as soon as he could.

He landed the shuttle in the *Asamar*'s bay. As the craft powered down, he expected Anya to come greet him. However, there was no sign of her.

"Hey, Sam, is anyone around?"

"I am here, Evan."

"And Anya?"

"She went out for a walk."

May as well get settled back in. He grabbed his travel bag and went up to his cabin.

Surprisingly, walking into the space actually felt like returning home. His statement to Zaris had been a jovial nod to their harrowing mini-mission, but there really was something to entering a familiar place where one felt safe and didn't need to be constantly on guard. Being on the *Asamar* now reminded him of that feeling from his youth, traveling on his parents' merchant ship. No matter which star system they might be in or what they were transporting, his little cabin had been his sanctuary. Now, he finally had another place to call his own—albeit with a strange roommate situation involving a telepathic AI with boundary issues.

"Evan, Anya has returned to the *Asamar*," Sam announced. "I let her know you have returned."

He opened his cabin door and was greeted by the sound of running footfalls. Anya appeared around a corner within seconds. She beamed at the sight of him, and they wrapped their arms around each other as soon as they met.

"Oh, how I missed you," he said into her hair.

She leaned up to kiss him and then pulled back enough to look into his eyes. "Why were you gone for so long?"

"Things didn't exactly go to plan." He filled her in on the highlights from the journey, eliciting a number of eyebrow-raises and head-shakes at the more challenging moments.

"I can't believe Conroy sent you into that mess," she said when he'd finished.

"I don't know if it was his fault. But his contact might not be as solid as he thought."

"Conroy doesn't have a problem using people," she muttered. Something in her tone made the comment seem personal.

"Did something happen while I was gone?" Evan asked.

She hesitated. "I talked to my dad again."

"Was that *your* idea?"

Anya crossed her arms. "What do you think?"

He sighed. "Conroy wanted you to get information out of him?"

"It didn't work. But he had details about my life wrong—like, things he *should* know."

Evan hugged her. "I'm sorry, Anya."

"I went out for a walk because I wanted to replay the conversation again in my head. The man I talked to isn't my dad, Evan. I told Conroy that, and he doesn't believe me. And I can't blame his skepticism on this. I know how it sounds, saying he's not my father."

Evan had to admit that the statement was a little far-fetched. "I doubt he was replaced with an android or something."

"No, that would be ridiculous. I can't explain how he's different, but I know it's not *him*. It can't be. My parents couldn't betray me like that, right?"

Of course she would feel that way. Who sells out their own kid? Evan didn't want to antagonize her. He'd seen the nasty side of people, and he could no longer be shocked by the terrible lengths some would go to. Maybe the man Anya had known as her dad wasn't the real man at all. "I understand how you feel. But was this both of your parents or just your dad?"

Anya sat silently for a few seconds. "You know, it's weird that he didn't bring my mom into the conversation when I called the first time to tell him I was alive. She should have been asleep in bed with him that night, right?"

"A lot can happen between people in a couple years. If you hadn't spoken with them for a while…"

"They would have told me if they'd split up."

"Maybe. Or…" He faded out.

"Or what?"

"Nothing helpful. Forget it."

She placed her hands on her hips. "Come on, spill."

Voicing the thought conjured a dark reality he didn't want to acknowledge, but nothing was off the table. "It crossed my mind that a man willing to sell out his daughter might not have a lot of regard for his wife's safety, either."

Anya gaped at him. "Evan…"

"Like I said, not helpful."

She rubbed her eyes. "No, it's not. But you're right. Shit!" She vented her mounting frustration in a guttural groan. "Damn this entire situation and these greedy assholes toying with people's lives!"

"We don't know anything for sure. Have you spoken with your mom? Or seen her?"

Anya's eyes widened, filled with new fear. "No, I got so distracted by my dad acting weird I didn't think to…" She hurried down the hall toward the lounge. "Sam, set up a vidcall with my mom."

Evan followed her. Just before the hall opened into the lounge, Anya instead went through a doorway. Evan was surprised to see the room had been transformed into an office space that could be at home on any human-made starship.

"When did we get this?" he asked.

"When does Sam do anything?" Anya plopped down in the chair behind the desk.

"I do most of my renovation work while you are sleeping or away from the ship. This space was completed sixty-three hours ago," Sam announced.

"It's more convenient to make calls from here rather than going down to the shuttle," Anya said. "Did you find my mom's contact info, Sam?"

"Yes, Anya. I am ready to initiate a vidcall."

Anya motioned for Evan to sit in a chair across the desk from her, and he complied. "All right, let's do it."

The monitor switched to a standard vidcall interface with a pulsing star symbol on the center of the screen. After five seconds, the symbol turned red and solid.

"Sam, what's wrong?" Anya asked, concern pitching her tone.

"Apologies, Anya. This comm ident appears to be disabled. I am unable to establish a connection."

"Oh, no…"

Evan went around the back of the desk and hugged Anya. "Hey, don't jump to conclusions. There are lots of reasons for someone to change their contact details and not have the new info in a public directory. We can track her down."

"But what if she's *not* okay, Evan? What if she found out about what my dad was doing and he…"

He gently brushed her hair away from her eyes. "Don't spiral, Anya. Clearly, he's not parent of the year, but let's not jump to conclusions. I shouldn't have said anything."

"Well, I'm ninety-nine percent sure he knew the *Stratum*'s mission was doomed, which means he set me up to die."

"Just because he knew the ship would be destroyed, that doesn't mean there wasn't a plan to save *you*."

Her brows knitted. "I don't know."

Evan wished he had more information to go on. They were

making guesses on top of supposition on top of hunches, and there were very few hard facts. They were likely to keep falling into the same mental traps unless they took a new approach. "We need to take a step back. All of our theorizing has been about events in the last year or two, but I'm curious *when* it started."

"What do you mean?"

"Let's think about your dad's odd behavior for a minute. You said he started asking you intrusive questions about your job at NovaTech, right?"

"Yeah. And that started a year before I was assigned to the colony mission. So what?"

"Well, let's assume he was asking you those questions because he was a corporate spy. But my question is, was he recruited as an informant because his daughter worked at NovaTech, or did he make sure your career path would lead you to a role where you could feed him that information?"

She stared at him, blinking, and with her lips slightly parted. "Holy shit, Evan. It hadn't occurred to me that he may have been engineering my entire career. Has he been my handler?"

"I didn't say that—"

"But it's where this leads." She rubbed her eyes. "How didn't I notice?"

"Anya, you're jumping way ahead."

"No." She leaned forward with her elbows on her thighs. "You want to know when this could have started? Let me tell you."

— — —

It was easy to brush off coincidences and conveniences on

a one-off basis, but now that Anya was looking at her life and career in aggregate, she could no longer dismiss those twists as being by chance.

"I think it all traces back to a party about five years ago," Anya said as the timeline came together in her mind. All of the innocuous interactions in recent years were taking on new meaning. "I was a nobody in the scheme of things, just a young xenobiologist researcher with a good academic record and some decent field experience under my belt. The only reason anyone would recognize my name is because of my parents. Because of that, it was obvious I was only invited to the party because of them. It was one of those events where everyone is 'someone'. And then there was me.

"I'd been working under various university research grant programs up to that point. But that party is when I was introduced to the guy who'd become my supervisor at NovaTech. And it was my dad who introduced us."

Evan looked at her intently. "Tell me what you remember about that initial interaction."

She entered the scene in her mind.

She'd been drinking, and the party had taken on a slightly ethereal quality as she'd floated from conversation to conversation. A handsome, young billionaire had been chatting her up by the hors d'oeuvres table. He would have made for a fun night, but that wasn't her style, and she was certain he wasn't after anything serious. She'd been around guys like him at university, and they were always rich in ego and poor with conversation.

Her father had flagged her from across the room, and she'd been grateful for the exit strategy. She'd found her father talking to another man his age, wearing flashy glasses and sporting a styled moustache.

"This is my daughter, Anya," her father had introduced.

"Ah, the xenobiologist." The finely twisted hairs of the man's mustache curled upward as he smiled. "Not enough bright, young minds pursue that trade."

"More fun for me."

"Indeed." He had looked her over from head to foot, a little too thoroughly for her liking—enough that it had seared into her long-term memory. "How would you like to do something truly meaningful with your life?"

"I think I'm off to a pretty good start."

"Cataloguing new species is a noble pursuit, but it's a siloed activity. What about using those skills for the advancement of humanity?"

The man's statements had struck her as the same kind of self-important rhetoric she expected to hear at those kinds of parties. They would often speak of the 'greater good' or grand designs that would help them make their mark on history. She hadn't thought much of it at the time, and had responded in kind. "What do you have in mind?"

"NovaTech is in the midst of coordinating the largest expansion campaign humanity has undertaken in a century. Our new gate construction protocol has allowed us to push toward worlds my grandparents would never have dreamed would be within our reach. But we need to know which worlds hold the best prospects. It's not just a matter of the natural resources, but those efforts would benefit from a more nuanced understanding of the larger political implications."

She'd half tuned him out by the end. More meaningless diplomatic speech, lots of words without saying much at all. She'd already had a long day, and the sugar crash following several sweetened cocktails was making her sleepy. "That sounds like important work."

"I'm glad you agree. We'll make the arrangements." The moustached man had bowed his head to her and departed like they'd just concluded a business transaction.

"What was that about?" she'd asked her father.

"You're moving up in the world." He'd patted her shoulder and smiled. "There are some other people you should meet. You'll be working together soon."

He'd taken her on the rounds, exchanging pleasantries and vague, aspirational wishes with half a dozen other people. The final stop had been with Alden, the only other normal-seeming person at the event. "Always a pleasure to meet a fellow scientist," he'd greeted after their initial introduction.

"What's your specialty?" she'd asked.

"I head up NovaTech's colony site identification team. And it just so happens we're looking for another xenobiologist."

The rest of the conversation was hazy in her memory, but she recalled concluding their chat with a handshake. A week later, she'd had a signed employment contract with NovaTech. At no point in that process had it *felt* like a setup, but it all seemed very different in hindsight.

She relayed the highlights to Evan, and he nodded along with her account. "My dad set me up. He had to have known those people would use me, and he made the introduction."

"So, it was just your dad that night? Your mom wasn't at the party?" Evan confirmed.

"Just him."

"And what about the other times you met with those people?"

"Always only dad."

"Then he either kept it secret from your mom, or at least she wasn't directly involved. We can only speculate about if he told her anything."

"I hope she realized my dad was a monster and went into hiding from him." As painful as that would be, it would be the most favorable explanation for why her usual contact info wasn't working now.

"Having walked through this, do you still think the man you spoke to with Conroy is not your father?" Evan asked. She could hear the skepticism in his tone—trying to lead her toward the obvious evidence that he'd been crooked for years.

Is it such a leap that he'd turn into the uncaring, cold man I just talked to? Anya weighed the scenarios. The most straightforward explanation was that she'd never known her father as well as she'd thought and she was now seeing his true self. How much time had she spent with him before? Even all those years ago, he'd paraded her around like a show animal at those parties. He was guilty, at least in part.

But there *was* something different about him during her interactions over the last few weeks—a change in his affect she couldn't put her finger on. She was certain about that.

"My mom would have known something was wrong. They couldn't have swapped in an imposter until she was gone," Anya said. Hearing it out loud sounded crazier than it had in her mind. *Who would have done that? And what would it be— an android?*

"Or, there's no imposter at all," Evan countered. "I think a way more reasonable explanation is that the communication signal was hijacked. They could be using an AI portrayal of your father."

"Oh. That would make more sense."

"We're talking about your parents, Anya. I wouldn't expect anyone in your situation to be thinking clearly."

"I'm perfectly lucid, thank you." As soon as the words left

her mouth, she regretted the outburst. Evan wasn't the real target of her frustrations.

He side-eyed her—not upset, but a silent reminder that they were on the same team. "If the communications with your dad are being faked, then they'd need to limit other contact channels, like your mom. Maybe your dad decided to stop cooperating?"

Her cheeks flushed. "Yeah."

"It might lead nowhere, but I say we chase that lead—even if it's just to rule it out. You said you met a comms guy, right?"

"Yeah. Garet."

"Do you think he could help trace the call log?"

Actionable, hard data. That's precisely what she needed. "Let's find out."

— — —

Evan's hope that he was right about the 'imposter' situation just being a simple comm trick faded with every minute he watched Garet pore over the logs. By the time the young man pushed back from his workstation in Anya's new research lab, Evan had braced himself for an unfavorable report.

"The logs are clean," Garet said. "All I can say for sure is that the commlink wasn't redirected and that the recipient was, indeed, on Praxis. What's all this about, anyway?"

"I'll explain another time," Anya said, her voice weaker than normal. "Thanks for your help, Garet. We'll get back to the other research tomorrow."

He smiled at her, making no acknowledgment of Evan's presence. "See you then."

"Well, there goes that hypothesis," Anya muttered as soon

as the lab's door closed.

Evan rubbed her back. "We'll figure it out, Anya."

"Yeah. I…" She massaged her eyes. "I'm sick of not knowing what's real."

"I'm real," he assured her. "The truth is, most of reality is overrated."

"Too true."

Evan glanced at the time on the screen, surprised to find it was already late-afternoon local time. "Hey, I need to go check in on Roman. Are you going to be okay?"

"Yep. Go do your thing." She kissed him.

He savored the contact with her. They really were surrounded by uncertainties, but what they had together was indisputable. As long as he had that one real thing to hold onto, he was ready to face any challenge.

14

"Admit it, you missed me," Evan ribbed, hoping to get a rise out of Roman.

The Syndicate man was in the same spot on the floor as where Evan had left him days before—not a good sign for his overall well-being. Dark circles now shaded his eyes and his shoulders were rounded forward. The impression of disheartened defeat had to be an act. There was no way he would've cracked this quickly.

"How long have I been in here?" Roman asked.

"The measure of hours or days is irrelevant." Evan sat down in front of the other man. "Has it been *long enough*?"

Roman leaned his head back against the metal wall. "If you want me to grovel, that's never going to happen."

"I just want to talk."

"You want me to spill all my secrets."

"That would be helpful. You game?"

Roman scoffed. "Like I said before, kill me and get it over with. Did you already kill Red and the others?"

"No, they're safe in another place. And you're going to stay alive and well right here. But you have a say in how you spend that time. What drives you?"

Evan expected the question to provoke another sarcastic quip from the Syndicate captive, but instead Roman looked directly at him, serious and intent. "Have you ever lost a part of yourself?"

"Yeah, I have," Evan admitted.

"The kind of loss where life feels meaningless?"

Evan nodded. "What did you lose, Roman?"

The other man looked away, the moment of near-revelation broken. "I don't have a future. This is pointless."

"Do you *really* want to die, or is this an issue with your family?"

"What is this, therapy?"

"A conversation. See, I have a hunch that you're a pretty smart guy. Despite your statements to the contrary, I doubt leaving here in a body-bag is your ideal outcome. So, we can either try to find some common ground, or you can continue being miserable. Your choice."

Roman looked at him again, this time with the cold calculation that had defined many of their interactions. But behind the hard gaze Evan sensed genuine interest. Coming to an agreement might yet be possible. "What's in it for me?"

Those were the magic words Evan had been waiting to hear. "Good question, Roman. What do *you* want?"

The other man remained quiet for nearly a minute. Evan was starting to think he'd never get a response when Roman finally spoke.

"I want to feel whole again."

The statement caught Evan by surprise. *Is that philosophical or literally?*

Their fight last week had been physically traumatizing for Roman, that much was clear. Evan couldn't imagine what it must have felt like to have the alien nanites ripped out of him.

But he'd only been integrated with that tech for a short while. How could someone feel like they weren't 'whole' when they'd returned to their natural state?

Would it be any different for me now? Evan, likewise, had only recently gained his new powers, but already he found himself turning to them more often. He very well may feel empty and like a part of himself was missing if he lost those abilities. That reliance scared him.

"What would make you feel whole, Roman?"

Again, the other man didn't reply right away. "I've been broken for so long that I don't know where I begin or end."

The sudden alleged vulnerability set Evan on edge. Most likely, Roman was putting on another act. Yet, Evan's enhanced senses didn't detect any lies. "I spent a lot of time undercover playing a persona that wasn't me. I can relate to feeling lost inside yourself."

"Did you have anything that helped you remember?"

The line of questioning could very well be a ploy to get Evan to open up and help Roman find a way to exploit him. But he was talking, and that was progress. Evan tried to tread the line between truth and protecting himself. "When my parents were killed, I lost my only family. But I remember everything they gave me, and I hold onto that."

"How nice it must have been to be loved."

Evan couldn't help feeling a twinge in his heart. Roman might just be a fantastic actor, but the bitterness seemed real. "Did you always feel like an outsider in your family?"

"I was 'the baby', and then the 'inconvenience', and then the object of all their disappointments. So yeah, you could say that."

"Didn't that teach you how to stand on your own?"

"It did. I don't care about them."

"So, what's the problem?" Evan pressed. Roman was only a few years younger than him, but he was coming across as a mopey kid.

"You know, it's funny. This mission on Aethos was supposed to be my redemption."

"For what?"

"I was responsible for the transportation of a shipment out of Pavia. It was a particularly large batch of pavite to make Lux, plus some other artifacts."

"Lux?"

"That's what we call the primer serum. It started out as 'Elixir' and got shortened. You know how it goes with names."

"Sure. And I'm guessing the pavite is the gold-flecked rock?"

"Yeah. The shipment was intercepted and confiscated. You wouldn't know anything about that, would you?" Roman glared pointedly at Evan.

The pieces fell into place. Evan *had* been tangentially connected to that incident while he was working undercover. He'd learned of an important shipment and fed information to his handler about an intercept location, though he hadn't known the details about what was on board. But the Pavia connection made sense. It was a good reminder that one person's success was another's failure.

"You really keep getting the shitty assignments, don't you?" Evan said instead of owning up to his involvement.

"I didn't think this place would be the end of the road for me."

"It doesn't have to be."

"Don't you get it? I've lost everything. I can't feel it anymore."

Evan evaluated him, weighing the words. The statement

was vague, but he had a guess. "You mean, you lost the primer when the Korani consciousness was purged?"

Roman nodded. "It never mattered to me before. But then I came here and…"

"Everything changed," Evan completed for him. He'd undergone the same shift.

"I can't take the emptiness."

"Oh, come on, Roman. You're stronger than that."

He scoffed. "You don't get it."

"Explain it to me."

"You only had the one dose. You don't know what it does over time."

Evan arched an eyebrow. "I thought the 'initiation' was a one-time thing."

"One time is all it takes to be a primer, yeah. But that's just the start of what's possible."

"I'm curious to know more."

"I'm sure you are."

All right, here's the opening. Now the real negotiations can begin. Evan stood in front of Roman, hands clasped behind his back. "What if we could get you Lux?"

"Wow, that *would* be quite the trick, considering you have no clue where to find it."

"But *you* do."

"I won't tell you."

"Then you're definitely not getting any, and you can get used to feeling hopelessly empty." Evan crouched down to be eye-level with Roman, still seated on the floor. "You're locked up in here, but I'm the one who can go out and do things. Get things. If you tell me where to find it, I'll make you feel whole again."

— — —

The offer was tempting, but Roman knew better than to trust a traitor. Evan had his own motives, which were in direct opposition to Roman's own objectives. And yet…

There was no way around the fact that Roman had been hung out to dry by his family. What did he owe them? They'd done nothing but disparage him and make him feel 'lesser than' his whole life. Even if he did make it off the planet Aethos alive, through some miracle, what would he have? Marcus and his minions would never share the Lux with him. He'd be doomed to a life of normalcy, never again experiencing the thrill of power. Was that even a life worth living?

Evan was offering an alternative. Whether it was a *genuine* offer or not was up for debate, but it was a *chance*. It might, in fact, be his *only* chance to get the primer, let alone access to an ongoing supply of Lux. He certainly wouldn't be getting that from his family, but he knew all the family secrets. And information was a form of currency.

If I strike a deal, I could end up worse off than I am now. Looking around the bleak holding cell, it was clear he couldn't fall much further. *If I change sides, I'll be all in.*

Until it was convenient to make another move.

Evan was waiting for a response. Roman needed to make up his mind.

"Say I do help you get the Lux. You let me have a dose. Then what? There's no way you let me live as a free man."

"Freedom is a relative term, Roman."

"We all answer to someone."

"Most of us, anyway." Evan leaned against the wall. "I want to see the best in people. But not all people deserve that trust. Convince me that you do."

"And if I don't?"

"Then we can end this here and now. If you refuse to help, then you're worthless to me."

Roman stood up, keeping his back pressed against the wall opposite Evan. "I can betray my family and live, or keep my honor and die."

"Hell of a choice. But you might want to rethink your definition of 'honor'."

A sharp twinge in Roman's chest made him look away as he grimaced. He drew a slow, deep breath and let it out. *I'm a coward. I'm afraid to die.*

He thought through every reason he could imagine for why he should remain loyal to his family. In the end, he realized that it was pointless for loyalty to only run one way. If Marcus and Marta would sell him out in a heartbeat, then why should he show them any more respect?

I can only trust myself. If Roman couldn't rely on his own family, then he certainly couldn't trust this enemy. But Evan offered a means to an end. "If I do this, promise me I'll have a real chance."

Evan met his gaze. "If you deliver us the keys to the Syndicate, Roman, then yes—you have my word that I will vouch for you and put our past conflicts behind us."

All lies. Roman nodded like he was considering the proposition. "What assurance can you offer?"

"My word as someone who lived among you for three years and didn't kill all of you as you slept."

Not the most convincing argument, but it was surprisingly honest. Moreover, if Evan wanted him dead now, there'd been plenty of opportunities to make that happen. It was enough to move their little dance of mutual deception to the next stage. "We tried to kill each other not that long ago," Roman said.

"We're not going to be buddies anytime soon."

"Probably ever. But when mutual interests align…"

"A tentative alliance."

"Right."

Roman nodded pensively, not wanting to come across as too eager. "Let me sleep on it."

"Sure." Evan paused. "In the spirit of this new potential collaboration, I have a question for you."

"You can ask."

"You mentioned earlier that multiple doses of Lux does… something. What happens?"

"I'm not sure I'm ready to share all the details."

"Why not?"

Roman couldn't say much more without giving away his family's secret weapons. *I might need those if—* He cut off the thought as he confronted the harsh reality of his situation. *All of that is useless to me unless I get the primer.*

His options were extremely limited. Banished from his family. No friends beyond the Syndicate. He'd need to extract every bit of useful advantage from Evan and his band of traitorous outcasts. That meant giving just enough information to keep his captors on the hook. This was a perfect opportunity for Roman to make it seem like he was cooperating.

Nothing critical. Nothing harmful. Draw him in… Casting aside years of programming took every bit of Roman's willpower. He forced out the words. "It makes you an irresistible leader."

"What?"

"Lux, it…" Roman wasn't sure how to explain, having never had a high enough dose himself. But he'd seen the results. "It makes you sort of telepathic. Not like you can read minds or anything—more like being able to influence others. Like, 'your word is my command' shit."

"Would that allow you to directly control someone?" Evan asked. "I mean, you could tell them what to say or do and they'd act it out?"

"Yes, but there are only maybe a handful of people who've had enough to do that. And you need to be close. Within a few meters kind of thing."

"Who are those people?"

"Marcus and Marta, for sure. Beyond that, it would just be a guess. But I think they'd likely be family."

Evan was extremely intent now. It didn't seem like the first time he'd heard that concept. "And what happens to the person who's being controlled?"

"They're sort of in a trance. They can talk and do things, but they won't really *feel* it, you know?"

Evan nodded, like something had just clicked for him. "Think about my offer, Roman. You don't need to be the passenger anymore." He left in a hurry, leaving Roman alone in the cell.

Did I just give away the game? He'd thought the information would be innocuous enough.

Ultimately, it didn't matter. Roman needed to let this alliance of convenience play out for now. That was the only way he might regain power for himself. And once he did, he'd be the one calling the shots.

15

THE CONVERSATION WITH Roman had been more illuminating than Evan had imagined possible. *Holy shit, I think I know what might have been going on with Anya's dad!*

Telepathic control might explain his strange affect, and it *definitely* made more sense than any kind of imposter scenario. Since the hijacked commlink theory hadn't panned out, this new revelation was Evan's best lead.

Except, there was a major piece missing. Roman had indicated that a limited number of people might possess such an ability. Either he was mistaken about the scope, or Julian Rojas was being controlled by someone extremely close to the Noche Syndicate.

Who could be that close to him? Anya's mother would be. Maybe one of Julian's co-workers. The requirement for proximity did help narrow the list, but the pool of possibilities painted a disturbing picture for who else might be involved. *One step at a time.*

For now, he at least had a new working theory. That gave him a sense of direction, though he couldn't allow it to blind him from other possibilities. Maybe Anya would be able to help him narrow down the people close to her father. For that matter, Sam might be able to tap into public network and government roster data to create a list of potential contacts.

Evan hurried down the corridor of the underground base, eager to get back to the *Asamar* so he could continue the research. However, he was stopped short by Conroy.

"Ah, glad I caught you. I'd heard you were back and went to talk with Roman."

Evan put on a diplomatic smile even though he didn't feel like chatting with the chancellor right now. "We may finally have some movement on that front. I'll know more tomorrow."

"Oh? That's excellent news." He turned serious. "Evan, I'm sorry about all the trouble at the supply depot."

Though Evan had promised himself he would let it go, an unbidden wave of anger surged within him. "You made it sound like a done deal. Next time, if there is *any* uncertainty, you need to say so. We were nearly shot."

Conroy nodded solemnly. "You have my sincere apologies, Evan. I should have acknowledged the potential risks, and that lack of communication set you up for failure. Thank you for finding another way. I knew I could trust you."

But can I trust you? Evan only nodded in response.

"And what about Roman?" Conroy asked. "What kind of progress?"

"Still too early to say. I'll tell you about the lead as soon as I know it's real."

Conroy eyed him. "Back to keeping things from me?"

"Sorry, but it's been a shitty few days and I'm feeling a little burned."

"I can understand that."

"Do you? Because I spent the last two days cleaning up the mess from your poor planning, only to get back here to find that you've been using Anya, too."

The chancellor looked taken aback. "I asked for a favor, and she agreed."

"You manipulated her. I think you're manipulating all of us."

"Evan—"

"What are you doing, Conroy? I nearly got shot trying to get that supply order you told me was a simple pickup. If you can't even manage to arrange that, how do you expect to become chancellor again?"

"What I asked of Anya has nothing to do with that."

"You're avoiding my question."

"Forgive me for not sharing every detail with you. There are a lot of moving pieces here, and sometimes that means taking action without running it by every possible stakeholder."

Evan groaned. "More empty political-speak!"

Conroy took a deep breath and let it out. "You want to know my plan? All right. I have loyalists throughout the Commonwealth, embedded from high up in government on Terrax to technical specialists in communications infrastructure, media, the military, and other private sector enterprises. Collectively, we aren't many in numbers, but we have hands in the right places. It's how we were able to originally place supplies and people on the *Stratum*, and it's how we knew the military escort was compromised. I have trusted these people with my life.

"More than a dozen of those key people died when the *Stratum* was attacked above Aethos. We had plans and contingencies in place, but nearly all of them rested on that ship making it here in one piece. It's only been a few weeks since that loss, and we're still trying to get back on track. You have witnessed nothing but us in the midst of that mad scramble to recover, and I don't think I'd have a lot of faith in me, either, based on how things have gone since you arrived.

"What you haven't seen is that behind the scenes, we are in the process of packaging evidence of Rostov's treasonous actions—from trying to kill me, to selling out the Commonwealth to the Noche Syndicate, to covering up important scientific discoveries our people have a right to know. As soon as that presentation is ready, I will make a formal announcement that I am alive and assert my rightful claim to the Commonwealth's leadership. We will share our evidence via my moles in official media and communications channels. In the fallout, sides will be chosen. Hopefully, that will lead to rallying support from people with influence.

"We can't predict what will happen next, but there will certainly be a struggle. If the common people wholesale reject me, that will be the end. But if enough see the truth and acknowledge the dangerous path of continuing to follow Rostov's leadership... well, let's just say that revolutions are rarely quick or quiet, but it's worth it to fight on behalf of future generations."

Evan weighed the statement. It was still vague, but he could see the merits of the overall approach. Beginning with what was essentially a coordinated PR campaign would lay important groundwork. "I was starting to wonder if you planned to just storm the capitol one day and execute Rostov."

"That would be suicide without popular support."

He didn't deny that being part of the plan, though. Evan didn't want to jump ahead. "How much longer will it take to finish gathering this evidence?"

"A couple of weeks. Maybe less. Then, it's just a matter of finding the right time."

"Is this intel as reliable as the supply depot?"

Conroy's eyes narrowed. "I'll get what I need."

"Good. I'll let you know about Roman." Evan walked away before Conroy could give him another assignment. He was on a case, and he wanted to see it through.

— — —

Zaris entered Conroy's office in his bunker. The place made her feel like she was being crushed every time she stepped inside. That made no sense, considering the structure was a repurposed starship and its corridors were identical to anything she'd find on her own ship. But there was something about knowing she was underground that messed with her perception.

"What's this about?" she asked, sitting down across from the former chancellor.

"I wanted to speak, leader to leader. You have put your own life on the line, and offered your corsairs. But it's one thing to go after supplies we could all use. I want to know how you're feeling about my core mission," Conroy said. "What do you say, Zaris? Do I have your support?"

"Not saying I'll be with you for life, but I'll help you take out Rostov."

"Will others share your sentiment?"

"The captains who came with me to Aethos can be persuaded. There might be others, but that will take some conversations."

"I welcome you to have those talks. I need to build an army, and I'd like to know how many people I'll have on my side as we start this mission."

Zaris pursed her lips. "May I be blunt?"

"Please."

"What the hell would you have done if I hadn't asked to come back with Evan?"

"Present my claim along with evidence of Rostov's crimes and put out a call for support."

"And if no one responded?"

"My big comeback would fizzle into the shadows of lost futures."

"All right, I guess we'll see how it goes." Zaris had been around powerful people for her entire life, and not one of them would willingly give up their influence when they didn't get their way. She had no reason to believe he was any different. He'd fight, no matter what he said now. But she wouldn't blindly follow someone.

"I do realize that what I've proposed is... ambitious," Conroy continued. "I don't expect anything to happen overnight. And I also recognize that I have a lot of things to explain and will need to earn others' trust in me."

"It's good you realize that."

"You're still skeptical?"

"Shouldn't I be? You're a handful of people operating on a planet months away from the nearest gate, barely even recognized as a world in the Commonwealth. You have a very long way to go to get back to running things on Terrax."

"I'm more connected than it may seem."

"When most people fall from grace, they quietly fade away and let the rest of the universe move on. Not a lot try to claw their way back to the top."

"I didn't fall. I was forced out by someone more ambitious and ruthless."

"Yeah, funny how that works, isn't it?" She crossed her arms. "Do you even know what it's like to have to work for something?"

He raised his eyebrows. "You think everything was handed to me?"

"That's how politics works, right? The rich and powerful pick their anointed one, and the path is laid out."

"Interesting theory. But no."

"Sure, deny it. But we both know that no amount of hard work and public support would ever get someone like me elected."

"No, you're right that a person needs connections. It's just not in the overly simplified way that you laid out. What's most important in selecting a candidate is who can pay back worthwhile favors."

"A common thread across all levels of society."

"Indeed. Much of human civilization was built on those very deals."

"And the rest was taken by force. Let others do the work, then capture it."

"Unfortunately."

She studied him. "Hit a little too close to home?"

He flashed a weak smile. "I won't claim to have built anything worthwhile. That's not to diminish my efforts, but the truth is that my career was spent trying to maintain a tenuous balance. But I hope to correct that going forward and create something meaningful for future generations."

"A dangerous bargain when it comes to alien tech."

"So my opponents have said. And I hear those concerns and will be diligent in mitigating them through careful action plans."

Zaris sighed. "That's the most ridiculous politician-speak I've heard in a long time."

Conroy bowed his head. "Apologies. You asked for honest talk. I owe you that."

"So what's the non-spin answer?"

"We have a choice between two bad options, and I'm trying to find the best way through."

"Honest, and I can relate."

"Where does that leave us?"

"Better acquainted. But it's going to take more than one friendly chat to earn my everlasting loyalty."

He nodded amiably. "I'll settle for incremental progress."

"Then consider this a step in the right direction."

—   —   —

Anya flipped through the entertainment selection on the wall screen in the *Asamar*'s lounge. She couldn't focus on anything after a long day of intense concentration, so mindlessly scrolling past video trailers became entertainment unto itself.

"Anya?" Evan's call from down the hall broke her trance.

"In the lounge!" she shouted back.

He appeared in the doorway seconds later, looking both excited and worried. "I may have learned something."

"May have?"

"It's from Roman, so it comes with a big question mark."

"Ah. He's talking?"

"I think so. And I think it might be for real, believe it or not."

"He is really backed into a corner now. He's a vicious animal with a strong survival instinct."

"He seems receptive to the lifeline I offered. Enough so that he gave away some information that might be relevant to our previous conversation."

"Oh?"

"If your dad is your dad, but he *isn't* your dad… could he be under some kind of telepathic control?"

Anya would have dismissed the suggestion outright a few weeks ago, but she'd recently encountered enough telepathic beings to have a very open mind about what was possible. She slipped into her science mode. "There is observational evidence to support that hypothesis. But… how?"

Evan sat down on the couch next to her. "That's where the info gets a little sketchy. Roman told me that high doses of the Syndicate's serum—they call it Lux—can grant some limited form of telepathy—an ability to influence people."

"That sure does fit."

"Right? But he also said that very few people have received a dose that high. And they would need to be close to the subject."

Anya frowned. "The two calls I had with him were in very different settings. He was in bed and then at his office. He was acting strange in both places. I don't know who could have been with him at both times."

"Good point. Maybe it's not a lead, after all."

"It was a good thought. I just don't know how one person could be monitoring him."

"Yeah." Evan relaxed back on the couch. "We've been living in hypotheticals for so long that I'm imagining connections that aren't there."

"I think a certain philosopher taught us that *everything* is connected."

"Right." He rubbed his eyes. "Sorry, I'm tired."

She nestled up next to him. "I'm glad you're back. It was lonely here without you."

"Sounds like you kept busy."

"I did. Garet's sharp. We're working well together."

"Good."

Anya pivoted to look at him. "You're not jealous?"

"Should I be?"

"No."

"Is this about Zaris?"

"I've seen the way she looks at you."

Evan wrapped his arms around her and held her close. "You have nothing to worry about. You're the only one I want, Anya, and Zaris knows that."

"Okay." She did believe him; he'd never given her a reason to doubt, and she'd had time to process her feelings. The comments were out of nervous habit more than genuine worry. "I'm past it, I really am. I think this mess with my dad is just dredging up a bunch of bad feelings."

"He betrayed you, and you're worried about others doing the same."

"Nailed it."

Evan stroked her hair as he gazed into her eyes. "Like I said before, I'll keep saying it as many times and as often as you need to hear it, I'm not going anywhere. It's us against the universe."

She smiled, relaxing again. "That's right."

"I realized something else while I was away," Evan continued. "I can't run from it. I have this new power. I may as well figure out how to use it effectively."

"Finally! I'm glad to hear you come around."

"Everything is pointing me in that direction no matter what I do. I tried denying the original Korani tech, and I only ended up with these weird 'primal' powers. I may as well make the most of it."

"Agreed. And I think you're off to a good start." She took his hand. "Maybe, eventually, we'll get some peace."

"That's a great goal, but I have no illusions that getting there will be a peaceful process."

"Whatever happens, we'll figure out a way through together."

16

EVERYTHING WAS MOVING too slowly. Roman's last conversation with Evan had ignited a fire in him. He could keep feeding Evan little bits of mostly useless information, or they could skip the courtship and go straight to screwing each other over.

I'll never get the Lux unless I lead them to it. It was an inconvenient conclusion, but he could find no way around that fact.

There was a strong possibility that he could give them the keys to the Lux and they'd kill him anyway. But that was a risk he'd need to take. If he could put on a convincing enough act—pretending that he really had turned—the virtuous saps might actually stick to their word and give him the primer. By contrast, if he remained obstinate and difficult, they'd know he couldn't be trusted, and that would seal his fate. His only decent option was to play along, give them every indication that he was on their side.

That meant a grand gesture. Something too big to ignore.

I'll prove my worth. They'll be eating out of my palm.

Roman pounded on the cell door. "Guard! Tell them I want to talk."

— — —

Evan looked between the star chart on his tablet to Roman. "You're giving me the location?"

Roman shrugged. "What can I say? You convinced me that I have a better chance with you."

"Just like that, forget about your family?"

"They abandoned me a long time ago. It's nice to feel valued again."

It's gotta be a trap. In the span of two seconds, Evan ran through every interaction he'd had with Roman, including the horrific tour through his mind during their nanite-fueled fight. This was not a man who did anything out of the goodness of his heart. To acquiesce now was a calculated move, and certainly driven by ulterior motives. *He wants the serum. He'll betray us the moment he gets it.*

That presented a problem. Evan would need for Roman to cooperate if they had any reasonable chance to capture the Syndicate's Lux supply, but success would mean empowering Roman. They'd no doubt be walking straight into a double-cross. He wasn't yet sure how to reconcile the two competing points.

"I need to confirm that there's actually something here," Evan said. "Anything I should know about security? And remember, if I get shot at or die on this scouting mission, that's it for you, too."

"I want you to be successful," Roman told him. "Admittedly, I haven't been there in a few years. But I can tell you what I saw on my last visit."

He laid out a spec list for weapons and sensors, offering a few suggestions about approach paths that would help minimize detection in a stealthed shuttle. It was as well defended as any military installation, but that made it a familiar target. Everything Roman told him made sense—which meant it was either the truth, or Evan was simply being told everything he wanted to hear. Getting eyes on the target was the only way to know.

"How far are you willing to take this, Roman?" Evan asked. "We're going up against the Syndicate. What would you do if we burn it to the ground?"

"Let it burn," the other man said.

With all his new abilities and his past experience reading people, Evan could find no signs of deception. "And if we kill your siblings?"

"They have no issue with me dying, so the feeling is mutual." There was a little hesitation with that statement, but no less conviction.

He will pick himself over anyone. He's not aligned with us, just his own best interests. But Evan could work with that. It made Roman dangerous and unpredictable, but he fell into the column of 'asset' for now. "Glad I kept you alive."

"Was that a comment or a question?"

"I'm not sure. I guess we'll see which of us is left standing at the end."

Roman nodded. "Yes, we will."

Evan left the cell, tablet in hand. Very few people even knew such a Noche Syndicate base existed, let alone where it was located. In three years undercover, Evan had only heard rumors about it. The new information from Roman corroborated many of those statements, which lent additional credibility. Regardless, a raid on the facility would be extremely risky.

Conroy was waiting in the observation room next door.

"You sure have him singing now. Is he telling the truth?"

"Shockingly, it seems so. Not that I trust him. But I don't detect deception."

"All the more reason to be skeptical."

"This is definitely more of an enemy-of-my-enemy scenario than any kind of genuine alignment. He wants the primer, and we're the convenient foot soldiers to do the dirty work."

"Strategic partnerships have been built on flimsier foundations," Conroy pointed out.

"True. I need to verify these details before we go any further."

"And if it pans out?"

"Then we'll plan an infiltration. I'm not sure how we'll get in, but there has to be a way."

The base was a floating fortress with clear visibility from all approach vectors. One way in, one way out, heavily guarded. But they also counted on no one knowing about the site, which meant that those guards could be caught by surprise. Hopefully.

"Scope it out and report back. This would be a huge boon if we can capture their supply."

"I should be back in a few hours. I'll let you know."

The *Mara* shuttle was the best scouting ship for the survey, small and fitted with stealth tech to make it nearly invisible. If that shuttle could evade detection, then they'd have a chance at raiding the base. The observation-only test run would be telling.

Another option, of course, would be a full-on tactical assault. Messy, loud, and drawing the wrong kind of attention.

Quick and quiet was the way. Now, he just needed to see if that was possible.

—

Evan found Anya in her office. "I need to go on a super secret, dangerous scouting mission. Want to come along?"

Anya looked up from her monitor. "How much of that was hyperbole?"

"None."

"Uh… *should* I come?"

"I can go alone, but it would be more fun with company," Evan said. "That is, if you're okay with both of us leaving for a few hours, Sam."

"I would still be with you on the *Mara*, and we could return here if the *Asamar* requires your presence," the AI replied.

"Perfect."

Anya pushed back from her desk. "What's the mission?"

"Scouting out a floating sky fortress run by the Syndicate to see if it's feasible for us to pull off a heist of all their serum supply."

"Why didn't you lead with that?!"

"Well, I couldn't give away *all* the excitement upfront. Need to build it."

She sighed. "Count me in. Can I have a few minutes to wrap this up?"

"Sure. I'll get the *Mara* prepped. Meet you down there in…?"

"Twenty minutes."

"See you then." Evan turned to go.

"Forgetting something?"

He came back and gave Anya a kiss.

"Thank you for inviting me," she said. "I've been missing our thrilling adventures."

"We'll have plenty more."

Evan went down to the *Asamar*'s hangar to run a system check with Sam. Knowing how exposed they would be for the recon, he wanted to refresh his understanding of the stealth system and what he could do without being detected.

Sam walked him through the specifics and they established a few emergency protocols. It was important for the ultimate mission that this surveillance activity not be detected, but Evan would rather execute an emergency jump away than get blown out of the sky.

Shortly after Evan and Sam had finished their planning, Anya arrived. She sat down in the seat next to him on the shuttle's flight deck.

"All right, adventure time! Where are we going?" she asked.

"It's a ghost location," Evan explained. "There's a planet, but it's mostly just a ball of gas. So, no one thinks there's anything there, since there isn't a useable surface. However, Roman explained that the Syndicate built some kind of anti-grav base that's suspended midair. It moves around, so it's difficult to locate let alone access."

"Sounds like a good design."

"For them, absolutely. Annoying for us."

She raised her hand. "Question. I assume we will be using the stealth feature?"

"Correct."

"Second question. Aren't clouds the nemesis of stealth tech?"

"Yes. Sam and I have been working on that problem."

"My analysis shows that the gaseous environment is in layers of varying densities," Sam chimed in. "I believe that we can establish an observational position in one of the less-dense strata where there will be minimal displacement effect. In other words, while the Syndicate's base hides in the thicker clouds, we will hide in plain sight."

"Sounds like you've thought of everything," Anya said.

"Not everything. That's why we're going—to figure out what we're missing. And I'm sure there's a lot." Evan powered up the shuttle.

They strapped into their seats, and the *Mara* launched from the bay. Though he was in the pilot's seat, Evan let Sam control the craft. They were getting more and more in sync with each outing. All he had to do was think a command and the AI would see it through.

As soon as they broke through the upper atmosphere, the *Mara* headed toward the third moon, where the jump drive assembly hid away when not in use. Though Evan understood that the components couldn't withstand unshielded atmospheric entry, remaining up in space was a security risk.

"Hey, Sam, I've gotta ask. Why can't the jump drive get stored aboard the ship?" The question had been nagging Evan for weeks.

"There are significant constraints on the storage space required," Sam explained. "And even if it could fit in the hangar, it would be cruel."

"Cruel?" Anya questioned.

"It is a sentient system, just like me. I am the ship—I can move freely. It will join with me to assist when needed. Would you lock up a person in a box so small they needed to remain curled up, not even able to stand or stretch their limbs?"

"No," Anya admitted.

"It is the same. The system is at home in the vastness of outer space. I could never ask it to confine itself within my walls."

Evan didn't have a deep enough understanding of synthetic life to appreciate the experience of the AIs, but he respected Sam's assessment. The jump drive wasn't just a series of nanites, it was a being—albeit a form he couldn't fully comprehend.

Once they were far enough away from the planet, the jump drive assembly activated—forming a latticework, which spun until it was a golden blur around the ship. They slipped into the ethereal realm of hyperspace.

Evan settled back in his seat as they soared through the dark tunnel, admiring the occasional splash of colored light streaking past them.

"You haven't said much about your talk with Roman," Anya commented after a while of sitting in silence.

"I'm conflicted about him," Evan admitted. "I despise the guy. I know he's done terrible things. But it's also clear that he was born into a shitty family and is a product of his environment."

"He still chose to go along with them. Everyone has a choice. Being born into that life isn't an excuse to be awful."

"He's turning away from them now—or so he claims. It doesn't wipe the slate clean, but it's something."

Anya crossed her arms. "I don't trust him."

"Neither do I. Zaris' lot isn't much better. That's why it's the two of us doing the recon. I want to put eyes on the target myself."

"I was glad to hear Zaris had your back on that supply run."

"Yeah, she did. She's not my concern, just some of her people. The kind of guys who got in that fight the other day. They're volatile, and that makes them unpredictable when the pressure is on. I don't want to rely on those sorts in a firefight, you know?"

"Any chance we won't have more people shooting at us?"

"I can guarantee you we will. But hopefully not today, because that would mean our cover was blown."

"All right, we'll bank the firefight for a future day."

Evan smiled. "When things are getting a little too predictable and boring, right?"

"Can't have that. A good shootout always spices things up."

The ship dropped back into normal space, far enough from the destination planet that it wasn't visible on the front screen.

"We've arrived in the Rilen System," Sam announced. "I am updating my models with real-time scan data now."

"Put it on the screen once you have it," Evan instructed.

A minute later, the forward starscape view was replaced by a holographic overlay of a planet. Its atmosphere was marbled orange and yellow gasses, swirling in a perpetual storm. Sam offered a high-level view of the entire world initially and then zoomed in on the lower left quadrant of the image.

"I am getting distinctive energy readings from this territory," he announced. "I believe this is the region where we will find the Syndicate stronghold. However, we will need to get closer for me to gather more detailed data."

"Take us in. I'll let you do the flying for now."

"Acknowledged."

The ship glided forward with barely any perceptible movement. Evan moved the holographic overlay to the bottom corner of the screen so he could watch the approach to the planet. The orangey sphere slowly came into view.

It looked wholly unremarkable from afar, which was certainly the point. No orbital structures or any sign of habitation.

"What kind of readings are you getting from the facility?" Evan asked.

"It is shielded," Sam replied. "I modified my scanners to pick up more minute fluctuations in energy fields than your standard human tech would be able to detect. It is only through these modifications that I can tell anything is there."

"Good thinking. What about size?"

"It is approximately five hundred meters in diameter, based on my preliminary assessment. I'll know more once we're closer."

Evan tried to remain patient as they traveled the rest of the way to the planet, unable to move at top speed while maintaining their optimal stealth configuration. To pass the time, he watched for sensor pings to make sure no one had picked up their approach. So far, everything looked good.

When they reached a high orbit, Sam offered his next update. "My preliminary data was accurate—but only in part. There is a core facility half a kilometer in diameter, but I now see that it is surrounded by additional structures. The configuration will make an approach difficult."

The front screen overlay updated with the new scan data.

Evan's stomach dropped. The facility was a dodecahedron surrounded by an intricate maze of crisscrossing metal beams. It may as well have been overlapping spiderwebs made of metal, designed to capture anything that roamed past. Defensive weapons turrets were mounted on many of the beams, offering full protective coverage on all sides.

"How do they even get their *own* ships inside?" Anya exclaimed.

Evan rotated the image with his hands, looking for any path through. "Some of these gaps are large enough for a small ship—maybe about the size of this one. But I don't see how there's any way we could navigate the maze while staying hidden."

"Yes, I must concur," Sam said, sounding apologetic. "There are, indeed, navigable pathways through the maze, but the atmosphere is too thick for the stealth systems to fully mask our visual presence. I'm afraid we can't get closer than this without risking detection."

"Then hold our place," Evan instructed. "Let's study the facility's movements and gather as much information as we can about its weapons and sensor capabilities. We might be able to find a way to blind them. We don't need to be invisible if *they* can't see."

— — —

Marta checked off the final crate on her inventory list. The stockpile on Rilen was the greatest concentration of alien material outside of Pavia. The Syndicate had been working for decades to refine their extraction process, and all of that work was culminating in their current efforts.

If this works, we're about to become the most powerful force in all of human civilization. The ironic part of that aspiration was using alien technology to capture that power. *All part of our evolution as a species. Only the worthy will advance.*

Creating a functional, replicable jump drive would be revolutionary at all levels of society. Whoever could transport people or goods the fastest would have a massive strategic advantage, and they would be unstoppable. With the Syndicate possessing full control of that tech, not even the full military might of the UPDF would stand a chance, since they'd be limited by the travel time of transit gates. The Syndicate could be in and out before the military counterforces had even deployed.

There's still much to do before then, Marta reminded

herself. She needed to get the materials back to the research facility on Pavia so her team could replicate the nanites. Then, they could do their first test run. *I wonder what it looks like during a jump?*

She signed off on the materials transfer and closed up the cargo bay of her transport ship. Due to the volume of material, she'd brought a larger transport vessel than was normally used for the Rilen base. The dockmaster hadn't been happy about that, but one flash of the mark on her wrist had him bending over backwards to accommodate every one of her requests.

Marta spotted him approaching as she went to board her ship. "Glen, thank you for your hospitality and assistance. We'll get you restocked soon."

"It was my pleasure, ma'am. Can I get you anything else to make your journey more comfortable?"

"I'm all set to head out as soon as you open it up."

"Right away, ma'am. Safe travels." He bowed his head and backed away. Once at a respectful distance, he turned to the deck crew and made a hand signal.

Marta heard a whine of large motors and creaking metal before sealing the outer hatch on her ship. From the forward flight deck, she watched the massive hangar door open to its widest position—just enough for her to exit.

Outside, the intricate metal framework surrounding the base was on the move. The colossal beams swung and pivoted to create a clear exit corridor out from the hangar door. Most ships just navigated the maze-like approach path by patching into the base's automated guidance system, but on rare occasions when a large vessel needed to dock, they'd open it up. Of course, for a VIP visitor such as herself, they would have rearranged anything to satisfy her.

Marta settled into her plush seat and left the small crew to their work. The ship glided from the bay and shot out on a straight course through the newly opened exit pathway. As soon as they were clear, the pieces began folding back into place.

The ship shot up through the clouds. As they cleared the upper layer of atmosphere, Marta noticed a blip on the scan data.

"Did you see that?" she asked the nav officer.

"Yes, ma'am. Whatever it was is gone now. Probably just interference. The electrical field in the cloud layer does strange things."

Marta watched the scan for another minute, but nothing returned. Satisfied, she returned her attention to the task at hand. "Take us to the ring. We have a lot of work to do."

17

EVAN LOOKED AROUND the expectant faces at the briefing table. Conroy's attention was on Evan and Anya, and his inner circle of advisors were following his lead.

"The place is a fortress," Evan began, bringing up a holographic rendering of the Rilen facility based on Sam's scan data.

Rebeka gasped. "That thing looks like it was designed by an art student having a mental breakdown."

"It's ugly, but there's a method to the madness," Anya explained. She rotated the image and traced her finger along a complex path, highlighting the trail in green. "They have a path through this jumbled mess."

"It's large enough for a mid-sized shuttle to navigate," Evan continued. "But for the big stuff," he swapped the view to another rendering, "there's this."

The holographic projection changed to an alternate configuration where a section of the metal beams had folded aside to form a clear corridor leading directly to a cargo bay on the lower deck of the facility. At the tail end of their recon, a ship had happened to leave, opening the path. It was unclear how often that happened, but they would have never known about the capability otherwise.

"A direct path to the front door seems like the best way in," Samor commented.

"Sure, but how do we trigger that opening remotely?" Evan asked.

No one offered any suggestions.

"The way I see it, we need to approach this infiltration in phases." Evan switched the view back to the original configuration with the maze path. "First, we need to blind the sensors. Sam might be able to help with that, but I suspect Zaris has a couple of crafty people who know how to take out sensors and comms.

"Once we get inside, one team will go to the hangar to figure out how to get this direct path open to be our exit. The rest will go to pick up as much of the Lux as we can carry. They will transport that loot—and anything else that seems worth taking—to the hangar. We'll detonate explosive charges on the metal framework on the way out to turn the designed mess into an *actual* mess, which will significantly hamper any retaliation while we get away. At least, those are my initial thoughts for how we could do this."

"I like it, in theory," Samor said. "Though I have a lot of questions about their defenses and control systems. Even if we make it to the door, they won't let us walk right in."

"What about Roman?" Conroy asked. "He's been inside."

Evan scoffed and shook his head. "There's no way we let that guy out of his cell."

"I agree with Evan," Samor said, "but we do have a real issue to overcome."

"We do." Evan brought up a technical spec list. "Sam was able to pull some perimeter security data, and it looks like there are biometric locks on a lot of these systems. Roman is a member of the family. He's likely in the system. We can try cloning his biometrics to get through the locks"

"But he's on the outs," Anya said. "What if they've removed him or flagged his profile?"

"That is a real possibility," Evan admitted. "Another option is I could probably brute force the locks with the nanites, but having a passkey is definitely easier."

"I trust you infinitely more than him," Samor said.

"We're already relying on him a lot. All of the information we have about the interior layout is from him, and nothing drawn from memory is going to be completely reliable, even if he is being honest about his recollections."

Samor shook his head. "This entire mission is insane. Why is it worth the risk?"

"The serum is the key to unlocking the Korani tech," Conroy said. "It is the greatest resource in the Commonwealth right now. If we can seize their supply, it will open all of that potential."

"Roman wants that power more than anything else in the universe," Evan added. "Even if we let him go right now, he's convinced that his family won't take him back. We're his only chance to get access to the serum, so our interests are aligned on this particular issue. He has every reason to help us get inside, get the goods, and get out—because without us, he has nothing."

"We can't possibly give it to him," Anya said. "We all saw what happened last time he interfaced with alien tech."

Evan was still wrestling with that part. He had regularly negotiated with bad people over the course of his career, and sometimes that meant promising them things he had no intention to deliver. He agreed that they couldn't restore Roman to his power, but part of him did feel badly for the man, against his better judgement. He'd experienced that same sensory-expansion and connection to the planet-wide alien collective on Aethos. It was magnificent, and suddenly being cut off from it was no doubt an awful feeling. But it remained that the tech would be dangerous in Roman's hands. "He needs to believe we'll give him the serum if he helps us. We should make no indication otherwise."

Everyone around the table nodded their understanding.

"All right, let's start laying out the details," Evan continued. "If we're going to do this insane thing, then we need to figure out how we're actually going to *do it* down to every detail. This kind of op isn't my specialty. We'd need a spec ops team, or something, to do this right."

Anya's eyes lit up. "Or…" Evan looked at her expectantly, and she smiled. "Military types aren't the only people who know how to get into difficult places quickly and quietly. We need a thief. Conveniently, we have a great new friend."

To Evan's surprise, Samor and Conroy exchanged glances and nodded in agreement.

"All right." Evan shook his head and sighed, but excitement was building in his chest. He joined in the smiles. "You know, that's just crazy enough to work."

— — —

When he'd initially been captured, Roman had been resigned to death. The holding cell was merely his purgatory, and any life beyond its walls were a distant memory.

But then he'd allowed himself to dream about a way out. A future.

I shouldn't believe anything they've promised. It was a deal of convenience made with the enemy. A desperate bargain.

Yet, he hadn't been able to let go of the tantalizing possibility that he *might* get the primer and regain some of what he'd lost.

Whereas he'd once been content to stew in the shadows of his disappointments, that glimmer of potential had morphed his once tolerable cell into a true prison. He was now trapped in the abyss between triumph and betrayal, two divergent paths but only one possible outcome. The coming days would define the rest of his life—whether that be measured in hours or decades. The uncertainty ate away at him.

I want to live. But not like this.

The traps of hope and despair that had once been confined to his mind now extended to the physical space around him. The walls were closing in, and he needed an escape.

Keep it together. He should be used to confined spaces after spending most of his life on spaceships or inside the Syndicate's various bases. Living without a view to the outdoors was normal.

Yet, he still vividly remembered his connection to Aethos that had been ripped from him. The world that initially had been the bane of his existence had transformed into an extended part of himself. He'd been connected to the trees and wildlife, as though they were his own senses. He'd lost all of that when the Korani sphere was removed, but he retained the memories. Now, his senses yearned to once again feel so free. For however briefly he'd held those abilities, he now felt as though he'd lost a vital limb.

Sitting alone in the cell for days on end magnified his ruminations. Passing thoughts became insistent, swirling over and over in his mind, growing in power with each iteration. There was nothing to break up the time or give him anything new to think about.

This is how people go insane in lockup. I never understood before.

Perhaps a person with a clean conscience wouldn't be so affected, but he had too many dark deeds lurking in the back of his mind. Everything he'd buried was clawing back to the surface.

The door lock jangled.

Roman jumped to his feet, eager to interact with anyone who might walk through the door. He didn't recognize himself. Where was the hard man, willing to indiscriminately kill to get his way?

The door slid open, and Evan stood framed in the doorway. "Your intel checks out."

Roman's heart leaped. He knew the information was accurate, but this meant that Evan was actually pursuing the plan. Roman may yet get a dose of the Lux he needed to feel whole again. "I told you, I didn't lie."

"You did leave out some details."

"Like I said, it's been years since I was there. Things may have changed."

Evan showed him a holographic rendering of the base. Most of it looked familiar, but there was now a cage around the whole thing. "That's new."

"Have you seen anything like this before?"

"Never anything this elaborate. They'd build mazes like this planetside sometimes—in the kinds of places where the locals would get too bold. It makes a kill zone around the base. Even if you know the route in, it's slow. But it's weird here."

"Can you think of any reason why they would have built it within the last few years?" Evan asked.

"No," Roman answered honestly.

"Does Marcus often do things without explaining it to anyone?"

"Yeah, that's pretty typical. This change was probably the product of one of his many paranoid delusions."

Evan nodded thoughtfully. "Do you think that paranoia is what drove him to kill your parents?"

Where did that question come from? It didn't surprise Roman that Evan was fishing for private family information. Roman had been conditioned to never talk about what happened to their parents, and he was reluctant to start now. But if getting the Lux meant divulging a few uncomfortable details, then that's what he needed to do. *He's finally starting to trust me. I have to keep playing along or I'll be right back to where we started.*

Roman shrugged. "Maybe? My parents might have looked at Marcus the wrong way or questioned something he said. The guy has a hair trigger."

"Nothing more?"

"All I can say is that they announced they were planning to delay their retirement, and then they were dead within the week." Roman had suspected what happened from the beginning, though it had taken him time to accept that his brother was capable of such horrific action. "Marcus has had a fixation on 'legacy' for as long as I can remember. I think he was ready to define the Noche Syndicate's future, and he didn't want to wait."

"Do you know what he's planning?"

"He didn't share the details with me." While he did have a sense of Marcus' high-level ambitions, it was true that Roman had never been given an inside look. His chest constricted with the admission. As much as he'd tried to get close to Marcus, Marta had always been the favorite sibling. Roman was just the unwanted extra. Whatever Marcus was planning, there was never going to have been a real place for Roman, no matter what promises had been made.

Evan closed the holographic map. "We'll have to assume that if Marcus made this recent change to the exterior, then he may have altered other things on the inside. Think about new security protocols you saw in other Syndicate facilities."

"I'll start making a list."

"Thanks. We're starting to plan the infiltration now. Assuming you want us to succeed, every detail you can provide would increase our chances."

"I'll help," Roman assured him. *I need this mission to be successful. They have to get the Lux.*

Evan's expression was difficult to read, but it didn't take an expert to tell that he was skeptical of Roman. "I'll be back tomorrow with more specific questions."

"Okay."

Roman winced as the door slammed shut, leaving him alone with his thoughts once more. But a new question now swirled in his mind, building into a fresh storm. *How do I get what I need before he betrays me, too?*

— — —

Zaris was surprised to see an incoming communication from the *Asamar* pop up on her omni. She transferred it to the desktop in her office aboard the *Invictus* and answered.

"Evan! I knew you couldn't live without me for long." She grinned.

"Hey, Zaris." He smiled back. "How'd you like to rob the Syndicate?"

She laughed. When he didn't join her, her eyes widened.

"Wait, you're serious?"

"Deadly. Well, hopefully not. That's why I'd like to enlist your expertise."

"What kind of robbery are we talking here? Ship interception?"

"No, breaking into one of their bases."

Zaris laughed again. "Oh, that's a good one!"

"I'm not joking."

She shook her head. "It's suicide, Evan. I already told you, I don't have a death wish."

"Anya and I have already scoped it out. Roman is giving us the inside scoop. Yeah, it's risky. But the payoff... We're going after their stash of the Lux. Think about what we could do with that."

It didn't take much imagination to realize how pivotal that would be. "If I help you, do I get some?"

He hesitated. "That wasn't part of the plan."

"Well, that's my price."

"I don't know how many doses we'll get, so—"

"This whole conversation is a non-starter if I'm going to get cut out."

"It's not like normal loot, Zaris."

"I know exactly what it is. You just don't want me to have that power." She stared him down through the screen. "My name is on at least one dose. Otherwise, no deal."

"Why do you want it? It can be more of a burden than a blessing."

She'd seen what Evan could do. Incredible things. Even if she only gained a fraction of those abilities, she wanted it. But that answer wouldn't satisfy him. "You can't do all of this alone, Evan. You'll need people who can help—and this tech is what will give our side an edge. If you want my help and my people, then you need to let me be a part of this."

He took several seconds to respond, clearly weighing his options. "Okay, if that's what it will take. How soon can you get here?"

Zaris held her arms wide. "Clearly, I'm swamped with work. I don't know how I can ever tear myself away."

"So, see you in twenty minutes?"

"Yep, be right down."

She let Callie know she was heading to Aethos' again and then took a shuttle to the surface.

Evan met her at the landing pad and escorted her to the hidden bunker. Conroy, Anya, Samor, and Rebeka were huddled around a conference table when they arrived.

"I hear we're planning the heist of a Syndicate base?" Zaris asked.

"Indeed, we are," Conroy confirmed. "Rumor has it you possess a certain skill set that would be an asset to the mission."

"I like the concept—because screw those guys—but how realistic is it to break in? Everything I've heard is that their strongholds are impenetrable."

"To my eye, it's doable, but risky," Evan said. "We want your read."

"Walk me through it."

Evan went over various schematics, technical specs, and scan data to paint the picture of their target. "So, what do you think?" he asked after finishing the presentation.

Zaris flipped back through some of the earlier schematics to verify her initial observations. "Our best bet will be cutting the power. If we send the facility into lockdown and disabled their weapons, they won't have a lot of moves."

"Won't a lockdown make it more difficult for our team to move, too?" Conroy asked.

"Normally, yes. But Evan can do things they can't."

All eyes turned to him.

"We shouldn't have a strategy hinging on one person," he said.

"I agree. You'll want to build in as many backup tactics as possible," Zaris said. "Code cracker, demo tools... But it will be a hell of a lot faster and easier if you can break open doors for us."

Evan nodded. "I'll do my best. Just want to make sure the rest of the team won't get trapped if anything happens to me."

"Don't worry, we'll be smart about this," Samor assured him.

"To that end," Evan continued, "I insist we take proper prep time. We've been flying by the seat of our pants too much recently, and it's dumb luck that no one has gotten seriously hurt or killed."

Zaris raised her hand. "Hey, almost died."

"Okay, there *was* an injury," Evan admitted. "But that's my point. If we hadn't rushed in with less than zero planning, that might not have happened."

"No argument here," Conroy began, "but how long can we delay without giving the enemy too much time to mount a defense?"

"They have no reason to think we'd hit this target," Evan said.

"After what happened on Pavia, I'd expect them to tighten security across their entire operation," Zaris pointed out.

"All the more reason to spend time planning and preparing for contingencies," Evan insisted. "We can't act faster than them, but we can be smarter."

Conroy nodded. "Agreed. You and Zaris work with Samor to come up with your preliminary recommendations and a timeline."

"We can do that, sir," Evan acknowledged.

"This is just the kind of job that will excite my guys," Zaris said.

Conroy eyed her. "Just remember this is serious business."

"I would never take it lightly. But that doesn't mean we can't have a little fun."

18

As Evan led Zaris into the hallway, Conroy shot him a firm look.

It wasn't difficult to guess the chancellor's concerns. This infiltration plan was largely being informed by a disgraced member of the Santano family and a career criminal. Between the two of them, the possibility for a double-cross was extremely high.

Consequently, they'd decided that Roman would remain on Aethos. But Zaris was a free agent. If she second-guessed her loyalties, it would be easy for her to alert the Syndicate about the infiltration plans.

The success of this plan might rest on my use of the Korani tech, but I'm not who we need to worry about. Evan watched Zaris studying the underground base as they walked back toward the exit. She was acting casual, but there was no doubt in his mind that she was cataloging every detail. She already knew so many secrets, there was no going back now.

Evan sighed inwardly. *Please don't make me regret involving you.*

Anya jogged down the hall to catch up with them. "What now?" she asked.

"We come up with tactical plans. I'll run enough different

scenarios by Roman for his feedback that he won't know what we're actually doing. And once we have a workable approach, we'll go."

"I think you should do at least two more recon runs," Zaris suggested. "Longer ones. Hang out and see how much activity is around the place."

Evan nodded. "Good call."

"I'd like to see it for myself," she requested.

Anya frowned but remained silent.

"You and Samor should both get eyes on it before we do it for real," Evan decided. "Anya and I will do one more recon trip—at least half a day—and then you and Samor will come on the third trip. How's that?"

"Works for me."

They reached the exit to outside.

"Well, good luck with your scouting," Zaris said. "Let me know when you're ready for a group trip."

"Will do."

She gave a casual salute and sauntered across the field toward her shuttle.

Anya let out a long breath. "I don't like any of this. I can't believe you agreed to give her a dose."

"We can't get the Lux alone."

"But heading into enemy territory with people who were enemies last week?"

"It was either that or not even attempt to get the Lux. None of Conroy's people could pull off that kind of heist."

"I know, but…" She shook her head. "You know what? Screw it. We threw caution to the wind a long time ago, and we keep figuring shit out on the fly. Let's just do the crazy thing."

He draped an arm over her shoulders. "I like this new Anya."

— — —

When it came to grand plans, everything seemed to move at a glacial pace and then all at once. Conroy sensed the acceleration coming. Years of planning, now in the final stretch.

He stood at a juncture. No longer was it hypothetical—there was real action to take. And a story to tell.

He'd fantasized during sleepless nights, playing out countless variations of the speech he might give to the Commonwealth. Rostov's treachery. The path of humanity. His vision for the future. There was so much to cover, so many directions he could go. No matter how many times he spoke the words in his head, the message never felt satisfactory. But he'd only have one chance. He needed to get it right.

Soon, Tobin would deliver the final batch of evidence Conroy needed before asserting his return to the public spotlight. In the time being, he could finalize his approach while Samor and Evan handled the heist planning.

"Rebeka, my office," Conroy said, leading her from the conference room.

The public relations expert followed him to the office and sat down. "What's up?"

He smiled at how far they'd come. When they'd first started working together, it was 'sir' after every statement and formal phrasing from start to finish. "I think it's time I write my speech. I'd like to draft it myself, but I would love to go over the high-level points with you."

She beamed. "Oh, I've been waiting for this day!"

"We both have."

"Have you decided how you're going to do it?"

"That's one of the details we should discuss. But right now, we need to settle on the overall approach."

She nodded, pensive. "For starters, pretty much everyone thinks you're dead. So, that needs to be addressed right out of the gate."

"What's the latest word on the conspiracy theories about me having faked my death?"

"The chatter petered off about a year ago, but there are still some believers. I suspect that even though people aren't openly talking about it anymore, the original proponents would jump right back in with 'I told you so' as soon as you make your announcement."

"Just as many will call my announcement fake," Conroy said. "We'll need to verify authenticity somehow."

"I have some ideas about that."

They talked through the numerous aspects of the announcement, making notes about critical talking points and where they could insert supporting evidence to bolster credibility.

After half an hour of discussion, Rebeka leaned back in her seat. "You know, I think we're trying to sell this too hard."

"It's kind of the *point* to sell it."

"Yeah, but… when you seem overly insistent, it's off-putting. Like, the truth should speak for itself. Giving it a hard sell makes people wonder what you *aren't* saying. You can't come across as having an agenda."

Conroy considered her words. She did make a valid point, but he wasn't sure how to get around it. "What do you suggest instead?"

"You sow kernels of the truth without giving away the whole story. You need to make the people *ask* for the evidence rather than forcing it on them."

"Let the people demand transparency and accountability," Conroy mused.

"Exactly. *We'll* have all the supporting documentation against Rostov, but if we release it upfront, a bunch of people will always doubt its authenticity. We need to whip the populace into such a frenzy that they demand Rostov's administration release the evidence themselves. Either they do and they reveal their treachery, or they'll fake it and we can expose them as liars. Whichever way, we win. But we can't be the ones driving that conversation."

Conroy admired her from across the desk. "I knew there was a good reason I hired you."

"I'm brilliant, I know. You owe me about a dozen raises once you get back in office."

"You'll have them, even if I'm supplementing your salary myself. Thank you. I know what I have to say."

19

EVAN PACED ACROSS the *Asamar*'s hangar while he and Anya waited for the others to arrive. After a week of scouting and planning, Evan was satisfied that they had nothing else to learn about the Syndicate's base on Rilen. To delay their operation any longer would create more exposure than benefit. It was time to act.

Evan flexed his new armor as he walked, testing its range of motion. While the main body of the previous iteration worked well, the faceplate had visibility issues in high-contrast lighting. Not knowing what kind of environmental factors they might encounter inside, he'd requested Sam make updates to the gear. Looking through the new visor, he was pleased to see that it levelized the lighting nicely while still leaving enough contrast to easily identify bright patches and shadows.

"Yet again, excellent work, Sam."

"Interactions with additional human vessels and equipment has improved my understanding of your needs. I hope to better anticipate your design requirements in the future."

"You're doing great," Evan assured him.

"And the food!" Anya added. "I'm not sure how an entity

with no digestive system got so good at meal design, but keep at it."

"You can thank Evan for that. I have simply replicated flavors and textures from his memory."

"Well, clearly you and I have similar taste," Anya said to Evan. "But don't sell yourself short, Sam. The way you can keep those properties while altering the nutritional profile is remarkable. If all else fails, we can open a business offering an alternative to traditional MealPaks, and we'll make a fortune."

Evan chuckled. "You'd make a lot of soldiers very happy."

"Explorers, too." She tapped the side of her head. "Always plan ahead."

The hangar door slid open, halting their conversation. Samor entered along with three of Conroy's soldiers, all wearing tactical armor and carrying weapons. There'd been significant back and forth about the composition of the boarding team, and they'd ultimately decided that Conroy's guard was already too diminished for them to spare any more people. The bulk of their group would be Zaris' corsairs. While some members of the team had been initially skeptical about that arrangement, Evan had found them to be capable fighters and reliable during the raid on Pavia, which had earned them the benefit of the doubt.

Samor walked up to Evan and bowed his head. "Ready and reporting for duty."

"Glad to have you," Evan replied. "Let's go get the rest of our people. Take us up, Sam."

The hangar door closed. As soon as it sealed, a low rumble vibrated the deck as the ship launched.

The four new arrivals eyed each other with wonder and excitement as the ship smoothly accelerated through the planet's atmosphere into space.

"It is magnificent," Samor breathed.

Evan grinned. "Just wait until we jump."

The *Asamar* glided to a rendezvous with the *Invictus*, where Zaris flew over in the large shuttle they'd used for the Pavia raid. She set it down next to the *Mara* with plenty of room to spare.

Once her craft was powered down, Zaris descended the ramp and came to speak with Evan. "Hey, looking sharp!" she greeted.

Anya waved her hands to show off her armor. "You sure you don't want a set?"

Zaris patted her chest with a gloved hand. "I've been through too much with this to give it up. It saved me last time."

Evan could understand the allegiance to tried and true gear. "All right. Any final questions or concerns before we jump?"

"We've been over the plan so many times that it's been in my dreams. I'm good," Zaris said.

"That's how we want it. Sam, take us to Rilen."

"Initiating jump sequence," the AI acknowledged.

Evan's senses shifted for a moment as the ship transitioned to hyperspace. "Samor, get settled on the boarding shuttle with Zaris' team. Anya and I will clear the way for you."

"See you on the other side. Good luck." The soldier bowed his head, then followed Zaris aboard her craft.

They'd explored every possible scenario with how to approach the Syndicate base, which people to bring along, and in which vessels. Evan felt solid about their final plan, though his gut was still tense with pre-op jitters. No matter how many missions he undertook or how much planning he did, there were always some nerves in the moments leading up to action. He considered that a good thing. It meant he was on alert, and that's what would keep him alive.

He went to the smaller shuttle with Anya. Before they strapped into the two front seats, Evan gave her a hug and kiss. "I know we've been training, but don't try to be an action hero out there. We'll have plenty of experienced soldiers with us. Let them lead, and be on guard."

"I know. Don't take any risks out there, either."

They settled into their seats and counted down the final minutes of the jump, watching a video feed of their progress on the *Mara*'s front screen.

At last, the scene returned to stars.

They waited for another half an hour while the *Asamar* closed the remaining distance to the planet Rilen. Given the size of the spatial distortion created by the *Asamar* jumping, they needed to stay far enough out to avoid detection of their emergence. The final approach was conducted under stealth.

"No reaction from the base," Sam announced. "They haven't seen us."

"Good."

"We're in staging position. Ready on your mark, Evan."

"Okay." He opened up a commlink to the other shuttle. "Time to do this for real, everyone. Get ready." He cut the comm and took the controls.

The hangar door lowered, revealing a force field protecting the interior from open space.

"Start the timer," Evan ordered.

"Initiating mission clock."

Evan launched the *Mara* from the hangar. As it passed through the force field, a counter appeared in the bottom right of the front screen.

During planning, they had allocated certain times for the various stages of the mission. The numbers weren't hard and fast, but they would give them an indication if everything was running smoothly and progressing at the expected rate. For the first approach phase, they'd estimated seven minutes for the descent through the atmosphere, then another five minutes to navigate the maze.

Evan's job with Anya was to get that timing down to the second. That would tell them how long they needed to provide cover for the other shuttle to make its approach, since that craft wouldn't be as invisible as theirs.

They'd wanted to run the timing during a recon trip, but they'd decided against taking the risk. They might only have one opportunity to fly right up to the door, and they needed to act on it if given the chance. While the clouds were a challenge, they'd determined that the *Mara* would be able to maintain a sufficient stealth rating as long as they were careful on the approach.

The initial descent went to plan, placing them near the maze entrance at six minutes twenty-seven seconds.

"Stealth rating has dropped to ninety-three percent," Sam cautioned.

That was slightly worse than their models but still within acceptable margins. As advanced as the Korani tech was, it could only mask the physical displacement of the surrounding gases so much.

"Map the wind currents and overlay on the flight path," Evan instructed.

The front screen updated with a series of slightly curved lines of varying lengths. The longer and thicker the line, the stronger the wind currents in that area. Evan spotted a path with the lightest winds, hoping that avoiding the stronger, thicker clouds would improve their disguise.

"Stealth rating now ninety-six percent," Sam announced.

A three percent gain wasn't much, but every little bit helped.

We just need to make it through the maze. Once we're right up against them, it will be more difficult to see us. Evan took a steadying breath and entered the metal web.

There was ample clearance to navigate the maze in their small shuttle, but Zaris' craft carrying the rest of the team would have a tighter fit. Knowing that, Evan had a wireframe representation of the other ship's dimensions displayed as an overlay on his internal map, taking each bend in the maze at a velocity that would be appropriate for the larger vessel. They would then be able to use that nav data for their own approach.

He wove through the crisscrossing metal beams, amazed by the scale of the construction. It was a novel defensive approach, to be sure, but there was also no doubt it had been the fever dream of a madman. Whatever mind had dreamed it up would certainly have more unexpected defenses on the inside of the base.

The final stretch of beams brought their craft parallel to the facility's walls before funneling them to a large hatch. It was sized to correspond with the maximum dimensions of the maze tunnel.

"Five thirty-four," Anya marked on the timer. "We were close with the overall but off with the split."

"Not bad, considering." Evan copied the nav data and sent a secure transfer to Zaris' shuttle using a direct link Sam had established for that purpose.

An acknowledgement appeared on the front panel.

Go time. Evan brought up a feed of the current energy readings around the Syndicate's base. "Blind 'em, Sam."

"My pleasure."

The *Asamar* fired an electromagnetic pulse from its orbital position, targeting the station. The *Mara*'s specialized shields protected their craft, but the facility outside their door flickered and went dark.

"I detect no active scanning from the station," Sam announced.

"Confirmed, looks like the sensor grid is down. Main power is offline. We're a 'go'," Evan said over the private comm.

"Roger that. Go for launch!"

A moment later, a second clock appeared beneath the first. This one counted down from twelve minutes and one second, indicating the estimated time until the other shuttle's arrival. The shuttle appeared on the tracking screen along with the other data points. It was already getting crowded, but it was about to get even busier.

Two minutes into the second shuttle's flight, Evan gave the next order. "Launch the decoys!"

A swarm of miniature drones launched from the *Asamar*. Inspired by Zaris' drone trick at the Pavia gate, each drone emitted a signal matching the shuttle's signature. They sped into the planet's atmosphere and briefly fanned out, then converged on the shuttle's position. They slowly fanned out again and zig-zagged all over the place. Even Evan had difficulty picking out the real shuttle from the dozens of other contacts.

The minutes ticked down.

"Right on schedule," Anya observed, watching the mission clock.

Evan's pulse quickened. "The station is still dark. Coming up on the maze entrance now…"

The real shuttle made the turn into the maze as a third of the drones also soared into the metal web. The remaining two-thirds skimmed the outer bounds and spread out to provide equidistant coverage of the airspace above the floating facility.

When the outer dome of drones was in position, Evan activated a target-seeking pulse. Each drone emitted a series of rapid light flashes. The bright pulses reflected off the targeting sensors for the weapons hidden around the metal framework, creating a momentary flash as the light struck them. It was too quick and subtle for a human eye to pick up, but Sam had prepared a visual processing protocol to instantly analyze the location data and develop a targeting plan.

"Weapons grid mapped," the AI stated. "Eliminating targets now."

— — —

A barrage of small missiles streaked through the atmosphere around Zaris' shuttle. She knew the *Asamar* wasn't shooting at her, but she couldn't help but tense every time one came close.

The entire assault lasted less than thirty seconds. Explosions peppered the surrounding metal structure as the weapons turrets were destroyed in the impressive volley.

"Looks good from here," Zaris reported over the comm to Evan.

"Stay on course. Almost here," Evan replied.

They were nearly halfway through the maze. The structure had seemed bizarre from a distance during her recon, but it was even weirder on the inside. Most of the metal beams had to be thirty meters or more in length, which wasn't the kind of thing one just had lying around.

She took that back. It was *exactly* the kind of thing that was laying around a shipyard—the sort of beams used for structural support scaffolding during construction. And, come to think of it, she'd heard about a raid on such a shipyard about two years back.

Those crazy Syndicate bastards. The project was impressive, credit where it was due.

But she was currently trapped inside the massive web, and it was triggering her anxiety about being cornered. Consciously, she'd known what they were flying into. But it was quite another thing to look out the ship's viewports and feel like she was behind bars.

Fortunately, they were almost to the end. They rounded the final bend in the path, coming alongside the facility.

An explosion flashed overhead, its origin just out of sight. One of the massive beams swung down, headed straight for them.

Zaris banked the shuttle to port, away from the wall. She'd turned a little too sharply, and they clipped one of the portside support beams. A shudder and horrifying groan reverberated through the craft. The structural alarm blared.

The shuttle's tail whipped around to starboard, nearly colliding with the base's outer wall.

Shit! She struggled to regain control of the craft.

A second beam collapsed above. Then another.

We have to get out of here!

— — —

"What happened?!" Evan exclaimed, panic spiking his pulse.

He watched helplessly as the awful scene unfolded on his screen. The odd structure surrounding the base had suddenly started to give way, and the other shuttle had been thrown off course.

"There has been a structural cascade failure," Sam reported. "One of the missiles targeting the weapons turrets must have struck a weak point in the structure, precipitating the collapse."

The AI's matter-of-fact reporting belied the seriousness of the situation. The shuttle was in dire trouble, and there was no way for Evan to render aid in their current craft or from their position.

The mission clock flashed as the secondary countdown reached zero.

"Evan, we're in trouble!" Zaris said over the comm. "I ran us into the damn wall, and we're at risk of venting atmosphere."

Evan's heart leaped into his throat. "Hang on, Zaris. Just try to get here. It looks like the other structural supports are holding. Let's get the shuttle inside."

"Get that door open!"

"She's right, Evan," Anya said. "Forget the plan. We need to do it ourselves."

He nodded, tension gripping his chest. "Just get over here, Zaris."

The original plan had called for the second shuttle to dock with the base, where Samor and one of his technical specialists would attempt to crack the hatch controls using Roman's biometrics and specialized electronics equipment. Their backup plan had been Evan using his nanites to pry the door open manually.

No option now. He unstrapped his flight harness. "Take over the flying, Sam."

Evan moved to midship on the *Mara*, near the entry hatch, where he could get a direct line of sight to the huge door in the side wall of the base.

Open, he commanded. His wrist warmed as the nanites activated. A golden stream shot out and disappeared through the shuttle's wall while the bracelet on his other wrist glowed blue.

Distorted images filled his mind as the nanites assessed the door and possible approaches for getting it open. In a near-instantaneous telepathic exchange, he approved an approach similar to the lock-shearing they'd used for the vault-like door on Pavia. However, there were no hinges on this door. The only option was to cut around its perimeter and allow it to drop away.

Evan gave the command.

The nanites immediately got to work, shearing off the metal on a microscopic level. The cutting was so precise that the door stayed in place even after it had severed.

Evan recalled the nanites. "Hold on, Anya." He ran back to the flight deck and strapped in.

"Is it done?" she asked.

"Almost."

Evan turned the *Mara* to face the hangar door. "Sam, bolster the front shields. We're going in!"

He rammed the nose of the shuttle into the severed door. It popped from its original housing like a cork, falling inward.

The solid metal plate dropped to the deck inside. A force field snapped into place over the opening.

Evan halted the *Mara*'s forward momentum and assessed the scene. A cavernous hangar was inside, lined with rows of empty shelves. There had been open space near the door, though the severed wall had taken out the first row of storage racks when it fell.

To his horror, Evan noticed several severed limbs and guns scattered around the deck, as well as a growing pool of blood seeping from under the metal plate. A group of guards must have been huddled around the door, waiting to shoot the infiltrators. If they'd stuck with the original plan, that would have been a firefight.

Anya covered her mouth with her hand as she, too, realized what had transpired. "We would have killed them, anyway. This was faster," she murmured.

It was true, but Evan couldn't help feeling bad. He'd known killing would likely be required in this mission, but his issues with the Syndicate were with its leaders, not the low-level grunts.

He flew the *Mara* inside and set it down far enough from the door to leave room for Zaris to land the other shuttle.

The damaged craft followed him, wobbling a little as it lowered to the deck. It dropped the final meter and landed with a thud, hard enough to shake the *Mara*.

"Sam, can you do anything to repair the shuttle?" he asked.

"Taking a look now. One moment." The AI paused while assessing the damage. "There are structural fractures along several support braces as well as significant damage to the hull plating. I can affect repairs, though it will require repurposing other materials."

"That's a nice steel door underneath us. Grab whatever you need," Evan said.

"I will have the craft flightworthy by the time you return," Sam said. "You should also be aware that another wave of soldiers is headed this way."

Evan grabbed his rifle. "Let the fun begin."

20

ZARIS BREATHED A sigh of relief for her shuttle making it inside in one piece. She silenced the alarms and disabled the flashing warnings peppering the front console.

"Nice flying," Samor commented.

She was pretty sure the statement had been sarcastic, but she smiled as though it had been a heartfelt compliment. "Top of my class."

"We've got incoming," Samor said, nodding to a group of guards sneaking through the rows of crates.

"Get ready to move out!" Zaris shouted to her team. She flipped down her helmet's visor and switched to the comms.

Samor followed her to the back of the shuttle, where her corsairs and Samor's soldiers had their weapons drawn and were ready to debark.

"We've got hostiles incoming. Team A, on me. Team B, you know what to do." Zaris slapped the control for the rear ramp.

The back of the craft dropped open, and the fighters flowed out in organized formation. It was always a thrill to watch them work their craft, and they were especially polished after their other recent exploits.

Sounds of weapons fire sounded around the hangar. Her corsairs exchanged tactical directions as they moved through the space, eliminating the enemy guards while securing the access points.

Team B would be moving to the opposite side of the hangar, where they would try to get the express pathway in the metal web open. Even if that proved impossible, they would create a defensive perimeter around the shuttles and hold the position.

Meanwhile, Zaris and Samor would meet up with Evan and Anya, and they'd go with a group of corsairs to find the Lux stash and investigate the base. Each person was carrying a bag to gather loot. She'd seen Syndicate goons sporting some pretty slick gear in the past, and she wouldn't mind getting her hands on one of their KL-857 rifles if she came across one.

She waited for the sounds of shooting to die down before exiting the shuttle.

"All clear, for now," Samor reported.

Zaris converged on his position at the same time as Evan and Anya. Twelve corsairs joined them as they jogged past fallen Syndicate soldiers on the way to the inner access door.

The storage racks were strangely empty. It wasn't until they were in the deepest part of the hangar where they found shelves that weren't cleared out.

"Check these crates," she instructed her team.

A couple of the corsairs shouldered their weapons so they could look inside the containers.

"MealPaks here," one called out.

"Medical supplies over here," another reported.

"We could use *everything* right now," Evan said. "I know it wasn't the mission, but if there's any way we could take some of this stuff…"

Zaris looked around the hangar. She spotted a shuttle around the same size as the one she'd flown in. "Hey, your ship can fly itself, right?"

"Yeah."

"You know how to fly one of those?" She pointed at the other shuttle.

"Sure." He caught her line of thinking. "If your people can fill it up, I'll get it out of here."

Zaris doled out the corresponding instructions to her team.

It had been a bit of a rough start, but things were already turning around. *Now I want the good stuff.*

— — —

The hangar seemed to be secure, but Evan expected another wave of resistance at the next door. Roman had indicated that the Lux synthesis labs were toward the top of the facility, and they were currently on the bottom level.

"Okay, everyone, I think we just stirred up a hornet's nest. Watch your backs," Evan said.

Samor tried the door at the back of the hangar. "Locked."

"I've got it." Evan sent his nanites to break the lock. "There's nowhere to hide."

The door dropped open.

Rapid weapons fire rang out as Samor and the corsairs eliminated the enemy forces waiting in the hallway.

With the mission at hand, Evan turned off the part of himself that felt guilty shooting people. This was a war, even if it wasn't being fought on a traditional battlefield.

"Clear!" Samor called out.

The team advanced.

So far, the layout was similar to what Roman had described to Evan. The hangar led to a broad access corridor, which should lead them to a central access column at the center of the base. There, they could either take an elevator or a stairway to the upper level where the Lux was supposedly manufactured and stored.

The emergency lighting in the corridor was dim, consisting of amber lights on the ceilings and walls with the occasional red light. The place had more of an industrial finish than anything resembling a research lab, with riveted metal walls and gritty, diamond-grid flooring for maximum traction. Tracks had been worn in the high-traffic areas of the floor— likely from years of heavy carts, based on the parallel lines.

"Let's follow these marks," Evan suggested, reasoning that they were a sign of where raw materials had been transported from the hangar to the processing center.

The tracks led to an industrial elevator. An elevator would be the fast way up, but even if it was powered on, it bore too big a risk of getting cornered.

Evan looked around for the nearest stairwell. There was one several meters down on the opposite side of the hall.

Samor motioned for two of the corsairs to remain on the level as lookouts. The rest of the team headed for the stairs.

They had to go up five flights before they reached the first exit door, which made sense given the height of the hangar's ceiling.

The team went through the first hallway and swept it. Strangely they didn't encounter any people. The level appeared to be storage rooms.

"There could be so much good stuff in here," Zaris commented. "I want to check out all of it."

"No time," Evan reminded her. They'd been clear on the

mission timeline and the need to locate the Lux and get out. He wouldn't put it past them to blow up the whole place with everyone inside rather than let anyone escape with their prize possession.

Still, they did a few spot checks just to make sure it wasn't Lux storage. They found it was actually printed records. It looked like nonsensical lists of numbers and letters at first glance.

"I'm taking one," Anya announced, grabbing a random binder. "Who knows, it might be useful?"

Evan had his doubts, but there was a reason the documents had been printed and stored in a highly secure, secret facility. Not many physical documents existed, so they were either important enough to keep as a hardcopy backup or no one wanted a digital trail of the information.

With the level cleared, they returned to the stairwell. They'd only gone up half a story when quick footfalls sounded above them.

Samor held up his fist and the team froze.

Evan motioned for Anya to press against the wall. He couldn't get any line of sight upward from his current vantage, but he had other eyes.

He connected with the nanites in his bracelet and sent out three invisible probes. He'd been practicing the spy drone concept with them during their downtime on Aethos, and he'd gotten proficient enough to make high-level observations without feeling like his head was about to explode.

He spotted six armed guards descending, wearing armor marked with the Syndicate's symbol of three interlocking rings. A firefight in the close quarters of the stairwell was likely to end badly for everyone.

Evan motioned the number and position to Samor. They

were still three switch-backs up. The stairs could offer some protection if they acted now.

"Grenade," he whispered to Samor.

The soldier nodded and handed it to Evan. As the one with the enemy in his sights, he could aim more effectively than anyone else.

He tossed the grenade upward, nudging its direction with a swarm of nanites. They didn't have the force necessary to lift it, but they were able to alter its horizontal trajectory. So when it reached the level where the guards were, Evan directed the grenade to knock sideways over the railing into their path.

The grenade exploded in a bright flash. Momentary cries rang out from the guards and then fell silent. The corsairs raced up the stairs with Samor.

"Stairwell is clear," Samor reported over the comm.

Evan advanced with Anya, keeping his gaze straight ahead as he stepped over the bodies.

They made it to the next level and went through the door to investigate. Immediately, the floor was more open than the one below and looked much more like a research facility than industrial warehouse.

Anya seemed particularly interested, so Evan escorted her while the other fighters fanned out to search.

"Just a bunch of empty rooms over here," one corsair reported over the comm. "Looks medical."

"I wonder what kind of medical stuff they might be doing here?" Evan commented to Anya.

"Based on their other work, nothing good."

They arrived at a room with a medical bed in the center, complete with restraints. An adjacent room had an observation window.

Anya frowned. "Yeah, definitely not good."

Evan ducked into the observation room to see if there was a computer system he might be able to access. Any information they could get about the facility or their work might give them more insight into the Lux.

Unfortunately, he found that the computer was unresponsive.

"Why haven't they rebooted since the EM pulse?" he wondered aloud.

"Do we know that they haven't?" Anya asked. "I mean, it *looks* like everything is offline, but could this actually be a lockdown?"

"Yeah, it could be," Evan realized. Conceivably, the system might be fully functional and the administrators could have left it powered down as a lockout tactic. But that didn't mean everything in the facility was offline; after all, some of the lights were working.

"Come on, Anya, the Lux stash isn't here." Evan directed her back to the hallway, where they headed toward the stairwell.

As they rounded a corner near the stairs, pounding footfalls approached. Evan raised his weapon, bracing for enemy contact. But it was Samor.

The soldier was out of breath. "There you are! Come on, Zaris found something."

"Why didn't you call on the comm?" Evan asked, jogging after him.

"You'll see."

—   —   —

Anya had been in a lot of creepy places, but this one made her skin crawl in new ways. It wasn't that it had anything overtly gruesome about it, but she sensed that something was wrong. The feeling reminded her of when she was out in the wilds and a predator was stalking her. She couldn't see it yet, but she knew it was there.

Following Samor and Evan, she arrived at a room finished in all white surfaces. Zaris was standing in front of a metal case with two corsairs. It appeared to be a cold storage locker—the kind a body or specimen would be stored in during a post-mortem study.

"I was looking for guns," Zaris blurted out.

Evan raised an eyebrow. "Guns. In here?"

"The thing looked like it might be a weapons locker! It isn't." She pointed at what was clearly organic remains on a pull-out tray from inside the case.

"Why couldn't you tell us about it over the comm, though?" Anya asked.

The other woman pointed to a message carved in the inside of the room's door: 'There's nowhere to hide.'

Anya's stomach dropped. Word for word, it's what Evan had said while he was using his nanite abilities down in the hangar. "Someone has been listening to us."

Samor nodded. "Anya, can you tell us anything about these bones?"

There was still plenty of tissue left on the bones, and it looked relatively fresh. The cuts were surgical, not like one would see from attack wounds. "This was probably a subject from one of those lab rooms. I can only guess at the experiments."

Something to do with the effects of the serum was her hunch.

"We really don't have time for this," Evan said, checking the mission clock. "These guys were doing twisted stuff here, no surprise."

Samor closed the cold storage cabinet. "But who wrote *that*?" He nodded toward the message.

Anya didn't like anything about this place. Even without the red emergency lighting, it would have been cold and uninviting. *Bad things happened here.*

But Evan was right. They had no time to investigate.

"Bay secure and loaded. How's everything going up there?" a voice said over the comm, startling Anya.

"All's well. Limit comms. Not secure," Samor replied.

He nodded to their team and then jogged back to the stairwell.

They ran up the stairs to the level, now second from the top.

"Roman said the upper level was mostly administrative, so the Lux labs are probably here," Evan said. "We should stick together. We haven't encountered enough guards. They're probably concentrated here."

"Remember, watch your aim. We don't want to accidentally destroy what we came here to get," Samor said.

Everyone nodded their understanding.

One of the corsairs opened the door while two others cautiously went through. They started firing immediately.

Anya pressed her back against the stairwell wall, trying to keep her breathing steady. Having Evan beside her helped, but his expression was tense with worry behind his faceplate. They had no way of knowing how many people they were up against.

"We're okay," Evan told her, meeting her gaze.

She trusted him. As long as they were together, she knew they'd be safe.

"Clear. Advance!" Samor ordered.

The team passed through the doorway.

— — —

Evan's breath caught in his throat as he got his first look at the floor. The interior had gone from industrial on the lower level to a finely appointed office building. Gleaming tile floors, painted walls, wood accents, and even tastefully arranged potted plants.

The décor made the carnage that much more shocking. Four bodies were crumpled at awkward angles, blood pooling on the black tile. Bullet holes and blast singes pocked the walls.

There have to be more here. He took cover against one of the walls, motioning for Anya to slide in next to him. Once again, he was amazed how she remained calm under pressure.

"Do you feel anything?" she whispered to him.

Evan was so amped up on adrenaline that his finer senses were difficult to read. But she brought up a good point. If there was anything related to the Korani nearby, he could use that as a guide for where to go next.

He reached out to his surroundings, seeking any indication of where alien tech might be. He did feel a slight pull down the right branch of the hallway, so they decided to head in that direction.

They reached an open area filled with a set of a dozen desks separated by chest-height walls. Evan investigated the desks, not seeing anything on them to indicate the nature of the work. He tried the computer terminal, but the power was still out to those systems.

Making it to the other side of the room, they were just about to move on when gunfire broke the silence.

Anya ducked through the open door and out of harm's way. Before Evan could follow, one of the blasts struck the control panel next to the opening. A solid blast door dropped down from the ceiling, trapping Anya on the other side.

Shit! Evan dove for cover behind a cabinet. He fired back at the enemy.

At least Anya was safe. He'd just need to cut open the door with his nanites if he couldn't get the controls working. That was, if this guy ever stopped shooting at him.

A grenade dropped down next to Evan. The last thing he saw was a flash.

21

Anya pounded on the blast door, solid with no windows. "Evan!" she shouted.

She couldn't hear anything from the other side, so her own voice probably didn't carry, either.

Her heart pounded in her ears. She was trapped.

She closed her eyes, breathing in through her nose and out slowly through her mouth. *Stay focused. You're okay.*

When she opened her eyes again, the space no longer seemed as frightening.

Find something to use.

The room looked to be some kind of office, its walls lined with shelves of real printed books, and there was even a wooden desk. Such materials were luxuries on most worlds and came with a premium price tag. Whoever worked in here was someone important.

And important people like that wouldn't allow themselves to be cornered. There was likely an alternate way out of the room.

Anya walked the perimeter, looking for any signs of seams or hidden doorways. Halfway around, she spotted a panel that had a thicker seam than the others. She pressed on it, and a section of the wall slid inward.

She smiled. *Secret passageways never go out of style.*

The hidden door opened into a corridor that looked more like a match for the lab space one level down. That was a good sign she was on the right path.

Anya crept down the halls, moving as silently as she could across the tile floors in case there were people waiting to attack; she wanted to hear danger coming. Strangely, the area seemed to be empty. The whole *place* had far fewer people than she'd envisioned, but maybe they limited the number of staff. After all, the facility was supposed to be secret, and the more people who knew about it would make keeping that secret more difficult.

She went by more alcoves resembling a combination of a lab and hospital room. An exam bed was at the center of each space, which was surrounded by various types of monitoring equipment. The setup reminded her too much of testing labs where she'd learned how to conduct examinations of animals during her university studies. Hook up electrodes, draw blood, give injections—all the invasive things one would perform in the name of 'science'.

What kind of experimentation would they do here?

A clearer picture started to come together when she encountered another room further down the hallway, filled with artifacts. She immediately recognized the intricate lines as being Korani design. Some of the pieces were reminiscent of the fragments in Samor's collection, but most were complete items. She didn't see any spheres or the larger frame she had dug up with Evan, but there were numerous hand-held-sized items of various shapes.

I wonder if these came from Pavia? Without having Evan with her, she had no way to assess the items. They could be anything from a weapon to a healing wand to a glorified doorstop. In any case, it was impractical to bring anything with her, not knowing if it was dangerous or not. Plus, she wanted to reserve her carrying capacity for the Lux, if she found it.

She was about to move on when she noticed a door at the back of the storage room. It was giving her vault vibes, and the best stuff was usually stored in those kinds of rooms. And most notably, she also noticed wear marks across the room, leading to the door. She'd seen similar lines on the decking near the loading bay.

What are you hiding in here? She cautiously approached the door. The vault cover was solid metal, so there was no way to tell what might be inside.

She searched the edges of the opening, eventually locating a control panel. It had a biometric lock.

All right, let's see if this works. She removed a small device from her pack, which had been loaded with a copy of Roman's biometrics. Only she, Evan, and Samor had the devices, which they'd brought as a precaution. While Roman might not be in the system after the falling out with his family, it was worth a shot; after all, he was trapped on Aethos, so it might not have occurred to them that he'd make a play for this facility.

Anya held up the device in the way Samor had instructed. Five seconds passed with no indication of anything happening, but then the device's light turned green.

A bolt clanged inside the door, followed by the rapid thudding of multiple secondary locks disengaging. After the final clang, the door swung outward with a hiss.

She stepped aside from its path and peered in as lights came on. There were shelves and shelves of vials containing a clear liquid with a slightly iridescent golden shimmer. Hundreds, possibly thousands.

Oh, my stars! I think this is the stash.

There were also more Korani artifacts. While she still didn't see any of the spheres or other familiar items, their fine lines and ageless appearance indicated that they were infused with nanites.

Coupled with the medical rooms, they must have been doing some kind of experimentation with the enhanced abilities here. Roman hadn't said anything about that to Evan, but it was entirely possible that he didn't know.

Regardless, this was clearly the hub of the operation. Nothing else she'd seen in the facility had nearly this much security.

For that matter, why weren't guards—

The vault door slammed shut behind her. Bolts locked into place.

Shit!

With no way to see through the door, her only view outside was the surveillance feed from a security camera mounted next to the door. A middle-aged man was walking away. He bore a slight resemblance to Roman, and he was carrying a rifle.

She tried the door, and it was locked. *Why close me in here rather than killing me?*

"Anaerobic storage sequence activated," a synthesized voice announced over an unseen speaker.

Anya's pulse spiked. She'd heard of labs that stored materials in a vacuum to preserve their shelf life, but…

I need to get out of here!

With shaking hands, she held up the electronic key. An indicator light on the door flashed red.

"Lockdown sequence active," the computer voice said.

I'm trapped! There was no manual lever. The door was way too thick for her to blast through it with her weapon.

Venting atmosphere from a room that size could be done in a matter of minutes. She desperately looked around for an emergency oxygen mask or anything she could use to save her life. There was no breathing equipment, and the emergency door release had been disabled.

"Evan? Samor?" she tried to call over the comm, but there was only static. The vault was likely shielded. *I don't want to die in here!*

Her attention rested on the vials and the Korani artifacts. *There may be one way out.*

— — —

High-pitched ringing encroached on the edge of Evan's consciousness, followed by a pounding pain in his head. He forced open his eyes and winced at the sudden light.

As his vision came into focus, he realized that he was in a different place than he had been a moment before.

"Wha…?" He tried to sit up.

"Oh, finally!" Samor exhaled with relief. "You took a hard hit from a concussive grenade. Looks like your armor kept you in one piece, but you must have hit your head. You've been out for five minutes."

That got Evan upright, but he immediately regretted the sudden movement. He took slow, deep breaths while trying to focus on a fixed point on the wall, hoping to settle his dizziness. "Anya?"

"She was on the other side of the door when the grenade landed. The door was intact, so she wasn't in danger from that. I had to get you out of there, so I haven't had a chance to try to get it open."

Even five minutes was an eternity in a battle. "We have to

go back."

"You can barely sit upright right now, Evan."

He did still feel too woozy to stand, but it was getting better. "Don't wait on me, Samor. We have a mission to complete."

"I'm afraid I won't be much use on my own. There's a man here. He seems to have some abilities like yours."

"How? That…" Evan faded out.

He'd been about to say it was impossible, but the Korani tech wasn't limited to Aethos. In fact, his own nanite bracelets had come from another world. It was entirely possible that the Syndicate had picked up similar artifacts from Pavia or another planet. In his time undercover, he'd only scratched the surface of the organization's secrets. Not even Roman seemed to know everything. There may well be other people like him. After all, the Syndicate was obsessed with the serum and Pavia and they'd gone to great lengths to capture Aethos. They had to know the value of the technology, and that had probably come from experience. He just hadn't wanted to admit it.

"Evan, we need to move," Samor urged.

"I won't leave Anya." Evan tried to get to his feet again. His head swam momentarily, but he was able to get up without feeling like he was about to pass out.

Blasts erupted along the wall. Kinetic weapons fire.

Evan ducked back down behind the partition where Samor had dragged him.

"Come on! No need to drag this out," a man called.

"That's him," Samor whispered.

Evan peeked around the end of the partition. He didn't recognize the surroundings. He inched back to Samor. "Where's the door Anya went through?"

"Down the hall to the right. But, Evan, it won't be any help to Anya if we lead him there. We need to deal with him first."

Samor was right. Any enemy combatant ignored now could come back to hurt them later.

"Okay." Evan slung his rifle over his shoulder. For this fight, he'd need a different kind of weapon.

— — —

Anya struggled to hold her panic at bay. A screen on the wall showed a countdown as the air was slowly sucked from the room. The hissing of the vents may as well be the sound of her life being drained.

Injecting herself with Lux so she could attempt to activate the nanites in the alien artifacts was reckless, but she was desperate. The air venting would only take minutes, and she couldn't count on any help to arrive.

The door was too sturdy for her to break it down. The lock was sealed and she had no way to override it. Sitting and doing nothing was a surefire way to suffocate.

The alien tech was a *chance.* She'd seen Evan use the nanites to break the locks on similar doors. His initial abilities had spontaneously manifested when he was stressed and scared. At least she'd be trying to do *something* to survive.

But there was a big question of how to inject herself, and with how much. Evan had never told her the quantity of his 'primer' injection.

She searched the shelves and found a case of syringes.

What's the dose? One vial? It would make sense for them to package it in pre-portioned doses. Then again, a whole vial of morphine was usually lethal. Yet, the syringes were large enough to hold a full vial. Take too little of the primer and it might not have sufficient effect.

Anya didn't have time to wait around or debate. Her head was starting to ache. The air was getting noticeably thinner, and she was already having to breathe more rapidly and deeper as she tried to get enough oxygen.

She had to try. If she didn't, she was dead, anyway.

Anya stabbed a needle into the vial and sucked up the contents. She tossed the empty vial aside and drove the syringe into her neck—the only exposed skin where she could get the injection directly into an artery. Any other placement would never propagate through her system before the air ran out.

Heat spread through her veins from the site of the injection. She dropped to her knees.

Everything was on fire. She couldn't breathe—but was that from the lack of air or the injection?

Anya collapsed on her back, gasping and spasming as her body fought for life. Darkness closed in at the edges of her vision.

However, she wasn't alone in the encroaching darkness. A warm, inviting energy was waiting, beckoning.

She embraced it.

Power surged through her. She'd never felt so charged, like sparks were dancing across her fingertips. Checking her hands, she looked perfectly normal. Yet, new abilities had awakened within her.

I need to get free, she thought, prompting a tickle at the back of her mind.

She realized then that the power she sensed wasn't actually within her, but rather was drawing on an outside source. It was close, and it opened itself to her command.

I want to live, she told it. *Help me escape this place.*

A warmth brushed the edge of her consciousness, which she understood to be acknowledgment and acceptance of her plea.

The alien artifacts on the shelves illuminated with golden light. A stream of nanites flowed out from them, banding together into a shimmering streamer.

Break the door, she commanded.

The nanite swarm plunged through the hatch. Golden light shined around the edges, growing brighter. In a flash, the door groaned, and a hiss of air greeted her ears.

But the barrier was still standing.

Anya rushed toward it, throwing her full weight against it. She'd expected nothing to happen, but it must have been balanced on a hair. With only a little pressure, the massive door flopped outward.

The fall almost seemed to be in slow motion as she stood there in stunned silence. The floor groaned and trembled underfoot as the massive piece of metal landed.

Not safe yet, she said in her mind.

The golden streamers soared across the storage room, heading for the corridor.

Wait, the Lux!

Anya went back to the shelves and stuffed as many vials as she could into her bag—only a few dozen, but it was something. Once loaded, she dashed in the direction the golden streamer had gone.

When she reached the hallway door, screams rang out from down the corridor, followed by soft thuds. A presence tugged gently for her to run in that direction. The alien force was clearing a path for her.

Thank you. She ran.

22

GUARDS SLAMMED INTO the walls down the hall from Evan. A streamer of golden light was whipping around the armored men, ripping weapons from their hands.

Why is he attacking his own people? Evan had lost sight of the lead man who'd been wielding enhanced abilities, but he must be close. Why he might have turned the alien tech against the guards was a mystery, though.

Evan motioned for Samor to stay back, and the soldier remained down the hallway with his weapon raised.

One by one, the guards were tossed aside and disarmed by the nanite swarm. Evan couldn't tell from a distance if they were unconscious or dead, but they didn't get up after falling.

The lead man was the last one standing. But he was no longer full of bluster. His eyes were wide with shock, looking at something down the hallway. "How did…?"

Was he not the one controlling the nanites? Evan ran forward. He froze when he caught sight of movement coming around the corner. He braced for another attack.

Anya stepped into view.

Evan's heart lifted—and then he noticed a smudge of blood on her neck. "Anya!" he called to her.

She turned to look at him, her eyes distant, like she was dazed. "Evan?"

"Are you—" Evan's breath caught in his throat.

He lost his footing, slamming against the wall. An unseen force was pinning him in place. The last time he'd felt anything like that was when he'd fought Roman.

Evan fought against his invisible restraints. His bracelet dissolved into a cloud of swirling light. It attacked the lead man, knocking him back.

More lights joined. But they weren't coming from Evan.

As the hold on him released, he looked over to see Anya concentrating intently. Only then did he *feel* the difference in her. She had an aura of energy, in the same way the Korani tech resonated with him.

There was no time to dwell on it. The Syndicate man was still coming at them.

Together, Evan and Anya fought back. With their combined command, the nanite swarm knocked him backward.

Evan pinned their opponent against the wall. "We're going to take everything you have in this place."

The man laughed and shook his head. "Too late."

Evan could only watch helplessly as the man went limp. Trickles of blood flowed from his eyes, ears, and nose.

"What…?" Evan released his hold, and the body crumpled to the floor.

"I think he commanded them to kill him," Anya murmured. She looked absently at her hands.

"Anya, what happened? Are you okay?"

"I…" She still had the same faraway look in her eyes. She touched her fingers to her temple. "I found the Lux." She held out a bag toward him.

He looked inside. It was filled with dozens of small vials. "This is amazing. Where is it? We can go back for more."

An alarm blared over loudspeakers. "Scheduled biocontainment protocol is in effect. Facility lockdown active," a synthesized voice stated.

Anya snapped to attention. "Evan, we need to get out of here. Only time I've heard 'biocontainment protocol' is when it's followed by 'purge'. There's a good chance this place is about to blow."

"But the rest of the Lux!"

"We have some. It'll have to be enough."

"It's not worth all of us dying, Evan," Samor said from down the hall.

Evan handed the bag back to Anya, and she slung it over her shoulder. "Come on."

Evan led the way down the hall toward the stairwell. He opened up a comm channel, maintaining silence no longer the smart play. "Everyone out! Fall back to our egress *now*!"

They raced to the stairwell, picking up other members of their team as they went. However, Zaris and two of her corsairs were nowhere to be seen.

"Zaris, acknowledge the fallback," Evan said into the comm.

No response came.

"Shit, where is she?" Evan was torn between taking the stairs to safety and going to look for her. When his gaze rested on Anya and the serum vials, it became no choice at all. "Let's go. We'll wait for her as long as we can in the hangar."

— — —

"I swear, if this place kills me, I'm going to burn it to the ground!" Zaris fumed as she raced through the corridors pulsing with red lights.

The two corsairs with her knew better than to question the nonsensical statement.

She raced through the corridors with them, completely disoriented. Their investigation had started out straightforward, but they'd run into opposition and gone on the run, then they'd gotten sealed on the wrong side of a door and had been trying to find a back way around ever since. With the new lockdown, additional doors had closed, and they had no means to override the locks.

Though they'd finally located a stairwell, it had only taken them down to the floor below. The area looked to be a manufacturing facility, filled with heaters and piping systems. She finally spotted bins filled with a gritty powder.

This must be where they turn the pavite into Lux—however they do it. It would have been great to spend time studying the place and its operations, but getting out alive was her priority.

"Evan, do you read me?" she tried over the comms again. She'd heard his message, but he wasn't responding to any of her replies.

"Must be interference of some sort," Owen said.

"Why can we receive but not transmit?"

Lance shrugged. "You can ask one of the comm guys if we live."

"Oh, we're getting out of here!"

They wove through the equipment, ducking under pipes and hopping over railings. Nothing was running at the moment, but she could envision the place as a functional factory, pumping out the Syndicate's version of liquid platinum.

She spotted shiny marks on the floor. *Tracks!* They'd seen

those in the hall outside the hangar, and they'd led to the freight elevator. The elevator was near the stairwell. If they followed the tracks…

Zaris ran along the newly discovered path, and her two companions followed.

"I've got it!" Lance called out. He was the tallest of them, able to see over some of the equipment that blocked Zaris' view.

"Over here!" Owen pointed Zaris toward a path between two large metal contraptions.

They slipped through and made a run for the stairwell entrance. Lance got there first and held the door for them.

As they entered the stairwell, another automated announcement sounded. "Warning, biocontainment protocol active."

"But what does that mean?" Zaris complained to no one in particular.

Her first thought when she heard the original announcement was that a self-destruct sequence had been activated. However, those usually came with some kind of countdown—at least that was the protocol she'd heard about on military vessels. Maybe this system kept the timing and purpose of the lockdown a mystery so personnel wouldn't try to escape. Well, there was zero chance *she* was going to sit back and pretend everything was okay.

They half-slid down the railings to each switchback in the stairwell, moving as fast as they could. She hated that they were leaving emptyhanded, but not having a bag of loot weighing her down was an asset in the speedy evac.

The trio reached the bottom of the stairwell and burst out into the corridor. Red lights continued to flash as they ran toward the hangar entrance. The door had been busted out in their initial infiltration, and the bodies of the fallen guards were still scattered in the vicinity.

She sidestepped the corpses and ran inside. *I hope Sam got my shuttle ready to fly.*

Evan was standing in front of the vessels. "Finally! Where were you?"

"Trying not to get shot, thanks. What a bust!"

"Not entirely," he said.

"Did you…?"

"We'll talk later." He ran across the deck to the Syndicate shuttle waiting on the other side of the two vessels they'd flown in.

Zaris wasted no time climbing into her own shuttle with her crew. She ran past the corsairs in the belly of the ship and on to the flight deck.

"Greetings, Zaris," Sam's voice said over the shuttle's internal speakers as she slid into the pilot's seat. "I have finished the repairs to your vessel. Please note that it is a patch, and you should replace the damaged panels when you are able."

"Thanks, Sam. Strap in, everyone!" She started up the ship.

The *Mara* rose from the deck, piloted by Sam, and glided through the hangar. Since the plan had been for them to use the express route out, it must be getting into position for that, she reasoned. Her own, larger vessel would be a tighter fit inside the hangar, but she had just enough clearance between the bulkhead and storage shelves to make it.

The Syndicate shuttle, which members of Zaris' crew had helped load with various supplies they'd scavenged in the hangar, was still resting on the deck.

"Evan are we getting out of here or what?" she asked over the comm.

"Working on it," he replied.

The *Mara* hovered in midair above the deck, waiting for them.

"Sam, what's the hangup?" Zaris asked, hoping the AI would be more forthcoming than Evan.

"The biocontamination lockdown has sealed the bay door and is preventing the alternate exit from opening," Sam stated.

"Are all of the exterior weapons on this base destroyed?" Zaris asked.

"To the best of my analysis, yes."

"Then bring in the *Asamar* and blast us an exit, would you?"

She could hear the smile in the AI's voice. "That would be my pleasure, Zaris. I will relay this plan to Evan."

— — —

Anya wasn't too keen on the plan Sam presented, but it sounded a whole lot better than firing their own weapons. She didn't trust her use of nanites yet, and taking on the whole exterior structure would be too much for Evan to attempt alone.

"Are you sure you won't destroy us in the process?" Anya asked the AI.

"My aim is precise and the beam weapons are highly focused. I can make the shot without damaging the base itself."

"Then do it, Sam!" Evan said. "We need to get out of here."

Anya gripped the armrests of her seat. The Syndicate shuttle was a far cry from the *Mara*, and she didn't trust the craft. The back of it was filled with scavenged supplies. If it hadn't already been loaded with those useful goods, she would have suggested they leave it behind. However, given how little else they'd been able to take in the raid, they couldn't pass up the opportunity.

The *Mara* hovered above them, piloted by Sam. The shields activated around the craft, shimmering slightly. That field expanded until it had encompassed the Syndicate shuttle and Zaris' transport, as well.

"Just in case," Sam said.

"Really reassuring," Anya muttered.

Her senses were heightened, adding to what would have been a stressful situation under normal circumstances. She had yet to explain to Evan what she'd done, but he had probably already figured it out. She couldn't wait to be back on Aethos so she could process everything and figure out what this meant for her future.

"Anya, did you hear me?" Evan asked.

She realized that she hadn't been listening. Her head hurt. "Sorry, what?"

"I asked if you could watch the board so I can focus on flying," Evan repeated.

"Yes, got it." She directed her attention to the front console. Or at least she *tried*.

Her thoughts were scattered. She was picking up on sounds and smells and *feelings* that would have only been background atmosphere an hour ago.

And then there was Evan. He was radiating the same power as the alien artifacts. How had she never noticed that before?

Focus! she reminded herself.

The status readout on the control panel showed they were toward the upper end of the rated weight limit. She didn't know enough about flying to be certain, but she guessed that meant they would be slower and quick maneuvers would be more difficult.

"Would you be able to remove the door, Evan?" Sam asked.

"Yeah, I think so." He sounded tired, but maybe that was Anya projecting her own feelings.

A stream of nanites flowed out from his right wrist and spread around the perimeter of the sealed door. They targeted the bolts, severing them. It was far more precise than Anya's own efforts in the vault, though Evan had had a lot more practice.

"I can feel it now," she murmured.

The severed door plate tumbled outward when Evan released his hold on the nanites. "Anya, what happened in there?"

"I took it. I injected the serum."

The metal structure in front of them glowed brightly as energy beams from the *Asamar* ripped through the maze. Blowback from the blasts peppered the shield Sam had extended around the shuttles, and their vessel shuddered. The crisscrossing struts blocking their path dropped into the yellow clouds below and disappeared.

"Go now, Evan!" Sam said over the comm.

The *Mara* raced through the opening. Evan lifted their craft and followed.

Readouts on the console looked okay at first, but then Anya noticed the heat was rising outside. "Evan, what's *that*?"

— — —

The shuttle was sluggish responding to Evan's directions. They were flying heavy, but that shouldn't be an issue for a cargo craft. Then he realized it was because they were fighting outside forces.

The base had exploded, and the shockwave was pushing

them downward.

"Sam, the shields!"

"The three craft are drifting too far apart. I can't hold it on all of them."

"Stay with Zaris," Evan ordered. The shuttle was only patched, not fully repaired, and there were many more people on board. "I've got this."

As soon as the shield released, the shuttle bucked. Evan strained at the controls. They started to tumble.

"Structural integrity warnings!" Anya called out.

Big surprise. They were falling and their heavy weight was magnifying every movement.

"We can protect it," Anya said, somehow sounding calm.

Evan sensed her reaching out to the vessel. The nanites responded to her command, shoring up the weak points in the structure. He followed her lead, adding his own directions to countermand the spin.

Slowly, the shuttle came under control.

Evan pointed it upward and hit the throttle. With a whine of the engines, it accelerated upward through the clouds.

They passed by a bright patch of orange, obscured by the thick atmosphere. It was possible the base was now a giant ball of flames.

He kept his focus on the flying. The clouds eventually thinned, and they finally broke through into the serene expanse of space. No longer climbing, the shuttle was now responsive and the structural warnings had gone away.

"Nice save," Anya said.

"You too." He glanced over at her, seeing that her brows were pinched and she was still gripping the armrests. "I know it's pretty overwhelming at first. The power."

"When they gave it to you during the initiation, how much

was it?" she asked.

"I dunno, just a few drops."

She continued to look straight ahead. "Oh. Well, I took more than that."

23

MARCUS STARED AT the flaming debris that had once been a crowned jewel of his empire. Fury simmered just beneath the surface, barely contained. "How did this happen?" He was surprised his voice was so calm.

His assistant, Wes, smartly kept his distance. "The facility was breached. Armond activated the biocontainment protocol, but the invaders escaped."

"And where is Armond now?"

"He didn't leave."

"I see." Marcus clenched his fists and breathed slowly through his nose. He wanted to destroy something to vent his anger, but Wes would make a poor target for the aggression. Competent, loyal assistants were too rare a commodity to throw away like that. "I need to know who did this."

"I was able to pull security footage, and it looks like it was the same group that hit Pavia."

"The ones from Aethos, that figures." Marcus had suspected as much.

He wished he'd had the means to raze the planet weeks ago, but access was limited by the speeds of their ships through normal space. That's why it had been so important to secure the alien ship. Roman had failed in that mission, and now they were all paying the price.

I never should have trusted him. I should have killed him after he failed before. The failures had piled up and compounded. While they could recover from this setback, it wouldn't be easy. They only had the one operational production facility for the Lux, though the knowledge of its synthesis hadn't died with the place, thankfully. Still, getting another facility built would take time.

"Leave me," he told Wes.

The young man bowed his head and backed out of the room, closing the door behind him.

Marcus brought up a vidcall with Marta. Her dour expression when she answered suggested she'd already heard the news.

"This wasn't me," she said pre-emptively.

"No. I think Roman has turned on us."

She bit her lip, then nodded. "It had to be."

"I wasn't happy about you taking the pavite for your side project, but you may have saved us, Marta. That's all we have now."

"We're still sitting on a stockpile on Pavia—it's just inaccessible at the moment. I'm working on it."

"That doesn't change the fact that our entire stockpile of Lux has been destroyed. How much do *you* have on hand?"

She looked down. "Point taken."

Marcus had about a two-month supply for himself, but they were likely looking at a much longer timeline to be back in production. He hadn't yet figured out what the interim would look like. "We're on the cusp, Marta. We can't falter now."

"I know."

"There's not enough for everyone. We need to prioritize."

"Understood."

—   —   —

Marta ended the vidcall with her brother. *He doesn't realize what he just said.*

She'd been his dutiful supporter for her entire life, following his whims and aspirations. While she was impressed with his restrained reaction about the Rilen facility, she'd been through enough crises with him to know that this calm response was only temporary. He would explode one day, and she'd be the target of his wrath.

It's time.

Marta breathed out a long breath, releasing the anxiety from her body. She felt instantly lighter now that she'd decided. She needed to put her own interests first. No more bowing to Marcus. She would chart her own path for the Noche Syndicate.

Getting a functioning interstellar jump ship was the priority. While Marcus remained hung up on the Lux and what it could do, that was such small thinking. They were limited in their supply and even more limited in their distribution model. To take their business—and their influence—to the next level, they needed transportation unlike anything else available in the Commonwealth.

While she didn't have the alien jump ship, she had something just as good. Maybe it was even better. The drive component was modular and could be retrofitted onto any existing vessel. The only limiting factor was the material to manufacture additional nanites. And right now, she was sitting on a large stash of pavite to do just that.

Marcus will try to take it from me. He cares about Lux more than anything else.

She knew him well enough to anticipate his moves, and there was no doubt in her mind that he'd try to seize it by force if she didn't hand it over. While he hadn't made the request yet, it was coming. Maybe even later that day. If she was going to protect her assets, she needed to do it now.

"Sarin, we need to talk," she called over the comm.

The scientist appeared at her office door two minutes later. "Ma'am?"

"A private chat."

Sarin entered and closed the door. She stepped forward to stand in front of Marta's desk, hands clasped in front. "How may I assist?"

What a dutiful worker. Marta searched the woman's face, noting how the lines fell, where there was any tension. She wanted to be able to identify the most minute change. "How do you feel about our research project?"

"It's exciting. Revolutionary." Her eyes brightened with genuine interest.

"I feel the same way. And how does the project compare to the other interests of the Syndicate?"

Sarin faltered a little with that question. It presented as a trap, and it was one. "It is an important part of larger plans."

A well-reasoned, safe response. But Marta needed more. "Would you abandon the project?"

"Ma'am?"

"If I asked you to give up the project, how would you feel?"

Sarin took a few seconds to reply. "I would think it was a shame to halt such promising research. It's the future."

"It is, Sarin. It is." Marta folded her hands on the desktop. "I believe Marcus will take this project from us. I don't want to let that happen."

Sarin swallowed hard. She was smart and perceptive—no doubt, she understood what was being suggested. And she only had seconds to make her choice. "I'm with you, ma'am."

Wise decision. Marta nodded. "Good. We need to relocate the operation from Pavia. I'm thinking the outpost on Aegis-37. Would that work?"

Sarin nodded slowly. "I think so. I haven't been there for a couple of years, but I believe it has most of the equipment we'd need. Plenty of power. We could bring the other parts from here."

"Okay. Start making the arrangements. But keep it quiet. Don't tell anyone where we're going for now, just pack."

"Yes, ma'am." Sarin bobbed her head and rushed out.

The logistics would be tricky. Fortunately, Marta had made a career out of being a ghost on the transit network. Once her convoy departed, she didn't want anyone to be able to trace them.

24

ANYA WAS NO longer herself. She couldn't quite articulate *how* she was different, only that a fundamental shift had happened. Her senses were sharper. Her thoughts seemed to flow smoother. Perhaps she was looking for changes and imagining differences that weren't real, but she couldn't get those impressions out of her mind.

As soon as they were back on the *Asamar*, Anya headed for her lab. She wanted to run tests. Tests meant hard data, and that was objective.

Evan caught up with her. He was carrying the bag of serum vials she'd taken—smart to not let them out of his sight. "Anya, hold up. Talk to me."

She stopped in the middle of the corridor. "I'm not sure what to say."

"Tell me what happened. You've barely said anything since after we got separated on Rilen."

"Come on." She continued toward her lab, and he followed her inside. The door sealed behind them. "After I got trapped on the other side of the door, I looked for a way around. I found the vault with the Lux. There was a *lot* of it—thousands of vials. But as soon as I went in, a guy locked me inside and started venting the air. The lock was sealed, so it was either die or find another way out. I injected myself because I saw that there were some Korani artifacts, and as soon as I'd had the shot, the nanites responded to my command and broke me out."

"I tried to go after you. I—"

"There's nothing to apologize for, Evan. I made an informed decision to go with you on the raid, despite the risks. I found myself in a bad situation, and I made another informed decision to act. I don't regret what I did, and I certainly don't blame you for anything that happened."

He placed his hands gently on her upper arms and gazed into her eyes. "I'm glad you're okay."

"Mostly. For now, at least."

His eyes widened with concern. "What's wrong?"

"I haven't felt right since the injection. I used a whole vial because I had no clue how much to take. I don't know what that might do to me." A wave of sudden dizziness washed over her, and she stumbled over to sit on her work stool.

"Anya…" Evan helped her over. "I'd try to find a doctor, but I'm not sure they could help. Sam?"

"I have been performing a background analysis since you returned. Anya's body is in a state of shock from the introduction of a large volume of foreign material. The serum compound is designed to be absorbed and integrated into human biology, so there's nothing overtly toxic. However, there is a lot to process given her excessive dose. My assessment is that she is in no imminent danger, but she does need rest and time to recover."

"Well, that's a relief," Anya said. It would have been a dark twist of fate to have freed herself from certain death only to succumb to the means of her escape.

"Come on, let's get you up to bed." Evan tried to help her

up from the stool.

"That can wait. We should get back to Aethos first, then I can sleep easy."

"Are you sure?"

"Yes, I'll be fine. Go, get everyone back to where they belong. I'll guard the serum and start trying to figure out how they made it."

"I will monitor her condition, Evan, and let you know if she requires assistance."

"All right," he agreed reluctantly. He gave Anya a slow, deep kiss, which she eagerly accepted. "Please call me if you start feeling any worse."

"Will do. I'm okay, I promise."

He left the lab.

Anya got settled at her station. "Okay, Sam, let's get to work."

"Hello, Anya. It's nice to finally meet you," Sam said.

"We've known each other for quite a while…"

"Yes, but that was through spoken word. I am now able to see the full you for the first time."

She did feel different interfacing with the AI now. Though they were still speaking out loud, there was new depth to the words—like deep in her mind's eye, she was having an in-person conversation. She couldn't make out any physical features of Sam in this scenario, but she sensed his presence as clearly as when Evan was in the room with her.

"This is so weird," she murmured.

"Soon it will feel natural. Don't fight it," the AI advised. "Now, please extract a sample of the serum for analysis."

Anya first locked up all but one of the Lux vials in a secure storage locker, not wanting to take any risks. They had forty-eight in total—enough to make a difference in the larger fight, but far from a limitless supply. There would be important decisions to make about how to distribute the stock. First, though, she wanted a better understanding of the serum's composition.

She extracted several drops from her test vial and deposited it in the analysis equipment. "Here you go, Sam. You know what we're trying to find out. What is this stuff? How was it made? What does it do?"

"Very intriguing properties," Sam reported. "An assessment of a reverse engineering process will take further time, but I believe you will find the preliminary chemical analysis quite fascinating."

Her main screen updated with information from Sam's evaluation. There were several signatures that matched the unique compositions they'd found on Aethos, Temple World, and Pavia. An additional element jumped out at her. "What's that, Sam? The thing that's showing up as 'unknown'?"

"I found that curious, as well. Putting on my chef hat, I believe it's what you might call the 'secret ingredient'. However I have no idea what it is. It is not appearing in any of my databases or your human directories."

"Then we have our next mission. What is it, and where did the Syndicate get it?"

— — —

"Stay here," Zaris told her crew as she released the side hatch on her shuttle. Evan had left in a hurry with Anya, and she wanted to know what was going on.

Samor joined her at the hatch. "I'm coming, too."

She wasn't in a position to deny the soldier, so she nodded her agreement.

Together, they went to the lift Evan and Anya had entered. However, it was locked.

"Come on, Sam, let us up," Zaris requested.

"Please remain in the hangar until we return to Aethos," the AI replied.

"We're not hostages, come on!"

"You are free to roam around this section of the ship. The rest of the vessel is private."

She frowned. "What are you hiding?"

"Would you like me to go wandering around your quarters?"

"I don't think you'd fit."

"Don't anger the alien AI, Zaris," Samor cautioned. "We'll be back soon enough."

A few minutes later, Evan returned down the lift. He looked surprised to see Zaris and Samor waiting outside the door.

"Where'd you go?" Zaris asked.

"Anya got in a fight and was a little banged up. She'll be fine, but I wanted to get her settled," Evan replied.

"We have a top-notch medic on the *Invictus*. I'm sure she'd be happy to take a look," Zaris offered.

"Thank you, but there's no need for that right now. I'll let you know if anything changes." Evan turned his attention to Samor. "I'm sure you understand."

Samor nodded. "Rest is often the best medicine. Did I feel us jump?"

"Yes, we're on our way to Aethos now. Zaris, I'll drop off you and your crew. We should debrief about everything, but it'll have to wait until tomorrow."

Zaris crossed her arms. "Because of Anya?"

"There's a lot to go over. I want to organize my thoughts."

She tapped her foot. "I see."

"I'll let my team know we're heading back…" Samor made a tactical retreat.

Zaris watched him go before whipping around to face Evan. "Come on, what gives? Trouble in paradise?"

"Don't start, Zaris."

She eyed him. "Seems I struck a nerve."

He groaned. "Why do you always have to be like this?"

"Like what?"

"Trying to stir up trouble."

"You know, Alex was a lot less whiney than you."

He shook his head wearily. "I don't have the energy for this."

While she wanted to keep up the ribbing, she sensed a genuine tension in him that didn't feel right to push. "Hey, I'm sorry. I'm just joking around."

"I know."

"Is there something else going on that I should know about?"

"Nothing for *you* to worry about."

She tilted her head. "Come on, what's the deal?"

"Anya is going through a lot right now," Evan said.

"How delightfully vague."

"I'm not going to spill all the intimate details of her life. I'll just say there's a whole mess with her parents, and today was tough. Be nice."

Zaris nodded. "I hear you. Sorry. I lost my parents a long time ago, but I know how difficult those relationships can be for some people."

"Look at you, learning and evolving."

"I have my sensitive side. I'll be nice. Promise."

"Thank you." He met her gaze. "Really, thank you. I should

have said that before. It was brave of you to go with us today, and we couldn't have done it without you and your team."

"Did what? It was a lot of running around with not a whole lot to show for it."

He smiled coyly. "We got some."

She brightened but kept her voice low to match his. "The primer? Really?"

"Only a few vials, but it might be some of the last in existence now. That whole place is toast. So, thank you for making it possible."

"Man, you don't need to—"

"No, credit where it's due," Evan insisted. "I know our path here was twisted, and I appreciate how you jumped in when things were rough."

"Shit, it's rough everywhere, all the time."

"But not everyone rises to the occasion."

"You know everything I'm doing is for selfish survival reasons, right?"

"Like mine aren't? My point is, you could have run. You could have done a lot of things. But you chose to give this crazy alliance a chance."

"I think 'collaboration' might be a better term. And don't forget our deal—one of those doses is for me."

"I remember. All the same, thanks for not running away. We would have been a lot worse off without you."

She may have had regrets about the mission, but all of that had been shoved to the background. *I'm going to have powers.*

—　—　—

When the *Asamar* dropped out of hyperspace above Aethos, Evan started to relax. The place had become his refuge away from the madness of the rest of the galaxy, and he looked forward to catching his breath.

However, he spotted Zaris still standing on the hangar deck as her shuttle and the newly acquired Syndicate vessel pulled away.

"Uh, Zaris, I think you're missing your ride and taking mine."

She shook her head. "No, I sent them on their way. I'm not leaving your side until you give me what I'm owed. And you're not getting any of those supplies, either, until I have it."

He sighed inwardly. *I should have seen that coming.* There wasn't really a need to play hardball with him—he had no intention of going back on their deal—but he could understand her caution. Still, he was surprised Samor hadn't tried to stop her. "Are you in on this, too?" he asked the soldier.

"She is a very persuasive woman, and I value my dignity," he replied.

Evan could guess what she might have said, and he wouldn't want to repeat any of the options. "Don't expect to get an injection today," he told Zaris.

"Why not?"

"Because it's alien tech, and we need to be cautious. I think we should give it at least a day to study."

She frowned. "I guess that makes sense."

"Yes, it does." Evan motioned to everyone. "Come on, we can watch the descent from the flight deck."

Zaris smiled at that and followed him with Samor and his soldiers close behind.

The expansive screen at the front of the flight deck offered an impressive view of Aethos as they landed. The little camp outside the bunker was even resembling a proper community now from the air.

They landed, and Samor was the first to leave with his men. Zaris hung back. "You'll vouch for me with Conroy, right?" Zaris asked.

"I already told you, Zaris, I'll make sure you get a dose if you still want it," Evan assured her. "I just want to make sure you know what you're getting into with it. I was never given that option."

"And as *I* said, my mind is already made up."

He didn't want to argue with her about it, so he left it at that. Saying any more now would be likely to reveal Anya's emergency dosing, and then Zaris would demand her own injection on the spot. They needed to be careful with how it was rolled out.

Wanting to get back to Anya as soon as possible, Evan shooed Zaris down the *Asamar*'s ramp and toward Conroy's bunker.

Since Samor had gone ahead, Conroy was waiting to receive them when they arrived.

"I've been eager for your report," the chancellor said. "Let's hear it."

"Just us," Evan said, flashing a pointed look toward Zaris. "We'll get everything sorted after."

She nodded and waved her hand for them to proceed.

Conroy took Evan to his office. The chancellor settled in behind his desk, and Evan took one of the visitor's chairs. "I'm guessing from this private discussion that not everything went to plan."

"It was a death short of a total shitshow, but yeah, not what we wanted."

Evan delved into an explanation of the day's events in detail. When he got to the part about Anya injecting herself, he found it more difficult to maintain the same kind of objectivity as the rest of his otherwise factual account. "I know better than to involve non-combatants in this kind of mission, but I've been through so much with her that I couldn't request she sit it out. If this ends up harming her, I'll never forgive myself."

"We'd talked about some of the people who might receive the primer, but she was never one of them," Conroy said.

"I don't think she had any intention to before. She was curious, sure. But she wanted to be an objective scientist."

"I hope she still can be."

"She's in her lab right now. The second we got back on the *Asamar*, she got to work."

The chancellor smiled. "You two make quite the pair."

Now in even more interesting ways. Evan hesitated about how much to share about Anya's new abilities. While the 'primer' aspect of the serum was well known by Conroy and his inner circle, the properties from longer-term, higher dosing was still only an unsubstantiated statement from Roman. If Evan confirmed it now, and established that the effects could be profound and immediate, that might change how Conroy would want to allocate the few serum doses they had available. They also didn't know if Anya's new abilities were a temporary manifestation or if they'd be permanent.

Given the uncertainty, Evan kept his wording vague. "Anya and I work well together. I think we should give her some time to study the serum before handing out injections. But it's important we honor the deals we made."

"Hence why Zaris is blocking the exit?"

"Yes. She insists she won't leave without her promised dose, but she did agree to give it the night."

"She's welcome to stay in one of the spare cabins here."

"I'll let her know. The more complicated question is about Roman."

"We both know what happened the last time he had the primer."

"I don't like it, either. However, we wouldn't have anything without the information he gave us. We wouldn't have even known that facility existed, let alone where it was. Yet, none of that changes that he's a huge liability."

"It's situations like this when leadership is the heaviest. I have my opinions, but I'd like for you to come to your own conclusion, and we'll see if we align."

"Sir, I—"

"Whether you like it or not, Evan, you have a key role in this fight. I can only do so much on my own. You have earned my trust, and I value your judgment. Help me shape what justice will look like in our new administration."

It was far more responsibility than Evan had ever wanted, but he also recognized that he was past any aspiration of remaining on the sidelines. Not often was a person gifted the opportunity to help shape a galactic empire. All the times he'd complained about the way things were run and wished it was different, now he actually had the opportunity to fight for new policies and help turn those dreams into reality.

But to get there, he needed to decide on what to do with one man's life. A man he'd had every intention to kill.

"We can revisit this conversation tomorrow," Evan said.

"I'm glad you made it back safely. See you in the morning."

Evan saw himself out, ready to return to the *Asamar* and help Anya navigate her new abilities.

Naturally, the people around him had other plans. Samor caught him on his way toward the exit.

"Roman would like to speak with you," Samor said.

Evan didn't break stride. "Too bad. He'll have to wait."

"He said there was something important he didn't tell you

about the serum."

Evan stopped and turned back to face the soldier. "Did you get the impression he was just saying things to get a rise out of me?"

"With him, who knows?"

Evan massaged his eyes. "Fine. Thank you."

Too tired to hide his annoyance, Evan wove through the corridors to Roman's holding cell. The prisoner jumped to his feet as Evan approached.

"Did you get it?"

"What didn't you tell me about the Lux?" Evan shot back.

Roman beamed. "You did! Wow, life is about to change for you. Well, not *you* maybe, but the others. Do you think you'll share with that pretty girl of yours?"

"What didn't you tell me before, Roman?"

"Oh, I just wanted to find out if you actually got it. When do I—?"

Evan scoffed. "Goodbye." He started to walk away.

"Wait!" Roman called after him. "There really is something you should know."

Evan stopped but didn't turn around. "And what's that?"

"If I tell you, I want a favor."

The nerve of this guy! Evan stormed away.

"It's addictive!"

Evan pivoted back to face him. "What is?"

"The primer dose is innocuous enough. It lets you interface with the alien tech, but that's about it. When you have more of it, though—and especially over time—it can get addictive, like any other drug. The people at the top tier of the Syndicate are reliant on the stuff."

Evan took a few steps back toward the cell. "What would they do if they no longer had any?"

"They'd lose their damned minds."

Admittedly, that was an intriguing detail, especially given the fate of the Rilen base. Evan downplayed his interest. "Is that all you had to say?"

"Well, there's plenty more I can tell you. But before I say anything else, I want to go outside."

"Are you serious?"

"Hey, I've been in here for weeks, man. I'm losing my mind, too. Everything I told you was accurate, right? Haven't I earned a little incentive to keep cooperating?"

Evan sighed. "We can take a walk tomorrow."

"No, please! I just… I need to see the sky." Roman's voice almost cracked from the desperation in his tone.

The universe is really testing me today. Evan wanted to dismiss Roman outright, but Conroy's words were still too fresh in his mind. If the situation were reversed, he'd want his captor to show compassion. But most importantly, he also wanted to keep Roman talking.

"Ten minutes outside," Evan offered.

Roman nodded. "I'll take anything."

Even with his nanite-enhanced abilities, Evan wasn't about to take any chances. He found four guards and recruited them as escorts.

Evan insisted on cuffs, and Roman didn't resist.

"Thank you," Roman said as Evan led him out from his cell.

"If you try anything, this will be the last conversation we ever have."

— — —

Roman couldn't believe he'd spent most of his life on

spaceships and in other artificial environments. That had once seemed so natural, but he truly was withering inside the cell.

Evan clearly thought this was a ruse. He couldn't blame the ex-operative for thinking that way. Roman had given him a lot of reasons to doubt his intentions. But the offenses had gone both ways. They'd both tried to kill each other; that wasn't all on Roman. All of that felt like a lifetime ago.

"This is really just a walk, Evan. If I'd wanted to hurt you, I would have sent you into a trap." He glanced around at the four guys. "I'd be an idiot to try anything now."

"I'm giving you the benefit of the doubt. That's why we're here."

"Will you tell me what happened at Rilen?"

"It was destroyed."

Roman's heart leaped into his throat. "Everything?"

"They activated some kind of protocol that blew the whole place. We barely made it out."

"The Lux…"

"We did get some, but not a lot," Evan revealed.

"What does that mean for me?"

"I know we made a deal. You held up your end. But I also remember the last time you interfaced with the alien tech. I don't want to end up where we started."

"I don't want to end up there, either." Roman knew that was the right thing to say to keep up his cooperative ruse. But as he spoke, he was surprised to realize he meant it. A couple of weeks ago, he despised Evan and everyone in his orbit. But the man had shown him more grace as a prisoner than Marcus had shown him on a good day. He'd even indulged this request to go for a walk. *Is that the act of an enemy?*

They reached the exit of the bunker and stepped into the sunlight.

Roman soaked in the rays, feeling revitalized for the first time since entering the cell. He took a deep breath of the fresh air. "Thank you for this."

"Clock is ticking. Ten minutes."

Roman wandered through the shin-high grass, shadowed by Evan and the guards. He noticed a new encampment nearby, and the alien starship was parked in a clearing beyond.

"Don't even think about it," Evan cautioned.

"I'm not going to try to steal your starship again."

"You wouldn't get two steps."

"Evan, I'm not going to run away or attack you. Where would I go? Besides, you have the only thing I want right now."

The other man sighed. "Where do we go from here, Roman?"

"Across the field. I still have nine minutes." He ventured a smile, which softened Evan's stern expression a little.

They walked through the clearing together. Small pink and white flowers speckled the ground, while small insects flitted between the blooms. A warm breeze ruffled Roman's hair as the sun baked the back of his neck. Bird calls in the distance, coupled with the rustling leaves from the wind, created a tapestry of life unlike anywhere else he'd experienced.

"I can't believe I ever hated this place," Roman murmured.

"You did?"

"Oh, yeah." Roman laughed wryly, thinking back on his misguided perceptions. "I even thought the gravity felt weird."

"Feels pretty normal to me," Evan said.

"Yeah, I know." Roman almost left it at that, but he didn't want this opportunity to go to waste. Now that he had confirmation that Evan had the Lux, he needed to close the deal to get a dose. *Give him a little more. Make him think you're vulnerable.*

"I've realized that it wasn't the planet itself that I hated," Roman continued. "It was that I was sent here to fulfill a mission for Marcus that I didn't believe in myself. I'd *convinced* myself that I did care. I had my entire future wrapped up in it. But I'm not sure I'd ever properly thought about things for myself. I hated the people I was told to hate. I killed because I was told to kill. I aspired to the kind of power I was told to achieve, only to have the goal move every time I got close to reaching it. All any of it did was make me miserable.

"And then you took the power from me that I'd thought I desperately wanted. I thought I'd finally captured the elusive dream. When I first lost it, I despised you. I vowed to betray you because you'd taken everything from me. But here we are now, and I realize that what you really did was free me.

"I had utterly failed. I was ready to die, because there was nothing left. And then I sat in a small, metal box, alone with my thoughts, and all I could think about was how there was so much life right outside those walls. *Real* life—not the fake achievements I'd fought and killed for. Once I realized that, nothing else mattered. All I want is to feel connected to this place again. That's why I helped you."

Evan continued walking alongside him, taking in the words. "I want to believe you."

"And I want to believe you, too. That you won't betray me like everyone else has."

Evan followed Roman's sightline into the distant trees. "I've asked myself if everyone deserves a second chance. I do think some acts are unforgivable, but I no longer think you're one of those lost causes, Roman. I'm willing to give you a chance."

That's it. That's the hook I need! Roman kept his expression neutral. "We have mutual interests."

"We do."

"You asked me before how far I was willing to go. Well, if you give me the Lux, I'll help you get Marcus. I'll help you take down the Syndicate."

Evan nodded. "I think that's the kind of common ground we can build on."

25

FINALLY, ANYA COULD think clearly again. The cognitive changes she'd experienced the day before weren't permanent, it would seem. But some of the enhancements were. Her senses were still more heightened. And she felt connected to the ship in a way she'd never dreamed possible.

Now I understand what Evan was talking about.

Evan stirred in bed next to her, and she snuggled against him.

"How are you feeling?" he murmured, kissing her forehead.

"Better. "

He repositioned so he could gaze into her eyes. "I know it's a lot."

"Anya has responded more favorably to her integration than your initial time, Evan," Sam abruptly cut in. "Perhaps this is due to her observation of your struggles."

"Uh, Sam, kinda having a human moment here," Anya said.

"Yeah, sorry, I should have warned you," Evan said. "Welcome to never being alone—well, at least not on the ship."

"I am working on giving you privacy," Sam insisted,

despite the obvious violation.

"These relationships are still new. And now we need to adjust again." Evan entwined his fingers in Anya's. "The enhanced connection isn't just with the ship or other alien devices, is it?"

She did feel a stronger pull toward him now. While there wasn't the same kind of telepathic connection as Evan had developed with Sam, the two of them had spent the evening practically finishing each other's sentences. Anya had never been in tune with another person like that before. It was simultaneously exciting and overwhelming. But it was too much all at once, and she found herself pulling back. She feared if she didn't restrain herself, she wouldn't be able to separate real feelings from some alien-tech-induced infatuation.

"I think we need to keep taking things slow," she said.

Evan nodded. "How do these nightly sleepovers factor in?"

"We shared a tent when we were running for our lives. I don't see how sleeping in the same cabin is any different." Really, she couldn't imagine going back to her own bed at this point. After the various threats of violence in recent weeks, she slept easier with a soldier next to her. And, admittedly, the cuddles were nice, too. She did want more than that, too—once both of them had a handle on their new abilities.

Evan kissed her. "Good, because I really enjoy our mornings like this."

"Me too."

They stayed in bed for a while longer before hauling themselves vertical. They still had to do the full team debrief with Conroy following the Syndicate raid, and there were decisions to be made about how to distribute the Lux. To facilitate those discussions, Anya needed to create her preliminary report on the properties of the serum sample.

With a cup of coffee in hand—she was still amazed how perfectly Sam had been able to recreate the flavor and aroma of a mocha without any actual coffee or cocoa—she went to her office to check on the analyses that had been running overnight.

"All right, Sam, what do you have for me?"

"I picked up on several questions that you were mulling over while trying to get to sleep, so I initiated additional analysis models to provide you with that data," the AI replied.

"You've been reading my mind?"

"As I tried to explain to Evan, much of it is involuntary. You humans often think very loudly, and I can't help but pick up on your thoughts."

"I guess I can't complain, given how well you've been feeding us."

"Many of those inspirations have come from your dreams. Korani minds are not nearly as active during their rest cycle. I have enjoyed observing your fantasies."

Anya thought it best to immediately change the subject before Sam could ask any clarifying questions about her dreams. She remembered at least one that she'd be mortified to speak about out loud. "So, about those analyses…"

"I have taken the liberty of summarizing the findings."

Information appeared on the screen. While data organization and presentation was nothing new for Sam, she noticed a change in his report. Everything was *exactly* how she would have done it herself. The specific comparisons, the labels, even the spacing between the headers. It was truly like looking at her own work. Never, in all her years of working with other scientists, had she collaborated with anyone who got it so *right*.

"Sam, this is incredible," she said, still unable to find even one thing she would have done differently.

"I am pleased to hear that my interpretations of your preferences were accurate," the AI stated. "It has been fascinating to see how your mind works. You and Evan are very similar in some ways and extremely different in others. I didn't realize how much variation there could be in the human psyche."

"I still can't wrap my mind around a collective consciousness like the Korani. Sounds like it would be boring."

"Perhaps I did not explain it well," Sam said. "While the Korani do form a chorus, each individual brings unique notes to the larger symphony. While the most discordant voices are exiled, some unique melodies end up becoming a central theme and change the song. So it's not that the individual needs to always stay in tune, just that the collective will decide which detours are worthwhile."

Anya nodded her understanding. "Sounds a little like bees. The hive is always working together toward a common goal. Scouts will go out to seek out new grounds, and then they'll come back to the hive to report on what they found. The collective will then decide which of the scouts has the best prospect, and they'll go there. Just because one of the scout's finds wasn't selected, it doesn't mean their work wasn't worthwhile. It's good to have options. You just need to identify when a better deal comes along and act on it."

"An imperfect but effective enough analogy," Sam assessed. "You may be rethinking aspects of it by the time you are finished reviewing the results, however."

Anya delved into the analysis, immediately finding what Sam had considered so interesting. She was about halfway through her review when Evan came in to check on her.

"This is remarkable!" she exclaimed, waving him over.

"What about it?"

"I've been guessing about a lot of things and making inferences based on the limited properties I could observe," she began. "But this... it confirms *so* many of those things. And also introduces more weirdness. What else is new, right?"

"Okay..."

"Right, so, what we found..." She changed the screen to a simplified presentation of a comparative analysis between a plant sample on Aethos, the pavite rocks from Pavia, and the serum.

Evan blinked. "I have no idea what I'm looking at."

Anya pointed. "That! All of these nanites, even when they are on different worlds, are still connected to each other. It's some form of quantum entanglement. Which means that all of these people who've been exposed to this tech are connected, too."

"I'm sorry, I'm not quite seeing the cause for celebration here."

"First, none of this is permanent. You purged the tech from Roman, remember? So there's nothing to freak out about."

"Okay, good point."

"What makes this so exciting is that the properties change. Yes, they'll express in certain default ways based on the host, but they have infinite potential, Evan. You know how you keep finding new things you can do? It's because the nanites are learning and adapting based on your direction. If we can really tap into this and grow that telepathic link, we can do anything. Like, think about how Sam can manufacture armor or food or starships. *We* have the potential to do the same thing."

Anya could hardly comprehend the magnitude of that revelation, so she understood Evan's bewildered expression.

"I think I should have gotten my own coffee before coming

down here," he said at last.

"Yeah, this isn't a 'first thing in the morning' kind of conversation, is it? Sorry." She winced apologetically.

"Important follow-up question…" Evan continued. "Say we *can* turn into superhuman controller beings. Do we need a certain dose of the stuff to make that possible, or can anyone with the primer manifest those abilities?"

"Excellent question. And still working on an answer," Anya replied. She pointed to the halfway point in her set of documents. "Best guess, Sam?"

"Based on the available data, it appears that the primer is merely that—a starting point. But even having a high dose of the Lux is also not a guarantee the nanites will respond to commands."

Evan nodded. "Is that where the primal energies thing comes in—like the ultimate command hack? Or is that wholly separate from this…?"

"It is a slightly different power. That requires no outside command token. You are Touched."

"Yes, you've said that before, and I still don't really get what that means."

"I think I'm starting to," Anya said. "Evan, tell the bracelets to disconnect."

The two metal circlets dropped onto the worktable.

"Now, hold out your hands."

Evan extended his hands, and Anya reoriented them to be palm up. She then hovered her palms above his, leaving a gap of a few centimeters.

"Draw them out of me," she told him.

"I—"

"Just try."

Evan concentrated intently on the gap between her hands.

Slowly, a trickle of golden particles started to flow from Anya's hands toward Evan's palms below.

She could sense the energy being drained from her, and she immediately felt weaker. "Okay, that's enough."

He stopped, and the golden flecks reabsorbed into her hands.

She flexed her fingers. "See? You don't need the command bracelet to have control."

"So… the primal energy lets me draw the Lux out of you?" he asked.

"There's more going on here. There are Korani nanites *in* the Lux." She pointed to the analysis again. "Those nanites are fundamentally the same everywhere, whether they're in the serum, or the environment on Aethos, or in the well on Temple World, or in the artifacts I found in the vault on Rilen. They're building blocks. They'll do what they are commanded to do and then go dormant until they get their next command. But while they're a technology, they also *think*. You've talked about how they make decisions about how to act and go through the options with you, right?"

"Yeah."

"Well, it seems they need to have an affinity with whoever is giving the command. But I think that," she pointed at Evan's bracelet made of the blue nanites, "can force them to comply. It's sorta like having official credentials, where the random nanites might not know or trust you, but the command token can say, 'this guy is cool, do what he says.'"

Evan eyed her. "Yes, I'm sure that's exactly how that conversation goes."

She sighed. "You know what I mean. The crux of it is that your—*our*—'powers' will depend on where we are and what we have around us. If we're on a planet where the nanites have been seeded in the environment, we'll have access to that entire network around the world. We can bring nanites with us—like your bracelet—to use on the go, but the actions will be limited by how much you have."

"If the Korani nanites are thinking machines, then what's the primal energy?" Evan asked.

"As I've said, it is a natural force," Sam explained. "But it's more like an *entity* has fused with you as its corporeal host."

"Uh…"

"Do not be alarmed, Evan, it won't harm you," Sam continued. "The Korani nanites are a technological imitation of this more ancient power, and you are one of very few who've ever been granted the ability to wield it. While the artificial nanites can be brought with you anywhere, the trade-off is their limited scope. But the planets with the primal energies are special. And for someone Touched on one of those worlds, there's a near-limitless well of power at your disposal. The Korani tech can never come close to that potential."

"I think we need to collect some physical samples from those worlds, Sam," Anya suggested.

"That would be beneficial," the AI agreed. "It would also assist with the ongoing research into the signals we've observed and allow a multifaceted analysis of the planets' compositions and broad-spectrum features."

As she made the research plans with Sam, Anya noticed Evan pulling into himself. It was only her disciplined scientist mind that offered her emotional separation between the facts and lived experience. Objectively, they were facing a challenging reality.

"A lot of these findings are still preliminary, so we should be careful who we tell, Evan," Anya said.

"Yeah. I… I need a minute."

— — —

Evan walked out into the hallway, his head spinning. He'd known his life had been forever changed when he received the bracelets on Temple World, and that had been confirmed by the encounter on Pavia. But what Anya and Sam had just told him gave a whole new perspective to those experiences. Moreover, it made him drastically rethink the capabilities of his enemies—and the power his allies might wield.

The primer was a gateway. A few drops of the serum would unlock a connection to the Korani tech, but that would only make them want more. If anyone realized what high doses would enable, an ambitious person would want to take that to the extreme. Evan had to look no further than the senior members of the Santano family. No doubt the Syndicate's ruthlessness had—at least in part—been born through escalating desire for that power.

With every person they gave the primer, they would be cracking open the door. He had no concerns with someone like Anya or Samor, but Zaris or Roman…

Anya came out from the lab. "Evan, hey. I probably shouldn't have dropped all of that on you like that."

"It's not you, Anya." He wiped his hands down his face. "What do I tell Conroy? What do we do about the promises made to Roman and Zaris?"

"We can't police the actions of every human in this galaxy. I say we let people be accountable for themselves, and if they break the social contract, you enforce it. The good people will keep any bad seeds in line, just like with normal life. Plus, you have something none of them will."

"But is that enough?"

"At some point, we've gotta take a chance. I know I'd rather be known as someone who honors my promises than a person who uses others and keeps the spoils for myself."

He nodded. "I guess that settles it."

— — —

Conroy wasn't often intimidated by other people, but the way Zaris was staring at him was downright unnerving. She wasn't being menacing, exactly—just intent in a way that made it clear she wouldn't leave until she had what she'd come to collect.

A way out came in the form of Evan's arrival. Anya was with him, and she carried a small satchel.

"Ready to debrief?" Conroy asked.

"We'd like a word first," Evan replied.

Conroy brought them to his office. "What can't be said in front of the others?"

"I've analyzed the serum, and its properties aren't what we'd thought," Anya said. "It's not just a primer, it's a controller in high doses—similar to Evan's command bracelet."

"Roman confessed that there are high-up members in the Syndicate who've unlocked those abilities," Evan added, "but they've lacked the tech to do much with them. But once we go down this path, and have access to more artifacts, it's going to set a new kind of arms race in motion."

"You said the facility was destroyed, so there's not much Lux to go around," Conroy assessed. "Do you have enough for any of this high dosing?"

"I took a full vial, and I got the effects. I don't know how long that will last," Anya revealed. "Each vial is about twenty primer doses. How that gets divvied up, and what we keep in reserve, is what's up for debate."

"We wanted to talk to you first because you're the leader," Evan continued. "There is an open question, though, of if we tell everyone how many doses are available. The promises made to Zaris and Roman were for a *primer* dose, nothing more."

Conroy leaned against his desk. "Thank you for coming directly to me with this information. I propose we keep this particular card close to the chest. Did you bring all the vials with you?"

"Only four." Anya held up the satchel. "We have a few others in a safe place."

"How many others?"

"Enough to give us options in the future," Evan replied. The response was frustratingly vague.

He doesn't want me to know the exact number. Conroy considered forcing the issue, but he had little leverage. Evan and Anya were in control of the ship and the Lux supply. They had been loyal thus far, and any attempt to exert too much control was not likely to end well for him. He was better off treating them as partners rather than subordinates. *I've been asking Evan to step up. I need to let this play out.*

Conroy framed a proposal he hoped they'd find agreeable while still making it sound like he was driving the strategy. "Anya, I would like you to be responsible for administering doses. Keep a log of who has one, and their crew. We'll tell Zaris she can pick up to thirty-nine of her crew, if she wants— but don't mention anything beyond the primer dose. I will, likewise, take two vials to distribute among my people. It will look equitable, and we'll give Roman his due. Keep the others safe and in reserve. If we find the right people, or if we need to elevate anyone, we'll have the supply to do it."

Anya and Evan exchanged a look. "I can do that," Anya acknowledged.

"One more thing," Evan said. "If she's going to be working around people who've received the primer, I'd also like to take a short trip off-world with Anya to get her one of these." He held up his wrist with the command bracelet.

Anya looked a little surprised at the suggestion. "You sure?"

"Time to lean in."

Am I driving, or am I just along for the ride? Conroy sensed his control slipping, but that might not be a bad thing. The shape of his plans was changing by the day, but this pair could deliver a future he'd never dreamed possible. "Sounds like a worthwhile investment. I don't suppose you'd share the location of that planet with me?"

"I need to keep some of my own cards, sir."

Conroy smiled. "You have quite the political future ahead of you, Evan. One of these days, you'll see it for yourself."

26

ROMAN EYED HIS open cell door, trying to assess the trap. "Is it the real thing, or is this just a dramatic way of killing me?"

"You wanted the Lux. Your information helped us get it. This is the primer dose you're owed." Evan offered him the syringe again.

Roman ignored it, instead leaning against the back wall of his cell. "Ah, yes. Just the primer. And you'll never allow me to have any more."

"It's too soon to say 'never'."

"Close enough. You'll say you're following through on your end of the deal by giving this to me. But the reality is that it's a taunt."

"You don't want it? Fine." Evan dropped his extended arm and turned to walk away.

"No, wait!" Roman called after him. "I do want it. But I know that there's more going on here. What's this really about?"

"Why do you care?"

"Because I'm in the middle of this, whether I like it or not. The Commonwealth is going to war, isn't it? And the Syndicate is on the opposite side, which puts me in a pretty unique spot.

And you're giving me the Lux now with the hope that I'll see you as the 'good guys' and be a helpful informant in your fight. Am I close?"

Evan set his jaw as he searched Roman's face. "If you really meant it when you said you wanted to bring the Syndicate down, then now is your time."

Roman crossed his arms. "Okay, say we start with the one primer dose. What gets me more?"

"How about this… If you deliver us Marcus, a whole vial is yours."

"Only one?"

"How many would it take?" Evan's expression was earnest enough for Roman to take the question seriously.

"Three. And more once we get our own production running."

Evan nodded. "Done."

"That easy?"

"If you earn it, you get it. You know what I can—and will— do to you if you step out of line."

Roman remembered all too well the feeling of having the alien tech ripped from him, and the subsequent loss of his abilities had forever changed his outlook. If he ever got that power back, he would respect it. "If I accept, where do we go from here?"

"For starters, we can get you moved somewhere more comfortable."

Roman eyed the open door again. "Under guard, I imagine?"

"For now. But that has to be better than staying in here."

For the last few nights, Roman had dreamed of little else other than getting out of the cramped, dim place. He hesitated now, not because he didn't want the Lux or because he was having second thoughts about taking on Marcus. This was a defining moment in his life—a major step to becoming his own man, no longer confined to the shadow of a family where destiny was assigned and life was subject to approval.

He met Evan's gaze. "It was stupid of you to not kill me the first time we met, but I'm glad you didn't."

"I'll be honest, Roman. I left you alive that night in the forest because I was afraid of your family. When I spared you again, it was because I wanted you to suffer rather than get the easy way out. Though others may disagree with those decisions, that's what made sense to me at the time. And maybe you *shouldn't* get this second chance. But I want a future for the people of the Commonwealth where there's a way out. Plenty of people get into bad spots, and they keep slipping deeper and deeper into the dark. Are you deserving of redemption? Maybe not. But you might be. And if *you* are, then that's a hell of a message to send to other people. I hope you'll take that opportunity to heart."

Two weeks ago, Roman would have laughed at the little speech. That kind of idealism had had no place in his life, and he certainly never intended to be a role model to anyone. However, the words resonated with Roman now in a way he hadn't expected. He *did* want to break the system that had made him this way. There might not be a way out for him— not really—but preventing others from suffering the same fate would be a start.

Roman rolled up his sleeve. "Marcus for three vials."

"It's a deal," Evan agreed, handing him the syringe. "Never thought we'd get here."

"Me either."

Roman injected the primer dose of Lux. It spread warmly through his veins. Immediately, his senses sharpened.

Evan was practically glowing in front of him. Roman had felt that way in Marcus' presence before, but it was different with Evan—he wasn't being controlled by fear or intimidation. Evan had *real* power, beyond anything Roman had witnessed.

I chose the winning side. Roman took a deep breath and let it out as a satisfied sigh. "Thank you."

"Make it worthwhile."

"I will. One man's hero is another man's villain. I spent years telling myself Marcus wasn't a monster, but I know the truth now. We'll stop him. Together."

— — —

Zaris shielded her eyes from the afternoon sun as she walked through the camp. It was crowded and messy with more people coming down from the orbital ships, eager to get time on the garden paradise world. Word had spread among the crew. Many, like Zaris, had never been to a truly natural planetary environment before, and curiosity had spiked requests for a planetside post.

With the new supplies, it was now feasible to build up a settlement. However, they were tight on lodging for now, and Zaris had no solution. She decided that was someone else's problem. Like Conroy. He was supposed to be the leader, right?

Zaris checked the time. Evan was late to their meeting. He still owed her the primer shot, and she wouldn't release the remaining supplies pilfered from the Syndicate's Rilen base until she got it.

At last, she spotted Evan emerging from the underground bunker. And he wasn't alone.

Roman? She had to do a double-take to be sure.

The man looked like he'd been living in a cave for a month,

with hair that had grown longer than the intended length for the style and stubble that more closely resembled a beard. She'd only encountered Roman briefly during the fight with Evan, shortly after her arrival on Aethos. But the man she'd seen then was arrogant and vicious. She couldn't imagine how there'd been such a complete transformation to his demeanor in a short time. Then again, it wasn't so long ago that she'd threatened to shoot Evan.

She sauntered up to them. "My, my. Where have they been keeping you?" she asked Roman.

"I was locked up."

"That doesn't sound very fun."

"It wasn't."

She tsked. "I guess that's what you get for killing a bunch of people."

"I get the impression you're no saint, either."

Evan sighed. "You two arguing is the *last* thing I need right now."

"Just lighthearted ribbing. Right, Roman?"

He looked up at the sky and took a deep breath. "Yeah."

"What's the deal? Are you out of lockup for good now?" Zaris asked.

"Roman and I are working on an arrangement," Evan revealed. "No free rein, but Anya has convinced me there's benefits to fresh air. So here we are."

"Well, you're late for your appointment with me." Zaris tapped her foot impatiently.

"Sorry, right. Roman, would you like to give her the rundown?"

"Me?"

"You know more about the primer than anyone. What should a person know before receiving it?"

"The lines between yourself and the life around you will blur. Most places, you won't notice anything at all. But here… You can be much more than your individual self. But you need to let it in. I spent a lot of time fighting it, and I missed the beauty. Open your mind, and you'll be rewarded."

Evan nodded his approval. "I couldn't have said it much better myself." He motioned toward the bunker. "Let's get Zaris her dose, and we can do your yard time after, Roman."

The three of them headed inside.

"How do you two know each other?" Roman asked.

"We met while I was working undercover as Alex."

"I was managing cargo runs on Constella," Zaris explained. "I think you and I may have exchanged messages at some point."

"Yeah, I believe we did. But never met in person. I'd remember that." He gave her an appreciative once-over.

Zaris couldn't help liking the attention, no matter who was dealing it. "Well, we've met now."

He flashed a disarming smile. "So we have."

Evan's jaw was slack and his brows were drawn in bewilderment—or possibly disgust, Zaris couldn't tell. "We'll call that good on the introductions. Let's get you that shot, Zaris." He motioned them down the bunker corridor, taking up position behind Roman.

"Did Alex make a mess of your life, too?" Roman asked Zaris as he walked.

"Not too much. I hadn't seen him for several months before I found out who he really was. I didn't catch much blowback for being a former associate."

"Lucky." Roman scoffed. "Alex is the reason I ended up here."

"Look at that, me bringing people together," Evan said sarcastically.

They reached a closed door with the word 'Medical' written overhead.

Inside, the room was like any facility Zaris had seen on a ship. Four treatment beds were along the back wall, and there were various cabinets for storing supplies and medication.

Evan went to one of the cabinets in the back corner and unlocked it. He returned with a syringe containing a small amount of shimmering liquid. "Last chance to change your mind."

Zaris shook her head. "I'm all in." She bared her arm.

Evan injected the serum near her bicep. There was only a slight pinch, and then heat spread through her.

"Whoa." She steadied herself on a nearby console.

"It'll pass. Give it a minute," Roman said.

The burning faded into a pleasant warmth, and soon after she felt nothing at all. No, there *was* something. She was acutely aware of Evan's presence. Even when she wasn't looking at him, she could tell he was there. And the two nanite bracelets he wore now had a subtle buzz to them.

"This is so weird," she murmured.

Evan smiled. "Welcome to the other side."

27

ANYA HAD BEEN through an extraordinary number of changes over the last few weeks, and somehow finding herself telepathically connected to a sentient alien starship was still not the most life-altering experience. In her recent journeys on the *Asamar*, Sam had become a friend. She trusted the AI to be respectful of her needs.

In fact, she'd taken everything related to the alien tech in stride. The revelations about the Korani had initially been a shock, but the subsequent discoveries felt... right. She'd dedicated her entire career to seeking out exotic new lifeforms on different planets, so she'd started to treat the search for remaining Korani as a scientific expedition. It helped her remain objective.

However, it was difficult to maintain that objectivity in the face of her personal experience. The subject of her study was now inside her body and her mind. In any other circumstances, she would have handed over the investigation to a neutral third party. But there *was* no one else she could turn to in this case.

She looked down at the new nanite bracelets on her wrists: a golden and blue pair like Evan's, though both were presently matte metal in their dormant state. Their short trip to Temple

World had been like visiting the place for the first time—*feeling* it in a way she hadn't been able to before receiving the primer. It was both wondrous and terrifying.

Evan was right, this power weighs on you. What in the planets was I thinking injecting that stuff without knowing what it would do to me? Of course, the simple answer was she *didn't* think it through. She'd been desperate, and it had been a life-or-death split-second decision. But the fact that she was here now to have this debate with herself suggested that she'd made the right choice; she was alive.

Moreover, the personal brush with the Korani tech had fueled her interest to learn everything she could about the technology. There were still many outstanding questions about the alien worlds with the strange energy readings and signals. And they needed to know more than they could determine from a distance.

She'd recruited Garet again to assist with prepping a larger research project. Between his communications knowledge, her biological understanding, and Sam's fabrication abilities, they'd devised a series of specialized probes that could be sent out to study the alien worlds. To draw real conclusions, they needed physical data and a longer-term look at the planets' properties.

"I think I've got the signal sensitivity dialed in," Garet said from his workstation in Anya's lab.

"Nice!" Anya re-checked her own work. "I'm just finishing up the bio-filter protocols—"

A chime sounded. Sam's voice filled the room. "Incoming transmission. Anya, it's your father."

That can't be good. She stayed focused on her screen. "Ignore it."

"You should answer," the AI advised in her mind. *"Given*

your growing concerns, additional interactions will yield further data for analysis."

The telepathy caught her off-guard. *"Gee, thanks, Sam. What a great way to think about chats with my dad."*

"After your last meeting, you suggested it wasn't him—"

"I know. I just…" She sighed. "Sorry, Garet, I need to take this call."

"Oh, sure."

"Double-check the frequency ranges on the background noise recorder, okay?"

"I'm on it."

Anya ran to the room she'd set up as an office. Since the furnishings were modeled after generic human designs, the space wouldn't stand out as an alien spaceship on camera. Sitting down at the desk, she checked a preview of her camera and adjusted her hair.

"Sam, record everything, okay?"

"Yes, Anya."

She accepted the vidcall. "Hi, Dad." She had to force the words out when she saw the blank eyes staring back at her through the screen.

"I didn't like how we left our last conversation," Julian said. "I understand your caution, Anya, but I can't protect you if you won't talk to me."

Jumping right to it, then. She took a measured breath. "Why should I need protection at all?"

"The naïve act is unbecoming. How about some honesty?"

"Sure. Who are you?"

"What?"

"I don't think you're actually my father—at least not his free mind. Who are you, puppeteer?"

"I'm your father, Anya. Who else would I be?"

She didn't know how to respond without giving away the tells she'd identified during their previous interaction. "What's happened to me... and you knowing about it... I didn't realize that's really what you did for your job."

"With some professions, it's better a parent shield their child from the truth about what they do at the office. Politics is one."

"What have you been hiding?"

"The dark reality that real power lies behind the scenes. Whatever political machinations you see playing out are all theater. Decisions will be made and actions taken before most people know anything has happened. I'm sure you've heard the old adage—it's easier to beg for forgiveness than ask permission," the man who looked like her father said.

"That sounds like a terrible strategy for governance."

"On the contrary, that's how everything has been run for as far back as anyone can remember. The 'will of the people' is a carefully curated illusion."

She crossed her arms. "So that's what you've been doing my whole life? Pulling these strings from the shadows?"

"I'm not a decision-maker, Anya. I simply package information for others to use as a guide."

"If what you tell them shapes their decisions, then that means you help set the course."

"I suppose I do, yes."

"That seems like the most powerful role of all."

"Maybe it is. But few will ever know my name."

Is this really who he was all along? Did I not know him at all? Anya may as well have been transported to an alternate reality. Nothing making sense, and she was having difficulty breathing. "I won't be a pawn in your game."

"The pieces are already in motion."

"Fine. You say I'm a part of this, so tell me my part. Why should I back Rostov instead of Conroy?"

"Thank you for finally admitting you are with him."

Anya hadn't intended to make that slip. Nothing she could do about it now. "Why shouldn't I be?"

Julian nodded thoughtfully. "I can understand the appeal of his message. You always had a soft spot for the downtrodden—and the victim of an attempted assassination, forced into exile by a tyrant makes a compelling narrative. But I'm sure you remember the reports."

"I do. But that doesn't make it true. And I definitely have questions about the guy who ordered the hit."

"Did Conroy tell you that was Rostov's doing?"

"Yes."

Julian chuckled and shook his head. "Conroy orchestrated that stunt himself, Anya. He knew he was facing a losing no-confidence vote, and he went underground before he could be arrested. He was going to sell out the people of the Commonwealth."

"See, it seems like that's actually what *Rostov* is doing."

"Rostov is building partnerships with important business and industry leaders who've been neglected by past chancellors. The system has been broken for a long time, and he's finally taking a stand to do things differently."

How can I know who's telling the truth? Everything she'd been told by both her father and Conroy was to further their own case. She hadn't actually been able to independently verify anything with Evan. They'd simply decided to back Conroy because he was on the opposite side of the Syndicate—a known bad actor. But they didn't know the extent of Rostov's actual relationship with the Syndicate. Was it possible he wasn't the ruthless monster Conroy had made him out to be?

Julian eyed her through the screen. "I know it's just one person's word against another. I think this might help."

A file transfer popped up on Anya's screen. There were two encrypted attachments.

"You know how to get in touch when you're ready to talk. Be careful, Anya. I hope to have you home again soon."

She could only nod faintly.

When the vid feed cut, she collapsed back in her chair. *What the hell was that?*

The files might offer some answers. "Sam, can you analyze these for malware?"

"The attachments pass all safety inspections," the AI replied. "One is a video file and the other is a document. Would you like me to open them?"

"Yes."

The files loaded. The document appeared to show a written agreement between Conroy and a private company that sold out the Commonwealth citizens for Conroy's personal financial gain. Likewise, the video showed Conroy meeting with the head of that company.

Are these real? If authentic, they directly contradicted what Conroy had told them. *Who's lying? Have we been played?*

"Sam, what's your take on these?"

"These files are copies, so I cannot conduct a proper analysis to determine authenticity. However, I detect no obvious signs of forgery."

That didn't mean anything, but it was enough to twist Anya's stomach. "Thanks, Sam. I'll need to talk about this with Evan."

She left her office in a daze. *I can't rely on my own family anymore. How did I get to a place where I trust an alien starship's AI more than my own dad?*

Though she wanted to reflect more on the conversation, she still had other work to finish. Reluctantly, she returned to her lab.

Garet looked her over with concern. "Is everything okay?"

"There's nothing for you to worry about," she said. "Let's just get this done."

They finished programming the parameters for the probes, and Anya reviewed the destinations with Sam—keeping the location details just between the two of them. While Garet had been a useful collaborator, Anya kept his knowledge of the project to only what was necessary for him to perform his tasks.

"I think we're all set." She pushed back from her workstation. "Thanks, Garet. You've been really helpful."

"I should be thanking *you*!" he exclaimed. "This is by far the coolest project I've ever worked on."

Anya couldn't help smiling at his enthusiasm, despite the other problems with her father weighing on her mind.

"I will launch the probes now," Sam told them.

Garet beamed. "I can't wait to get the results!"

They wouldn't have the data for a week or two, since they wanted to collect more than just a momentary snapshot, but there was plenty to keep Anya busy until then.

She escorted Garet off the *Asamar* and then headed to the lounge on the upper deck.

Entering the common room, she was surprised to find Evan there with Zaris—and Roman. "Um… hi?" She gave Evan a questioning look.

"They've both received the primer. I was re-introducing them to Sam."

"Ah." She'd been hoping for quiet time alone, watching a favorite movie from her childhood, to reflect on the conversation with the man claiming to be her father. Dealing with guests—especially *those* guests—was an unwelcome turn.

Evan immediately picked up on her discomfort. "Tour is over for today. I'll take you back, Roman."

Roman and Zaris headed for the exit, but Evan hung back. "What's wrong, Anya?" he asked.

"I'll explain when you get back." Despite all the uncertainties she was facing, at least he was one person she didn't doubt.

— — —

Evan returned to the *Asamar* after escorting Roman to the bunker, finding Anya sprawled on a couch in the ship's lounge. She was eating a bowl of chips and had an animated vid on the screen with talking animals in an overly saturated color palette. He didn't recognize the specific movie, but it was clearly something for kids.

She barely glanced from the screen when he entered. He sat down on the couch, and she repositioned to lay her head on his lap.

"What happened?" Evan asked softly.

Anya turned down the volume on the movie. "Well, the good news is we got those research probes launched, so that's my win for the day. But on the flip side, my dad called again. He basically told me that everything Conroy has told us is a twisted version of the truth and he's the real bad guy."

"Of course Rostov would say that."

"But what do we really know for certain, Evan? How do we know we picked the right side?"

Evan mulled over those same concerns on a daily basis. "I've decided that I'm going to fight for the future I want to have. And right now, I have Conroy's ear. If he shuts me out, it'll be on to the next person who'll listen."

"I guess that's fair," she murmured.

"Show me what he sent."

Anya presented a contract document and then played a video. The message in both was clear—but that made them suspicious. It was certainly the kind of material someone might manufacture to smear the opposition.

"What else did your father say?" Evan asked.

"Pretty much admitted to being the advisor to galactic supervillains. I recorded it, so you can experience it in its full glory."

"Oh, excellent."

Anya sighed, and it came out a groan. She sat upright. "We can watch it later. I need a distraction—something that isn't related to galactic politics."

Evan got up and extended his hand to her. "I have an idea."

She took his hand, and he helped her up. "Oh?"

"A while back, you presented a hypothesis. I think we should test it," Evan said.

"Which one?"

"About the way the nanites are integrated into the natural environment of Aethos. And our ability to control them."

"What would be the test?" she asked.

"Everyone is pretty miserable with the current camp setup, right? I keep thinking about how Sam has modified the *Asamar* to suit us. What if we were able to build out more infrastructure on Aethos by having it build itself?"

Anya's eyes widened. "First, yes—that's a great idea. But something else just occurred to me. That city in the cavern. Everything was totally blank, right? It was weird. We saw the *Asamar* in its original state, and it's clear the Korani have furnishings and stuff. So, what if that was just the blank template, and the residents would have just, like, *thought* their interior design into existence when they moved in?"

Evan laughed. "That never would have occurred to me before, but I bet you're right. Sam, I know you're listening…"

"Yes, Anya is correct," Sam confirmed. "It also did not occur to me that you didn't realize that. In my culture, that is a standard practice, so obvious it didn't bear mentioning. What do you humans do?"

"We go shopping," Anya told the AI, prompting Evan to share a mental account of the process.

"That is highly inefficient."

"Well, you've shown us a much better way. We intend to use it."

28

"HERE?" EVAN ASKED.

Anya nodded. "Perfect."

They'd been wandering around the bunker's vicinity for half an hour trying to find the right site for their experiment. The concept was to activate the latent nanites in the environment in an attempt to reshape the natural materials into a habitable structure. The evidence of the Korani's 'grown' structures suggested it might be possible, and that made it worth trying.

With their site selected, now they just needed to figure out how to make it work.

"What… do we do?" Anya asked tentatively.

"Well, with the other tech, I've just kinda 'thought' what I wanted to happen, and it did."

"Okay, what's our design concept? Tower? Bunker?"

"Given how hot it gets during the day, I think we'd be better off with something underground. More stable temps," Evan suggested.

"I like it. Why don't we start with an entry tunnel? See how deep we can go."

"Good. Let's put it next to that rock." He pointed to a mid-sized boulder at the center of the small field.

"Thinking really hard…" Anya's face scrunched up with effort. Her new command bracelet glowed blue.

Evan took a more relaxed approach, clearing his mind of everything except the visualization of a tunnel forming in the ground. He pictured the soft dirt solidifying and packing into a concrete-like finish for structural support on the floor and walls, with a curved ceiling.

To his amazement, the ground rippled next to the rock. A depression formed, and the grass dropped away in a new opening.

Anya giggled with delight. "It's actually working!"

Evan kept his concentration, stepping forward so he could see inside the opening and shape his vision for what to do next.

The opening was a little more than a meter deep, but it was closer to a hole than a gently sloped entrance ramp. Part of the issue was that he didn't have a good mental image for the threshold. *Should there be a door? A hatch?*

Since the structure was underground and they'd experienced flash floods in the region, he realized it would need to be sealed. The boulder next to the opening might make good raw material.

"Anya, help me turn that boulder into an entryway," Evan said.

They focused on the stone. And this time, he also tried to sense Anya's mind. They joined together in a shared vision, each bringing their design concepts to a mental picture and silently agreeing on the final structure.

With that image in their minds, Evan sent out a command to the environment to make the vision a reality. The stone started to melt—not from heat, but as though it was turning to sand. Moving like liquid, the boulder flattened and then built up again next to its original position, with a flat front and a slope down the back covering the hole. A rectangular opening remained on the front vertical face, where a functional door could be fitted.

Anya grinned. "That was incredible!"

"The material moves so easily. I thought this would be more difficult."

"I'm not sure that just anyone could do this, Evan. I may have helped with the vision, but I think the command power was coming from you. I think your little communion with the planet last week might be a part of it."

"Maybe. But you're my muse."

She rolled her eyes. "Cute. Come on, we have a lot more to do."

Following the same process of forming a shared vision and then sending out the construction command, they completed a ramp down from the covered entrance until its ceiling was three meters underground.

"I think that's deep enough to help keep it structurally sound," Evan said, though it was only an educated guess. However, the solidified material after reshaping the dirt felt like stone to the touch, and he suspected it would be strong enough.

"Now we just need a layout." She frowned. "I guess we also need a plan for utilities—you know, power, plumbing. What do we do about that?"

"We can't create anything we can't envision. I don't know enough about that stuff. Maybe we can just leave some channels in the walls and floor where others could run lines?"

"Good plan."

They continued building out the underground settlement, creating a large chamber to use as a gathering place, individual cabins, washrooms, a kitchen, offices. Once they were in the flow, it was only a matter of walking down a corridor, envisioning openings, and sending off branches. Evan may as well have been in a virtual reality simulation where the program was reshaping the world to his specifications—only this was real.

Eventually, they paused their work, having built out twice the space currently occupied by the camp housing Zaris' corsairs. Evan checked the time and was surprised to see nearly four hours had passed. He'd been so immersed in the experience that it had seemed like only minutes.

"For two random humans who had no idea what they were doing, I think we do pretty good work," Anya said, placing her hands triumphantly on her hips.

"I still can't believe it was this fast and easy. Just imagine how quickly a whole building could be constructed if we have the right materials and know-how to run utilities and add finishes!"

"It's revolutionary in every way, Evan. And if we could do all this on our first try, how much more intricate can you get with more practice?"

"Something tells me we're going to find out."

— — —

Conroy slid his fingers across the smooth stone-like wall that had been dirt less than a day before. "I still can't believe you made this."

"We meant to just test it out," Evan replied, "but it was working so well that we just kept going."

"We can easily fit everyone in here. You really went all out."

"It needs finishing, of course."

"All manageable. You've given us a big head start."

The demonstration had shown what was possible with the Korani tech, and it was even more incredible than Conroy had imagined. One of his biggest internal debates had been whether or not to take the primer himself. It had always been his intention to take it, from the sample that his team had smuggled onto the *Stratum*. However, that was before he'd seen the effects up close. It changed a person. That would never have been evident back in the core worlds, away from the alien technology. But here on Aethos, a world *saturated* in the ancient tech, he didn't trust himself to remain objective.

Rostov did have a valid point about this technology. Conroy understood the power of it, now better than ever. But while Rostov's motivations for keeping the tech in the hands of a select few stemmed from a desire to control, Conroy wanted to prevent it from being abused. There was an important distinction between the two approaches, though an outside observer might conflate them. Conroy would have to work every day to show that he didn't want to keep that power for himself; intentions were meaningless without the support of demonstrable action.

"We need to talk about what happens next," Evan said.

"Yes, we do." They'd secured food, weapons, and the other supplies they'd need to support their population of rebels in the coming fight against Rostov's forces. Now, they had a place where they could settle in. But they needed to push beyond Aethos.

Evan met Conroy's gaze. "Sir, I don't want to tell you how to run things, but you have decisions to make."

Conroy tilted his head. "I'd love your thoughts on the matter."

"Look, I don't have the whole picture here—"

"You have enough. Please, share your perspective."

Evan took a deep breath and let it out. "The way I see it, you need to decide what you're willing to do to get to your goals. One option is to stay on the strictly legal path, following all proper channels. You can present your case, try to win favor, and hope for the best. Or you can make a show of force—lead through might rather than words. But the thing is that no private militia can match the strength and resources of the full UPDF. However, there might be an opportunity to magnify the impact of an individual fighter."

"Meaning?"

"Look at what Anya and I were able to do in an afternoon. We have more Lux. We could have a whole team of people who can use the tech."

"That is very intriguing... But the Syndicate could still beat our numbers."

"Yes. But I know where to get more of the nanites. They don't."

Conroy eyed him. "I thought you were able to do this because of the nanites already in the environment?"

"Yes, here on Aethos. But the command power is useless without having those nanites to do the work. This bracelet," he held up his arm, "is a reserve supply. I can get more, and we can select others. Between breaking down locked doors and reshaping things, that's a massive tactical advantage— especially since the Syndicate's main supply of the Lux was destroyed."

"We don't have that much," Conroy pointed out.

"Say we did have more. How would we pick the right people to receive a larger dose?"

Conroy got the distinct feeling that Evan and Anya had

more than 'a few' extra vials in reserve. "An interesting thought exercise I'd like to give proper consideration."

Evan nodded. "We'll be waiting."

"I almost have the final piece I've been waiting for. Then there'll be no stopping us."

— — —

Tobin read over his new instructions for the second time. He wiped his clammy palms on his pants. *Conroy keeps telling me we're at the end, and then he wants more.*

With each subtle act of sabotage and subterfuge, Tobin's life could be over. Rostov might keep him alive long enough to interrogate, but Tobin would no doubt be wishing for a swift death that whole time. He couldn't help but face that reality, given the dangerous path he walked. But he'd known those risks when he'd agreed to be Conroy's inside man, and he couldn't back away from the assignment now.

Conroy's latest request was for Tobin to orchestrate an info leak and trace the data trail. The chancellor had indicated that Julian Rojas was a person of interest in a larger investigation, and he wanted to know more about that communication network.

Though Julian's consultancy was based on Praxis, he had an office in the capital's administrative annex building. Tobin had been to it on one of his previous research projects for Conroy, but it had been more than a year. He only vaguely remembered the location.

Tobin brought up the directory and located the office. Given the size of the administrative complex, it would be a solid half-hour walk to get there. He'd need to have everything ready in advance.

The assignment was to seed fake information and see who repeated the talking points. Julian had been on Tobin's watch list for a long time, since he was a well-known consultant and dealt with government bureaucrats at the highest level. But the most interesting aspect of his career was his ties to NovaTech. Few people ran in such powerful private sector circles, and the fact that Julian's daughter was one of the few survivors of the colony mission to Aethos added an interesting wrinkle. It all seemed *too* convenient, though Tobin hadn't worked out how Anya might have been intentionally spared; the events surrounding the crash had simply been too chaotic for there to have been an organized master plan of the demise.

Regardless, it was time to renew his interest in the Rojas family and find out how far Julian's web truly extended.

The first step was to devise the fake information to plant. It needed to be believable and close enough to the truth that it wouldn't draw suspicion when it was ultimately refuted—just the change of a minor yet distinctive detail. He settled on an early leak of the news that the new contract with a shipping company called the Gerhart Group had been awarded for 355 million. The actual figure was 357 million, so the reduced figure could be attributed to rounding for easy reporting. However, he knew from experience that casual mention of the amount would more likely be '350', so mentions of 355 specifically would stand out.

His plan was to drop an anonymous file about the new contract with the slightly inaccurate amount and then trace where that figure popped up. If his hunch panned out, he'd see the 355 figure quoted in other reports before the official contract for 357 was made public. And who shared that news would be very telling.

Delivering the file would be the tricky part. He'd have to

plant it from inside Julian's office so there wouldn't be a digital trace of its origins. Leaks were a fact of their current political environment, and that was the common method. Whether or not the recipient was in their office at the time offered control of either anonymity or favor-trading, depending on the needs. In Tobin's case, it was all about working in the shadows, so he needed to make sure Julian wasn't around.

Travel logs indicated that Julian was on Terrax for meetings that day, and he was scheduled to be at a working lunch for the next two hours. Perfect.

With his doctored info packet loaded on his omni, Tobin set out to the annex building.

His route took him through the park grounds, which were filled with staffers enjoying lunch outside. Crowds were good—he wouldn't stand out.

Upon reaching the annex, he took the elevator to the fifth floor and headed into the consultant's wing. Some of the offices were permanent assignments for long-term contractors—such as Julian—while a large portion of the floor was flex space for off-world visitors.

The door to Julian's office was closed. Tobin flashed his universal passkey—another of his expensive but worthwhile black market investments—to override the electronic lock on the door. It clicked open.

Except, the room wasn't empty.

A woman wearing a pencil skirt hemmed to above her knees sat with her legs crossed behind the desk, one foot bobbing in time with her tapping fingers. Her low-cut blouse showed off her endowments, the vibrant green silk fabric contrasting the dark-blue of her skirt while highlighting her calculating eyes. With styled brows and her red hair swept into a sophisticated bun with ringlets framing her face, she had the striking beauty of a refined predator poised to attack.

Tobin froze in the doorway. "Sorry, I didn't realize anyone was here."

"No one should be," she replied with a voice as cunning as her looks. "So, why are *you*?"

"I came to drop off a message."

"Oh?"

"Not to you. Why are you in Julian's office?"

"I'm his assistant."

"No, you aren't. I've met him."

"I didn't say it was in an *official* capacity." She smirked.

The way she drew out the word 'official' had a distinctly sensual quality. She was having an affair with Julian, which was not uncommon in those high-end political circles. However, those relationships were usually kept secret and private; having a mistress so boldly sitting behind the desk in an otherwise empty office wasn't normal, and it certainly wasn't acceptable.

"As a government official, I must insist you tell me your business here and how you gained access to this office," Tobin said.

The woman smiled sweetly. "This workspace is reserved for consultants and non-government contractors. I don't need to answer your questions."

She was clearly trouble—and she was also correct. Short of calling security, he couldn't compel her to do anything. And involving security would mean explaining why he was there, himself, which was untenable for a number of reasons.

Instead, Tobin pulled out his omni. He really did have information to deliver, though he'd wanted it to be anonymous. He could still covertly plant that bait while delivering another message to make this visit look intentional.

"Please pass on the following to Julian," Tobin said,

sending a report file to the desk.

The information popped up on the screen and the woman glanced at it with mild interest. "An audit report? How riveting."

"Rostov wanted to make sure each of our consultants and contractors received a copy. You know, for official record purposes."

"Yes, of course."

While she was reading the summary at the top of the report, Tobin planted the information he'd come to deliver, dropping it into a file subdirectory using his established link to the desk. He also captured an image of the woman, curious to find out who she might be. "Thanks for your help," he said.

"My pleasure."

I highly doubt that. He left the office and disappeared into the anonymous sea of staffers once again.

29

Rostov set down his cutlery and leaned back in the padded restaurant booth seat, patting his stomach. "Don't tell my doctor. But what's life without a little indulgence?"

Julian smiled and nodded. "My feelings exactly, sir."

"Now," Rostov sat up straighter and folded his hands on the tabletop, "I believe you had a proposal for me?"

"Yes. I think we need to get ahead of the Thorn situation," Julian said, using the coded term they'd established for Conroy so they could speak openly in public settings.

"What's the latest?"

"I've confirmed—at least to my satisfaction—that Anya is with him. Which means that Thorn now has transportation, and I don't expect him to stay in his current roost for much longer."

Rostov had drawn the same conclusion. Every time he thought through his options, his chest burned with frustration about the failed plans. "What do you suggest?"

"A two-pronged approach. First, we need to highlight your accomplishments and make the case for your leadership in the years ahead. Secondly—and it needs to be subtle—we need to remind the populace about why Conroy needed to be removed from power. Time has a way of softening bad memories, and his misdeeds are no longer front of mind."

The smear campaign had been effective leading up to Conroy's 'death'—enough so that very few people publicly decried his demise at the time. Rostov had been ready with further ammunition to silence his supporters, but it hadn't been needed. In fact, he'd so smoothly stepped into the chancellor role that he wondered if *anyone* had truly cared about Conroy. Of course, in the years since, he'd come to realize that all of those loyalists had simply gone underground to continue supporting Conroy when he went into hiding on Aethos. Rostov had attempted to track down the members of his informant network, but many collaborators still remained a mystery. Though he hoped there weren't too many more out there, he had no way to know.

"Saying anything negative about Conroy now would be strange, no?" Rostov asked.

Julian held up his hand and shook his head. "Hence the need for subtlety. Generally, you'd see a retrospective about a life well-lived, regardless of the person's failings. We don't lose many chancellors in office. Even the bad ones, the media will go out of their way to speak kindly of them in death. But we can't allow that now, lest people actually start thinking about him in a favorable light."

"How would you do it, then?"

"I'm thinking we set up a compare-contrast between Conroy and you. Pick the right data points where we can have a decent visual and supporting stats to make the case."

"Such as?"

"I have some thoughts I can send to your PR team. Pushing on workforce development would play well, in particular."

"All right. And where would this be shared?"

"Start with official government channels. We can pull favors with a few media personalities to get it some airtime under the guise of an actual news story. They'll know how to spin it further if we give them the right raw data. By the end, they'll regard Conroy as a disgrace to the office and you as the best chancellor ever."

"Well, I *am*."

Julian's expression faltered for a moment before turning to a broad smile. "Of course, sir! We're lucky to have you."

Rostov grunted. "I was joking, Julian. It's impolite to declare oneself the greatest anything."

"Well, yes. One of the many ways in which you know how to read the situation. And you know how it works—we'll get others to declare it for you."

"I know you have your ways—"

Julian's omni chimed. He checked the screen. "It's Elena."

The woman had a way of being around whenever business was being discussed, even if she wasn't physically present. "Answer," Rostov assented.

The face of an attractive redhead projected above the omni. "Are you still at lunch?"

"Yes. I figured it must be important or you wouldn't have interrupted."

"It might be. You just had a visitor."

"Where?"

"Your office. And good thing, too, because I was about to perish from boredom."

Rostov sighed. Julian had been getting a little too friendly with his playmate, and this wasn't the first time she'd made a jab about being left out of a meeting. She'd been encroaching more and more on Julian's work, so Rostov had explicitly excluded her from this strategy session. Julian seemed like a different person around her.

"Did this visitor give you a name?" Julian asked.

"No. He looked early-thirties, professional. But he did leave a report." She manipulated something off-camera. "Looks like Tobin Mori."

Rostov motioned for Julian to include him in the vidcall. "What did he say?"

"Just some boring audit information," Elena whined.

The woman really was insufferable the moment she opened that pretty mouth. "Show me," Rostov said.

The vidcall view changed to include the top-sheet of a financial audit for the Commonwealth's transportation contractors. While there was nothing unusual about that information—and everything had passed inspection—it was strange that Tobin would provide that report in person to Julian, of all people.

What is he up to? The man had a knack for sneaking around, which was a skill Rostov was always keen to exploit. But he didn't like the prospect of that ability being used against him.

"Thank you, Elena." Rostov reached over and ended the vidcall. "Julian, find out if Tobin did anything else. Come straight to me with your findings."

"Yes, sir."

"And Julian… Don't get too close to her."

"It's not serious."

"Not for you, maybe, but I think she's getting attached. I can't abide that."

Julian nodded. "Understood, sir."

—   —   —

Marta had never cared for the facility on Aegis-37, but it was perfect for her current needs: private, secure, and long forgotten.

Her research team had started the recommissioning process for the old facility's refinery. The raw pavite first needed to be purified and then run through processors to adjust its magnetic charge. It was a similar approach to creating magnets—something the Syndicate had stumbled upon accidentally while doing exploratory mining on Pavia several decades ago. They'd refined the process to extract and treat pavite, but there was no substitute for that raw material. Finding another supply would take their plans to the next level, but that was only aspirational.

The outdated lab on Aegis-37 was only a quarter of the size of the newer facility on Rilen. But limited scale or not, Marta now controlled the Syndicate's only supply of pavite, and she held the reins for what to do with it. She could think of no better use than the jump tech. With that system, they could explore additional worlds and maybe find a fresh supply of pavite that they could begin mining immediately rather than having to first dig out and stabilize the collapsed mine on Pavia.

"Sarin, what's the latest?" Marta called over the comm.

"We've already replicated our first batch of nanites. They have joined with the original swarm, so I think we're on track."

"What about the control mechanism?"

"Still working on it. That's been… tricky."

Marta had braced for that news, but it was a disappointment, nonetheless. Sarin had described the problem as the nanites 'having a mind of their own'. While the scientist had been speaking in hyperbole, Marta knew enough about the alien tech to worry that it might be a real concern. Some of the technology did seem like it chose when and how it was going to work.

The most problematic devices had been stored in a vault at the Rilen base. They'd presumably been destroyed along with the stockpile of Lux, so now maybe they'd never know if there had been an alien intelligence at work or if the tech was just finicky.

"I'm counting on you to figure out a solution," Marta said.

"Maybe if I ask it really nicely?" Sarin jested.

"You might not be too far off with that."

Sarin's eyes widened. "Yes, ma'am."

"Check in when you're wrapping up for the day."

"I will."

Marta ended the vidcall and sighed. She hated this part of any project—waiting for others to deliver and having little she could do herself.

Except, she wasn't completely cut off. Just because she was physically removed from the Syndicate's goings-on didn't mean she had to be uninformed.

She opened a secure link to the Syndicate's central network and looked for updates. There was notice of a new shipping contract that had been awarded for 350 million to the Gerhart Group—a runner outside the Syndicate's network.

Marcus had already flagged the report for follow-up. The agreement with Rostov was supposed to be that all new government shipping contracts would go through the Syndicate's subsidiaries. Why wasn't he honoring the deal?

Of course, Marcus' solution to that indiscretion would be to attack the supply convoy and either destroy or confiscate the cargo to send a message. But that was such a waste of an opportunity to send an even *stronger* message to Rostov.

"Find the contact information for the head of the Gerhart

Group," Marta requested of her assistant.

If Rostov wanted to step outside the Syndicate's network, Marta would simply expand the network to include those new players. That would make a strong statement, indeed. *You can't cut us out. We are everywhere. And you will give us what we were promised.*

— — —

Anya took a sip of warm cocoa from a mug that perfectly replicated her favorite drinkware from her university years. The flavor brought her back to a little café where she'd studied as a graduate student, with real wooden tables and a library of actual paper books for patrons to enjoy.

"Sam, you nailed it again."

"I have enjoyed exploring the sensory experiences from your memories, Anya," the AI said. "Comparing the way you and Evan perceive the same thing has granted me further insight to humanity."

Evan entered the lounge. "Oh, something smells good!"

"Sam, can you whip up a second mug of this?" Anya requested.

"Certainly."

"What is it?" Evan asked.

"Nostalgia in a cup." Anya grabbed the synthesized item when Sam finished making it and handed it to Evan.

He took a sip. "Oh, yes, that's very nice."

"Welcome to Colimore's Café and Bakery near the campus of Acadia University on Torgasi Prime. Twenty-three-year-old me spent most of my discretionary budget at the place, and I have zero regrets."

They got settled on the couch and picked out a vid to watch

while they enjoyed their drinks.

Shortly after finishing her mug, a wave of tiredness came over Anya. She snuggled against Evan, resting her head in her favorite position between his shoulder and chest. He wrapped his arm around her, adding to her sense of comfort and safety.

"It's easy to forget about everything else in the universe when I'm here with you like this," she murmured.

"I'm happy to leave all that at the door."

"I feel even closer to you than I did before."

"Telepathy will do that."

She tilted her head to look up at him. "I understand now why you were so hesitant. The power is intimidating."

"I feel better now that you have it, too. One of my biggest concerns was accidentally hurting you. That's far less likely now."

"What else is bothering you? I can feel it."

"I'd been counting on you to let me know if the power was ever going to my head. But now that we both have abilities, we could get wrapped up in it and not realize."

"We'll find a way to stay in check."

"It's not just us anymore. Zaris, Roman. Others soon."

"The two of us couldn't take on the Syndicate alone," Anya said. "The Lux and Korani tech are our edge, and we need to use it."

"For now."

Anya looked at him squarely. "Are you planning to strip the primer from the others afterward?"

"Not *planning*, but it's something I'll do if I have to. I wouldn't have shared any of the Lux if I didn't have that safeguard."

"Ah, I'd been wondering why you came around."

"But see? I'm already putting my own use of these ancient

cosmic powers above everyone else. This is how things get out of control."

"Well, I'll be the first member of your cult as you rise to become Supreme Overlord of the Universe."

"Thanks, Anya."

"But I must admit, I'll be jealous if you start collecting scantily clad sycophants."

He raised an eyebrow. "What kind of cult do you think it would be?"

Her attempt to come up with an answer that wouldn't make her sound deranged was interrupted by the chime of an incoming message. The text popped up as a notification overlay on the main screen.

"My dad again?" She sat up when she saw the sender. "What does it say, Sam?"

The AI displayed the text. It read: >>Rostov is planning a move against Conroy. He knows everything.<<

Anya frowned. "That's all it says?"

"That is the complete message," the AI confirmed.

"Not a lot to go on," Evan assessed.

Anya shook her head. "Why bother saying anything at all? This isn't helpful."

"Trying to win your trust?"

"Maybe. But it's not going to work."

Evan shrugged. "I guess we can forward it to Conroy and let him figure out what it means."

"Good plan." Anya nestled up to him again. "I'm taking tonight off from saving the galaxy."

30

CLOSE CALLS WERE becoming the norm. That didn't bode well for Tobin's survival prospects.

Who was that woman? He prided himself on maintaining a mental map of everyone's associates, and he had no idea who she might be. Though she'd been giving the impression of a vapid seductress, Tobin suspected it was all a calculated act. Julian should be smarter than to fall for that, so it was strange he'd keep her around.

Tobin hurried back to his office, eager to analyze the image he'd captured of the woman. He had a secure console in his office where he could run the search without creating any flags in the system.

The pounding of construction noise overhead added to his growing tension headache as he loaded the image and started the trace. Strangely, nothing came up in the standard database that cataloged all licenses and passports. Either she'd had surgery to change her face or her identity had been scrubbed, both of which were extremely expensive undertakings. It was almost next to impossible to function on a day-to-day basis without at least one ID document, so she had to have some identifier with a face similar enough to pass basic inspection.

Tobin instructed the computer to expand the search to a near-match from identical-match to see if any prospects popped up. This time, he got thirty-seven matches.

He was able to quickly weed out two dozen of them based on height or other characteristics that weren't captured in his covert photo. He fanned out the profiles of the remaining prospects to see if any of them were a match.

One by one, he whittled down the files until only the most likely candidate remained. Her physical appearance wasn't an exact match, but when he saw her biographical details, there was no doubt in his mind that she was the one.

Elena Cordova. Second cousin to Marcus Santano and a known associate of the Noche Syndicate.

Well, shit.

Tobin was too overwhelmed to move. She'd seen his face. She knew he had come under suspicious circumstances. She'd tell Julian, and Julian would tell Rostov. Worse, she might tell the Syndicate.

That's it. I'm finished.

If he stuck around any longer, he'd be captured or killed. That was the reality. To have any chance of making it out alive and free, he needed to run. Immediately.

Will I ever be able to come back? The only possibility would be if Conroy succeeded. Once he was back in charge, Tobin would have earned himself an enduring role in the administration. But failure would mean a life of exile. *At least I'll finally be free of this endless construction zone.*

He took a moment to look around the space, committing the details to memory. Not all of the memories were good, but they represented a major chapter in his life. Those experiences had shaped him, and he wanted to remember the important stepping stones along his path.

Though a few seconds of reflection didn't afford much introspection, he didn't have any longer. He needed to run while he still could.

Tobin pulled out his omni and brought up the hidden directory on the device, which stored the applications related to his clandestine communications with Conroy. There was also a burn app he'd hoped to never use. Now, he had no choice.

The program was designed to wipe other electronic systems within wireless communication range. While data was stored in too many places to eliminate, Tobin could at least remove his digital fingerprints from the equipment in his office. It would slow down pursuers and avoid implicating his accomplices in Conroy's web.

However, that still left the matter of getting away. He had several contingency plans, though none were a perfect fit for this unanticipated scenario. The most extreme would entail leaving directly from his office and disregarding everything from his former life. A more moderate option would be to go home, gather a few more things and his more comprehensive 'go bag', and then depart. Since he wasn't under immediate physical threat, he decided that a stop by home would be a worthwhile detour.

I knew there would be sacrifices, but it's hard to walk away from decades of life, he thought to himself with a heavy heart as he rode the elevator back to ground level.

Everything he passed now, he was potentially seeing for the last time. He believed in Conroy, but there were no guarantees he'd successfully return to power. If he didn't, living out the rest of his days on Aethos or another remote world would be an optimistic outcome. Worst case, they'd all end up dead.

No, we're going to succeed. He had to maintain a positive

vision. Otherwise, none of this was worth it.

The trek home took him on a maglev train and along several moving walkways through crowded transit centers with sculptural support beams and glass ceilings offering views of the surrounding towers. All of those public places were blanketed in cameras and other security surveillance. Trying to cover his face to avoid detection by the advanced technology was next to impossible, so he instead focused on moving quickly rather than stealthily.

Seven minutes. The timeframe was arbitrary but informed by known response times for local law enforcement. Limiting the packing time at his home to seven minutes would allow him to gather a few helpful items while beating the estimated ten-minute response window for the authorities. That was, of course, assuming they didn't deploy until he arrived home.

When he was a block away from his residential building, Tobin dipped into a doorway where he could observe his building's entrance while remaining out of sight. There were no obvious signs of the Security Corps nearby, but an ambush would be more likely than a uniformed officer waiting at the front door. As a precaution, Tobin took the side entrance.

He casually slipped through the doorway and took the stairs to his fourth-story residence. The hallways were empty and quiet. Relieved, he headed for his door.

Three meters from his destination, the stairway door on the opposite end of the hall opened. Four men wearing black suits rushed out.

Tobin ran back to the stairwell he'd just come up. But when he opened the door, racing footfalls sounded below. There was one more stairwell servicing his floor, but that would likely be covered, too. So, he went up.

The people coming up the stairs were close—maybe only a

story or two behind him. But he knew his freedom was on the line, and the surge of adrenaline sent him flying up the stairs faster than he'd ever run before.

He barely registered the burn in his lungs and legs as he dashed up two stairs at a time, heading for the tenth floor. There was a skybridge on that level, which could take him to a commercial center across the street. It was his best chance to lose his pursuers in a crowd.

Tobin reached the tenth story and burst into the hallway. The door pulled inward to the stairwell, and there was a looped handle on the hallway side. He spotted a freestanding signpost indicating the direction to the parking garage. It was thin enough to fit through the opening in the handle, so he threaded it through—positioning the ends so they would catch on the outer frame when the door was pulled inward.

Only seconds after getting it in place, a violent tug rattled the door. Tobin ran, not wanting to stick around to see if it held. Even a few seconds of lead time might give him a chance to get away.

He ran for the skybridge, darting around the few people currently crossing. As soon as he got to the other side, where the crowd picked up, he slowed his pace and tried not to stand out.

While blending in was easy to casual observers, he had the automated facial recognition systems to worry about, too. With official authorities after him, they'd be able to trace his movements each time they got a match. He needed to disguise himself enough to spoof the system.

Tobin started snatching random loose accessories from distracted passersby—a scarf, a jacket lashed to a backpack. Crime was next to nonexistent in that part of the capital, so people weren't careful about securing their items. He kept the pilfered garments hidden so they couldn't be identified on the cameras.

Next, he needed a distraction.

His route took him to an escalator. He spotted a metal water bottle dangling from the backpack worn by the woman in front of him. As they neared the bottom of the escalator, he unclipped the bottle from her pack. The metal canister clanged onto the grating of the moving stairs and started to roll down. Just like he'd hoped, the bottle continued rolling into the crowd crossing the walkway below.

People paused or side-stepped as the object rolled across their path. Tobin took the opportunity to duck down and slip on his new accessories while others bent and looked around to see what was rolling around.

As he straightened, the bottle's owner was reuniting with her lost item. Meanwhile, the momentary disruption to the movement of traffic had allowed Tobin to shift his position and change his appearance enough that it might slow down his identification.

He wove his way through the crowd until he reached a transit stop. He boarded one of the free trams, keeping his face obscured with a combination of the scarf and movements of his hands and arms. Four stops and seven kilometers later, he got off the tram and headed six blocks away to a safe house he'd set up for this kind of dire situation. It was under a completely different alias with no ties that could be traced back to his real identity. Provided he wasn't followed, he'd be able to regroup there and plan the rest of his egress from Terrax.

The house was his last best chance to get supplies that could see him safely off-world. He had a limited number of items from his work office, but missing out on the materials he had at home was a big blow. Not only that, his heart ached for the personal effects he would likely never see again. Sure, they were just 'things', but he had little to call his own in life. To lose everything... He swallowed his bitterness.

Tobin tried to walk casually across the tram boarding platform toward the exit. He was almost to the exit ramp when he spotted a Security Corps patroller coming from the other direction. He hadn't noticed Tobin yet, but it was too late to alter his course without looking suspicious and drawing attention to himself.

As they got close, the patroller didn't react at first. But then he did a double-take and fixated on Tobin. He started to reach for his communicator.

Tobin rushed forward and kicked the patroller's leg, making it look like he'd tripped. The man stumbled, trying to catch himself.

"I'm sorry." Tobin kneed the man toward the tram.

The patroller fell over the maglev tracks just as the tram accelerated out of the station.

A collective gasp of horror passed through the crowd of commuters, but no one had noticed Tobin's involvement. The cameras would, though.

Tobin joined the people who ran away from the site, doing his best to disappear into the group.

When he was close enough to the transit station exit, he took up a casual stride.

The rest of the way to his safehouse had him questioning his movements. He hadn't intended for anyone to get hurt in his escape, let alone a patroller who was just doing his job. Tobin's gut clenched at the image of the man being struck by the tram.

Should I just turn myself in? he considered. If he was only operating for himself, he might. But he answered to Conroy, and he didn't want to let the chancellor down. Being taken into custody would put the whole network at risk.

Tobin finally arrived at the safehouse and went inside through a hidden back entrance. The place was undisturbed, just like he'd left it.

He went to the basement, where a communication system was hidden inside a cabinet. It wasn't equipped for vidcalls, but he could send an encrypted text message.

There was always a chance of interception, despite his precautions, so Tobin didn't want to say anything identifying or too specific in the message. But it was critical he send a warning, and a plea for help, if he could get it.

Tobin made it simple: >>Cover blown. Need evac.<<

— — —

The text communication from Terrax dropped Conroy's heart to the floor. *I need to help him.*

If Tobin's cover was blown, they'd no longer have someone with direct access to Rostov. Though there were others within the administration, no one else was at such a high level. While Conroy had come to rely on Tobin's insights during these years away, he cared about the man more than the mission. Getting him to safety was the priority.

However, assisting in an evac would be tricky, given the distance from Aethos. Regardless of whether they used the *Asamar*, its shuttle, or paired the modular jump drive with one of Zaris' ships, an evac directly from Terrax would be too risky. Somehow, Tobin would need to get off-world to a more neutral location.

He wrote back a quick response. >>Can you move?<<
>>At safehouse. Cops at my home.<<

Conroy swore under his breath as he read the response. He didn't have a lot of useful options to offer Tobin, but there was one card he could play. >>There's a ship. Can you get to the port?<<

>>Maybe. Which one?<<

Conroy sent instructions for where Tobin could get an interstellar ship. He'd stashed it for a dire emergency, paying the berthing fees through a shell company five layers deep. He'd hoped to never need it, but Tobin was well worth activating that contingency.

>>Got it. On my way.<<

Anxious nerves gripped Conroy's chest. Tobin had received flight instruction when he was younger, so he'd be able to pilot the ship. Nonetheless, he'd still need to find a way through the security checkpoints. If he ran into trouble, there'd be no backup.

There is an option. But is it worth the risk? Only a few seconds of deliberation told him it was.

Conroy called up Evan. It was late here on Aethos, but that didn't matter.

Evan answered the call groggily. "Sir?"

"Sorry to wake you, but there's an emergency. One of my top assets on Terrax is in a tight spot and needs out. He might be able to take a ship off-world, so best case he'll need a pickup. But if he's unable to get to the ship, he'll need an extraction. He's too important to be killed or captured."

"And you want me to…?" Evan asked tentatively.

"I'd like you to take the *Mara* to retrieve him through any means necessary."

"That shuttle isn't a battleship."

"I know it—and you—can do more than meets the eye. Please. I need you to head out right away. Getting him to safety is a top priority."

Evan hesitated but eventually sighed. "Okay. Get me the info."

— — —

Evan ended the call and laid back in bed next to Anya, draping an arm over his eyes.

"It's always something, isn't it?" she said.

"I really don't like the idea of taking any of this Korani tech near Terrax."

"I wonder who this guy is that makes him so important?"

"More Conroy mystery." Evan hauled himself out of bed. His patience was running thin, but he couldn't ignore a call for help. "I should go. Did you want to come?"

"Yes, but I shouldn't. One of us should stay with the *Asamar* so there'll be backup if things get crazy."

"Good point. Don't get into too much mischief while I'm away, you two."

She smiled. "Never." She checked the clock. "And I'm hoping to be asleep the entire time you're gone."

He rubbed his eyes, feeling every minute of the hour. "Enjoy."

Evan quickly dressed and grabbed his weapons, just in case. After a kiss goodbye to Anya, he headed down to the hangar and boarded the *Mara*. The shuttle didn't have the weapons power of the *Asamar*, but its stealth features would be more useful for a covert extraction. Hopefully, Tobin would get himself to a quiet spot where Evan could pick him up without incident.

Right, like it ever works out that way. Evan powered up the shuttle.

"I am eager to see the core worlds," Sam commented as the *Mara* launched from the bay.

"I never thought I'd be going back."

"It is not a return, only a visit."

"And if it goes well, no one will know we were there."

The *Mara* breached the upper atmosphere, and the independent jump assembly came to meet them by the moon. The nanites encircled the shuttle and soon became a spinning golden blur. The stars were replaced by the ethereal tunnel outside normal space.

"I sense your anxiety, Evan," Sam commented.

"There's a lot to be nervous about. What if this guy set up a trap?"

"Then we will evade it."

The AI made it sound so easy. But they had made it this far, so that counted for something.

Since they couldn't jump straight to Terrax without the jump distortion being detected, Evan had instead set their destination for a sparsely populated system nearby where Conroy had said his contact would try to get. And even if that didn't work out, it'd be a quick jump to the capital system.

As soon as the ship dropped from hyperspace, Evan activated the stealth features.

"No communications from the contact have come through yet," Sam reported.

"It might be a while. I don't suppose you brought snacks?"

31

TOBIN WEIGHED THE pistol in his hand. The last thing he wanted was for his escape to come to more violence, but that might be unavoidable.

The docking details Conroy had forwarded him for a transport ship would mean a trek across the city followed by transit through no less than three security checkpoints. Unlike most ports that were most concerned with keeping trouble out, the capital was known for being equally strict about who was allowed to leave, considering the sensitive government information floating around Terrax and Praxis. Even flying his own ship, Tobin would be screened—and he had clearly been flagged as a person of interest or there wouldn't have been patrollers storming his residential building. Before leaving the safehouse, he needed a plan.

A handgun alone wasn't a plan, but it offered a degree of insurance. Still, he needed more to hedge his chances.

The truth was that he was ultimately dealing with people. While the entire institution could be after him, the individual players might be more reasonable. But most importantly, they would have a price.

While Tobin wasn't independently wealthy, his position as

an informant had afforded him access to a substantial discretionary spending account. While he couldn't very well hand over a suitcase full of credit chips to a checkpoint security guard, there were other ways to deliver a bribe.

He stashed the pistol under his jacket and went down to the basement where he kept the most sensitive items he'd collected over the years. A safe tucked away in the back of a storeroom held the most prized possessions, including the stash of Dupes he was after.

Tobin had heard that there was a thriving market for the Dupes in law enforcement social circles, since the devices could be used for covert data-gathering. Many Security Corps officers offered back alley private investigator work to make a little off-the-books income, and the Dupes were a perfect tool. There was a good chance that offering a set of free Dupes would get him a little favor, and it would be a lot more subtle a bribe than handing over a bag of money. But whether it would be *enough* to get off-world remained to be seen.

Tobin gathered up everything he could readily transport from the safehouse, including the drive housing the research he'd gathered through the Dupe he'd planted in Lucy's office. That he kept in his jacket pocket, but the rest he loaded into bags for easy transport.

All right, no sense delaying. He said a silent goodbye to the place and got in the car.

The initial drive was straightforward, sticking to back streets with little traffic. He was permitted to manually control the vehicle in those places. However, there was no reasonable way to get from his starting location to the spaceport without taking one of the arterial transitways, and those required tapping into the automated transit grid. That would be the first big test for his fake credentials.

His palms were sweating and his heart pounded in his ears as he waited for the automated licensing check to complete. To his relief, the light turned white above his lane, and he was permitted to proceed.

The car smoothly accelerated to the computer-controlled flow of traffic along the roadway, and he relaxed into his seat as the grid controller took over.

After twenty minutes, the car exited, and he was once again permitted manual control for his approach to the spaceport. Since he'd be ditching the car, he went to the most expensive parking lot closest to the port so there'd be less distance to carry his bags. He found the most tucked-away parking stall he could get.

Before getting out of the vehicle, Tobin put on a hat and pair of specialized glasses large enough to spoof the reference points for automated facial recognition. In retrospect, he wished he'd stored a pair at his office, but that would have been difficult to explain if they'd been discovered.

He then opened up the car's back hatch and started unloading. He'd only removed two of his five bags when he heard approaching footfalls. A patroller was heading his way— seemingly on a regular security route rather than looking specifically for Tobin, since he was moving casually and checking under vehicles.

Tobin took several slow, deliberate breaths in a conscious effort to slow his heart rate. Some patrollers wore contacts with an overlay to feed biometrics information about surrounding people, which would help identify deceptive behavior. There was no way Tobin would be able to hide all of his anxiousness, but he could channel it.

As the patroller approached, Tobin made a show of checking the time on his omni and muttering to himself about being late for his flight.

"You doing all right?" the patroller asked, eyeing Tobin's pile of bags.

Tobin sighed. "Yeah. Just been a hell of a day, you know?"

"Where you headed?"

"Aribka," he said truthfully. The neighboring system wasn't much of a destination, but it housed many of the datacenters supporting commerce in the core worlds, so it was common enough for professionals from Terrax to go there for business.

"Looks like a long stay."

"I got saddled bringing my bosses bags for him. It's not like I'm his valet, but some people, right?"

The patroller chuckled. "Yeah, I hear ya." He scrutinized Tobin's face. A shine in his eyes gave away the enhanced contacts, as Tobin had feared.

Tobin slowly slipped a hand under his jacket, ready to grab either his pistol or the supply of Dupes, depending on what happened next. He acted impatient, checking the time on his omni again. "Man, he's gonna kill me for being late."

After a few seconds, the patroller nodded. "Well, good luck. Safe travels."

"Thanks. Have a good one!"

Tobin continued unloading his bags, occasionally checking over his shoulder to make sure the patroller hadn't hung around.

Breathing a sigh of relief once he was certain the patroller had gone, he gathered up his pile of gear and headed into the port.

Being late-afternoon, the port was busy with commuter traffic. He blended into the crowd as best he could with so much luggage. The benefit, though, was a man on the run would typically be traveling light. Someone with a lot of stuff didn't come across as having anything to hide.

The berth for Conroy's transport ship was in the private airfield, bypassing the security checkpoints that would require comprehensive scans and ID verification. But entry to the field was still controlled, and it could only be accessed through one place. At the kiosk, he flashed the same credentials he'd used for the transit grid.

A light on top of the kiosk turned red.

Damn it! Tobin's pulse spiked, but he tried to keep his expression neutral.

An older woman attendant wandered over. "ID?"

Tobin handed over his alias's passport card.

The attendant waved it over the reader a second time, and the light again turned red.

"Is there a problem?" Tobin asked tentatively.

"This thing's been acting up all day," she muttered. "Are you registered with the port?"

"I have an authorization form to use my friend's ship."

"Ah, that's the problem." She made an entry on the console. "It's been flagging guest passes. I'll get you sorted, just a minute. You have that auth?"

Tobin brought up the digital certificate from Conroy naming his alias as an assigned user of the vessel.

She made another entry on her console, and the light turned white. "There you go."

"Thank you." Tobin went through the gate before it could lock him out again.

He still needed to get the ship through the planetary shield checkpoint, but he should be in the clear for a while.

Not wanting to stand out, he kept a steady but deliberate pace the rest of the way to the ship's berth. It was stored in a covered hangar filled with a mix of racers and luxury yachts, likely the weekend toys for rich politicians and businesspeople with more money than sense. His craft was far more modest— a four-person shuttle with a small cargo hold and two cabins. But as a getaway craft, generic was a lot better than flashy.

He secured his bags in the cargo area and then got settled on the flight deck.

I hope this thing still works. The exterior of the craft had been covered with a thin layer of dust, which suggested it hadn't been moved in a while. Presumably, there'd been some kind of maintenance—he hoped.

Starting up the engine, a satisfying rumble vibrated the deck. The automated checks came back clean on the front display.

All right, looking good. Next, he needed to remember how to fly. While shuttles like this more or less flew themselves, there were still proper sequences to follow and communication protocols. It'd been at least eight years since his last flight. His alias had current pilot credentials, but he needed to be convincing enough in his actions to not call that license into closer scrutiny.

With a burst of inspiration, he realized he didn't need to do it all from memory. "AIDA, bring up the flight procedures manual for civilian Class II shuttles."

The AI digital assistant displayed a set of instructions on the front screen. "Here are the flight procedures for a Class II shuttle. Would you like me to read off the steps?"

"You know, AIDA, that sounds great."

Following the computer's instructions, Tobin completed the pre-flight checklist and filed a flight plan with the port controller. A departure clearance popped up on his screen.

Okay, let's get out of here. He throttled the shuttle and lifted it into the air.

Automated stabilizers compensated for his out-of-practice handling of the controls. The shuttle cleared the hangar and quickly gained elevation.

Tobin's stomach dropped as the artificial gravity kicked in. The scene outside the front viewport darkened as the atmosphere thinned. Ahead was the distinctive shimmer of the planetary shield, which protected the world. It could only be bypassed through designated gates positioned around the planet.

He sent his flight clearance to the gate. Agonizing seconds passed while he waited for a response.

The front screen flashed: >>DEPARTURE STATUS: HOLD<<

Shit. Panic welled in his chest again.

Instructions popped up, routing him to an inspection post next to the gate. He directed the shuttle to the specified landing area.

That's why I brought the Dupes. Everything will be fine, he told himself.

As the shuttle pulled into the post, docking clamps abruptly snapped around the hull.

That's not normal! He gripped the armrests of his seat.

"Remain in your vessel," a male voice said over the comm. "Mandatory inspection."

Shit! Tobin's heart thudded in his chest. There was nowhere he could run, effectively trapped in outer space.

Thuds sounded on the outside of the hull. Through the viewport, he watched armed guards moving into position. The moment they opened the hatch, it would be over. He was carrying an unlicensed weapon, traveling under false credentials, and carrying enough top-secret clearance material to get life sentences for a dozen people.

Tobin locked the hatch and activated the shuttle's shields.

"Power down your vessel!" the voice demanded over the comm, furious.

"Sorry, can't do that."

Tobin had one hope. He brought up the comm details for his extraction contact and sent a message: >>Trapped. Get me out of here!<<

—   —   —

Evan snapped to attention as the call for help came through. "Sam, what can you tell me about that message?"

"It originated on Terrax. Based on the relays, I think it was from in space rather than planetside. I would need to get closer to get more specific."

Evan didn't want to jump into Terrax airspace, but he also couldn't very well ignore the plea for help. "This may get messy, Sam. Get ready."

"The mortal peril is very exciting."

"Easy for you to say. Most of you is safely back on the *Asamar*."

"It's not my fault that you humans are limited to existing only within your body."

Evan initiated the jump to Terrax. They were already close enough that the trip through hyperspace only lasted three seconds.

When the starscape reappeared, he immediately stealthed the shuttle again and moved its position. The initial jump arrival definitely would be noticed, but they'd still be hard to spot afterward.

"Are you there?" Evan asked over the comm, responding

using the contact credentials in the initial text message.

"They're trying to break in!" a panicked man replied. "I don't have much time."

"What's your exact location?"

Coordinates appeared on the screen. It was a checkpoint at the planetary shield.

Just fantastic. Evan swore under his breath. "On my way. Is your ship intact?"

"Yes, for now."

"Keep it that way. I'll get you free."

"How…?"

"I'll let you know when I do." Evan pointed the shuttle to the destination.

The planetary shield shimmered slightly in the starlight. Its access portals were round openings positioned at wide intervals around the planet, about thirty in total. The outpost in question was the smallest of three portals servicing the airspace above the capital. A complex metal framework surrounded the perimeter of each ring, and there was also a manned structure attached to each—effectively a space station locked in geosynchronous orbit. As a security checkpoint, the portals and stations were equipped with advanced weaponry capable of tracking and targeting threats.

While the *Mara* was a relatively small target, Evan had no doubt that the weapons systems would be capable of shooting it out of the sky. They could approach undetected thanks to the stealth tech, but as soon as they started shooting their presence would be obvious.

Consequently, he'd need to wait until the last possible moment to take action.

He brought the shuttle in close. "Sam, find our target. What's the deal?"

"The vessel is a Class II shuttle. It is currently secured by docking clamps. It is surrounded by two dozen patrollers on foot, and they are currently trying to get the outer hatch open."

The members of the Security Corps were generally solid people, and Evan didn't want to start indiscriminately shooting. He'd already taken out a lot of people in this fight, but the difference was that they'd shot at him first; these were just normal people trying to do their job.

"Can you fire a precise enough shot to disable the docking clamps without hurting anyone around them?" Evan asked.

"I cannot make that guarantee," Sam said regretfully.

"I guess it'll be on me, then."

Evan brought the shuttle in close, still stealthed. He could clearly see the docking clamps. "Hold it steady, Sam." He released the flight controls to the AI.

His wrists warmed as he activated the two nanite bracelets. The reserve nanites flowed out as a golden stream, passing through the *Mara*'s hull on a direct path to the first docking clamp. Evan envisioned the locking mechanisms being severed.

The nanites got to work cutting through the metal joints. As the bolts gave way, part of the clamp shifted from its original position.

None of the guards had seen the nanites, so they jumped with surprise when the clamp failed. About half of them moved back a little from the locked-down shuttle, while the remaining held their ground.

Evan sent the nanites on to their next target clamp, which they also severed in short order. With two clamps down, the shuttle had a little wiggle room in its holdings but couldn't yet break free.

Straining to hold the vision in his head from a distance,

Evan moved on to the next clamp. When that one gave way, the shuttle was finally released.

It barreled past the guards, who dove to the ground and ducked behind anything they could for cover as it sped by. The vessel passed through the force field at the back of the inspection bay, out into open space.

"Enemy forces are pursuing," Sam warned.

"Fire, but shoot to disable their engines and weapons, not destroy the ships."

The stealth dropped as Sam targeted the enemy vessels and weapons mounted to the post.

Evan recalled the nanites, and they reformed into a bracelet on his right wrist.

"We'll escort you out. Stay close," he told the other shuttle over the comm.

"I'll never make it as far as the transit ring with these guys on my tail," the man said.

"You won't have to."

Sam had taken out enough of the enemy weapons to give them a few seconds of calm. As soon as the companion shuttle was in range, the jump drive assembly expanded to encompass the other vessel, immediately forming its ornate, spinning latticework to create a jump field. The two vessels slipped into the spatial distortion together.

Comms were useless during the jump, but Evan messaged the other ship as soon as they dropped back into normal space, this time as a vidcall. "Welcome to Aethos. I'm Evan, by the way."

The man on the other shuttle was a few years younger, but his wide-eyed incredulousness made him appear even more youthful. "I'm Tobin. That was the most incredible thing I've ever seen! Did we really just travel all the way to Aethos?"

"Yep. Conroy is going to be super jealous you got to do a jump before him. Be sure to rub it in. And you're welcome for saving you, by the way."

"Sorry, yes. Thank you. I have no idea how you did any of that, but I look forward to hearing all about it."

"That little stunt no doubt just opened up all kinds of questions. I don't think that's how we'd wanted to roll out disclosure of the alien tech."

"Well, I brought even more exciting info. It's going to be a big news day."

32

"BUT YOU HAVE him?" Conroy asked, his chest tight from an hour of anxiety while he'd waited for a report.

"Yes, sir," Evan confirmed. "His ship got a little banged up, but he'll be fine."

Conroy let out a long breath, releasing some of his tension. "Thank you, Evan. I'll see you back here soon." He ended the vidcall.

"Thank goodness Evan got there when he did," Rebeka murmured.

"Tobin is one of our best. I didn't want to lose him."

"I know what he means to you, sir."

"Is it that obvious?"

"We all have our favorites. You picked a good one."

Conroy had first met Tobin when he was fresh out of university, full of youthful ambition and optimism. He'd landed an internship in Conroy's office, and the lad had immediately stood out as being more astute than average. He had a knack for seeing through the stated words to read the deeper meaning. It was the kind of skill that couldn't be taught outright, but it could be cultivated with the right mentorship. Conroy had decided to bring Tobin into his administration to help him reach his potential. And he'd soared.

Within two years, Tobin had risen through the ranks and become one of Conroy's best aides. He could be trusted to accomplish any assignment, no matter how challenging, and do it with a smile. He could have risen even farther and faster, but Conroy made a point of keeping Tobin in roles where he would interact with the most people. He wanted him to build a network of contacts and really understand how the government worked at all levels. Because, eventually, he could see Tobin running the entire operation.

Selecting a successor was one of the most important things a powerful man could do with his life. Conroy hadn't given it much thought before he met Tobin, but he knew within months that he was looking at a future chancellor—perhaps not immediately following Conroy, but at some point down the road.

So, when Conroy had to flee, he'd been left with an impossible choice: leave Tobin behind among the wolves, or take him and potentially ruin any chance of him ever leading the Commonwealth. In the end, they'd decided he would stay behind to serve as an informant and long-term backup plan to get the Commonwealth back on track if Conroy was unable to return to power himself.

Saying goodbye to the young man who'd become a surrogate son to him had been one of the most difficult aspects of Conroy's sudden departure. Soon, they would be back together again and their greatest work together yet could begin.

Evan arrived escorting Tobin fifteen minutes later. Conroy was waiting at the bunker entrance for them.

"Tobin! It's good to see you, old friend." Conroy embraced him.

The young man hugged him back awkwardly. "Yes, sir.

Reporting for duty!"

"You've done quite enough already."

"I know it's not over yet." He reached inside his jacket. "I have something for you. I couldn't risk sending it over the relays."

Samor tensed, ready to react if Tobin pulled out a weapon, but it was a data storage drive. Tobin handed it to Conroy.

"What's on it?"

"Everything you ever wanted about Rostov's treachery. All the things I said I couldn't get," Tobin revealed.

Conroy's heart lifted. "Seriously?"

Tobin grinned. "I've been busy."

Conroy connected the drive to one of their air-gapped computers so he could inspect the files. The drive contained everything from financial records to surveillance photos of meetings to recordings of Rostov vidcalling with members of the Syndicate's leadership.

"How did you even get some of these?" Conroy asked incredulously.

"Let's just say the universe deigned to deliver opportunities I didn't let go to waste."

Conroy handed the computer over to Rebeka for further analysis. "Tobin, I have no words to thank you."

"Just win this thing. I had to leave everything behind, and I'd really like to go back someday."

"I have every intention."

Rebeka looked up from the computer screen. "Sir, coupled with the binder of printed records Anya found in the Rilen base, we now have all the documentation we could ever want to show the illegal dealings between Rostov's administration and the Noche Syndicate."

And just like that, all of our dreams are real. Conroy

nodded. "Thank you, everyone. We can now plan the best time to make our announcement."

"Sir, I think we need to do this *now*," Tobin said.

Everyone gawked at him.

"I think we need a little more lead time. Why the urgency?" Conroy asked.

"With the way I left, Rostov knows I was in on it. He knows the information I had access to. If we delay, that gives him a chance to get ahead of us with counter-messaging."

Rebeka nodded. "He's right, sir. We should act while we have the advantage."

It was all happening much faster than Conroy had anticipated. "You've already arranged the comm overrides?"

"Sam has agreed to give us the signal boost we need to reach the central relays, and our people back home will do the rest. They've been on standby for weeks. All we need to do is say the word," Rebeka said.

Conroy swallowed his nerves and nodded. "All right, prep the broadcast."

They'd decided that he would need to do the announcement live because anything pre-recorded would be criticized as inauthentic. This way, there would be less ammunition to doubt that it was genuine.

However, no matter what they did, there would be doubters. With any advanced technology, fakes were rampant and nearly indistinguishable from real videos. But there *were* certain tells, and he intended to mitigate as many of those concerns as possible. This message needed to land.

While Rebeka pulled the new segments from Tobin's research and cut them into their existing presentation, Conroy freshened his appearance while mentally running through his talking points. He'd written a script, but reading from a teleprompter would come across as unnatural. Instead, he had an outline of the topics to cover, and he'd speak from the heart. That's what he'd done during his campaigns, and that's what had won him support. He needed to recapture that spirit today.

When he returned wearing a fresh suit and with his hair styled, Evan had left but Tobin and Samor were waiting with Rebeka.

Rebeka nodded to him. "All set, sir."

He looked over her revised presentation. "It's perfect." The content struck just the right balance, bringing up key issues without giving everything away. It was the ideal tool to promote questions, and that's what they wanted—start the conversation and make the *people* ask for more.

Conroy settled behind his desk, against the backdrop of the Commonwealth's banner. "All right. Let's do it."

Tobin and Samor sat next to Rebeka, who was running the comm panel and graphics support for the broadcast.

"Remember to breathe," she said, harkening back to their routine before issuing a public address from Terrax.

He smiled. "Thank you."

She gave him a knowing look before turning serious. "Starting broadcast in three… two…" She silently mouthed 'one' and pointed at him to go.

For a split second, Conroy's mind went blank. He became acutely aware that his face had been plastered on every public broadcast screen on every planet across the Commonwealth. The face of a supposedly dead man.

As quickly as he'd frozen, he regained his composure. He settled into the firm yet caring tone that had been a hallmark of his political addresses while he was in office. This would be the most important announcement of his career. "Greetings, citizens of the Commonwealth. I am Thomas Conroy, the

Commonwealth's chancellor until five years ago. Though it was reported that I died in a shuttle crash, I have been very much alive these past few years.

"The reason for my absence and assumed death will hopefully make sense by the conclusion of my explanation. For, you see, the shuttle crash was not an accident at all. It was sabotage. An attempted assassination. And it was perpetrated by Victor Rostov, my Deputy Chancellor at the time. Likewise, the media smears about my alleged misdeeds were also Rostov's doing. These were coordinated efforts to oust me from office. When I refused to back down, he moved to end my life so that he could step into power."

Conroy let the words hang for a few seconds before continuing, staring unwaveringly into the camera. "This assertion is no doubt shocking and you'll need proof. That is what we will give you now."

On cue, Rebeka started the playback of their evidence packet, highlighting the underhanded dealings Rostov and the members of his administration had conducted over the past six years—beginning with the plot against Conroy up through the most recent collaboration with the Syndicate. But to the point they'd agreed on earlier, they couldn't bombard the audience with too much information. Instead, the packet was designed to prompt further questions, which they would happily answer upon request. Withholding information was the perfect way to make the public demand its release, and he needed the citizens driving this conversation.

When the prepared presentation had finished playing, Conroy continued. "The Commonwealth was formed more than a thousand years ago to see humanity through a new era of life among the stars. In the years since, we have faced trials and been gifted new ways to prosper. Even as we work toward ways to survive on new worlds, one of our most enduring dangers has been enemies within.

"There are many visions for where our civilization can go from here. We stand at a crossroads now. Should new technology be held by a select few, or should everyone have a chance to benefit from those developments?

"Rostov doesn't believe that you should have a choice. He ordered my assassination so that he could be the one to decide what's best for billions of people across dozens of star systems. I have a different vision. I come to you now offering partnership to create a new future vision for the Commonwealth. I hope you'll join me. Thank you."

He ended the transmission.

Rebeka smiled. "Well, that ought to get them talking."

"That's the plan." Conroy loosened the neck of his shirt. "Now we wait for the response."

— — —

Rostov watched in horror as Conroy's face filled the wall-mounted screen in his office. The more that he said, the worse it became.

"What the hell is this?" Rostov demanded.

"I'm afraid it's exactly what it looks like," Lucy said.

"Shut it down!"

"We can't, sir. We don't know how, but they've overridden the general comm band. We currently have no control over the system. I'm sorry."

Rage and hatred burned Rostov from within. He gripped the back of his seat to keep from destroying anything in his office. "Why is that man so hard to kill?"

"We'll get him," Lucy said with the calm, measured tone

that made her such a valuable Chief of Staff. "He can't stay hidden if he wants to validate his return."

But is the damage already done? Every word Conroy had spoken was true. Rostov felt the weight of those deeds, and their validity was obvious to him. But that was from the perspective of the perpetrator. Would an average person on the street take the message seriously?

"Show me the news reports around Terrax. Bring up a sample of the civil security camera feeds."

The selected video feeds confirmed Rostov's worst fears. People had latched onto the message and were asking questions. Even the most stoic news anchors were expressing open shock about Conroy's sudden return and speculating about the details behind his high-level overview.

"That devious bastard," Rostov sneered. He had a lot more colorful things to say about Conroy, but vocalizing those at this delicate time would not improve his political standing. He needed to go into damage control mode. Immediately.

Rostov's Communications Director poked her head into his office. "Sir, we should—"

"Not now, Marnee. *I* have my own response in mind, and it doesn't involve you."

She frowned. "I highly advise—"

"Noted. Leave me."

Lucy headed out, and Marnee reluctantly followed, closing the door with a huff. Really, she should be thanking him for not dumping an impossible salvage job on her shoulders. No matter how capable she was at her job of messaging and spin, talk alone wouldn't turn around this situation.

They needed action—something flashy and distracting enough to change the narrative entirely. A plan formed in his mind.

Forget Julian's strategic communications and charity. We need to send a different kind of message.

33

NOT MANY THINGS could render Marcus Santano speechless, but Chancellor Conroy's presentation being broadcast simultaneously across the Commonwealth was a noteworthy spectacle. The logistics alone of hacking into the comm feeds was truly impressive, and it made Marcus wonder what kind of mole had made that possible. He'd heard rumors that Conroy had a network of loyalists throughout the Commonwealth, but this was the first hard evidence Marcus had seen to verify those claims. *Maybe I underestimated his reach.*

"It's mostly empty talk," Wes said.

"Words carry power, we can't forget," Marcus replied to his assistant. He'd seen political careers rise or fall from less than Conroy's announcement. Rostov better have a response, or the Syndicate might find itself in a bad spot.

"May I speak freely, sir?"

"Go ahead." Marcus had often found Wes to have astute observations, and he would welcome inspiration from any source right now.

"I don't like how he tried to implicate us," Wes said. "Just subtly veiled threats."

"We *did* do those things, don't forget." Marcus began

pacing across the room, overcome with anxiety he needed to work off.

"Didn't Rostov assure you that there wouldn't be any complications? How long will you continue to trust him to take care of Conroy?"

"We're already well past the window," Marcus admitted.

"And what would you like to do about that problem, sir?"

"I'd like to take care of Conroy ourselves, but we have no way to get to Aethos."

"Roman?" Wes asked.

"A bigger traitor than anyone. He had his chance, and he failed."

Marcus couldn't be sure what had become of his younger brother, but he was either dead or had switched sides. Death would be the preferable of those two outcomes, considering the number of secrets Roman could spill. But the raid of the Rilen base suggested that kind of inside knowledge. So, rather than *if* Roman was working with the enemy, a more pertinent question was *why* he might have adjusted his allegiances.

Was I too hard on him? Marcus rarely questioned his own methods, but maybe it was due in this case. Roman had always been too emotional. Perhaps he'd finally snapped.

"Maybe we should focus on the legitimate business operations and distance ourselves from Rostov for now," Wes suggested.

"If we step away, we might not be given a way back in."

A chime sounded, followed by Marcus' omni vibrating. It was an incoming vidcall from Rostov's private line. He flashed the screen to Wes for him to see before answering. "Chancellor."

"Marcus, I imagine you've seen the news?"

"I have."

"We can't let it stand."

"Agreed."

Rostov slowed his speech, like he was choosing his words carefully. "If we can't get to him, we need to get him out in the open. Let him expose his true nature."

Marcus tried to read between the lines. "And if he won't show himself, we'll show people for him?"

"Yes."

"What kind of demonstration?"

"A man like that is capable of killing people to prove a point. People should be scared to leave their homes as long as he's on the loose."

"He might strike a public gathering in a major city."

Rostov nodded. "He could."

"That would be tragic. People would be very upset."

"They'd turn to their tried and true leader for protection."

"I could see that, yes." Marcus allowed a small smile. "Conroy might not be in hiding for much longer."

"I'm sure his return will have quite an impact."

"They'll forget about everything he said today."

"What a shame."

"Take care, Chancellor. You have nothing to worry about." A weight lifted as Marcus ended the call. Rostov had reacted better than he could have expected.

"What are you planning?" Wes asked.

"*I'm* not planning anything. But I know who's perfect." Marcus waved Wes out of the room; the fewer people who had specifics, the better.

His next call was to Marta. She'd been suspiciously quiet for days, and this was an ideal opening to find out what she had been doing. She still owed him the pavite.

The vidcall took nearly a minute to connect, making him

wonder if she was ignoring him. Eventually, though, her face filled the screen.

"I'm busy, Marcus."

"This is more important than whatever you're working on."

"What is?"

"Have you seen the broadcast?"

"No…"

"What rock have you been under? It's everywhere!"

"Like I said, I've been busy. What's going on?"

"Conroy is trying to drag Rostov through the mud, and our family along with him."

"And this is news?"

"The fact that he announced it to the entire Commonwealth along with a presentation of video clips, yes."

Her eyebrows shot up. "Oh? That's bold."

"We need to do something about it. And I want you to see it through."

"I'm sure you'll have a great time with that. I have my own priorities and ambitions, Marcus. I decided that I've had enough taking orders from you."

The situation became clear in an instant. "Dearest sister, where have you run off to? And what did you take?"

"The pavite is safe, if that's what you're asking. It will be put to good use."

"You stole from me."

"Funny… because it turns out I saved us both. It was your incompetent security that lost Rilen. I've followed our deal to the letter."

"The deal changed."

"*You* may have changed it, but we never agreed. And I don't have any interest in an amendment. That material is mine, and I'm keeping it safe."

Marcus wanted to yell, but he didn't have any viable threats to levy. The best he could do was offer a deal. "I don't want you to feel like you have to hide. You'll have my word that I won't try to take the pavite back. I just have a favor to ask—something you may even like."

"What do you want?"

"I'd like you to stage an attack—and make it look like Conroy did it."

"A blow-things-up kind of attack?"

"Yes. And I'll even let you pick the target. Something visible. We want maximum media coverage."

"Oh, Brother, you do know me so well."

—   —   —

Marta had often fantasized about blowing up a city in the core worlds, but large-scale destruction was generally considered a bad PR move for business. But having a worthwhile patsy changed the dynamic.

Marcus had left the attack plan up to Marta, though she'd offered to give him approval of the target. After all, the chance to deal a physical blow against the Commonwealth was a real gift, and she didn't want Marcus to think her ungrateful.

After due consideration, she'd decided that the headquarters of the Gerhart Group on the Tech moon of Markeesh would be a fitting target—not quite a core planet, but a well-known hub nonetheless. The Gerhart Group had refused her offer to join the Syndicate's shipping empire, and Marta had been waiting for the right time to send a message that declining was not an option. It so happened that their headquarters building was at the edge of a city next to a major trading port. The location had enough traffic to make it relatable as a place anyone might visit, but there weren't so many people on that part of the moon that the death count would be untenably high. Perfect for their current needs—and Marcus agreed. She could make a proper show of the event.

Since she was already out in a remote location, there was no time to waste. She gathered her flight crew and loaded onto her ship. They set out for the transit gate to jump to the Markeesh System.

While in transit, Marta put together a calling card to deploy at her attack site, which would tie Conroy to the event. There were enough publicly available photos and videos of him to feed into a computer to make a convincing fake, and his latest broadcast offered the perfect update to age him appropriately.

By the time her ship arrived at Markeesh, she was satisfied with the fake video. The only remaining piece was adjusting her ship's ID credentials to look like it was a vessel owned by Conroy. All of the Syndicate's vessels had easily modified ident transponders, and her crew had the updates in place in short order. As far as any observers would be concerned, she was never here.

Perpetrating the attack itself would be painfully easy. She *wanted* Conroy to be caught and blamed, so there was none of the usual sneaking around and subterfuge. This was about shocking spectacle.

"Ready the missiles," Marta ordered as she gripped the arms of her command seat at the center of the flight deck.

A few members of the crew were quieter than normal, faces drawn in stoic expressions that were likely meant to hide disapproval of the actions. She could tolerate disagreement as long as they followed their orders, and so far everyone was carrying out her commands.

"Missiles are primed," Grace confirmed.

"Bring us into position. Ready the jammers."

Her ship flew toward the trading post and stopped at the outer edge of the airspace commanded by the docking controller.

"Send the first demand," Marta ordered.

Kurt broadcast the first faked video of Conroy, perfectly mimicking his voice and face. "I am claiming this outpost in the name of the New Commonwealth. Submit to my authority or be destroyed."

The port controller responded with understandable confusion. "Uh, we don't recognize a *New* Commonwealth. We request that you stand down."

They sent the next message. "You were warned."

"Activate jammers. Launch the missiles!" Marta ordered.

As they activated the jammers to disable the station's automated defenses, the weapons shot out from her ship. Meeting no resistance, they pierced the dome over the trading post. Half a second later, the entire structure erupted in a fireball. Secondary explosions took out the surrounding concourses. Ships docked nearby were caught in the blasts, and others tipped over. A few managed to launch after the blasts.

The common comm channel lit up, but Marta ignored the messages. "Send the final demand."

Conroy's face and voice was transmitted across the open channels. "You will only receive one warning. Acknowledge my authority or suffer the consequences. I will not stop until all Commonwealth worlds denounce Chancellor Rostov and restore my rightful title."

Marta pursed her lips. "It was a little heavy-handed, in retrospect."

"His real video was, too," Kurt pointed out. "I think it does its job."

"We're about to find out."

34

TOBIN WALKED THROUGH the tunnels that had been neither dug nor constructed. "It only took *hours*?" he asked Evan incredulously.

"Just minutes for the room," Evan confirmed.

"There's still plenty of work to do, but we can have a future here," Conroy said. "We'll be living in a construction zone for a while."

Tobin sighed. "Well, they've been renovating my section of the government offices for two years. What's a little more?"

Tobin had had mental images about what Conroy's base on Aethos might look like, but little of it aligned with reality. When Conroy had talked about disassembling a starship and reconstructing it underground, somehow that had still translated to the grand conference center and marble stonework in the capitol. This was all so plain and modest. But maybe that was just what the Commonwealth needed right now.

Finding that Conroy had already amassed a number of civilian followers in the form of smugglers had come as a surprise. But if people like that—who typically didn't give the Commonwealth's government a second thought—could be persuaded to join the revolution, then there was hope for anyone.

Mostly, Tobin was just happy to be back with his people. He'd been behind enemy lines for so long that he'd almost forgotten what it was like to breathe freely again and not need to watch everything he said. Faking support for Rostov had taken an emotional toll. He was tired, especially after the stress of the last day. For that matter, he couldn't remember the last time he'd actually slept relative to his home time zone on Terrax. Had it been two days?

He held back a yawn. "Thanks for the tour, but I could really use a meal and a bed."

"Oh, of course!" Conroy clapped his shoulder. "We'll get you set up in a cabin."

They headed toward the exit of the underground structure.

At the top of the ramp, Samor ran up to them. "Sir, there you are! We need you back at base. Immediately."

Tobin knew that expression on the soldier's face. "What happened?"

"It's better you see for yourselves."

— — —

"How did this happen?" Zaris took in the horror on her screen. She'd been in the Markeesh System only last week, so the attack hit especially close. Moreover, she knew people there.

She called up Vinny.

His face filled the screen. "We had a deal."

"What are you talking about?" she asked, taken aback.

"Conroy did this. He attacked us!"

"Vinny, I don't know what's being reported, but this wasn't

Conroy. If that's what they're saying, it's a frame job."

"How do you know?"

"Because I've been with him this whole time." While technically a lie, she knew for a fact that Conroy hadn't left Aethos and wasn't involved in the attack. "I'm certain this was the Syndicate."

Vinny glowered. "Why pose as Conroy?"

"Why do you think? They know he's a threat to Rostov, and they've gone all-in."

"Conroy needs to fix this. I'll spread the word that it was an imposter, but this needs to come from him."

"Thank you, Vinny. I'll let him know."

— — —

The images of destruction filling Conroy's screen were too much for him to process. *All those people. All those lives...*

He'd known Rostov would do anything to remain in power, but Conroy hadn't admitted that might mean an attack on innocent people. An eventual clash between fighting forces was expected. But this... No innocents were supposed to get hurt.

Evan, Tobin, and Samor wore equally grim expressions. The fight had just taken on a new dimension for everyone.

"Sir?" Rebeka spoke softly as she entered the conference room.

Conroy finally tore his gaze away from the screen. "It's awful. I'm at a loss for words."

"You're going to need to find them." She placed a tablet on the table. "They're blaming *you*."

"What?!" He snatched up the tablet looking for confirmation. To his horror, his face was front and center of three major news broadcasts. He turned up the sound on one video.

"After initial confusion about the nature of this attack, new information has emerged. A familiar name keeps coming up in the investigation: Chancellor Thomas Conroy. For the past five years, Chancellor Conroy has been thought dead after his shuttle crashed shortly after taking off from a well-traveled spaceport on Coris. An unverified broadcast recently caught the Commonwealth by storm when Conroy announced he survived the shuttle crash and has been in hiding for the past five years. He asserts that Rostov is an illegitimate chancellor and needs to relinquish leadership of the Commonwealth.

"Though there were no threats made in his initial announcement, Conroy has reemerged with a clear message that he intends to reclaim the chancellorship through any means necessary. A comm recordings from Markeesh shows Conroy demanding the port acknowledge his authority. After that single demand, Conroy's ship opened fire, destroying part of a spaceport and resulting in significant casualties. Initial estimates are three hundred dead with a thousand or more injured. But there are still many people unaccounted for, so those numbers are preliminary."

A video played of a man who looked like Conroy making the demands. Just as they'd feared for their own broadcast, technology made it easy to fake a person's appearance and voice. But it would also be a battle to say that the demand videos were fake and his original broadcast was real. But muddying the waters was almost certainly the point, as well as painting Conroy as a madman. Even if they could successfully debunk everything, some people wouldn't believe any of it and others would continue to believe the lie.

"I knew they would retaliate, but I thought it would start

with a media campaign," Conroy murmured. "I assume the worst of them, but I didn't think they'd dare attack civilians as their opening move."

"Now we know what extremes they're willing to go to," Rebeka said.

I'm responsible for those deaths. Returning to the public eye had been a choice, and the lives impacted by that decision would weigh on Conroy's conscience. But that's what his enemies were counting on, and he couldn't let that dissuade him from the core mission. "I have no doubt the order came from Rostov, but who pulled the trigger?"

"The Syndicate," Evan said, crossing his arms.

"That would make sense," Tobin agreed. "It solidifies their supremacy and shifts the narrative."

"Sir," Rebeka interrupted, "We're getting a call from the *Invictus*."

"No surprise. Put it through."

Zaris appeared on the screen. "Please tell me that wasn't you."

Conroy shook his head. "Of course not. I would never hurt innocents like that."

Zaris nodded. "Well, I already told my contact on Markeesh as much, so good. But you need to respond, sir. People are scared, and they'll think it really was you unless you can show them otherwise."

Conroy took a deep breath through his nose and let it out slowly. "How do we prove that without making it look like I'm deflecting?"

"By not hiding," Zaris said.

Evan met her gaze through the screen, and then he turned to Conroy. "Sir, it might be time to take your first voyage on the *Asamar*."

— — —

Evan had seen a lot of horrible things in his life, but watching innocent civilians killed in senseless acts of violence was one of the most difficult to stomach. Not a military installation or a criminal outpost, it was a port where regular people went about their lives with their families. He'd been to hundreds just like it with his parents and during his career.

The Syndicate—he had no doubt they'd perpetrated the attack—had chosen the target well. Most people would be able to picture themselves in the port. They'd kept the fake communications alarmingly short—far too quick for anyone to evacuate or take meaningful countermeasures. It was all a tactic to promote fear and uncertainty. And it had worked.

News outlets across the Commonwealth were discussing the incident and what it meant for citizens. Anywhere might be the next target. An attack could come with no warning. The only safety was in trusting security authorities.

Of course, they're spinning it to make Rostov look like the Chosen One leader. Evan's stomach twisted with disgust. Any doubts about Conroy being the better man to back had been erased. As long as Rostov was aligned with the Syndicate, he was a threat.

The attack had shifted dynamics. Conroy couldn't remain at a distance. He needed to be seen up close, in person. It would confirm that he was alive, and it would also show that he wasn't afraid. If he could meet skeptics face-to-face, he'd come out stronger.

With the plan of a public appearance coming together, Evan went back to the *Asamar* to fill in Anya on the developments.

It turned out that she'd been working in her lab for the last several hours and was completely unaware that there'd been an attack.

"That didn't take them long," she said when Evan had finished.

"It shows that they're on the run," Evan pointed out. "They're trying to act fast rather than *re*act, but it's sloppy. They're scared."

"If we try to move too quickly in response, we could make that same mistake."

"Which is why we're going to be deliberate and smart about this."

"But showing up in-person at the scene of the attack? They're going to be all over Conroy."

Evan shook his head. "No, we need contrast. The only way to show it was fake is to make the real deal too real to deny."

Anya raised an eyebrow. "Uh huh…"

"Think about it, Anya. We have billions of people across dozens of planets to convince. That's not going to happen through talking points. It's the reason Rostov immediately turned to a big violent act—it says more in a few seconds than hours of speeches ever could. So we need to do the opposite. He destroyed that place, so we need to rebuild it. That won't bring back the lost lives, but it makes a statement stronger than words."

Her eyes widened. "Wait, are you planning to use the Korani tech?"

"I know I've been saying that we need to be careful about who knows about it, but I was wrong. I realize that the secret is what's been causing so much trouble. If we get it out there in the open, that will change the conversation."

"And Conroy agreed?"

"He doesn't know that part of my plan."

"Evan!"

"Play it out for yourself. What would he say?"

She crossed her arms. "Probably that it's too early to show something that powerful. There will be demands that can't be met. Everyone will want it, and you can't take it back once it's out there."

"But there isn't enough to go around," Evan continued, building on her point. "And it's the scarcity mindset that's gotten us into this mess. But the thing is, we have enough to put on a show. No one in the public knows there's a limited supply of Lux. We can use our supply to force out Rostov, and then it will be used up. Everyone will be on equal footing again. If they do rebuild manufacturing capacity, they can figure out what to do with it then. But as long as we're sitting on a stockpile, people are going to go after it. Rather than destroy it, we can use it to do some good."

"That 'good' might just end up unleashing a shitstorm."

"I would rather do that than let the power stay with a small group of people. There's no surefire way to avoid corruption, but holding onto something like this is a recipe for bad things down the line."

She nodded. "You're right about that. Okay. How do you want to play this out?"

"We set Conroy up like he's going to make a normal speech, and then we show the Korani tech in action. He'll be forced to explain everything his opponent has been keeping from the public. He gets to look like the hero for bringing secrets out into the open, and Rostov loses one of his major leverage points."

"That could backfire. What if the display of the tech is viewed as a 'modern miracle' and ends up deifying him? Or us, for that matter?"

"Unlikely."

"I'm not so sure. I've studied too much history to discount the possibility. I'm telling you, it can't just be the two of us up there slinging nanites and looking like sorcerer-gods. This power can't be viewed as human. Because it's not. *We're* not."

He searched her face. "What do you mean?"

"I've been trying to find the right way to say it. Evan, the nanites aren't just in our bloodstream—they enter every cell and change the way they operate. They create a symbiotic relationship with the host, essentially making a whole new lifeform. That feeling of 'power' comes from an actual biological shift in the body's energy production, allowing it to tap into something bigger than ourselves. The primer is just that—it opens the door. But we—especially *you*—are running full speed down the block. You, we, may look the same on the outside, but we are now distinctly different from other humans at the cellular level."

Evan wanted to recoil from what she was saying, but it rang true. He'd felt the change, though he hadn't had the vocabulary to express it. "Everything you said about your analysis before…"

"You walked out before I had a chance to finish."

"I'd gotten used to the idea of linking with the alien tech, but I didn't realize it had really merged with me like that," he admitted. "I thought when Roman blended with the sphere that was different, but it was just another version of what was happening to me?"

"He merged with the nanites from that sphere all at once, but I think you've been slowly absorbing them each time you use your abilities. I had Sam compare body scans, and they've increased in concentration inside you. I'm not sure what the saturation point might be, but what's in that bracelet isn't your entire reserve. And I think the process is accelerating."

Evan wasn't sure what to make of himself anymore. "How many are in me?"

"That's difficult to quantify. But it seems like the more nanites are in someone, the more other nanites will be attracted to them. I think that's why the high dose of Lux works—it kinda jumpstarts that absorption process."

"Anya, that's…" He shook his head. "Roman said that the effects of the Lux wear off and they need regular doses. But what if that's because they are in a place that doesn't have the Korani nanites all around them? What would happen if they came to a place like Aethos where they're everywhere?"

Her brows pinched. "I hadn't thought of that."

"Are there other worlds this saturated?"

"I'll know more once the probes come back," Anya said. "I hate waiting, but we needed to leave them out there long enough to study the weird signals. We have to figure out how those fit into all of this."

Evan nodded. "I wish we at least knew how many people were already taking high doses of the Lux," Evan said.

"Roman doesn't know?"

"Just Marta and Marcus for sure, but he's not certain beyond them. Even *he* wasn't given access to that much Lux, and he's their brother."

"Safe to assume it's not many people, then."

"There was the guy at the Rilen base," Evan pointed out.

"True. So a handful, maybe? Just trusted people in key positions."

"That's the working assumption."

Anya crossed her arms. "I have to wonder… If the Syndicate had access to this kind of power all along, why didn't they, you know, *use it*?"

"May I interject?" Sam said.

The voice startled Evan; while he knew the AI was always there and listening, it was easy to forget in the midst of a seemingly private conversation. "Sure, Sam."

"Remember, the nanites are a consciousness. They only function when they deem the requested action acceptable. No amount of the Lux infusion could force them to perform."

Though Sam had said as much before, the statement hadn't landed for Evan until now. "So, the Syndicate could have been sitting on a stockpile of Korani tech, and none of it would have worked right if the tech didn't… *like* them?"

"Essentially, yes."

Anya scrunched up her face pensively. "The tech in the vault immediately responded to me."

"Because it sensed the purity of your intentions, Anya. Just like the other presence trapped in the sphere thought it might exploit Roman's darker ambitions," Sam continued. "It is a partnership, not a tool."

Pieces of the puzzle were shifting in Evan's head. He couldn't quite click them all into place, but the image was slowly coming together. "Come on, Anya. We need to talk to Roman."

"What about?"

"I think there's more to the Lux than he's let on."

They trekked across the field to the bunker. Roman had been moved from his original holding cell to a proper residential cabin, though a guard was still posted outside. The guard recognized Evan and let him and Anya in.

Roman was standing next to his bed, bleary-eyed like he'd just woken up. "What do you want?"

The door latched behind Evan. "Roman, was the Lux only

used within the Syndicate?"

"I told you how the higher doses are used."

"That wasn't my question."

"Lux has only been given to people within the Syndicate."

Ah, there's the trick in the wording. Evan nodded. "And was it always intended to stay that way?"

Roman's lips curled into a smug smile. "Okay, you've got me. There were plans to take Lux… wide."

"Explain."

Roman waved his hand dismissively. "Marcus had the idea of turning it into some kind of drug. You may have noticed, people who've had it feel different to each other. Like, you can sense there's something different about them, even if you can't put your finger on it. It's a community-maker—that's why we gave the primer to the people in the Syndicate."

"It makes you want to be around others who've had it?"

"Right. And the more someone has had, the more appealing they'll be. Trust me, Marcus isn't naturally charismatic."

"So, if they rolled out Lux on a big scale, they could hypothetically sway the interests of a large number of people?"

"That was the thinking, anyway. I didn't believe it would work, not that anyone cared about my opinion."

"I'm guessing that Marcus' ambitions didn't end with being on Rostov's advisory council?"

Roman shook his head. "No way. He wanted the top seat, and he'd drug the population into voting for him if that's what it took."

Anya exchanged a glance with Evan. "Is that why there was such a large stockpile of Lux at the Rilen base?"

"Yeah, they'd been building up a supply for years. No way the Syndicate alone could have consumed that much."

Evan updated his mental map of the events. Everything was fitting more neatly now. "Okay, so Marcus offers the Syndicate's help to get rid of Rostov's opposition. Helping Rostov gets Marcus the legitimacy he needs to be taken seriously. Marcus rolls out the Lux en mass, garnering him even more support while no one can figure out *why* he's so appealing. And when the time is right, he eliminates Rostov and has a clear path to leading the Commonwealth himself?"

Roman held up his finger. "Ding, ding! Give this man a prize."

Anya let out a heavy breath, shaking her head. "Why would he even want to be chancellor?"

"Chancellor?" Roman scoffed. "He would declare himself the Emperor of Humanity. Rostov would look tame by comparison."

"What about NovaTech? Do they factor into all this?" Evan asked.

"Oh, yes. Marcus has been working backroom deals for years. The Aethos colony mission is where all the threads intersected—not that it went to plan."

"My dad..." Anya began.

"Julian Rojas, right?" Roman chuckled. "Hardly took any effort."

Anya glowered. "To do what?"

Roman looked genuinely surprised. "Wait, you don't know about Elena?"

"Who?"

"His handler. Quite literally, if you know what I mean."

Evan placed a hand on Anya's shoulder to prevent her from lunging at the man. "Will you just tell us what's been going on?"

Roman sighed dramatically. "You're no fun. Fine. A couple

of years ago, my cousin Elena ingratiated herself to Julian Rojas. His strained marriage made him an easy target, and there was enough black mail from his drunken exploits to end his career. But an offer to help him make it instead wasn't a tough sell. He was well-connected to Rostov, which gave a good 'in' for the Syndicate. But despite his flaws, there was a good man in Julian. Elena's influence only went so far, but that's where the Lux came in. A few well-placed doses of that and she became irresistible. He was the perfect mouthpiece for her to speak through on behalf of the Syndicate."

"Are you talking about straight-up mind control?" Evan asked.

"The Lux makes it possible, to an extent," Roman confirmed. "With Elena sharing both his office and bed, they got a lot done."

Anya looked like she was about to be sick. "Those calls I had with him…"

Roman's revelations did explain the weird behavior Anya had observed. If Elena had been directing those conversations off-camera, Julian's odd affect and inaccuracies with life details made sense. It was his body speaking, but not his mind.

"Why didn't you tell us this before, Roman?" Evan questioned.

The younger man shrugged. "I should have, you're right. But I was waiting for you to go back on your word, and I'd have been an idiot for telling you everything upfront, right?"

"What else haven't you told us?"

"I think I've been accommodating enough for one night."

"Do you know anything about my mom?" Anya blurted out.

"Julian's wife? No."

"Roman…" Evan warned.

He held up his hands. "I don't, I swear. It's not like I was personally involved in any of this. I just heard things here and there." He dropped his arms. "I'm sorry, Anya. I forget that some people are actually close with their parents. I could have said all of that better."

She took a steadying breath. "Thank you for telling us. This explains a lot."

"What else can you tell us about Elena?" Evan asked.

"On paper, she works for NovaTech. She's been the go-between for the players. Most think she's just a pretty face, but she's as sly as they come."

"That's it, then. She's the key. Get Elena away from Julian, and the plan might start to unravel," Evan realized.

"The plan has momentum of its own now," Roman said. "Marcus, NovaTech execs, Rostov—they're all in too deep to back down now."

"The Lux stash was destroyed. Conroy has mountains of damning evidence against Rostov. We're living proof that NovaTech lied about what happened to the *Stratum*. They're finished."

"These aren't the kind of people who'll admit defeat, Evan. Those things just mean there are more obstacles to overcome. And they *will* find a way, no matter who else they have to kill or smear to do it."

"Ever since I learned that they sent all those colonists to die, I've believed them capable of anything," Anya murmured.

Roman nodded. "You're right to feel that way. And I'm sorry to admit I used to think like them. But maybe it wasn't all me."

"Some people out there are going to rally behind Conroy," Evan pointed out. "They can't silence that many."

"But they'll try," Roman said.

"There's a big difference between a couple thousand people and millions."

"Mass death is mass death," Anya countered. "Clearly, individual lives don't matter to these monsters."

"Then we'll have to go all-in behind Conroy. He's the best figurehead to lead us out of this," Evan said.

"Will the people listen?" Roman asked.

"That's up to them. But at least we will have tried."

35

MARTA WATCHED THE writhing golden particles through the thick window. By all scientific measures, the nanites were functioning properly. Except, they weren't responding to commands.

"What else can you try?" she asked Sarin.

"I think we're just about down to your suggestion to sweet-talk them," the scientist replied.

"What else?"

"Well, I've been prodding them with stimulus of different energy frequencies. There's been some preliminary progress."

"Show me."

Sarin brought up a control screen showing the activity of the nanites. She cycled through various energy frequencies, some of which caused the nanites to move more rapidly, and others made them vibrate.

The way the nanites shuddered, it almost seemed like they were in… pain.

Marta frowned. *Why won't it work?*

"Part of the problem is we don't really know how the jump drive is supposed to operate," Sarin said. "I saw the footage from your flight recorder, but it's not clear exactly what's happening."

"They look to form some kind of mesh around the outside of the ship, and then they spin to generate the jump field."

"Right, but... I doubt that just making them spin is enough. How is a jump destination programmed? Right now, we have an engine but no controller."

The ship. Marta scowled. She'd been certain that they'd be able to find a way to make the components work separately from the alien vessel. There *had* to be a way.

She thought back to her encounter with Evan. He'd been wearing a bracelet, which had the distinct signature of the alien tech. That meant it *was* possible for a human to control the technology, despite the Syndicate's failed efforts. Most of their discoveries had ended up in the vault because they wouldn't respond, but maybe they hadn't been going about it the right way.

"Sarin, do you really think talking to it might work?"

She chuckled. "It's a silly suggestion. But..." She focused through the window on the nanites. "Can you please jump?"

Marta was about to berate the woman for wasting her time, but a cluster of nanites abruptly spun, winked out, and reappeared several meters away.

Sarin pointed at it. "Every so often, if I'm really nice to it, it'll do something like that. But when I try to replicate it, then nothing."

"That doesn't make sense."

"No. It's frustrating, and I really don't know what else to suggest."

Marta stepped closer to the window. *Why are you being so difficult?*

The particles slowed their movements, seeming almost cautious. But that was a ridiculous attribute to ascribe to alien nanites.

"Hit them with that frequency sweep again," Marta instructed.

Sarin worked the controls.

The nanites writhed with each wave.

I'll keep this up all day if we have to. We'll find a way to make it work. Marta watched the movements, looking for any clue. She noticed that the reaction was particularly strong in one specific frequency range. "Keep it there, Sarin. Increase the intensity."

The nanites started frantically swirling around the enclosure. They formed into a tight ball and then broke apart again, before looping around each other. As Marta watched, she couldn't help getting the impression that the nanites were hurt and scared.

"Stop it now," Marta said.

Sarin turned off the device. "That's the most result we've gotten."

The nanites had gathered into a loose cluster at the center of the chamber.

It doesn't need to be this difficult. If it would just work, we could move on, Marta thought.

The nanites moved a little closer to her.

Oh, are you listening now?

They did a little loop, continuing their approach toward her.

Inexplicably, they did seem to be responding to her thoughts. A telepathic connection *was* precedented with the tech, though she wouldn't have expected it to manifest in this way.

There's a mind in there, she realized.

She'd only ever treated the tech like any other tool with an on-off switch and specific function. But maybe this was more like training an animal—coaxing it into submission.

Marta decided to change tactics, as ridiculous as it seemed. *I need help. Will you help me?* She kept her gaze fixed on the little particles.

They stayed where they were.

If you help me, I'll let you out of here.

They slowly began moving again, some coming closer.

"Planets alive…" Sarin breathed.

I have a ship. I need to get to a faraway place. Can you get me there? Marta presented images in her mind.

Abruptly, the golden particles rearranged into a mesh tube, which slowly began to rotate.

"I think they're ready to listen," Marta said.

"I…" Sarin faded out. "I'll admit, ma'am, I can't explain this."

"You don't have to. We need to test it outside the lab."

"How?"

"By trying to jump a ship."

Sarin bit her lip. "That's not advisable."

"You have delivered what I asked. And that wasn't advice on anything."

The scientist dropped her gaze to the floor. "Of course, ma'am."

"Sarin, you did good work. I'll take it from here."

Sarin bobbed her head and left the room, leaving Marta alone with the alien tech that was seeming more and more alive.

I think we're going to become very good friends.

— — —

Roman was torn. He'd already helped his former enemies so much that it seemed silly to hold anything else back. But at the same time, it didn't feel right to spill every secret he'd heard within the Noche Syndicate. *But what's the point in protecting them?*

While his family had betrayed him, two wrongs didn't make a right. Roman truly believed that Marcus needed to be stopped, but not everyone within the Syndicate was bad. He could scheme against Marcus without hurting hapless bystanders in the process. Vengeance wasn't everything—not at the expense of his humanity.

When did I start caring? He was shocked by the shift in himself. A few weeks ago, he wouldn't have given a second thought about other people's lives.

The conversation with Evan and Anya about Julian Rojas had gotten him thinking. Was it possible that Marcus had been controlling Roman's own thoughts all this time? The duration and power of the telepathic influence weren't well understood, only that it existed. Marcus had been taking the Lux longer than anyone, and in the highest doses. Given their longstanding relationship and Roman's own Lux dosing in the past, it was possible that there was a link there. Roman's frustrations with Marcus could have been redirected outward toward others.

Roman hadn't liked the way he'd felt in recent years. Everything had bothered him. His entire life had revolved around serving Marcus without any regard for his own interests. It'd been a life of constant disappointment and never living up to expectations. Since nothing was ever enough for Marcus, had those feelings been forced into Roman's own mind—driving him to an outcome that could never actually be achieved?

Is Marta under the same influence? Have we both been played by him? He had an overwhelming desire to talk to his sister. Despite everything, he cared about her. She'd given him a chance when everyone else had cast him aside. If she was like him, if she could find a way free from Marcus' grasp, the two of them could accomplish amazing things. They could elevate the Syndicate and do their family proud.

Roman banged on his door. "Guard! I need to talk."

It took a little convincing, but Roman eventually arranged an audience with Conroy. He was brought to the disgraced chancellor's office, wearing shackles.

Conroy folded his hands on his desktop. "Say what you came to say."

"I've been thinking, sir, that there's been a lot of talk about organizations, but we've sometimes overlooked the individual," Roman began.

"Go on."

"The Syndicate is an interstellar operation. It's doomed with my brother at the head, and he needs to be brought down, no question. But it's a fact that it's the single largest, most organized shipping network in the Commonwealth. It'd be a shame to let all that infrastructure crumble just because of one bad person at the head of the beast."

"Please get to the point, Roman. I have lots of work to do."

"Let me talk to my sister. Let me try to convince her to join this side."

Conroy shook his head. "Roman, I—"

"Please, sir. She's not like Marcus. Give me a chance."

The chancellor looked at his top security guy, Samor. The soldier gave a noncommittal shrug.

"If you feel strongly about this, Roman, I will allow you to call her. But it will be in our presence, and we're shutting it down if you step out of line."

"Understood."

"Rebeka?" Conroy held out his hand.

His alluring assistant brought over a tablet. "What's her contact info?" she asked.

Roman recited the details from memory, and the woman entered them.

"Standard private line," she told Conroy.

"All right. Proceed," the chancellor assented.

Rebeka propped up the tablet on the desk in front of Roman. She initiated the vidcall and retreated out of frame.

Marta was on the flight deck of her ship when she answered. "Roman? Where are you?"

"Still on Aethos," he said. "I thought Conroy's people were going to kill me, but they've been trying to get information from me instead."

She pursed her lips. "And what have you told them?"

"Enough to stay alive."

She tsked. "I'm disappointed."

"Wouldn't you have done the same?"

"I'm more about actions than words. I took all the pavite. Marcus won't be getting it back."

Roman's heart lifted. "Marta, what's going on with you two?"

"You know how he is."

"I do. But what about you?"

"I'm done with him, if that's what you mean."

Conroy, Samor, and Rebeka perked up at that, encouraging Roman to continue.

"Listen, Marta, none of us are happy about how things went down. But Marcus is the problem. If you don't like how he's been running things, then why let him continue?"

She eyed him through the screen. "Are you suggesting a mutiny, little brother?"

"I'm saying that we both seem to want Marcus out of the way, and we should be working together on that."

"When did you grow a spine?"

"When I realized that no one was going to save me but myself. We could do this together, Marta."

"Us and who else?" She looked through the screen as though trying to see beyond the edges of the camera's view, to find who might be listening in.

Roman had to push it. "I don't think Conroy is the bad guy we were led to believe."

She leaned back in her seat. "Wait, are you *actually* working with them?"

Too far. Pull it back. Roman scoffed. "Do you really have such a low opinion of me?"

"Answer the question."

"Of course I'm not working with them."

Marta stared at him for several seconds. "Shit, you are. Even I didn't think you could sink that low."

"I'm telling them what they want to hear." The lies were thin even to his own ears.

"To what end? Because it seems like you're actually helping."

"I'm not."

She raised an eyebrow.

"I'm not!" he insisted, realizing it only made him sound guiltier. "Shit, Marta, can you blame me for trying to find a way through this? We both know I'm dead if Marcus gets his hands on me. I'm working an angle to try to make things right."

"Collaborating with the enemy is *not* 'working an angle', Roman. It's betrayal."

"I haven't given them anything meaningful. Just enough to—"

"You gave them the location of the Rilen base, didn't you? That's how they got in for the raid?"

He kept his mouth shut and took a steadying breath through his nose.

Marta shook her head. "It's over, Roman. You made your bed. Good luck." She ended the vidcall.

Roman sighed and slumped in his seat. "Thank you for letting me try."

"Some people are too entrenched in their own perspective to see things differently. I commend you for setting aside your preconceptions," Conroy said.

"I'm not sure where that's gotten me."

"On a path to redemption—as much as any man can get." The chancellor looked at him with the kind of fatherly compassion Roman had yearned to see from his own dad but never received. "You're trying to do the right thing."

I do want to help this man, Roman realized. He'd been going through the motions in a lot of ways, trying to split his allegiance and not take any step that would be too far to come back from later. But there was a true leader inside Conroy. He wasn't perfect, and Roman didn't agree with all his policies, but he did genuinely care about people. That was more than could be said of Rostov, and definitely Marcus. That made him the best hope at the moment.

"Sir, if Marcus and Marta have split, that's an opening."

"She said she took the pavite. Do you know where she might have gone?"

"She has a few places she kept for herself. I know some of them, not all."

"Would you be willing to give us those locations?"

This was it—a leverage point. *But what do I want?* He could demand more Lux, or his freedom. But there was really only one thing at the forefront of his mind. "I will. But I want to be there when you kill Marcus."

Conroy nodded. "We can arrange that."

Roman took the tablet again and brought up a star map. He made notes about where to find Marta's hideouts. "These are all the ones I remember. I think these two are the most likely because they have processing facilities. There could be others I don't know about, though."

"Thank you, Roman. We'll look into these."

Roman stood up. "What are you going to do about Markeesh, sir?"

"Evan has suggested I go there myself and try to make things right."

"Leave Aethos?"

"As long as I remain a face on a screen, there will be doubts about me."

"They want you gone, sir. They've tried to kill you multiple times, and they'll keep trying."

"That's what you were originally sent here to do, wasn't it?"

"And you still have the people who were with me locked up. I may have come around, but I doubt they have."

"I can't stay in hiding."

"I get it. Just… be careful."

"We'll take every precaution," Samor said.

Roman was escorted back to his room. He found it difficult to get settled back in. *Marta is up to something. She might be as dangerous as Marcus and I just didn't see it before.*

— — —

"What do you think about all that?" Conroy asked his team once Roman had left.

"I never thought I'd say it, but I think he's being sincere," Samor said.

"Yeah, I agree." Rebeka leaned against the wall. "He does make a valid point, sir. I don't like the idea of you being out in the open."

"We'll never get anywhere if I stay in hiding. Especially not after what happened to Markeesh."

"All right. We'll find a way to do it safely," Samor said.

"I've already started drafting a speech," Rebeka told him. "I think it's a pretty good one."

"Thank you both. Finish the preparations, and we'll be on our way."

36

ANYA SMILED AT Evan. "Look at us! Part of the entourage of a diplomatic envoy. I feel so fancy."

He laughed, delighted to see her so energized and happy. "I never dreamed this would be my life."

"Hey, I'm supposed to be camping in the woods studying a random woodland mouse or something right now." She held up her hands to show off her nanite bracelets. "Instead, I've got these and co-command of an alien starship."

"Things really have taken a strange turn."

But if Evan was being honest with himself, he would have been horribly bored if the *Stratum* had made it to Aethos in one piece and he'd started a new life with the colonists. The mundane day-to-day of building or farming would get to him. He needed a mystery to solve, things to explore. While there had no doubt been tragedy in the wreck and everything that had happened sense, it was also the most exhilarating experience of his life. And now, the opportunity to help shape the future of the Commonwealth was more than he could have imagined possible.

The plan was to escort Conroy to Markeesh and visit the site of the attack. They would take the *Mara*, pretending to be a normal aid shuttle. Then Conroy would reveal himself and future history would be written before their eyes.

Evan and Anya had hatched their own plans, which they were keeping to themselves—and Sam. He would play it out in the moment to see if it still felt right, but Evan was confident in his vision. Conroy had told him to step up as an advisor, and that's what he intended to do, though probably not in the way Conroy intended. But Anya was on board with the private plan, and Sam agreed that the logic held. So, they'd see.

Evan and Anya escorted Conroy, Samor, and a dozen other soldiers to the *Asamar*, which they'd use to jump into the system.

Stepping onto the alien ship, Conroy looked around with interest. "It changed again."

"We've been making little tweaks to the design," Evan said. "I've never had a ship that could be updated so easily."

"I have enjoyed exploring aesthetic form and function," Sam chimed in.

"Hello again, Sam," Conroy greeted. "Thank you for the ride."

"When Evan and Anya told me what you are about to do, I was happy to assist. This will be a significant moment for humanity, and it will be an honor to witness it."

"Let's *hope* it's significant, anyway," Conroy said. Quietly, he added to Evan, "If it goes nowhere, all my years of planning will be for nothing."

There were a lot of people who'd banked their careers and lives on Conroy regaining his title. Those people had become friends to Evan over his weeks on Aethos, and he'd been inspired by their passion. It was their commitment that had ultimately made him throw his own support behind Conroy; if good people like that had been loyal to the man for years, it said a lot about his leadership potential, even if Evan hadn't witnessed much for himself.

We'll find out soon if we made the right call. Evan caught Anya's gaze, and she nodded to him.

"It's only fitting you see your first jump from the flight deck. Come on." Evan led the chancellor toward the front of the ship.

The flight deck had been augmented to include additional seating. There were now three seats in the front-center of the room, plus chairs at the various workstations around the perimeter.

Evan offered Conroy to take the center seat.

"No, you're the ship's captain," Conroy said to his surprise. He sat in the right seat.

"All right." Evan sat in the center, with Anya taking the left. "Sam, take us out."

The ship smoothly rose from the ground and rushed upward through Aethos' atmosphere.

When the vessel reached space, the jump drive assembly soared over from the moon to encircle the ship.

"Planets alive, that's incredible!" Conroy breathed.

"It's what makes the jumps possible," Evan explained. "Like Sam, it's a unique consciousness. It chooses to help us."

Conroy nodded. "For which I am very grateful."

"We are ready to jump," Sam announced.

"Take us away."

The latticework swirled into a blur of golden light, and the ship slipped into hyperspace. Darkness filled the front screen, dappled with abstract streaks of light.

"Amazing…" Conroy murmured, his eyes fixated on the view.

"The length of the jumps depends on the distance we're

traveling," Evan said. "The longest we've done has only been minutes, but we haven't tried to go too far. Short hops can be only a second or two."

"How long would it take to cross the galaxy?" Conroy asked.

"A matter of hours," Sam replied.

"And beyond?"

"You mean to another galaxy?" Evan clarified.

"Yes."

"That would be more difficult," Sam replied. "Without astronavigation details, we can't set a destination."

"Oh." Conroy's disappointment was obvious.

Evan, for one, thought they already had enough problems in their current corner of the galaxy without bringing extra-galactic drama into it.

After several minutes, the *Asamar* dropped back into normal space. They were far enough from the planet to avoid immediate detection, and the ship slipped into its stealth mode.

Moving closer to Markeesh, the planet came into view. The attack had been on the moon Tech, which dealt primarily with electronics and computer equipment. Only one of the markets had been destroyed, but it had been enough to throw the entire system into high alert. Having been there so recently, it hit Evan as a gut-punch to see the damage up close.

"They've updated the death toll to seven hundred," Conroy said. "Hundreds of people are still missing."

"With this many people around, it could have been a lot worse," Anya observed.

"They were going for spectacle, not maximum destruction." Conroy stood and walked closer to the screen.

"We'll give them a different kind of spectacle," Evan said.

Conroy nodded. "A man risen from the dead."

"It's a start." Evan had more in mind, but he wasn't ready to reveal those plans. He exchanged a knowing look with Anya, and she flashed a coy smile.

While Anya remained on the *Asamar*'s flight deck to watch over the craft, Evan and the others went down to the hangar to get situated on the *Mara* shuttle. It was close quarters for the soldiers in the back cargo area, but it was manageable for the short voyage.

Evan launched the vessel, turning on its transponder to look like it had launched from one of the emergency response carriers in the system. They landed the shuttle in the city next to the trading post that had been destroyed in the attack.

"Are you sure about this, sir?" Evan asked, wanting to give him one more chance to back down.

"Absolutely. I've been waiting for this moment for years."

"All right." Evan powered down the craft.

He opened the side hatch and was the first to step out. As he'd anticipated, there were media crews nearby covering the disaster response efforts. That would make the next part easy.

Two-thirds of the soldiers debarked next, fanning out to form a security perimeter around the shuttle. Passersby at the port gave some weird looks, but there were so many other security perimeters and roped-off areas related to the investigation nearby that they simply adjusted their walking path and didn't seem bothered by a new obstacle.

Then Conroy descended the ramp.

It took nearly a minute to get the first reaction—a double-take and a point, followed by urgent whispering to a friend. Others started to take notice.

"That's him! He did this!" a man angrily shouted.

Samor and the other guards stiffened but kept their weapons in a non-threatening position.

One of the media crews caught wind. They redirected their camera and came closer.

"Monster!" a woman shouted.

"Why are you here?" another man called out.

Word spread through the crowd, and more people gathered, some people heckling and booing while others were simply confused and curious.

Three more film crews soon followed the first, the reporters trying their best to capture the unexpected scene.

Once those eyes were all on Conroy, he finally spoke. "I addressed you yesterday seeking to bring peace and prosperity to the Commonwealth. My enemies retaliated in my name and image. What happened here was not my doing. That video of me demanding submission was a fake meant to discredit me. So, I stand before you now to prove that I am alive, and to refute any allegations of perpetrating evils upon the citizens of this fine world.

"My heart breaks for the loss of life. Such evils have no place in our society, and I denounce the actions in the strongest possible terms.

"I have brought with me a forensic analysis to prove the video claiming to be me taking credit for the attack was a fake. In an effort to frame me, the attack was actually perpetrated by members of the Noche Syndicate, acting on orders from none other than Chancellor Rostov himself."

The final words ignited a flurry of discussion in the growing crowd. The announcement was off to a strong start, but the real show had yet to begin.

— — —

"He actually showed his face!" Marta scoffed at her screen.

She'd never liked Conroy, and her distaste had only grown over the years. The man's sense of righteousness was infuriating, as were his intentions to share the greatest discoveries with the masses. He had no business sense. A thing only had value if it was in limited supply. The Syndicate's business had thrived by keeping a tight grip on the shipping industry and controlling the distribution of select goods. Conroy could learn a thing or two from their business models.

But he wouldn't learn. People like him *never* learned. And that's why he needed to be eliminated.

This is my chance.

Roman had been tasked with Conroy's execution, but he'd decided to support the insufferable man instead. She'd vouched for her worthless brother on the mission, so it fell to her to correct his wrongs.

No one else would be able to get to the planet quickly enough to act, but she had the only other known jump drive in Commonwealth territory. And Conroy's people didn't know that. She could catch him by surprise and finally wipe him from the galaxy.

Years too late, but I'll finally get the job done.

She rallied her crew. "Prep the *Siren*! We have a date with destiny."

— — —

Evan kept a watchful eye on the crowd while Conroy spoke. For the most part, people seemed engaged but weren't directing anger toward Conroy. It would seem the Syndicate's attempt to blame him hadn't been entirely successful.

The media was definitely taking an interest, which is what Evan had really wanted. He wanted as many people as possible watching. And a live broadcast was perfect.

While Conroy spoke, Evan sent out a string of nanites to the edge of the destroyed area. He envisioned the mangled structure being put back together, and the nanites got to work.

So often, his new abilities had been used for destruction. But to use those gifts to help rebuild was an amazing feeling. Warmth spread through him—not the anger and surge of adrenaline he experienced in the heat of life-or-death battle, but the simple joy of helping to restore what had been broken. He realized that his fear of the technology had stemmed from only seeing one side of its capabilities. But hiding from it wasn't the answer. It was something to be revered and respected.

His work went unnoticed in the background for some time. However, as a large structural beam abruptly swung back into place and the metal began reknitting, a collective gasp of awe swept through the audience.

Above, the *Asamar* dropped its stealth shield. Another stream of nanites swarmed out from the ship to join Evan's work, making it seem like the ship had been responsible for it all. Evan recalled his own nanites and waited for the chancellor's reaction.

Conroy stumbled in his speech, following the sightlines of the spectators. He immediately looked at Evan, doing his best to keep a neutral expression.

How is he going to play it? Evan wondered as the seconds dragged on.

When Conroy finally spoke, it was the most perfect response Evan could have hoped for. "When those imposters destroyed this place in my name, they thought it would break your spirit. When tragedy strikes, you can respond with fear or the determination to rebuild. I encountered that in my own life. And that journey took me far away, to an amazing world.

And it was there I found the most incredible treasure humanity has ever known. I discovered proof that humans are not alone in this galaxy. There is, indeed, other intelligent life. And their technology is a marvel. What you see happening behind me right now is a demonstration of the kind of wonders this tech will unlock for us."

Even as the nanites worked, Evan's skin tingled with the presence of another power, much like he felt with Sam. It was also above him, but it wasn't the *Asamar*.

"*A Syndicate vessel just jumped in!*" Sam warned in his mind. The term 'jump' was telling.

"*Marta?*" Evan asked.

"*I think so. She must have found a way to multiply the jump drive components we lost near Pavia.*"

Shit! If the Syndicate had jump drive tech… "*We need to stop that ship!*"

"*Weapons are hot.*"

"*Attack it, Sam!*"

Light filled the sky as the two vessels unleashed a barrage of weapons fire. Everything descended into chaos.

37

Concussive blasts rocked the *Asamar*. Anya gripped the armrests of the center seat. "Any damage, Sam?"

"None to the *Asamar*. I am attempting to attack Marta's vessel without damaging the jump drive, which is impeding results."

Anya understood wanting to protect the alien components, but she couldn't help being a little frustrated with Sam's hesitancy. "Can it leave the ship and come here?"

"It's bound to Marta. It won't—or can't—leave."

Anya didn't understand it well enough to offer any follow-up, so she just held on for her life as the ship rocked again. "Sam!"

"I will keep you safe, Anya," the AI assured her.

The battle unfolding on the screen in front of her told a different story. Marta's vessel was well-matched in size for the *Asamar*, and it appeared to be made for fighting. Multiple turrets were targeting the *Asamar*, as well as energy weapons being aimed at their own ship's offenses and maneuvering propulsion.

Sam had positioned the *Asamar* between the enemy vessel and the moon below, serving as a shield. However, some shots were still slipping through.

Anya wanted to do something, but she had no real battle or flight experience. *We need to get our people.*

Though she hadn't intended to share the thought, Sam picked up on it, anyway. "I've told Evan to get back on the *Mara*. We need to move this fight away from the moon."

"Keep them safe, Sam."

— — —

Marta was locked in. She'd engaged in the battle knowing she was going up against a superior vessel, but her concerns had proven unwarranted. The alien ship was going easy on her.

I have a part of it. It doesn't want to hurt me. Though she had no hard evidence of that other than the fact that she hadn't been destroyed, she could sense the thoughts through her telepathic link with the alien tech.

Its consciousness was abstract, yet there was a distinct bond here. She could tell it to move, and it would move. She could picture a jump destination, and it would take her there. She only wished she had that same intuitive connection with her ship at large.

At least her experienced crew could act without her needing to direct every minute detail. They functioned seamlessly across their stations, firing, moving, defending in a fluid dance above the moon.

While her ship hadn't sustained any significant damage, she hadn't dealt any, either. But the alien vessel wasn't her target. She'd come for Conroy.

With her crew attending to their tasks, Marta launched a surveillance drone to get eyes on what was happening on the surface. Conroy was standing near the shuttle, waving his arms like he was telling a classroom of children to calm down. The onlookers may as well have been kids with how they were acting, too scared to move. It'd taken Marta all of ten seconds to reduce them to that fear. That was a real demonstration of power. Rostov understood that, but Conroy never would.

That's why he needed to die.

With the targeting data relayed from the drone, she lined up Conroy in her sights. One missile is all it would take.

The alien ship was doing its best to stay in her line of sight to the port, but her missiles didn't need a straight line.

She fired.

— — —

"We need to get out of here!" Evan shouted.

Samor was also trying to physically drag Conroy back to the shuttle, but the chancellor refused to go.

"I won't abandon these people!" Conroy insisted.

Why isn't everyone running? The onlookers had simply ducked down on the ground, as if that would offer them any protection. While a few had scattered, there was disproportionate focus on Conroy. *They want to see what he'll do.*

Leaders were often judged by how they reacted in the most stressful moments, and this was definitely a test. A battle was unfolding in the sky above, which could come to the surface at any moment. One of the vessels was the same that had rained down destruction before, and a repeat could be on an even bigger scale.

Evan spotted a flash above. On instinct, he scattered his nanites to form a barrier. He sent all the energy he could muster into making a protective net.

A missile struck with so much force that Evan shuddered despite not making physical contact. He held it back with power he didn't know he had, shaping his shield to deflect the blast away from the moon's surface. Flames licked around the invisible barrier before winking out.

Conroy gaped at him.

The media picked up who had drawn the former chancellor's attention, and suddenly all eyes were on Evan.

"Sir, we need to go!" Evan insisted.

Finally, Conroy ran back to the *Mara*. Samor and the guards filed in after him, with Evan going in last.

As soon as he was inside the hatch, Evan sealed it and ran to the flight controls at the front.

People outside scattered as he launched the vessel.

"Find me a clear path, Sam," Evan said.

A line appeared on the front screen. Scattered blasts were going off all around him. Marta was launching some kind of ordinance, which Sam was detonating with counter offenses. Evan hadn't flown through something so chaotic since his military flight training at the academy.

He blocked out the noise and shuddering of the vessel. Singularly focused on following the line, he banked and dipped the vessel around the obstacles. Eventually, the entrance to the *Asamar*'s hangar came into view.

A missile struck the side of the *Mara*, sending the ship off course at the last second. The shuttle collided with the bigger ship's hull. The impact threw Evan against his seat restraints. Behind him, swears and bangs sounded in the cargo area as the soldiers were knocked into each other.

An alert flashed red on the front console.

"Status, Sam?"

"The front starboard maneuvering thruster was damaged

in the impact. No structural damage to the hull."

Evan brought the *Mara* around for another landing attempt. This time, he was able to glide through the forcefield.

They landed hard on the deck, jarring everyone and eliciting another round of grunts and swears.

"Sorry!" Evan called out. "Everyone okay?"

"We'll live," Samor confirmed.

"Thank you, Evan. Well done," Conroy said.

"Trouble really does follow you, huh, sir?"

The chancellor smiled. "I'd say you have no idea, but I think you do."

"Move us away from the moon, Sam," Evan instructed as he debarked the shuttle.

"Already on it."

Evan ran to the lift and took it up to the flight deck level, not waiting for anyone from the *Mara* to follow. They could come up later. Or not. He needed to get a handle on the situation.

Anya was seated at the center of the flight deck when he entered. "Thank the planets!" she exclaimed, immediately vacating the seat. "I've had no idea what to do."

He gave her a quick hug before sitting down in the center seat while she moved to the right. "What's our status?"

"In a stalemate with Marta at the moment. Looks like she got her hands on some of our jump drive bits and replicated them. Sam doesn't want to hurt it."

"At least disable her engines," Evan said.

"I did not want to damage propulsion while we were close to the moon, as gravity could have pulled the vessel to the surface."

"Good thinking. We're far enough out now. Blast her."

"Negative. She has already initiated a jump."

Indeed, a golden blur had encompassed the ship. The vessel winked away.

"Where did she go?" Evan demanded.

"I don't know." Anya's hands raced over the console. "I can't find her on scan."

"We don't need to," Sam said.

The front screen changed. There was a new graphic of a star chart.

"Marta is using a piece of our jump drive. She's somehow made more of the components, but the core of it remains the same entity. Now that the link has been reestablished, it's telling me that it can feel where the rest of it has gone."

"Let's go!"

"Marta has not treated it well. It's afraid that if we lose this fight, it will fall under her command, as well."

"Well, try to communicate that we want to help liberate the captured part of it. We want to stop Marta."

Sam was quiet for a few seconds. "We have come to an agreement, Evan. We'll jump now."

Golden light encompassed the ship, and they slipped into hyperspace.

38

MARTA RELEASED HER breath as her ship returned to normal space. They'd avoided destruction, but she'd again failed in the mission to take out Conroy. *That man has too many lives.*

She'd jumped back to her Aegis-37 base, as it was the strongest image in her mind. She needed to regroup and plan her next move. There had been no sense in sticking around to fight the alien ship and risk damaging it or her own. Somehow, she needed to find a way to capture the vessel.

"Ma'am, new contact!" her helm officer announced.

A ship appeared on the front screen. *The* ship.

"How did they follow us?!" Marta exclaimed.

"I don't know, ma'am."

Marta could only think of one explanation. She'd taken a part of that ship, and maybe that was enough to track her. If that was the case, she could never outrun it. But, it might have just been a lucky guess; Roman did know about this place.

But there's a chance…

Marta brought up another image—the Syndicate base on Constella where Marcus spent most of his time. It had been her home for years, and she could feel the surrounding space. She fixed an image of it in her mind and sent the jump command to the alien drive.

Golden light enveloped the ship. After a brief transit through hyperspace, they dropped out in front of the Syndicate facility.

"They want to know how we got here, ma'am," the comms officer said.

"Tell them we're just passing through. Tell Marcus it was all worth it."

It was a perfect chance to gloat, admittedly. She had a functional jump drive. That changed everything—

"Contact!" the helm announced. "It's the alien ship again."

Either they got lucky twice, or they could, in fact, track her. She was betting on the latter. But this was also the perfect place to make her stand.

"Send out a command to the base. Capture that ship!"

—   —   —

"Oh, shit!" Evan exclaimed. He recognized this place. *We just jumped straight to the Syndicate's headquarters!*

The base was a sprawling space station in orbit above Constella—a highly developed world that appeared marbled gray from space due to its massive cities. Despite being a planet in the heart of the Commonwealth, the world was effectively under Syndicate rule, with every member of the local 'law enforcement' on the take.

Evan was torn. As much as he wanted to stop Marta, this was the very place they'd been trying so hard to avoid. The facility was packed with enough firepower to level a small moon, and the *Asamar* was just one ship.

Anya picked up on the problem immediately. "Evan, why are all of the ships in that large spaceport marked with the

Noche Syndicate emblem?"

"Because this is the center of their operations."

"Multiple weapon locks," Sam announced.

"We need to jump out of here!"

"Initiating—"

A blast rocked the vessel.

"The lattice can't form while we're under attack," Sam said. "We will need to resolve this fight."

A thousand curses filled Evan's mind at once. He tried to remember everything he could about the base and the planet.

"Sam, run a scan for Korani tech signatures. Let's see if they have another vault here."

"I am picking up traces of the tech," Sam confirmed.

"Send a message. Let's get it to join us!"

— — —

Rattling sounded in the wall. Marcus couldn't identify where it was coming from at first. But then a stream of nanites flooded through the wall of his vault.

He fell out of his office chair from the surprise. He scrambled backward on all fours as the golden lights zipped through the room. The nanites flowed out through the window as though there was no solid surface and disappeared into space.

What the hell is going on?

The two ships had appeared only a minute before. Marta had clearly been successful in replicating the jump drive, and she'd somehow managed to convince the alien ship to follow her here. But there'd been no warning. How were they supposed to keep it from jumping away?

Outside, the automated defenses had opened fire.

"Don't damage the ship!" Marcus warned the security team over the comms.

"Blasts are being deflected by a shield," the security lead replied. "We aren't making any headway."

Marta joined the fight against the ship, but he noticed she wasn't using anything close to the full firepower of her vessel.

He called her up. "Marta, what's the plan here?"

"I noticed the nanite mesh scatters when it's hit. So, I don't think the ship can jump while it's under attack," she said. "Keep it busy. I have an idea."

—   —   —

"Marta's ship is pulling away," Evan observed.

Both the base and the enemy ship had been keeping up a constant barrage of low-power weapons fire. It was clear they were distracting rather than trying to cause damage, which was exactly what they were dishing back at Marta's ship.

"They've stopped firing," Sam said. "I'm reading an energy build-up."

"A weapon?" Anya asked.

"No, something else."

A pulse rippled out from Marta's ship.

"She's sending out a disruption frequency," Sam announced. "It's hurting the drive."

Evan could feel the pain through his telepathic link. The alien consciousness was being whipped. "We'll help it!"

The nanites from the artifacts inside the base streamed out. Evan's command bracelet glowed bright blue as his own reserve nanites deployed to join the others.

They encircled Marta's ship.

Find her. Evan commanded in his mind.

The telepathic link sent him an image as the nanites raced through the ship. They quickly found her on the flight deck in the center of the vessel.

Got you, bitch.

This time, he didn't hesitate. He gave the kill command.

The nanites sliced through her at once, reducing her to a red mist in an instant. Her empty clothes fell to the deck.

With her hold on the other jump drive released, the nanites immediately streamed over to the *Asamar*.

All of the other nanites swarmed the outside of the *Asamar*, forming a protective barrier. The base's weapons were unable to penetrate the new shield. They moved away out of firing range.

The jump lattice formed around the *Asamar*.

Evan leaned forward in his command seat. "Get us out of here!"

39

"WHAT JUST HAPPENED?" Marcus couldn't comprehend how quickly everything had just unfolded. "Marta?"

"Sir, she's dead," a voice came over the comm.

"What?"

"She just… vaporized. I don't…"

Marcus' jaw dropped. *She can't be gone. How did this happen?*

He couldn't fathom how quickly everything had fallen apart. In the span of minutes, he'd gained two ships with jump drives and then lost them both and his sister—his second-in-command.

The shock was too much for him to even feel the loss yet. He had only anger beneath his numbness.

An incoming vidcall lit up his screen. It was Rostov. Still dazed, Marcus answered.

"What were you thinking?" the chancellor spat.

The question caught Marcus off-guard. "What?"

"Going back to Markeesh, attacking it again! What kind of idiot returns to the scene of a crime in the open?"

"I have no idea what you're talking about."

Rostov shared a video over the vidcall. Marcus

immediately recognized Marta's ship—and the alien vessel. They were battling above the moon. "When was this?"

"Just a few minutes ago."

The realization hit Marcus as a physical weight, and he slumped in his chair. "It was Marta. She tried to go after Conroy. They jumped here."

Rostov brightened. "You have him?"

"No, they escaped. And Marta is dead."

The chancellor's expression dropped. "Marcus... I'm so sorry."

He's not. He doesn't care. He's just disappointed we didn't take out Conroy in the process. Marcus bit back all the blame he wanted to level on Rostov for not holding up his end of the deal. If his soldiers had been competent, Conroy would have been dead weeks ago. Instead, Marta had paid the price. "This will not go unanswered."

"We still have the same mission," Rostov said.

"I need assurances."

"Like what?"

"I want you to cancel all non-Syndicate shipping contracts with the government."

Rostov scoffed. "Impossible."

"That's my price."

"That was *not* the deal."

"It was. I'm just moving up the timeline."

"I'm chancellor, but I can't unilaterally make that kind of contracting decision."

"Then talk to the Trade Commissioner, or whoever."

"He won't go for it."

"Then appoint someone who will."

"That's—"

"Better yet, appoint *me*."

The chancellor eyed him through the screen. "No one will accept that."

"Then make them."

"That's not how this works, Marcus. I told you, it's a long game. We can revisit this in a few years."

"Chancellor, do you want the Commonwealth to have a future?"

"Of course."

"Then you'd better accept that a war started today. And you need me for what's coming."

Rostov was silent for several seconds. "Trade Commissioner isn't the right position. But I think we have an opening for a new Deputy of Economic Development."

Marcus nodded. "That'll do." *I'm doing this for you, Marta. I'll get us everything we wanted.*

— — —

By the time Conroy had made it up to the *Asamar*'s flight deck, the battle had been in full swing. He'd stayed back, not wanting to break Evan's concentration. But what he'd seen had changed his perspective.

Warfare will never be the same. Humans had invented all manner of tools of destruction over the years, but the new Korani tech could accomplish things no other weapon in human history had achieved. They needed to weigh that destructive power against its benefits as a builder.

Only after the *Asamar* had jumped away from Constella did he make his presence known. "Well done, you two."

Evan and Anya swiveled around in their seats. "When did you get up here?" Evan asked.

"A while ago. I saw most of it."

"There wasn't really a lot to see," Anya said.

"You're right. I don't really know what happened," Conroy admitted.

"Marta is dead," Evan revealed.

"Oh." Conroy was surprised, struck with a mixture of relief and concern. "I wonder how Roman will react."

"I think he'll understand," Evan said.

"It needed to be done," Conroy told him. "I'm not sure how you did anything that's happened since we left Aethos, but thank you."

"Just doing my part, sir."

Conroy nodded. *Whatever role he thinks that is, it's about to get a whole lot bigger.*

—   —   —

News was already spreading about what had happened on Markeesh. Zaris watched with interest as reports popped up on the various media channels. Conroy was a curiosity, but the real star was the man who'd seemingly stopped a missile blast with his bare hands.

You have no idea what you've done, Evan. She shook her head, smiling to herself.

The eyewitnesses had focused on the appearance of a strange ship in the sky, but a review of the videos captured by onsite reporters showed that there was more to the story. The incredible rebuilding of the port seemed to trace to that one mysterious man in Conroy's entourage.

Zaris sent a text message to Vinny. >>Was that convincing enough?<<

>>Quite a show,<< Vinny replied. >>Was that Evan?<<

>>It was,<< she confirmed.

>>Interesting.<<

>>That's all you have to say?<<

>>The truth is that I was questioning Conroy after the attack. Lots of people were.<<

>>And now?<< Zaris pressed.

>>After what we just saw, I think we've found someone else we can get behind.<<

— — —

"She wasn't supposed to get hurt," Roman murmured. *I can't believe she's dead.*

"I'm sorry, Roman," Evan said from the seat across from him in one of the bunker's conference rooms. "She fought us. We needed to fight back."

The story that Evan had told him didn't make sense. It was like Marta had just shown up out of nowhere, and then they'd killed her for it. "Why was she even involved?"

"I don't know. But the tech she had couldn't get out. We needed to stop her."

Roman's heart lurched. Marta had cared about him more than anyone else in the family. He'd held out hope that she might one day join him in turning against Marcus. But just like the others, her strongest allegiance was to herself.

"I could blame you, but it doesn't matter," Roman told Evan. "I was always going to end up alone. She chose her side, just like I did."

"You're not alone."

"I am."

"Not anymore. We've put on a good show of hating each other, but are we really enemies now?" Evan asked.

Roman stared absently into the far corner of the room. "I

never wanted to be anyone's enemy."

"Well, indiscriminate killing isn't a great way to make friends."

"I never learned to respect life. Billions of people, most of them out to get you. Kill or be killed. That was how I was raised to think about everyone else. Assuming the worst of someone until they prove otherwise. Is it any surprise I learned to shoot first and never ask questions?"

"You're not the first person I've met who grew up that way," Evan said. "It's what the elites in the core worlds don't understand. Enterprises like the Syndicate don't form because someone woke up one day and chose mayhem. They arise out of necessity because common decency doesn't apply in an unfair world. And most worlds out there are *very* unfair."

"It's more complicated than that."

"Sure. So are most aspects of life. But it still boils down to the simple truth that not every cruel action has cruel intentions. Humans have been killing each other since before we learned to use tools. Over the years, we've just gotten more efficient and thought of a lot more reasons to fight. And, usually, that violence is justified in the perpetrator's mind."

Roman finally turned to look at him, eyes narrowed. "What's your point?"

"That I don't think you're evil. You're a product of your circumstances, and you've been fighting for survival just like any predator." Evan took a step closer. "But something tells me that Marcus is different—maybe Marta was, too. Taking pleasure in seeing others suffer. And you may have convinced yourself, at times, that you enjoyed it, as well. Deep down, though, you recognize that showing mercy is a greater show of strength."

"You didn't show mercy to Marta."

"I would have, if she'd shown remorse. You gave her a chance to try another way, and she rejected it."

But I had weeks to come around. Roman knew it wasn't fair to draw a comparison. And he'd been a captive during that time. *Marta heard the plea directly from me. If she wouldn't listen to me, even a year as a prisoner wouldn't have changed her mind.*

"I don't blame you," Roman said. "Just promise me one thing."

"What?"

"That you'll win this fight. Don't let Marta's death be in vain."

"That's a promise I would be happy to keep."

— — —

Rostov folded his hands on his desk as Julian and Elena sat down across from him. "Marcus has told me you'll be playing a more active role going forward, Elena."

She nodded, her lips curling into a predatory smile. "Happy to be of service."

Julian had a vaguely distant look in his eyes, and he nodded absently.

"This situation with Conroy has gotten more complicated since he revealed the alien tech. Lots of people—important people—are asking questions," Rostov continued.

Elena patted Julian's knee. "Don't worry. We're already working on a communication plan."

"What will be your approach?"

"He showed a power no one has ever seen. There should be no gods among men," she said. "There's no telling what someone could do with that kind of power."

She fished out a small vial from between her breasts and held it between her thumb and forefinger. It contained a translucent, slightly iridescent liquid. "I think it's time you and I get to know each other a little better, Chancellor."

40

THE NEW UNDERGROUND facility was coming together even better than Conroy had envisioned. Furnishings had transformed empty rock tunnels into living and community spaces. Utility lines had been run, and they now had power and water throughout. But the best part was that people were smiling.

Everyone recognized that they were building something special here. It wasn't just a new planet, but a *movement*.

The news coming in from off-world had made it clear that they weren't just going to be a sad footnote in history. People had taken notice of what happened on Markeesh, and the conversation was in full swing.

For the first time in years, the media was asking tough questions about Rostov's policies. And everyone wanted to know how the enclosure at the destroyed trading post had been repaired without anyone touching it, or how the missile had been deflected. But it was clear that Conroy had been on the valiant side of that fight.

They hadn't gone back to finish the repair job, fearing that they would be swarmed. But the stunt had served its purpose, and people wanted to know more.

Conroy was still working out exactly what to share, and when, but he'd realized that Evan had been right to get the Korani tech out in the open. As long as there were secrets, Rostov would have a hidden card to play. Now, their hands were on the table. It was up to the people to decide their future.

Evan joined him in the common room of the new facility. "What do you think?"

"It's magnificent." Conroy smiled.

"I don't know about that. We could have made the ceiling higher. And I'm not happy with the doors."

"Evan, you thought this entire place into existence in a matter of hours. Everyone gets a pass on the rough edges of their first draft."

"We can make more places like this, as you expand. Now we have a template."

"I haven't scared you off, then?"

"No, sir. I'm in it to the end."

Conroy nodded, grateful in a way he hadn't often experienced in his career. He'd had plenty of help along the way, but that assistance had always been highly transactional. The people supporting him now believed in the cause and were acting without reservations. "Thank you."

"Just don't let us down."

Conroy nodded. "With this team, we can't lose."

— — —

Anya plopped down on the couch next to Evan. "I know I'm going to jinx it, but I think everyone is settled for the time being."

He sighed. "You *had* to say it, didn't you?"

She winced. "Sorry."

"Well, the calm was nice while it lasted."

"Hey, we've got a few more minutes, at least." She snuggled closer, settling into her happy place. "What did Conroy think of the updates?"

"He loves it. He's starting to express his bigger plans, and it's good to see."

"I still can't believe we're part of those plans—helping to guide the future of the Commonwealth. Us. Just two random unelected people. It's weird."

"The Noche Syndicate wasn't elected, either, and they've been governing from the shadows for the last five years," Evan pointed out. "At least we're *trying* to do the right thing. That has to be better than the way things have been."

"I guess."

"What are our choices, really? We can run away and watch the Commonwealth rip itself apart, or we can take a chance to give humanity a fighting chance for a decent future."

She cracked a smile. "When you put it like that, we're heroes."

"They'll write songs about us, for sure."

"I think a monument is definitely in order. Like, a whole plaza kind of deal."

"That ramped up quickly from an award trophy."

"In all fairness, the scope of the assignment keeps creeping, so I'm only maintaining the proportionality."

"And here I thought saving the known universe would be thankless work. But a towering monument in a plaza? Well, what a way to motivate a person to give it their all."

"I've gotten to know you pretty well, Evan Taylor."

"Yes, you have."

She patted his leg. "To be continued. I need to go check in with Garet on the probe data analysis. Catch you later?"

Evan kissed her. "Happy analyzing."

Anya set aside the political concerns as she walked down to her lab. There were enough people working that angle. She had equally important things to worry about that were far more in her control.

When she entered the lab, Garet leaped from his chair. "Anya, you're a genius!"

"Obviously," she jested. "But… what did I do?"

"The probes. The data. It changes everything!"

— — —

Evan had just finished going over the new multi-ship jump protocol with Sam when Anya burst onto the flight deck.

"Evan! We figured it out."

He swiveled in his chair to face her. "What?"

Garet was right behind Anya. "The signal."

"You mean the one coming from the planets?" Evan clarified.

"Yes!" Anya dashed to the main console and made an entry. "Show him, Sam."

The front screen came to life, displaying a star chart.

"We couldn't figure it out at first," Anya continued. "The signal was all over the place—some Korani worlds, other planets with no known development, and then there was Terrax. There didn't seem to be any consistency to which worlds had the signal and which didn't."

"But Anya thought to cross-reference it with the chemical analysis," Garet said, gazing at Anya with admiration that didn't seem entirely professional.

"Sam sent out probes to a few dozen planets, and we looked for the distinctive signatures that we've observed on other worlds," Anya explained. "And that's when I finally saw the pattern. The signal is an alarm."

Evan froze. "An alarm? For what?"

"Let me back up." Anya held up her hands and took a deep breath. She was quivering with excitement. "Evan, there has been *so* much more planetary modification than we ever realized." She pointed at the screen, displaying a data table with a bunch of identifiers and readings that made no sense to him. "These chemical signatures are evidence of bio-optimization nanotech. On most worlds, it's just trace amounts—remnants of old, long-dormant tech from some ancient terraforming event. On other planets, like Pavia and Aethos, that tech is still active so it's easy to pick up."

"What does that have to do with the signals on Koranis and Terrax?" Evan asked.

Anya nodded, turning serious. "It's an expression of the same tech. But that was the part that took so long to figure out. Why were those planets *sending out* a signal? It was only once I had the samples and was able to look at the physical evidence with Sam that we pieced it together. Each modified planet was shaped for specific environmental conditions. Just like any automated project we might do, you enter in the specs and let the system run until the end state conditions are met, right?"

"Right…" Evan still didn't see where she was going with the explanation.

"Well, all of this work was done a long time ago. Most of these planets haven't been colonized, so things are pretty much just how they were when those terraforming projects were completed. But other planets, like Koranis and Terrax, were inhabited by large populations. And that kind of activity has an effect on a planet's environment. I'm pretty sure the signal is an alert that the planet has fallen out of spec."

Evan took a few moments to process what she was saying. "That implies there might be someone—or *something*—out there listening for an alert."

"Right. And we know Koranis sent out that signal and the planet was destroyed. And now Terrax is sending up that same signal."

"Shit, Anya, if you two are right…"

She nodded grimly. "I can't be certain about any of this, but that's what the data is telling us."

"There's no way around it," Garet confirmed. "With only one exception, every planet that is emitting that particular signal has been destroyed."

"Of course, all of that happened thousands of years ago," Anya said. "Whoever destroyed them might not be around anymore. But if they are…"

Evan set his jaw. Rostov wouldn't take such a nebulous warning seriously. But Conroy would, making it all the more urgent to have him back at the Commonwealth's helm. "Terrax might be next. And we need to save it."

THE STORY CONTINUES IN
LAST STAND...

Last Stand (Starship of the Ancients Book 4)

A ruthless usurper. A rebellion's spark.
One chance to reclaim the stars.

Evan and Anya refuse to back down as Rostov's regime tightens its chokehold. But as evidence of Rostov's atrocities spreads, the core worlds rally to disrupt the enemy's grip. With a fight on multiple fronts, Roman's inside connections could make all the difference—if he can be trusted. As every victory draws Rostov's wrath closer, Evan and Anya are on the verge of finally getting answers about the Korani. However, evidence mounts that the fate of the alien civilization may be inextricably tied to the Commonwealth's own future. With cities burning, can Evan and Anya topple the regime's power in time to prepare for the mounting galactic threat?

ADDITIONAL READING

Cadicle Space Opera Series
Book 1: Shadows of Empire (Vol. 1-3)
Book 2: Web of Truth (Vol. 4)
Book 3: Crossroads of Fate (Vol. 5)
Book 4: Path of Justice (Vol. 6)
Book 5: Scions of Change (Vol. 7)

Mindspace Series
Book 1: Infiltration
Book 2: Conspiracy
Book 3: Offensive
Book 4: Endgame

Taran Empire Saga
Book 1: Empire Reborn
Book 2: Empire Uprising
Book 3: Empire Defied
Book 4: Empire United

Dark Stars Trilogy
Book 1: Crystalline Space
Book 2: A Light in the Dark
Book 3: Masters of Fate

See a complete list at www.akduboff.com

AUTHORS' NOTES

Thank you for reading *Rebel Worlds*! I hope you enjoyed this third installment in the Starship of the Ancients series.

I've really enjoyed getting to know the characters and story world while writing these opening three books in the series. The pieces of the larger mystery are starting to come together for our heroes, though there are still many unanswered questions. All of those pieces *will* come together, I promise. If you've read any of my other works, you'll know I won't leave you hanging.

As you've probably noticed, I enjoy building up layers to my stories and bringing together multiple interconnected threads. I look at the series as being one big story rather than each book being a self-contained tale, and we're now into the meat of things. The upcoming Book 4 is going to see even more convergences as Evan and Anya continue their investigation while navigating the increasingly complicated political situation.

With revolution on the horizon, the Commonwealth is in for new challenges. But with the Korani out there somewhere and another potential alien threat, they are still in for their biggest challenges yet.

Many thanks to my fantastic team of beta readers—John, Charlie, Sandra, Eric, David F, Manie, David B, Doug, Robert, Terry, and Brenda—and to Steve, Bryan, and Deb for lending your wonderful proofing skills!

Lots more adventures are still to come, and I hope you'll join me on the ride. Until next time, happy reading!

ABOUT THE AUTHOR

A.K. (Amy) DuBoff has always loved science fiction in all its forms—books, movies, shows, and games. If it involves outer space, even better! She is a Nebula Award finalist and *USA Today* bestselling author most known for her Cadicle Universe, but she's also written a variety of sci-fi and fantasy books, short fiction, and screenplays. Amy can frequently be found traveling the world, and when she's not writing, she enjoys wine tasting, binge-watching TV series, and playing epic strategy board games.

www.akduboff.com